I0763323

Business Secrets from the Stars

Books by David Dvorkin

Fiction

The Arm and Flanagan
Budspy
Business Secrets from the Stars
The Cavaradossi Killings
Central Heat
The Children of Shiny Mountain
Children of the Undead
Damon the Caiman
Dawn Crescent (with Daniel Dvorkin)
Earthmen and Other Aliens
The Green God
Pit Planet
The Prisoner of the Blood series
- *Insatiable*
- *Unquenchable*

The Seekers
Slit
Star Trek novels
- *The Trellisane Confrontation*
- *Time Trap*
- *The Captains' Honor (with Daniel Dvorkin)*

Time and the Soldier
Time for Sherlock Holmes
Ursus

Non-Fiction

At Home with Solar Energy
The Dead Hand of Mrs. Stifle
Dust Net
Once a Jew, Always a Jew?
Self-Publishing Tools, Tips, and Techniques
The Surprising Benefits of Being Unemployed
When We Landed on the Moon: A Memoir

Business Secrets from the Stars

David Dvorkin

ISBN: 978-1-7345636-3-4

Dedication:

To Democracy
You were the best.

CHAPTER ONE

It was on a lovely spring day in the Rockies, as I sat in meditation atop a fourteen-thousand-foot peak, that Lukas of Aldebaran first came into my mind and spoke to me soul to soul.

—Business Secrets from the Stars

Actually, Malcolm's great idea came to him after lunch at a Mexican restaurant.

The waitress was not as young and pretty as the fantasy Chicana on the cover of the menu, but she came close enough in Malcolm's view and his present mood.

Not that she seemed interested in Malcolm's opinion. Although the restaurant was almost empty, she was distant and inattentive. She put the bill on the table, smiled mechanically, and asked, "Do you want anything else?"

Malcolm and the friend he was having lunch with thought the same thing, but both said no.

For a moment, Malcolm had the odd feeling that the waitress knew what he was thinking and was about to slap him. She looked at him coldly and turned her attention to another table. The two men watched her walk away and muttered to each other abbreviated versions of the something else they wished they had had the courage to ask for.

Both men were approaching forty, both were divorced, and both were lonely. Neither had seen his life work out as he had once thought it would.

Steve Golden, Malcolm's companion, and a fellow Western Bell employee, scanned the bill, then threw down six dollars. "Wish it was five o'clock already," he said.

"Yeah. Wish it was five o'clock ten years from now, and I was free and successful."

"Well, if you're wishing," Steve pointed out, "why wish it was ten years from now? Why not wish it was now, and you were already free and successful?"

"Right, right. After all, Shirley MacLaine says we make our own reality. God, what crap. I've been wishing for years, and reality still hasn't changed."

They walked from the restaurant and down the street discussing the unfairness of Shirley MacLaine's making vast amounts of money peddling New Age nonsense. The sky was cloudless, the sun was fierce, the Gypper was in the White House, and drunks littered the sidewalk. Malcolm and Steve were too engrossed in their conversation to think about the heat, and they stepped automatically around the splayed legs of the drunks. This area near downtown contained a lot of the sort of local color the Chamber of Commerce neglected to advertise.

"She churns out that bilge," Malcolm complained, "and the yahoos snap it up. While I write good, serious novels, and I can't even sell the damned things. Life isn't fair. But you already knew that."

"It's not just her," Steve said. "It would be bad enough if it was. But there're others doing the same thing. The bookstores are full of the stuff, and those guys are giving workshops and charging people a fortune to attend." He shook his head. "It just goes on and on. I guess we're writing the wrong sort of stuff."

"Maybe so."

"It's not just non-fiction," Steve said. "Fiction, too. Angels. Indians. Hell, I don't know, novels dictated by aliens. Maybe I should try writing under a pseudonym. Running Eagle Horsefeathers, or something."

"You're part Indian?"

"Everyone's part Indian. Just about every American is part Indian and part black. Anyway, it doesn't really matter, does it? You can just say you are. You can make up all the Indian stuff. No one knows what's real and what isn't. Or cares."

"You think that would work?"

Steve sighed the sigh of the eternally defeated. "No."

After a while, Steve said, "Fakes. We're a country of fakes. Style over substance. Mythology instead of history. P. T. Barnum was the quintessential American. There's a sucker born every minute."

"But you can't fool all of the people all of the time."

"You don't have to. You only have to fool a majority for long enough to get into office or become a zillionaire."

Malcolm had heard all this before. It was Steve's one obsession. "Heavy, man."

"Yeah, damned heavy. This is a nation of people who live in cities and are descended from immigrants but think they're cowboys and like to be told by television commercials that their grandparents live on a farm in Iowa. One of our most popular movie stars was a guy who couldn't act, had never been a cowboy, had never been in uniform, but he played cowboys and war heroes, and everyone thought he really was a cowboy and soldier–warrior. One of his buddies, another bad actor who played the same kind of roles, is now our Figurehead in Chief. We have a guy in the White House who chuckles and drools and wears a cowboy hat for his publicity photos even though he never was a cowboy, and the public swallows it and loves him. He's the lovable, braindead, cowboy grandpa they like to pretend they all had. Why, man, he doth bestride the narrow world like a Colossus–shaped helium balloon."

"On the bright side," Malcolm pointed out, "it'll never get any worse than this. The Gypper is the nadir. We'll never have a worse, fakier President than this. It's got to get better from here."

"I suppose." Steve was silent for a moment. Then he said, "The Big Gypper. The Deceptor in Chief. The Great Deluminator. The Supreme Mystifier." Steve's voice began to rise. "The Deceiver in Chief!"

"Steve, Steve, calm down. I keep telling you, you've got to stop thinking about politics all the time. It only depresses you."

Golden laughed. "I suppose that instead I should think all the time about getting published, the way you do. Yeah, sure, that doesn't depress *you* at all."

They walked on in silent, companionable gloom for a block or two. They had left the area where drunks littered the sidewalk and they were now entering the region littered by overdressed, rising young men and women. The two men had often debated which kind of litter was worse. At least the drunks were genuine. The yuppies were all playing grownup, whereas the drunks were just being drunks.

This was a topic that often diverted Malcolm and Steve, but today they were both too depressed to bother with it.

Both men had been writing stories and novels for years and making little progress.

Steve had yet to sell anything.

Malcolm had had two stories and three novels published. All were science fiction.

One of the stories had appeared in a men's magazine of so sleazy a nature, and bearing a cover which proclaimed that sleaziness so loudly, that he had never intentionally shown the magazine to anyone. Marlene had found it once and had burst into hysterical laughter, after which Malcolm had hidden the magazine.

His novels had been, as his then–editor had kindly put it, "quietly received." The first time he heard that phrase, Malcolm was pleased. He imagined his book being thoughtfully discussed in low tones in quiet, dignified surroundings. Eventually he came to understand that "quietly received" was a New York publishing euphemism for "totally ignored." As Malcolm was nowadays by New York editors.

He fantasized about the editor who would say, "This is a work of genius, Mr. Erskine, sir! Where have you been all my life? How much money do you want?" The editor of his dreams!

"How much money do you have?" Malcolm would reply.

Malcolm could not understand why Steve had not yet sold anything. He liked what he had read of Steve's work. It tended to be a bit heavy on political philosophizing, but it was well written. But then, neither could Malcolm understand why he had not sold more of his own work, or why what he had sold had been ignored by critics and readers.

Failure made Malcolm despair.

Despair made him whine.

His whining had already driven away one wife and one agent and seemed on the verge of driving away a second agent. When pressed, he had to admit that it was difficult to say which loss was the more painful. Charlie, the first agent, had been ineffective but a nice guy. Marlene, the ex–wife, had been quite effective but not at all nice. She had, though, looked awfully good in underwear. Now the only human being Malcolm ever saw in nothing but underwear was himself, reflected in the bedroom mirror. The sight never excited him. As the years passed, he began to doubt that it would ever again excite anyone.

"Yeah," Malcolm said after a while. "Workshops. The yahoos are so gullible. Everyone's gullible. It's all about gullibility. Look at those workshops. Someone advertises a workshop that will tell you how to start a successful business or whatever, and all the idiots rush to sign up and pay a couple of thousand bucks for a few hours of empty talk and some glossy slides and a fancy binder full of illiterate nonsense. Workshops..."

Maybe I could combine all of this crap, he thought. Use my fiction-writing background. Run a workshop while dressed as a gray space alien with big eyes. I could practically write the material in my sleep. How to start a successful business. Secret inside information from an alien.

Suddenly he stopped walking and spoke aloud the title that had just sprung into his head: *"Business Secrets from the Stars."*

"Huh?"

Malcolm looked around quickly to make sure no one else had heard him. "Er, nothing. Nothing important. Well, actually, I may have just hit on something. Wow." The more he thought about it, the better it sounded.

"You want to take the long way around, along the Mall?" Steve asked. "The girls in their summer dresses."

"What? Oh, no, not today. I've got to get back to the orifice. You'll just have to be horny and frustrated on your own."

"Oh, I'm used to that."

Malcolm practically ran back to the office.

With each step, it all became clearer.

Tens of thousands of years ago, and vast numbers of light years away, a mighty business empire had existed. The Andromeda Corporation was its name, and one of its top executives was Lukas of Aldebaran, a member of a noble, admirable, handsome race known as the Merskeenians.

Lukas of Aldebaran, star-dwelling Merskeenian! What a ring that had to it!

The Merskeenians were the ancestors of mankind. Now, across the immense distances of time and space, Lukas was communicating mind-to-mind with the only human being of a moral, spiritual, and intellectual fiber sufficiently refined to receive his messages: Malcolm Erskine. Lukas wanted to pour into the mind of his descendant the secret business wisdom that had made the Andromeda Corporation so great and so revered. It was Malcolm's duty to share this wisdom, these secrets, these business secrets from the stars, with his fellow human beings. Who in return would share their paychecks with Malcolm.

Oh, this was dynamite!

Of course, that first contact and all the astonishing revelations that followed it could not come to Malcolm in a cubicle or his apartment or out here on the street. The place had to match the experience.

Malcolm pondered for a while as he raced back to his office. Finally he came up with the image of himself sitting in lonely contemplation in the solitude, the clean, pure air of a Rocky Mountain peak.

That would be believable given that Malcolm lived in a city snuggled up against the Rocky Mountains and containing many enthusiastic mountain climbers and hikers among its citizens. Malcolm was not one of them. For him, the mountains were just an interesting backdrop, those jaggedy things off to the west that the sun set behind. Malcom preferred city life. If he sweated and strained, he wanted it to be because of a beautiful girl with shoulder-length black hair and not because of a mountainside. But he'd leave that out of the book.

In the real world, Malcolm lived in a cubicle. He was a man-shaped rat surrounded by thin, movable four—and six-foot walls. He was required to sit in one place for hours on end, with his back to the cubicle opening, staring at his computer screen, churning out unspeakably boring computer programs for use by other cubicle rats trapped in the vast maze of the telephone company.

Some of the cubicle rats liked to call themselves cubicle cowboys. They had convinced themselves that they were autonomous, in control of their lives, spending their days in a maze because it was their choice to do so and that it was moreover a strong and admirable choice. They were macho, they were manly, they were warriors in a great capitalist battle. Malcolm, excellent though he usually was at fooling himself, was immune to this particular delusion.

The cubicle rats shared each other's lives unwillingly. Malcolm knew more about his fellow rats' personal relationships than he had any wish to. He had heard—could not shut out—their loudly angry or explicitly affectionate telephone conversations. He had always tried not to broadcast his own telephone arguments with Marlene, but she had a way of making him forget where he was and lose all self-control. "Oh, it's you," was usually the last thing he said at low volume.

At his first job, after being shown his assigned cubicle, he had immediately decorated the walls with photos and a calendar, making it his space, converting it from anonymous gray to something welcoming. Using a hook rigged from a bent paperclip, he had hung a cheap plastic clock where he could watch it. The next morning, his second day on the job, he had arrived to find the pictures and calendars taken down and dumped in the trashcan and the clock on his desk, its face cracked. There was a note taped to his computer monitor reminding him that, as stated on page fourteen of the employees' manual he had been given the previous day, only company-provided and approved material was to be placed on the walls of his cubicle. He had later decided that that was just as well, given how often he and his fellow rats were shifted from cubicle to cubicle.

So he settled for the gray, supposedly sound-absorbing walls. He never looked at them, anyway. All day long, his attention was—or was supposed to be—focused on the screen of his computer.

Malcolm's desk was just a shelf attached to the cubicle walls, and the computer was placed so that its screen faced toward the cubicle opening. Sometimes, to give himself the illusion of privacy, Malcolm would swivel the monitor as much to one side as he could and would do his work with his upper body leaning awkwardly on the desk. That way, the screen wasn't quite so visible to anyone walking by or sneaking up behind him.

It was a good thing he had worked this method out. When he got back from his Mexican lunch, Malcolm swiveled the monitor to one side even more than usual, shoved aside a stack of already long-neglected requests for new programs, and began writing what was destined to become his first and only bestseller.

This, at any rate, was how Malcolm remembered the genesis of his great idea. He liked to think that his grand conception had come to him while he was digesting refried beans and a side order of menudo and that it had sprung from his existential headache like a New Age Athena. But the truth was that important seeds had been sown earlier.

Five weeks earlier, in the case of the first seed.

Malcolm had been ordered to attend a one-day workshop which was guaranteed to make him a more dynamic employee, a better salesman, and a more satisfied human being. His doubts about the utility of the whole thing were aroused as soon as he read the pamphlet which both announced the workshop and explained that no one was excused from going.

"Attendance at the voluntary loyalty meetings is compulsory," Malcolm muttered, quoting from one of his own novels.

The compulsoriness of the workshop was enough by itself to excite his skepticism. In his experience, management always made compulsory those gatherings that no employee in his right mind would attend voluntarily.

Although it was a depressing fact that a surprisingly large number of his fellow employees were enthusiastic volunteers at indoctrination events that he considered stunningly inane. What all of that might signify, Malcolm had no idea.

More to the point, Malcolm's job did not involve selling, so the workshop could scarcely make him a better salesman.

Nor could any workshop make him satisfied. Only a best-selling book, followed by a cascade of dollars and sexual delights, could do that.

And finally, he had no wish to become a more dynamic employee. He was happy being the narcoleptic employee he now was, and if he ever did achieve writing success, he would instantly become an ex-employee. He had already worked for the telephone company for ten years, and he didn't see why any reasonably law-abiding citizen should have to serve a longer term than that.

As if all of this were not enough, the pamphlet advertising the workshop was written in what Malcolm had come to call Corporate English, a subliterate variant of the language that filled him with helpless fury whenever he was forced to read it.

> *Are you being all that you can be? All that you should be? When you lay in bed at night, do you sleep happily because you're Career's "right on track?" Or do you "toss and turn" because your worried about it's path? Don't worry any longer! Come join you're Successful Coworkers for a 3 day Workshop where you will learn to "factor Success" into you're Daily Life!*

The temptation to mark the pamphlet up with spelling and punctuation and usage corrections in red ink and then mail it back to the 55th-floor office where it had originated was almost overwhelming, but Malcolm managed to resist the temptation.

No, he reminded himself, to the place where the pamphlet's writer officed. The word of the month was "office" used as a verb. Thus, Malcolm and all his fellow employees had recently received a memo announcing that Ted Jones had been put in charge of In–House Career Enhancement and that he would be officing on the 55th floor. It was from that very office that the pamphlet announcing the workshop had come.

According to the intramural grapevine, Ted Jones was currently sleeping with a very important company vice president. It was clearly unwise to belittle this man who officed on the 55th floor and sexed in a power bed. Some of Malcolm's fellow employees, conflating a useful British expression with a useful American one and coming up with something meaningless, liked to say that Western Bell was run by a good old boy network. They would have come closer to the truth if they'd said it was run by a good old bed network. Malcolm saw no point in endangering his job now, while literary success was still a distant dream.

The pamphlet went on and on, for page after slick page, with photographs of happy groups of Successful Coworkers who had attended previous sessions of the workshop, and with quotations from them attesting to the impact of the workshop on their lives and their work. All in all, the telephone ratepayers of the state of Arapahoe had been soaked a pretty penny for this workshop even before it got under way. It was the kind of company extravagance that made Malcolm grind his teeth every time he encountered it. The thought of it filled him with guilt when he deposited his biweekly paycheck. Not that he would ever not deposit it. The monthly payments he had to make to keep Marlene in the manner to which the court had said she was entitled gave him little choice.

Wednesday of the next week found Malcolm the lone wearer of blue jeans and running shoes in a room full of overdressed and overeager Successful Coworkers.

They sat around an oval table of some heavy wood, a handsome piece of furniture, highly polished, and paid for by the long-suffering telephone ratepayers, who had no idea what their money had bought. The same, Malcolm thought, looking around the room and feeling out of place and trapped, could be said for the souls of his fellow workers. Those souls were also dense, impenetrable, well polished, and completely for sale. He pondered that analogy for a while, but it led him nowhere and he abandoned it.

At nine on the dot, the instructor bounded into the room, grinning frantically. "Hi, everyone!"

He was a young man, smooth of cheek and forehead, and, Malcolm felt sure, of brain. He was also tall, slender, handsome in a clean-cut way, with clear eyes and perfect teeth. His head was covered with thick, wavy dark hair and his clothes hung on him perfectly. He was every woman's dream and every man's nightmare.

"Hi!" he said again. He sprang from the doorway to the front of the room and said, "I'll be your facilitator today. My name's Jack Jackson, but you can call me 'Jack.'"

And my parents grew me in a vat from alien spores, Malcolm thought. Or maybe it's plastic surgery. Christ, look at them. They think this guy's great!

All the Successful Coworkers around him were staring at Jack "Jack" Jackson worshipfully. This was the man with the answers, the secrets of success, the holy knowledge. This was Important Stuff.

"Now that *you* know *my* name," Jack "Jack" Jackson said, "I think we ought to go around the table and introduce ourselves." He pointed at a woman near him, who looked first flustered and then flattered. "We'll start with you."

She pointed at herself and raised her eyebrows and batted her eyes at the facilitator, who was probably twenty years her junior.

"Yes, that's right, you," Jack-Jack-Jack said. "Just give us your name, dear, and the name of your organization."

"Oh," she said breathlessly, "I'm Rebecca Ortiz, and I work in New Products Marketing, and we're right here on the 14th floor!"

The facilitator nodded. "Becky. That's great. And you?" He bent his boyish gaze on the man next to Rebecca Ortiz. The man answered, and Jack–Jack–Jack shortened his name immediately as well.

Malcolm ground his teeth. Compulsive nicknamery. Another nickname nincompoop. How was he going to get through eight hours of this idiocy?

When his turn came, he said, "My name is Malcolm Erskine, and I work in the New Ways to Get Money from the Widows and Orphans Office, more popularly known as the Waffen SS. We office down in the 25th subbasement. Our motto is, 'If you've got a last penny hidden somewhere, we'll find it.'"

His coworkers looked at him in consternation, confusion, or hostility, depending on each individual's degree of company loyalty and intelligence. However, JackJackJack was unfazed. Obviously, he didn't listen to what anyone said. He heard only the name and then nicked it. "Mal," he said, nodding, and turned his attention to the next Successful Coworker.

"Yeah," Malcolm muttered. "Mal. Short for Malcontent."

A lunch break was scheduled for noon. It seemed ten hours away, rather than three. Since only his body's presence was required and not his brain's, Malcolm tried to spend the rest of the morning working out plot details in the novel he was currently writing. It worked surprisingly well, and for him the morning was productive. He felt that he had indeed become a more satisfied human being. He was almost sorry to see noon arrive.

Lunchtime! Teacher J–J–J says, "See ya in an hour! Have a good lunch, you guys!"

The Successful Coworkers laugh.

Why the laughter? Malcolm wondered. Was there a joke I missed? It was a feeling he had often had, going back to his childhood. Nowadays, Marlene and the court system played a renewed joke on him every month, and he still didn't get the punchline.

Bell rings! Captives free for one hour, rush to the playground!

Malcolm fretted as he waited for the elevator. There was good stuff in his head from his morning's musings and he knew that it would drift away if he didn't get it into some permanent form soon. The elevator bell *pinged,* and Malcolm bulled his way to the front of the crowd so as to get on the elevator first. "Sorry, sorry, sorry," he muttered insincerely. "Running shoes. Won't hurt your toes."

A flash of insight: if all execudroids wore running shoes, there'd be fewer mortal injuries as they scrambled over one another on the road to the top. Perhaps he could use that insight in a book some day.

Back at his desk (fifty–five minutes left), Malcolm yanked open the drawer in which he kept personal matters, pulled out a Tupperware container, pulled off the top, and began eating the lunch he had brought from home. Then he turned to his desktop computer and began processing words.

Eating, typing, eating, typing. Just a writin' fool. The outside world had vanished.

The outside world hadn't vanished entirely. Boss–radar alerted him to the passage of Jim Leiter, a man who had stopped climbing the corporate ladder a decade earlier and whom others now climbed over. Malcolm kept typing but also kept watching Leiter out of the corner of his eye, ready to save the chapter he was working on and substitute some work on his screen.

Leiter passed by, deep in conversation with another boss of the same level. Malcolm heard the other man say to Leiter, "You're lucky with Erskine. Works hard right through lunch, even in the middle of a workshop. Wish *I* had..." At which point they passed out of earshot.

Yeah, that's me, Malcolm thought. Just call me "Mal." Short for "Malfeasance."

Uh-oh, the bell's ringing again! The sad bell, the dolorous bell, the bell that calls the little barbarians back to the classroom.

Malcolm's face was appropriately long. The book—a tragic, gripping drama about an unsuccessful science-fiction writer—was going well and he hated to leave it in mid-grip.

His Successful Coworkers, however, looked happy and chattered together about their eagerness to get back into the room and hear more wonders from Teach. Out of the mouth of a babe and suckling, Malcolm thought, wondering briefly what the rest of the quotation was and where it came from.

J-J-J stood at the door to welcome them, each and every one, and he addressed each and every one by nickname, proving the value of the memory-aiding tips he had spewed out during the morning session. "Mal," he said, nodding.

Malcolm grinned brightly. "That's me. 'Mal.' Short for 'Maleficent.'"

Christ, he thought, what a jerk, what a twerp, what a dork. This is endless. It's all endless. Life is endless. Failure is endless.

Failure is endless, he repeated, savoring the line. Not bad. Have to use it in a book some time.

Post-prandial sleepiness took over. There was to be no working out of plot details this afternoon. Instead, J-J-J's nattering kept merging with dreams, out of which Malcolm would jerk suddenly awake, looking around in short-lived panic to see if anyone had noticed his drooping eyelids and bowing head.

But his Successful Coworkers were all too absorbed in listening to JJJ to notice Malcolm. Their pens scratched busily on their burgundy-leather-encased ruled tablets.

Oh, God, Malcolm cried within the safety of his mind, they're taking notes!

While he was nodding with sleepiness, they were nodding in agreement with JJJ's insights into the business world—a world which Malcolm believed to be so lacking in depth that insights into it are physically impossible. The shock of seeing everyone else take all of this nonsense so seriously kept Malcolm awake for a full ten minutes.

During that time, JJJ was able to rattle off three points of vital importance for becoming more dynamic, a better salesman, and a happier person within the telephone company environment. With each point, he extended another finger, starting with his index finger, and waved his hand in the air, so that at the end he was giving a manic Boy Scout salute.

"One!" JJJ cried happily to the roomful of wide–eyed, small–brained, busily scribbling listeners. "A customer never *buys* anything. You *sell* him something!"

Scribble, scribble, scribble.

"Two! You can go just as far in this company as *you* decide to! No one promotes you! You promote yourself! Golly! Look at Ted Jones! He started out as a lineman, and look at him now! You can do the same thing he did!"

There was a slight pause as all the Successful Coworkers thought about Ted Jones's route to the top and wondered if they really wanted to take it themselves, but then the scribble, scribble, scribble began again.

"Three! Capitalism was ordained by God, right there in the Bible, so the more you do to advance it in the world and in your personal lives, the better everything will go for you now and in the afterlife."

Malcolm expected an even longer pause after this bomb, but there was no pause at all. The Successful Coworkers nodded vigorously and scribbled furiously.

Malcolm sighed in defeat and drifted back into sleep.

He was rushing down a long corridor toward a gigantic old man sitting in judgment over the souls of the newly dead. The old man sat behind a battered gray-painted metal desk. He had a very long, white beard splattered with food stains.

"Who's this?" the old man roared in a voice that shook the Heavens. "Malcolm Erskine, eh?"

Malcolm recognized him immediately. It was his grandfather, old Tibbs Erskine, source of childhood nightmares, a ghastly ancient whose death fifteen years earlier Malcolm had celebrated with a bottle of fairly good champagne.

The real Tibbs Erskine had had a hoarse, gravelly voice. Not this Tibbs.

"Gotcha now," Tibbs bawled, leering at his hated grandson. He peeled back his thin lips, exposing those big, pointed, grayish yellow teeth that Malcolm had seen so often in nightmares much like this one. Tibbs opened and closed his mouth rapidly a few times, his powerful teeth snapping together. "Heh, heh, heh. Filthy kid. Cleanliness is next to godliness. Lesson you never learned."

He wagged his long forefinger at Malcolm, displaying a ragged, dirty fingernail. "Lessee, now. Questions for the defendant. Yes, indeedy. Number one: 'Dja ever resist being sold a bill of goods, eh? Didja? Ever in your life?"

Not that Malcolm could remember. And even if he had ever resisted being conned, falling for Marlene more than made up for that. He looked at his feet and muttered, "No."

"Hah!" Tibbs Erskine checked something off on a clipboard that materialized in his hand. "Did you go just as far in your career as you wanted to, rather than let other people decide how far you could go? Huh? Didja, huh?"

Malcolm glared at the ground and shuffled his feet. "No."

"Speak up, you godawful little turd!" The very ground shook. Those teeth snapped and snapped, sounding like thunder. "I can't hear you! You're as worthless as your father was at your age. Speak up!"

"NO!"

Tibbs Erskine glared down from his immense height. "Don't raise your voice to me, Sonny. Must be your damned mother's blood. Okay, last question. Have you always and ever and in every way and in every place and at every opportunity preached capitalism and condemned all forms of collectivism?"

"N—"

"Ah hah!" Tibbs Erskine bellowed, cutting off his grandson's reply. He jammed his thumb down on the desk, depressing a huge red button that Malcolm was sure hadn't been there before.

The floor beneath Malcolm vanished and he started falling. Far below him, a great pit of fire roared, its flames writhing up toward him eagerly.

He kicked in reflexive panic and awoke. He looked around quickly, but his Successful Coworkers were still intent on JJJ's words of wisdom, and no one had noticed his movement.

The dream, he realized—and it was a very depressing realization—was better than anything he had ever written.

The second seed was provided by Malcolm's still-new agent, a young woman named Judith Tillen, who was quickly learning why both Malcolm's first agent and his wife had dumped him.

"I wanna be rich," Malcolm whined. "Why aren't I rich?"

Why aren't I? Judith thought. Why don't I have at least one fabulously successful client, fifteen percent of whose royalties would make *me* rich, too? Then I could handle only those clients I really liked. Which is to say, those who don't whine.

"Because you've never had a hit, Malcolm. In fact, you've never even had a moderate success."

Malcolm glared at her for a moment, then relaxed against his side of the booth. "Yeah, you're right."

They were in the coffee shop of the hotel where the World Science Fiction Convention was being held. The hotel was filled with the socially unusual young readers of the fiction and the embittered middle-aged writers of it. The former came to these conventions to see the latter and to socialize with each other. The latter came to pretend that they were there to get to know the former, but they were really there to booze with each other, to badger their agents, and to lick the boots of any editors in attendance. The agents attended to do business with the editors and to let their clients get their badgering and whining out of their systems. The editors attended because their boots needed a spit shine.

The convention was usually held on Labor Day weekend, usually in America, and usually in some city where the heat and humidity in early September are frightful. This year, it was being held in Indianapolis, and the heat and humidity were frightful.

Malcolm had gone to college only fifty miles from here, at Indiana University. He remembered the summers as being hot and humid, but not this oppressive. His body must be having more and more trouble dealing with the heat because of age. God, he thought, now I'm getting old, too. Old *and* unsuccessful. I'll be one of those unshaven, drunken wrecks I see stumbling around these conventions. Look, someone will say, isn't that what's-his-name? And someone else will say, Oh, yeah, Erskine. Didn't he sell a few books a few decades ago that no one ever read?

"And every year," he told Judith, "there's a whole batch of new, young writers coming up that everyone goes ga-ga over, which pushes people like me further and further down on the publishers' lists. This is a young man's genre."

"That's not really fair. There are plenty of older writers doing very well."

"Yeah, but they became famous when they were still young. I don't mean that only young writers can write this stuff. I mean that publishers aren't interested in discovering anyone who's already past thirty, or who's had books published that didn't do well. How well you write has nothing to do with that. If you don't hit it young, and on the first try, they aren't interested."

Embarrassed, Judith looked down at her dessert. Pecan pie, and far from the wonderful variety she had found only in the South, but at least she was closer to the South here than she was in New York.

"There's a lot of truth in that, Malcolm. But you really are a fine writer, with a polished technique and all the other craftsmanship an experienced writer develops." She meant that quite sincerely, and saying it made her feel—for the moment, anyway—warmer toward her luckless client. He *was* a pretty good writer, and he *did* deserve greater success, and acknowledging that to herself made her more sympathetic toward his whining and self-pity. "I don't know what to tell you, Malcolm. Maybe you ought to try something in a different genre."

"Well, I *have* thought about doing an expose of the software business. Rip the lid off it and show all the nasty little wriggling white things hiding in the darkness."

Oh, God, Judith thought. "I think the audience might be a bit limited."

"Oh, I suppose so. And the little nasty wriggling white things are few and far between. The main ugly truth about the software business is that it's so fucking boring, and that wouldn't make for much of an expose."

"It certainly sounds boring," Judith agreed. "I think you ought to stick to fiction. That's more your *metier."*

Metier, Malcolm repeated to himself. Jesus, I've got an agent who knows more words than I do. "You're right. Okay, listen to this. This is much better. I've been thinking of writing a satirical pseudo–Western. I keep hearing that Westerns are about to make a comeback any day now."

"I keep hearing that, too," Judith said. "But I've been hearing that for as long as I can remember. I bet you have, too, and I know you can remember a lot further back than I can. Anyway, just what do you mean by a 'satirical pseudo–Western,' or do I even want to know?"

She had ordered the pecan pie before finishing the main course, a truly awful fish sandwich, in the almost superstitious belief that this would make her late lunch meeting with Malcolm end sooner. Now she poked at the dry, tasteless, flaky white sandwich filling and thought again about the South. For an instant, a memory of succulent, tasty, lightly breaded fried river catfish came back to her. She could smell it. She closed her eyes and smiled. But then in her mind the dead fish assumed Malcolm's pouty face. She opened her eyes again and faced reality.

For a moment, Malcolm's pout disappeared and he displayed some enthusiasm. He leaned forward slightly. "This was my idea. I'd call it *The James Boys,* and the gimmick would be that it would *seem* to be a straight historical Western about Frank and Jesse James, but in fact, as the reader—pardon me, the *intelligent* reader—would eventually come to realize, the two gunslinging brothers are really Henry James, the novelist, and his brother, the psychiatrist, whatever his name was."

"William. I don't—"

"Wait, wait," Malcolm said, rushing on. "See, the plot would be one of the real–life escapades of Frank and Jesse. Robbing a bank, or whatever. But one of the characters, the older brother, would speak in Henry James's impossible sentences, and the younger brother would ponder everyone's inner motivations and psychological problems while he was shooting them." He leaned back, smiling with pleasure at his own idea.

"The more I think about it, the more I like it. Or a variant of it would be to have Frank and Jesse fake Jesse's murder and escape from the law by moving East and assuming new identities, becoming the other James brothers. Or maybe *vice-versa* if the dates work out the other way around. Have Henry and William move West and become criminals. Sounds like a blockbuster to me."

"Sounds impossible to sell, to me. How many editors would even get the joke? It's a bit obscure." Judith congratulated herself on her tact. Her first impulse had been to tell Malcolm that his idea sucked with teeth.

Malcolm deflated immediately. "Yeah, maybe you're right. Not to mention that I'd have to read a bunch of Henry James novels to really get the feel for his prose, which is a pretty awful thought. Ah, well, maybe some day, when I'm famous and can write anything I want to, I'll give the idea a try."

I'm desperate to be famous, he thought. It's loosening my normally ferocious grip on reality.

Judith, he realized, might be the only agent or editor at this convention who even knew who Malcolm Erskine was.

The evening before, on the way up to his hotel room for the night, Malcolm had shared the elevator with a famous editor. Just the two of them, alone in a small elevator for who knew how many minutes! It had struck Malcolm as a gift from the gods, a golden opportunity for the kind of professional schmoozing that he had told himself was the main reason for attending the convention. He had smiled at the man and said hello in as warm and familiar a tone as he could manage.

The editor had smiled uncertainly and peered at Malcom's convention attendee badge, pinned to his shirt pocket. Malcolm's name was on the badge, and a red ribbon was attached to it, indicating that he was a professional writer.

"Um, hi," the editor had said, frowning, concentrating on the name on the badge. "I'm sorry. Do I know you?"

"Not yet, ha, ha! Malcolm Erskine." He stuck out his hand.

The editor took his hand reluctantly and let it go quickly. "I'm afraid I don't...I'm sorry, I...What have you written?"

Malcolm told him. It didn't take very long.

"Ah, yes. I see. Well..."

There was a silence that seemed eternal.

The elevator bell *dinged.*

"Ah, my floor," the editor said, not hiding his relief very well. "Well. Have a nice convention."

The door opened onto a brightly lit hotel hallway filled with happy, laughing people who greeted the editor with cries of welcome uttered in rich, successful voices. Then the door closed, and Malcolm continued alone up to his floor, which was quiet and dusty and ill lit, where were located the rooms the convention had reserved for failed authors who really shouldn't have bothered attending.

He's just clutching at straws, Judith realized. Poor man. He really *is* depressed and worried about his career. With good reason, she admitted to herself. To what degree Malcolm's situation was her fault for not selling his work, and to what degree it was Malcolm's for not sending her work she could sell, she could not have said. She was sure that agents and their clients would always have different answers to that question.

"I'm not sure you should spend too much time thinking about Westerns."

"Maybe so," Malcolm said. "I suppose science fiction really is my *metier."*

This is going to go on forever, Judith thought. I'll never get to enjoy my pecan pie. I'll never even get back to my room. How do I stop it?

She looked at her watch. "Why, it's three o'clock already!" she said brightly. "So that means it's already four o'clock in New York! This whole time zone thing seems strange to me. I always have trouble keeping track of it. Here we are, eating," she sighed, "pecan pie, and in New York it's already almost dinner time. It's really quite late."

"Time zones are shit," Malcolm said.

"What?"

"They make no sense at all. The whole world should just be on Greenwich time. So instead of setting my alarm for 6 a.m. to get up for work, I'd set it for 1 p.m. So what? I'd still be tired and filled with resentment and anger when it went off. Anyway, it'd be less confusing for everyone, in the long run." Maybe that way agents wouldn't call their clients at 5 a.m., thinking they must be up already because it was 8 a.m. in New York, as Judith had once done to him.

"But wait a minute!" he said suddenly. "Why stop there? The world's moving toward decimal measurements in everything, so why should time be sacred? Why don't we divide the day into ten parts? Divide that into ten parts and so on. So that way, a milliday would be, um..." He drifted off into calculation.

Judith played with her pecan pie. She could of course eat it and ignore Malcolm as he rattled on, but she knew she wouldn't really enjoy it until he finally shut up. And, preferably, left.

"Just under a minute and a half," he said. "So that would be convenient. People could get used to thinking in those terms."

"I couldn't."

"No, they couldn't. You're right. They wouldn't accept it. People are idiots." He didn't notice Judith's sudden stiffening or her glare. That editors and agents are also people with feelings was a fact that too often eluded Malcolm. "The only way to make such a radical change stick would be to kill everyone off and start fresh. No parents to bias the new kids. Brew the next generation in vats."

Oh, no, Judith thought, he's about to come up with another hackneyed, derivative, unsellable idea for a science-fiction novel.

"I could do a non-fiction book suggesting all of this," Malcolm said thoughtfully, surprising her slightly. "Maybe make a bit of stir. Or maybe I'd just be dismissed as a kook. Probably not even publishable, right?"

Judith shook her head, feeling a vast sense of relief.

"Maybe I should do it as a novel, instead. A whole new world of new people. All speaking the same language, all using rational measurements. The only holiday all over the world would be the first day of the new year, which would be called Vat Day."

"And everyone would look the same and act the same?"

"Oh, no. There'd still be lots of genetic diversity." Malcolm laughed. "But they'd all read the same books. Mine!" He could imagine himself being happy in such a world. A rational world. A peaceful world. A prosperous world. A world in which he was the top bestselling author. Or maybe the only bestselling author. It wouldn't be a very rational world otherwise.

Everyone would be physically perfect. Especially the women. Who would also be perfectly infatuated with Malcolm Erskine.

Too simple, Malcolm realized. You have to have tension and an antagonist. So maybe the bestselling writer turns out to be the world's only defense against a seemingly sexy woman who somehow emerged from the vat mentally warped. Marlinga is her name. Maybe the temperature control went bad while Marlinga was still being formed. Or someone accidentally poured too much or too little of some important chemical into the mix. So she's outwardly a hot number, with a firm little body that looks terrific in panties, and she can do pretty remarkable things with her mouth, as the author hero finds out before he discovers that she's a criminal genius intent on destroying the world and especially him.

There'd have to be an even hotter babe involved, a girl who had emerged from the vats without a single flaw. All the temperature controls and chemical mixtures were absolutely optimum. She'd be a dusky goddess with shoulder-length black hair. She'd be rescued from Marlinga by the hero writer at the very end and would fling her arms around his neck and kiss him passionately. End of book, but not end of story.

Gazing off into space, smiling slightly, Malcolm sighed.

"Well, actually," Judith said, "I was thinking that maybe you should give science fiction a rest. Maybe you need to get some distance from it for a while. Crime, mystery, suspense—that's more what I had in mind. All very big right now."

Malcolm sneered. "So are New Age and self-help. Maybe I should invent some new kind of woo-woo."

Foolishly, Judith asked, "For example?" Maybe he had a germ of an idea for something useful. Infected by his desperation, she found herself wanting to help him even while she was desperate to get away from him.

"Oh, I don't know. I don't..." Then he chuckled. "Here's one. It just came to me. You know how idiotic astrology is?"

"Um," Judith said. One of her clients was selling a couple of hundred thousand paperback copies a year of an astrological cookbook, *Stars in Your Kitchen.*

"Right. Even if the theories weren't just pulled out of thin air and based on the sun's positions in the Zodiac thousands of years ago, how would the effect work? Not gravity. Someone calculated that the gravitational effect of the doctor standing next to a mother giving birth is far greater than the pull of the planets on the baby at the same time. I mean, it just makes no sense at all. But how about magma?"

How about those Yankees, Judith wanted to say. "What about magma?"

"Well, it's close by. Right under our feet. Almost. Sort of. It probably does have a gravitational effect on us. It flows in huge currents. Maybe it even releases gases that we aren't aware of. So in other words, where you're born and when may affect your personality because of the magma flows underneath you at the time."

"It's novel," Judith said uncertainly.

The gimmick began to appeal to Malcolm more as he thought about it. "Magmamancy," he said. "Magmoscopy. No, that sounds medical. Anyway, I'd have to come up with a good name for this new pseudo-science. I could tie it to primitive religions. Maybe that's why they used to throw virgins into volcanoes! They wanted to connect the tribe to the magma! They understood all of this intuitively."

"I bet that never happened except in a movie," Judith said.

Malcolm scarcely heard her. He had been transported into a fantasy in which he rescued a beautiful black-haired, dusky-skinned maiden from a terrible death in some Polynesian volcano. She turned to him, her almond-shaped eyes wide with gratitude and desire, and flung her arms around his neck and her legs around his waist and kissed him passionately.

That sexual fantasy gave way to an even more potent one: the cover of a bestselling book with Malcolm's name on it. Across the top it said MAGMAMANCY. Beneath that was a painting of a volcano in full eruption.

Malcom frowned. He had seen that cover before, in real life. Hadn't it been used for L. Ron Hubbard's book about his invented religion?

Then he saw the look on Judith Tillen's face, and both the book cover and the luscious mouth of the almond-eyed maiden faded away.

"Crap," Malcolm said. "Maybe I should start a new religion, like Hubbard. Now even his awful science-fiction series is a smash, because all those Scientologists rush out and buy each new installment. And he's dead! He's writing bestsellers from the grave! Do I have to die to make it? I can't become young again, but I can still die. Then you could hire some young guy to write more novels under my name and pretend they've just been discovered among my papers. Maybe then you could even sell my real novels, once they're reeking of the tomb and decaying flesh and wriggling piles of maggots."

Judith pushed her uneaten slice of pecan pie away and signaled for the check.

Malcolm found himself utterly caught up in his new literary project.

At work, he lied bald facedly about what he was really doing, and he worked on his new book instead of producing programs. He realized that eventually there would be a day of reckoning. He was counting on literary success coming first.

When someone approached close enough to see the monitor of the computer on his desk, close enough to see that the screen was covered with English text rather than lines of source code, he would say something about documentation. "Suppose a truck runs over me some day," Malcolm would say, repeating one of the oldest clichés in the programming business. "You guys would be left with having to figure out how all my programs work. I thought it was about time I started churning out detailed documentation, just in case of that truck."

Once, Jim Leiter, worried by how much time Malcolm was spending on this self–assigned documentation project, asked just how long all this text would turn out to be.

Into Malcolm's mind suddenly sprang a clear, solid, full–color picture of his book filling a window display in a Barnes & Noble outlet. It was a thick book. People of both sexes, various ages, and a range of income levels and professions were rushing into the store to buy it. It was as close to a religious experience as he ever wanted to come.

He closed his eyes to see his vision more clearly, watching one of the dream people pick up the book and read the back and front inside covers. He guessed the expensive hardcover to be around four hundred pages long. Meaning six hundred double-spaced manuscript pages. "Six hundred pages," he said.

Leiter stared at him in horror. "Six—!"

"Double spaced," Malcolm said quickly. "And with wide margins. Twenty-five lines per page, ten words per line. Say two hundred and fifty words per page, for the sake of argument."

Leiter looked dazed. "Huh? Why?"

"Because that's the way I do documentation," Malcolm explained.

"It'll take you forever! What are you doing to my schedule? I've got to hand in the next quarter's estimates to Jab. I'm screwed!"

Malcolm suspected that Leiter had never been screwed and never would be. "Give him anything," he told his boss, thinking this would soothe him. "He probably can't read, anyway."

Alarm filled Leiter's round face. He looked quickly to either side and then shook his head warningly at Malcolm. In a low voice, he said, "Don't be ridiculous. Of course he can."

"The guy's not even human," Malcolm said, although he did lower his voice.

Jab, as Leiter insisted on calling him, obeying the Western Bell dictum that everyone was to be addressed by first name or nickname, furthering the pretense of equality, democracy, and doors that were always open, was Leiter's boss. Malcolm had glimpsed him on a few of Jab's rare visits to what was supposed to be his office, and Malcolm really wasn't sure he was human.

"Look at him," Malcolm said. He kept his voice low, for until he achieved the success and wealth he was increasingly sure *Business Secrets from the Stars* would bring him, he needed a paycheck, and jobs were hard to come by in an America presided over by the Great

Defibrillator. "He's like two feet tall and covered with hair. And he doesn't speak. He makes strange noises."

"You've spoken to him?" Leiter looked even more alarmed.

"No. But I heard that weird babbling outside my cubicle one day, so I stepped out into the corridor and I saw him walking away. He looked like a little monkey wearing a suit."

Leiter glared at. "Well, you're wrong, okay? I've talked to him. He has kind of a strange accent, but he's brilliant. He's just what this company needs. And you..." He pointed at Malcolm. His finger shook with agitation, possibly anger, possibly just his usual nervousness. "Just do your damned job, okay?" He spun around and stalked out of Malcolm's cubicle and away.

Malcolm closed his eyes again.

The dream reader was still there, waiting in line to pay for the book and avidly reading it while waiting. Fuzzy and indistinct before, the dream reader now solidified into a stunningly, exotically beautiful young woman with shoulder-length black hair and olive skin. She looked at Malcolm's photograph on the inside back cover (the author: pensive, frightfully intelligent, yet dashing and with an intriguing glint in his otherwise quiet eyes) and she said to the woman waiting in line behind her, "Wow! Isn't he wonderful? I'd give anything to meet him and throw myself on him and wrap my arms and legs around him and kiss him nearly to suffocation and become his sex slave." She sighed. "But of course it will never happen. Especially if he doesn't get this book finished."

Malcolm opened his eyes and threw himself into his task with even greater enthusiasm.

At home he pushed aside the novel he had been working on and devoted all of his writing time to *Business Secrets from the Stars.* When he wasn't working on the book, he thought about it. When he slept, he dreamed about it, visions of the Andromeda Corporation and Lukas and his fellow Merskeenians drifting through his slumbering mind.

He was following the pathway blazed decades before by L. Ron Hubbard. He hoped, wished, prayed that he would have commensurate success.

For just a moment, Malcolm's conscience bothered him. He had been a basically honest person all his life, and yet now he was planning to earn a considerable amount of money with what amounted to a confidence game. But it was the work of a moment to rationalize his feelings away and stuff his conscience back into the tiny cranny where it belonged.

CHAPTER TWO

O beloved descendants, never let your history be a barrier to your future success. Old failures are buried in the past. You are blessed to live in the land of infinite personal reinvention and the limitless worship of form over substance. It is presentation that matters, not what underlies or does not underlie the surface. Do not let yourself fear because of what you were or were not. Forget your history. History, as one of your great thinkers told you long ago, is bunk.

—Lukas of Aldebaran, trying to be encouraging

Decades before Malcolm Erskine had his life–altering moment of illumination, indeed before Malcolm was born, young Daddy Longlegs came home from the war.

Daddy's postwar plans, formulated even before he had shipped out, were quite simple. He would marry Grammy, his fiancée, move from New England to Texas, start an oil company with the help of his daddy's friends, make a few million dollars with the further help of his daddy's friends, and live happily ever after.

But when he reached New England, he discovered that his daddy had changed the last part of the plan. Rather than live happily ever after, Daddy's daddy said, Daddy would have to become President of the United States.

Most immediately, this required that Daddy travel to Africa and murder some animals.

This quest for blood was driven by the careful calculations of his daddy's advisers, and most especially by the calculations of Mr. Umbral, an old Longlegs family retainer. For despite Daddy's wartime record, it was obvious to Daddy's daddy's men that Daddy gave anyone who met him the immediate impression that he was a wimp. If Daddy was ever to be President, it was imperative that he start working immediately to establish his non-wimphood. The advisers had agreed that Daddy should emulate Teddy Roosevelt. In a few respects, at any rate.

Daddy had another problem. With the possible exception of Grammy, no one who met him liked him. But that wouldn't matter so much politically, the advisers thought. The time was coming when no voter would ever actually meet a Presidential candidate in any meaningful sense. The image alone would matter, and they wanted Daddy's image to be that of a virile huntin', shootin' kinda guy. A man's man. A Teddy Roosevelt. Again, in some respects.

Fortunately, Mr. Umbral felt that it wasn't really necessary for Daddy to do his killing in, say, the Belgian Congo or even British East Africa. Some place safer and more civilized would be much better. So, accompanied by Mr. Umbral, Daddy went to South Africa, spent a few days enjoying Capetown's old-fashioned pleasures, and then drove up to Southwest Africa in a well-stocked Ford GPW.

Mr. Umbral stayed behind in Capetown to discuss family business with some local oilmen.

Daddy, on his trip into the relative wilderness, was accompanied by a number of South Africans. They were all friends or business acquaintances of his father. All of them worked for Shell Oil. They were all men, of course. They were all white, of course. They were all virile huntin', shootin', drinkin', and cursin' kinda guys.

It was June, the sky was clear, and except for the roughness of the unpaved roads in "The Southwest," as his companions called it, and the strange accents of those companions, and the odd shapes of the trees, and the chilly dryness of the air, and the dustiness of the terrain, and the occasional native village, Daddy could have imagined that he was in northern Texas.

"This is the real bushveld," his companions told him, rolling their r's and speaking in deep voices with a kind of manly, worldly self-assurance that Daddy envied enormously. Golly, this was the real place for a real man!

His companions' capacity for beer added to the north-Texas illusion. As did their attitude toward the natives. Each time they passed a native village or a black walking beside the road, they said something, always in an angry grumble, about "bloody Kaffirs," which they pronounced "bleddy Keffirs." As the miles increased and the supply of beer decreased, that changed to "blerrykeffirs."

Sometimes, Daddy, who did most of the driving because of the effect of the beer on his companions, felt like adding some racial pejorative of his own—not because he felt any animus toward the local blacks, or those back home, in fact he didn't, but rather as a way of becoming part of the gang, showing that he belonged in this company of older, hard-drinking, worldly-wise, tough, aggressive, virile men. But his nerve failed him and he said nothing.

They stopped a few times to spend the night—always in hotels, to Daddy's great disappointment, for he had been looking forward to camping out under the ancient African sky. But when he suggested this, his companions said scornfully, "And get robbed by blerrykeffirs? Maybe murdered in our sleep? Or just freeze to death? Man, you're crazy!"

In general, the driving toward the wilderness was taking far longer than Daddy had anticipated, in part because they stopped at every small town they passed through to buy more beer. Finally, though, the band of hunters found themselves a hundred miles inside Southwest Africa, in a wilderness with no other humans visible, and strange animal roars and cries coming from the surrounding bush.

It was twilight.

"Now we camp!" Daddy said with youthful enthusiasm. "No, er, dangerous blacks around. Real safe."

His companions laughed raucously. "Man, you think like a blerrykeffir! There're lions around. Lots of 'em. We're safest in here. We'll sleep in the bleddy car."

Daddy looked at his companions. He sniffed the air, rank with a combination of unwashed manly men and spilled beer, and he sighed. He said nothing, accepting their decree as he always had accepted the decrees of men of their generation.

But, darn it, he was annoyed!

One of the men waved in a general way. "Over there. Park under that bleddy tree."

Daddy let the clutch out. A bit too quickly, as it happened. The vehicle lurched forward, hit a huge tree root, and stalled.

Daddy smelled or saw or thought he smelled or saw smoke.

"Fire!" Daddy screamed. "Abandon! Ditch!"

The others laughed at him. "Blerrykeffir!" "Stalled it!" "Stupid boy!" "Worthless. Tell the old man about him."

Daddy flung his door open and scrambled out. In the rapidly fading light, he stumbled over tree roots and rocks, trying to get as far away from the crippled, doomed craft as he could.

The other men were now silhouettes inside the vehicle, waving their bottles in the air and shouting at him. He couldn't understand a word they said.

Other silhouettes slipped past him, big animal shapes heading for the noise. Two of the beasts turned their heads toward him. Giant cat's heads were just visible in the gloom, one with a shaggy fringe of hair.

Daddy had seen lions in a zoo. He froze in place.

The two lions glanced at each other, looked back at him, then dismissed him and joined their companions.

One by one, unhurriedly, the lions entered the vehicle through the door Daddy had left open. The shouts of his companions turned to screams.

Daddy turned and fled into the bush.

Which was a mistake, he realized immediately. He could see almost nothing here, and it was close to impossible to make headway. Maybe he'd be safer in the open.

He turned, intending to go back. But then he heard the roars of the lions and what sounded like one last, faint scream from a human throat, and he retreated into the tangled undergrowth.

Too late for them now, anyway, he told himself. Can't go back. Wouldn't be prudent. Guy's gotta save himself.

He thrashed about, hoping he was making some headway and moving away from the car.

He heard a low growl from behind him and the sound of something large moving through the brush.

He screamed, tried to run, crashed into a tree trunk.

By now he could see nothing.

He scrabbled frantically at the trunk. He felt a thick branch a foot above his head, grabbed it, and started to climb.

Lions, he told himself. Can't climb. I hope.

Daddy climbed until he was exhausted and the branches were too slender for him to pull himself up any further. He sat in a fork, wrapped his long arms and legs around one of the branches of the fork, and tried to stop thinking about lions.

This high up, the tree swayed slowly, gently. It was hypnotic.

Daddy had had a very long and tiring day. Astonishingly, he fell asleep. Fortunately, he held on even in his sleep.

Daylight woke Daddy from a delightful dream in which Grammy was searching through his hair for lice.

Something *was* searching through his hair for lice. Daddy froze in terror. Lions? Did they torment their prey this way before killing it? He kept his eyes squeezed shut and played dead.

No, that pleasant gibbering sound couldn't be a lion.

Slowly, Daddy opened his eyes. He was still in the tree, with his arms and legs still locked around the branch of the fork, but now he could see that he was at most fifteen feet above the ground. Lions could probably jump that high, he thought, annoyed at himself.

Cautiously he looked around. The movement elicited a louder gibbering and a rustling sound. Three little faces stared at him.

"Monkeys!" he exclaimed.

The sound startled them, and they leaped away, landing on more distant branches.

"Hey, it's okay! My, aren't you cute little monkeys?" Lowering his voice, Daddy spoke to them. "Look just like each other. Are you brothers? I bet you are."

Actually, they were brothers. Also cousins. All the little creatures in their small, isolated clan were simultaneously first cousins and second cousins and third cousins and so on. Incest was their way of life. Fortunately, they neither understood such concepts nor would they have been able to communicate the facts to Daddy if they had, which was just as well, for he probably would have been overwhelmed by a profound Republican disgust and fallen out of the tree.

In any case, they had no idea what he was saying. They liked the sound of his voice, though. Inch by inch, they crept closer to him.

By the time rescue arrived, some time around noon, Daddy had won the three little creatures over. The rescuers—all employees of Shell Oil—found him back on the ground with one of the little simians on each shoulder and the third one atop his head. Even in the presence of strange humans, they clung to Daddy.

"You'll have to leave them behind," one of the rescuers told him. "I think there are laws about that." The man stared at the three little creatures, who stared back at him. The man said, "I'll say this for them, though. They certainly are cute little monkeys."

"Sure are. Named 'em Jibber, Jabber, and Jebber. Going home with me."

It took numerous telephone calls to Pretoria and the intervention of the U.S. ambassador at the request of Mr. Umbral on behalf of Daddy's daddy, but of course the laws were bent. Laws are always crafted so that the rich and powerful are exempt from them. If that were not the case, how could we call ourselves civilized?

For a while, it seemed there might be a problem. A government biologist who happened to be in the area cataloging primates caught a glimpse of Jibber, Jabber, and Jebber and instantly declared them an unknown type of Greater Bush Baby. They were thus a national scientific treasure, he insisted, and must never be allowed to leave South Africa.

Fortunately for Daddy, the troublesome biologist, having returned to the bush to search for more of the new primates, disappeared. Once the biologist was out of the way, Mr. Umbral and Daddy's daddy's friends were able to produce a local biologist of their own who testified before a hastily assembled Crown commission that Jibber, Jabber, and Jebber were not Bush Babies at all. Rather, they were a branch of those mysterious Great Apes, native to the central west coast of Africa, that had famously adopted the infant Lord Greystoke in the romances of Edgar Rice Burroughs. Their possession of a language, albeit an indecipherable language, was sufficient proof of this assertion. As such, while they were certainly African treasures, they could hardly be said to be South African treasures. Therefore, if it was up to anyone to decide whether they could be removed from their native soil, it was up to, the biologist sniffed, the Belgians, and they were notorious for their lack of concern for native species. Anyone who doubted his conclusions, he added, delivering the rhetorical *coup de grâce,* clearly had the intellect of a bleddy keffir.

By August, Daddy, his new bride, and Jibber, Jabber, and Jebber were settling into their new home in Texas, which the three little brothers seemed to find satisfactorily primitive. Grammy Longlegs had loved them on sight, declared them almost unbearably cute little monkeys, and assured Daddy she'd raise them like her own children.

On a Sunday, the new family went to services at the local Church of the Moneyed Classes. Jibber, Jabber, and Jebber were dressed in little suits, custom made for their not–quite–human proportions, and the congregation was enchanted. After the service, Reverend Gregory descended to mingle with the crowd and get a closer look at the three brothers. He bent over and gravely shook hands with each of the three little simians.

This was Jibber, Jabber, and Jebber's first encounter with this human custom, and it delighted them. They would practice it with each other later in private for hours.

"My, my," said Reverend Gregory, "aren't they cute little monkeys?" He stared at the three of them for a few minutes, then said, "But they're not really the same as each other, are they? At first I thought they were, but the more I look at them, the more different they look."

Aware of the attention of a large and friendly crowd of humans, the three little simians, who were rapidly losing what fear they still had of these strange creatures, began to perform. Jebber covered his eyes and then spread his fingers so that he could look through them and gauge the crowd's reaction. Jabber covered his ears and crooned softly, a sweet and charming and meaningless sound. Jibber jumped up down, ran around trying to shake everyone's hand, and gibbered, making sounds that closely resembled but weren't quite English words.

"Kinda reminds me of the Big Three at Potsdam," Reverend Gregory said.

The congregation laughed appreciatively. Even though there was in fact no resemblance between the three little simians and the three big statesmen, the comparison could be taken as insulting to the Democrat in the White House, and that delighted this crowd.

"So which one's Truman?" someone asked.

Gregory pointed at Jibber. "Him. He's a gladhander, he's teeny, and he talks a lot but makes no sense."

The congregation applauded, but Daddy Longlegs looked at his three little boys and stroked his chin thoughtfully.

Many, many years later, probably at about the time Malcolm sold his third novel and was still feeling hopeful about his literary career and his marriage, Daddy had the family retainers assemble a family for Jibber.

On that fateful day when Reverend Gregory had pointed at Jibber and said he resembled Truman, Daddy had decided that after Daddy himself became President, Jibber would become President in his turn.

There were practical difficulties associated with this plan.

Daddy had an impressive pedigree and education and, increasingly, political experience. Jibber was some kind of animal. He had not been born in America. He couldn't speak any human tongue. He was short. He still occasionally forgot himself and defecated on the carpet. But Daddy knew that other Republicans had overcome even worse obstacles on the way to the White House. A paper trail could be manufactured. Jibber could be trained, or at least restrained when necessary. Speeches could be written for him and handed to the appropriate sycophants in the press beforehand.

The most serious lack was a family. A politician had to have one, and nowadays, they had to be photogenic and, increasingly, telegenic.

As always in moments of distress and doubt, Daddy consulted Mr. Umbral.

Daddy hadn't spoken to Mr. Umbral in a couple of months. The upward curve of one corner of Umbral's mouth seemed more noticeable than before. As always, Daddy tried not stare at it, and as always he spent much of the conversation thinking desperately about not staring at it and therefore kept snatching surreptitious glances at it. "He needs a family," he said abruptly. "Jibber. Political career. Requires a family."

Mr. Umbral nodded slightly. He pretended not to notice Daddy staring at his mouth. "We could bring one over from the area where you found him, but that wouldn't do."

"Wouldn't do," Daddy agreed. His gaze wondered around the room, came to light on Mr. Umbral's mouth, and skittered away again. "Wouldn't do at all. Has to be a human woman. And human kids. Gotta face it, though. Human woman would probably run away screaming."

"He's a cute little monkey."

"Even so."

"Well. I'll see what I can do."

At that, Daddy relaxed. When Mr. Umbral said he'd do something about a problem, something got done. The problem went away. It had always been that way, even before Daddy was born, judging by some photographs he had seen from his own father's youth. Daddy stole one quick glance at Umbral's twisted mouth as the old family retainer floated from the room. Yep, everything was okay again in the Longlegs world. Good old Umbral. Mr. U. Always there, always the same—well, except for the ever more twisted mouth—always reliable. Where would the family be without him?

Mr. Umbral—he hated being called Mr. U.—had connections.

He left the family compound immediately and flew to Los Angeles, where he met with some Disney people. They showed him their newest innovation, and it pleased him greatly. It reminded him of the old days, even though the artisans of those times had possessed skills modern man had yet to rediscover. Still, it was a start. He made his needs clear to the group of modern craftsmen. They expressed some doubts, but they were flattered by his confidence and the importance of his commission, and so they agreed.

Next, Mr. Umbral flew to London and met with a different group of craftsmen. These worked for Madame Tussaud's. They, too, were flattered by Umbral's compliments and at being asked to participate in something so novel and important.

Finally, Umbral headed for home. Along the way, he stopped in New York, where he spoke to officials in the city's child welfare agency and arrived at arrangements satisfactory to both him and them.

While Umbral paid attention to family values, Daddy paid attention to other aspects of Jibber's image. Cute was good, and his boy had the cute part down pat, but Daddy was sure that that wasn't enough. Jibber would need an appropriate image, something that would push the right emotional buttons in the electorate.

Religion usually worked.

Daddy set about training Jibber to simper and raise his eyes to Heaven whenever he heard the word "God." Unfortunately, Jibber couldn't distinguish between words with a similar sound. So while he learned to simper and look at the ceiling when he heard the word "God," he also simpered and looked up when he heard "dog" or "log" or "bod." That last one actually made some sense to Daddy, but he feared the public might not agree.

Scratch religion, then.

How about jingoism?

The public had always been quick to confuse excessive nationalism with patriotism and xenophobia with love of country. Any politician worth his salt knew that fact and exploited it constantly. The trick was not to go overboard. Even the American public could be pushed too far. You couldn't do something too obvious, such as wear a U.S. flag tie like some kind of used–car salesman. And while Daddy had a mental image of little Jibber wearing a Roman toga with stars and stripes all over it, like some kind of American emperor, he knew that would never fly. You had to wrap yourself in the flag symbolically, not literally.

Scratch jingoism.

No, he would have to be more subtle. More indirect. Strike the right balance, and you could be as absurd as you wanted to be, and Americans wouldn't even realize that their buttons were being pushed.

After casting about and looking at some popular magazines, Daddy settled on an old, reliable bit of fakery: the cowboy trail.

Daddy had a little cowboy hat and a little cowboy suit and a little cowboy hat and a little pair of cowboy boots custom made for his hairy little boy. Fortunately, Jibber took to them immediately. He only had to be shown once how to wear everything, and after that, he was rarely to be found wearing anything else, except for those days that he reverted to type and wore nothing at all.

The little cap–firing six guns were an even greater success. It reached the point that Grammy had to forbid Jibber to fire them in the house. The sound was giving her a headache.

The only failure was the horse.

Daddy took all three brothers to a stable whose owner could be trusted to keep his mouth shut and introduced them to the cowboy's best friend.

Jebber and Jabber disappeared immediately. Fortunately, they had scampered back to the car and hidden under it, and Daddy found them there later.

Jibber wasn't quite so swift. He stared at the horse, trying to figure out what this creature was. It wasn't a lion or baboon or leopard or anything else he knew he was scared of, so for the moment, he remained calm.

Then Daddy scooped him up and set him atop the saddle.

The horse shifted impatiently under him.

Jibber froze in terror.

Then he unfroze.

Rather, his bowels and his bladder unfroze. They unfroze so explosively that his little cowboy pants burst open in the front and the rear. The back of the cowboy's best friend was covered by the monkey's worst products.

The horse shook himself in violent disgust and turned his head around, fixing Jibber with an evil glare out of one eye.

Jibber leaped off the horse and zipped away after his brothers.

Daddy backed away quickly from the horse, who had now turned his evil glare on him. He turned and followed his three little cowboys' dusty trail out to the parking lot. Tomorrow he would tell the stable owner to have the horse taken away and shot. That'd teach him.

Oh, well, Daddy thought. The kid can still pretend to be a cowboy. Reality doesn't matter in this game.

Six months after his trip, Umbral introduced Daddy and Jibber and Grammy to the new Mrs. Jibber Longlegs and Jibber's and her two adorable children. Daddy was charmed, Grammy pretended to be charmed, and Jibber was bewildered.

"Allow me to introduce," Mr. Umbral said, "Tess."

On cue, a pretty young woman walked in from an adjoining room.

"More precisely," he added, "Tess Longlegs. Mrs. Jibber Longlegs. I have already created a good pedigree and personal history for her." He held up a looseleaf binder that looked quite full. "If you approve. We can change it, of course."

"Satisfactory," Daddy said. "Sure it is. Always is. You did a fine job with the three boys."

Grammy frowned doubtfully. She stepped up to the young woman and examined her carefully. "Tess, you say?"

"Yes," the young woman said. "Ma'am." She paused, then added, "Honored. To. Be. Your. Daughter. In. Law." Another pause. "Ma'am."

"Why does she talk that way?" Grammy asked.

Daddy had understood right away. "Suitable," he said. "Suitable. But Umbral, why not...Well, you know."

Umbral nodded. "Why not human?" He gestured with his chin toward Jibber.

Daddy squinted at his oldest boy, who wasn't really a boy at all, of course. For a moment, the illusion he had managed to convince even himself of fell away and he saw the little simian as he really was. "Ah. Yes. All right."

Grammy continued to examine her new daughter-in-law. "Oh, Hell," she said finally. She had accepted the three little simian brothers as her sons, so she supposed she could learn to accept this Tess person. At least she was human.

"Mr. U.," Daddy said suddenly, as usual not seeing the faint hint of a grimace that crossed Umbral's face at the sound of the hated nickname, "a wife is good. Politician needs kids, though. Cute ones. Told you that before."

Umbral smiled slightly. "Oh, yes," he said. Often, it was hard to tell that Mr. Umbral was smiling. His ancient internal machinery was slowly breaking down. In general, it didn't interfere with his efficient performance of his duties as chief Longlegs family retainer. The only visible side effect was that problem with his mouth, the left corner of which was slowly edging upward. Behind his back, some of the junior family retainers had taken to referring to him as "Mr. Sneer." They thought he had no way of knowing about this. They were wrong. Mr. Umbral had long ago perfected the art of biding his time.

Still wearing his faint smile, he vanished into the room from which Tess had emerged. A moment later, he returned, leading two small girls by the hand.

The kidlings were about five or six years old. They were dressed in frilly dresses and shiny patent leather shoes, their hair was shoulder length and curly, and they glared at everyone.

"New York's finest," Mr. Umbral announced. "I've named them Bip and Bop. Those are working names only. I'm sure you'll come up with something better."

"Hmm," Daddy said. "Like it. Fits with the J–J–J pattern for the boys. Bip and Bop. Yep. Those're their names."

Daddy and Grammy approached cautiously, trying to ooh and aah. These were wild kids, though. They curled back their lips and snarled, and the elder Longlegs were a bit scared of them. "Okay," Daddy said. "Enough with the grandparent crap. Take 'em away. Keep 'em in the nursery. Jibber, come here. Make nice with your new wife."

"He. Is. A. Cute. Little. Monkey."

When Tess said that, Grammy warmed to her a bit. Daddy warmed to her a lot. This was the kind of political wife a potential President needed! He watched with approval as Tess grabbed Jibber's hand in an unbreakable grip and dragged him away.

Jibber twisted his head around and looked at Daddy as though begging for rescue.

Daddy smiled and nodded encouragingly. "Time the boy grew up," he said to Grammy.

"Let's go upstairs," Grammy said. "Suddenly, I feel like breaking out the handcuffs."

Mr. Umbral felt a tiny stirring of doubt. He straightened his back. "I am determined that everything will go correctly this time," he told the family sternly. "I'm not going to repeat the mistakes I made with the Hapsburgs."

"The who?" Daddy said.

"Do they live over in Bar Harbor?" Grammy asked uncertainly.

Umbral grimaced and rubbed his chest. He wondered if he needed some work in there already. He also wondered if he had chosen the wrong family yet again.

He decided not to bother explaining about the Hapsburgs. He would press on, grimly doing his duty, no matter what. Head held high, he left the room.

Grammy pulled Daddy up the staircase to the master suite.

While Grammy and Daddy set about making sub–dom whoopee, Tess led Jibber into the bedroom she had been told was theirs. She locked the door behind them.

Jibber shrank back against the door.

Tess yanked her clothes off and stood naked before her lord and master. As wax–covered robots went, she was not unattractive.

She waited expectantly.

Jibber hugged the safety of the door.

Memory stirred in Tess's brain circuits. She heard Mr. Umbral's voice explaining, "We have had to make some assumptions about the mating habits of the unknown species to which the three J boys belong, based on the ways of other, presumably related, African animals. We have colored your appropriate parts in what we hope is a suitable manner. You should turn your back to him, bend over, and, er, present yourself. Nature will then take its somewhat unnatural course."

Tess followed those instructions. She turned and bent, pointing her rear end toward Jibber.

Jibber was filled with images of the females of his rare species. For a moment, he closed his eyes and imagined he was back among the scrubby trees of the veld. Safe in the branches, the cheerful females used to turn, bend over, and present their swollen red genitals to him. Jibber and his three brothers would shriek with glee and launch themselves upon the willing hairy little babes, commencing a night and a day and a night and a day and a night of delight.

Sniffling slightly, smiling nostalgically, he opened his eyes.

What he saw was rather larger than he remembered. And considerably less hairy. And the smell was odd. And it wasn't red. It was blue. At the center of the blue was a large white star. At the center of the star was an arrow pointing to the target.

Jibber burst into tears.

Tess waggled her star–imprinted loins at him.

Jibber straightened his back. He didn't understand much of what had happened to him since he'd been snatched away from his happy albeit lion–infested homeland and brought to this often horrifying place, but he felt a lot of warmth toward Daddy and Grammy Longlegs for their kindness to him and his brothers, and he enjoyed the act he had been taught to perform involving cowboy boots and six guns, and moreover he understood that Daddy wanted him to pretend to regard this terrifying creature as a female of his own species, and finally he was awfully, awfully good at pretending, and so he steeled himself and tried to do what had to be done.

He pulled off his cowboy boots.

He untied the leather laces that held his chaps in place and let the chaps fall to the floor.

He flung away his little Stetson.

He unbuckled the heavy belt that held his holstered, pearl-handled cap guns and let it slide down his legs.

He unzipped his sturdy jeans.

He unbuttoned his cowboy shirt and peeled it off.

He pulled down his pants and stepped out of them.

Naked, he advanced upon his mate.

Tess wiggled again.

Jibber paused, steeled himself, and moved forward again.

He felt himself stiffening and looked down and was surprised to see just how erected he was. Poor unlettered little simian, he was unacquainted with the ancient tradition of humans mating with beasts. For that matter, he had no idea that he was about to write a new chapter in those pornographic annals by becoming a beast who mated with a wax–covered animatronic machine.

Disney and Tussaud's had done their work well. The appearance and odor of the starry end of Tess were real enough that Jibber finally gave a cry of delight and triumph and leaped upon her, thrusting himself deep inside her.

Relatively speaking. He was rather small compared to her. He found himself straddling her like, well, like a cowboy straddling a horse. His feet were a foot off the floor. His penis, while enclosed entirely inside her, wasn't actually all that far in. Nonetheless, he did his determined best, holding onto her haunches with both hands and thrusting away valiantly.

Unlike the hairy little enthusiasts of his native land, Tess remained immobile.

Jibber's enthusiasm began to fade, and his movements became slower. Closing his eyes and thinking of Africa, he forced himself into rapid motion again and concluded triumphantly. He gibbered in high-pitched delight as his masculine juices shot out of him into the fairly good imitation of a human woman.

Exhausted, Jibber slid out and off. He landed on the floor in a crouch, dazed, confused, exhausted.

Tess straightened and turned around. She looked down at her husband. Jibber looked up at her. Her mouth expanded into a smile simulation. "Thank. You. Jibber," she said. Her metallic teeth glinted. She leaned down toward him, probably intending to simulate a kiss but looking as though she meant to eat him.

Jibber shrieked in terror and sprang away. He scampered up the expensive drapes beside the huge window, zippety zip, lickety split, as fast as any little simian ever did. He balanced for a moment on the heavy–duty curtain rod, testing his footing, then sprang a full fifteen feet to the fan rotating lazily in the middle of the ceiling.

Hanging onto one blade by his fingertips, going around slowly in a circle, Jibber stared down in horror at the creature he had just mated with. He gibbered even more meaninglessly than usual. His bowels loosened, and chimpy feces showered down on Tess and the expensive carpet beneath her.

The door opened and Mr. Umbral walked in. He looked the scene over, wrinkling his nose in disgust. At times like these, he really missed the Inquisition.

CHAPTER THREE

Oh, Starspawn of my star–begotten loins! How like unto a god art thou! How divine thy needs and wishes and desires, and how debased thine enemies and those who stand in thy way and keep thee from what thou deservest! Heed me, O distant descendant: you deserve it, they owe it to you, so grab it, and let no one stop you!

—Lukas of Aldebaran, stardwelling Merskeenian, as transcribed by Malcolm Erskine, after what might perhaps have been a few too many beers

The successful writers Malcolm had met had about them a lordliness, a self–assurance, an overly evident awareness of being at the top of the heap, that always drove him up the wall. It would have been bad enough if he had considered any of them his moral and intellectual superiors. Perhaps then he could have excused their superior manner. Most of them, though, were in his eyes measly scum.

Sometimes he wondered if they really had that air about them or if he was imagining it, creating it whole cloth out of his envy. But most of the time he didn't care whether they had that air or not. He just wanted to get there himself, to reach the point where Malcolm Erskine could look down his nose at anybody he chose to, and anyone observing him would say, "That's Malcolm Erskine. He's such a rich, famous, powerful writer that he's earned the right to look down his nose at anyone he wants to."

Malcolm already had his candidates for lofty nasal observation picked out.

Joe Hoffman, for example: fellow Piketonian, fellow science-fiction author, fellow alumnus of Indiana University, at one time even fellow computer programmer for Western Bell. That was all they had in common, though. Hoffman was up to about a dozen books vs. Malcolm's three. Hoffman had been the guest of honor at a couple of major science-fiction conventions, whereas Malcolm had yet to be invited even to pay his own way to a single one. Hoffman seemed to getting somewhere, edging toward real literary success, while Malcolm was still mired in the mid-list, perhaps forever. Hoffman had a sexy wife and a happy marriage, whereas Malcolm had memories of Marlene, the girl of his nightmares. Hoffman was self-confident and possessed considerable presence in public, but Malcolm was inundated by self-doubts and self-criticisms and could never hide that from others. In short, in Malcolm's view, Hoffman had been born with a silver spoon in his mouth, Malcolm with his foot in his.

Which part of all of that was the worst? Malcolm couldn't decide. Perhaps it was the guest of honor thing.

How he dreamed of being one some day! He imagined himself walking among the adoring fans, bestowing a gracious smile or two. Not too many. Keep them in their place.

It was common practice for the guest of honor to give a convention speech on the topic of his choice—a well attended speech, of course. Malcolm's speech would be brilliant. He had it planned out, written in his mind, just waiting to be delivered.

"Were I but King of Anglophonia." That was the speech's title. It would detail the linguistic atrocities Malcolm would outlaw if he had the royal power to do so. He would ban the words "respect" and "disrespect" so that no one would be able to use them as rhetorical clubs against those expressing opinions the club wielder disagreed with. He would require that anyone speaking English include the *w* sound in the pronunciation of "Quebec"—unless the speaker consistently used the French pronunciation of "Paris" and the Russian pronunciation of "Moscow" and so on for all other foreign place names. No one would be allowed to refer to committing a moral or legal transgression as "making a mistake."

And there was so much more! It would be a long speech. Amusing, of course, witty, entertaining, but leaving no doubt about Malcolm's firm opinions on how his subjects would be required to speak were he but King of Anglophonia.

At which point in his fantasizing, Malcolm would sigh and think, Were I but guest of honor at a science-fiction convention.

Like Joe Hoffman.

Once, during the final stage of their marriage's disintegration, Marlene had said to Malcolm, "Why don't you stop whining and turn out books, like Joe Hoffman does? And start doing some kind of exercise, like lifting weights like he does. He looks great. I'd sure be better off with him—in various senses."

To which Malcolm had replied, "Think you could compete with that gorgeous wife of his? Hah!"

Marlene had snarled. "At least *she* doesn't have to put up with whining from *her* husband!"

"Of *course* not. What does *he* have to whine *about?*"

Oh, what a lovely marriage it had been.

Its breakup had been delayed when Malcolm's third novel appeared on the stands. Marlene had privately decided to give her husband's career one more chance, to see if the third time was the charm, if Malcolm could finally hit the bestseller lists and bring her the wealth and ease she knew she deserved.

However, the stands on which the book appeared were very few, and Marlene immediately recognized the pattern set by Malcolm's first two books: high expectations followed by limited distribution followed by near-zero sales. She had ordered him out of the house and immediately filed for divorce on the grounds of mental cruelty. That, she had felt, was not an exaggeration.

Malcolm learned from a machine that his wife had chucked him out. The machine was a computer, something soulless and without any human feelings, which seemed appropriate.

The computer ran a voice messaging system that Western Bell had named SAM. Malcolm had no idea what that was an acronym for. A coworker had suggested that it stood for "Sadists and Masochists," since that covered everyone who worked for Western Bell.

At two o'clock in the afternoon, he got back to his desk from a long lunch with Steve Golden at their usual Mexican restaurant and checked for messages. He was hoping for the voice of his agent—his first one, at that time—brimming with eagerness, saying that Malcolm must call him immediately because numerous publishers were beating down his door with demands that they be allowed to give stupendous quantities of money to Malcolm Erskine.

SAM's voice was female. How many hours of intensive thought on the part of marketing executives—who are endowed at birth with only a limited ration of hours of thought, which must last them all their lives—had gone into the choice of the woman who had recorded the phrases and digits which the SAM computer combined to make up its spoken sentences? "You have...six...new messages. To listen to your messages, press one. For more options—"

Malcolm quickly punched the ONE button on the telephone's numeric pad, cutting off the recorded voice. If I must listen to a computer-generated female voice, he always thought, then I ought to at least be on the bridge of the Starship *Enterprise.* Beam me up a woman, Scotty.

And then Marlene's message began.

"Hello, you son of a bitch. I figured you'd be at lunch still, you lazy jerk. It's that attitude that explains why you're still a low-level programmer at your age, in case you're interested, you piece of shit. Anyway, I called during your three-hour lunch so that you wouldn't be there, because I didn't want to have to deal with your whining. This is to let you know that when you go home tonight, you're going to have to go to a different home. I've changed the locks. You don't live here any more."

The message continued for half an hour altogether. Since SAM wouldn't accept messages longer than five minutes, Marlene had had to keep calling back to complete her love note. Thus the six messages. Malcolm listened to all of them, following SAM's instructions mechanically as each one ended, absorbing with deadened feelings the insults and the promises of financial degradation. Marlene finished with, "Take good care of yourself, sweetie, because you're going to be taking good care of me for a long, long time to come. Shithead."

Buzz. "End of new messages. To erase messages, press seven. For more options..."

Malcolm and Marlene. A match made in Heaven. Or possibly in some other place.

Malcolm pressed SEVEN, erasing all of the six messages at once. If only Marlene could be erased so easily.

She could, of course. Murder is a simple and easy thing....

Malcolm shook his head. No, murder would not be simple and easy for him. He might get caught. Even worse, he might botch the job and leave Marlene alive.

Still, it was very pleasant to imagine her dying in various grotesque ways. One of the very few lines of critical praise Malcolm

Erskine the writer had received had been for the vividness of a violent death scene in his second novel. He might not have the courage to actually do anything gruesome to Marlene, but he did have the talent to imagine it well.

The dial tone interrupted his thoughts. Almost automatically, he dialed Steve Golden's number and told his friend what had just happened.

"Great!" Steve said. "This is just what you needed. I tell you, I never felt so good as I did when my own divorce was finalized. Now you're free. Now you'll have the time and energy to write much more than before, and you'll be able to chase women all you want. Now the fun begins, pal."

Like the fun life you lead? Malcolm was tempted to say. With Steve's example as a warning, he saw a long, dreary, and lonely few decades stretching ahead of him, a sad decline toward death.

"Tell you what," Steve said. "After work on Friday, I'll buy you a beer to celebrate."

"Sure." On the bright side, maybe he could now undertake an earnest pursuit of Joe Hoffman's wife. Maybe it was Ellie Hoffman who was somehow responsible for Joe's success. Perhaps she was a talisman. It couldn't be the quality of Hoffman's writing. Of that, Malcolm was sure. "How would you like to buy me about ten beers?"

"Ten—? Well, sure. If you're sure you really want that much."

"You bet. I've got the stomach for it." Malcolm winced suddenly as he imagined Marlene saying, "No, you don't have the stomach *for* lots of beer. You've got the stomach *from* lots of beer." What a sense of humor. "Bitch," Malcolm muttered. Yeah, well, he thought, Hoffman may have less stomach than I do, but he's also got less hair.

But he hung up the telephone and looked down at his paunch and was not happy. If he was to have a chance at a successful bachelorhood, that paunch would have to go. Joe Hoffman didn't have a paunch. Joe Hoffman also lifted weights, as Marlene had been so careful to remind him. Maybe *that* was Hoffman's secret. Maybe editors were all in love with his muscles. It wasn't the man's writing, he assured himself again. Surely not that.

There were perhaps a dozen science–fiction writers living in and around Piketon. Only two of them had had novels published, a few more had sold short stories, and most had never been published at all. They met once a month to critique each other's work and, after the verbal knives had been resheathed, to socialize at some area restaurant. Had it not been for Joe Hoffman, Malcolm would have been the undisputed star of the gathering by virtue of having had three novels published. The poor sales of the novels wouldn't have prevented the younger, less published writers in the group from being impressed by his achievement. As it was, the undisputed star was Joe Hoffman, with his dozen novels, his growing commercial and literary success, and his damned pleasantness.

Hoffman didn't exactly *try* to be in charge of the group or to be the mentor of the younger writers in it, but he certainly made no effort that Malcolm could see to turn down the role when the others thrust it on him. And so the rhythm and tone of the workshops were Hoffman's, and the standards of criticism were Hoffman's, and the literary paradigm was always what Hoffman had written, and Malcolm sank into the background and ground his teeth.

When he sold his third book, Malcolm had swallowed his pride and approached Joe Hoffman for a cover quote. This had actually been his editor's idea, not Malcolm's. Malcolm would have preferred to eat a bowl of hot tar.

"Let's see if we can do something," his editor had said, "to, well, frankly, break this third book out of the level of low sales expectations which the numbers for your first two books have probably preconditioned the chain buyers to base their calculations on."

Malcolm had had to chew that sentence over for a few minutes before he realized that what his editor was really saying was that the buyers for the bookstore chains would look at the sales figures for his first two books and would then decide not to bother picking up any copies of his third for sale in their stores. Which would be the kiss of death for his career. Whereas a favorable cover quote from some more famous, established, and respected science–fiction writer—such as Joe Hoffman, damn his eyes and his ears and every other part of him—might just possibly persuade them to give this latest Malcolm Erskine book a chance.

And so he had had to eat the bowl of hot tar.

He had looked up Hoffman's telephone number in the address list for the critique group and forced himself to dial the number. Ellie Hoffman answered in that low, warm voice that had always thrilled Malcolm. He could imagine what she looked like, standing there, holding the phone, those lively, intelligent eyes shining. Then he imagined her holding the phone while dressed only in panties, and he felt the beginnings of an erection, so he asked to speak to Joe, the undeserving bastard who got to paw her.

"Hello?" Hoffman said cautiously.

Don't worry, you shithead, Malcolm thought. My low sales numbers won't rub off on you over the wire. "Hi, Joe! It's Malcolm! Erskine! How's everything?"

"Just fine, Malcolm. Hope you're okay."

"Oh, I'm just great!"

"And your wife?"

"Oh, she's just fine, too, Joe!" This was, of course, before Malcolm knew just how perilous the state of his marriage was. Perhaps if he had realized the degree to which the future of his marriage was riding on getting a good quote from Hoffman and good sales figures for the novel, he would have been even more nervous. As it was, sweat was soaking his clothing. "And yours?" That lovely, sweet, intelligent creature, that paragon of a writer's wife, that angel whom I deserve so much more than you do.

"She's fine, Malcolm. Is there something I can do for you?"

Too fucking busy to spend any time chatting pleasantly with me, aren't you? Bastard. You're so goddamned superior. Shithead. "Well, actually, Joe, I called to ask a favor. It's a big favor, and I wouldn't blame you at all if you refused. Especially given how busy you must be, with the way your career is going. As I'm sure you know, my thir—my next novel will be coming out next summer, and my editor asked me to approach some of my friends and ask for cover quotes, so I was hoping, well, wondering if you'd be willing to read the manuscript and—if you like it, of course—say something that could be quoted on the cover. Front cover."

"Whom else have you asked?"

Why don't you say *who* like everyone else, you pretentious asshole? "No one else yet. You were the first person I thought of, of course."

"Hmm. Your publisher is Insignifica Press, correct?"

"Uh huh." After an awkward pause, Malcolm added, "They're based in New York."

"Hmm."

"They have national distribution."

"Umm."

"Some of their books have been mentioned as possibilities for some awards."

A heavy sigh came across the line. "I suppose you could send me a copy of the manuscript, and I'll try to look at it if I can. Of course, I can't promise anything."

Oh, thank you, thank you, Sahib. I kiss your shoes. I lick the ground you walk on. I abase myself before your awesome awesomeness, you shithead. "Wow, that's wonderful, Joe! Thanks so much!"

So Malcolm printed out a copy of his manuscript on the trusty printer at work and mailed it to Joe Hoffman, and in the fullness of time he received a letter couched in Hoffman's usual pretentious circumlocutions but containing one passage that Malcolm and his editor agreed would make a very suitable quote to put on the front cover of Malcolm's novel: "Erskine delivers precisely the kind of plot and characterization that those familiar with his previous work have come to expect. They will have anticipated the derring-do of the novel's writer-hero, the malice of its attractive female antagonist, and the passion of the dark-eyed, dark-haired heroine the writer just barely manages to rescue in the book's event-filled final scenes. It has been said by a far more accomplished and respected genre author than I that to be successful, science fiction should eschew character development, and certainly by this measure Erskine's latest effort achieves success."

Malcolm was delighted. His editor was delighted. They were both convinced that this quote alone would propel the book to the top of the bestseller lists, or at least the science-fiction bestseller lists.

The book came out, Malcolm and his editor waited eagerly for the success that would be so good—and was so necessary—to both their careers, for the gushing reviews, the remarkable sales figures. And they waited. And they waited....

Eventually Malcolm's editor stopped waiting, shrugged his shoulders, and turned his attention to another novel by another author, another book he hoped would make his career and get him the hell out of Insignifica Press.

Malcolm kept on waiting. Unlike his editor, he had no other options.

Alas, Book #3 was also quietly received, just like the two Malcolm

Erskine novels that had preceded it.

There were only three reviews. Two of them were lukewarm. In the third, Malcolm read this:

> *The only good thing about this book is the cover quote by the justly esteemed genre author, Joe Hoffman, to whose forthcoming novel this reviewer looks forward with anticipation whetted by frequent rereading of the excellent Mr. Hoffman's previous works. The quote from the highly acclaimed Hoffman amounts to saying, "For those few people who like the kind of garbage Malcolm Erskine keeps rewriting, this is the kind of garbage they like." Most amusing of all is the fact that neither Erskine nor his publisher seems to have understood just what the brilliant Joe Hoffman was really saying! But then, they wouldn't, would they?*

Malcolm wanted to scream, but he couldn't because Marlene was in the next room. He wanted to strangle Joe Hoffman, but he wouldn't have dared try because of the brilliant Hoffman's large muscles. He wanted to settle for stealing Joe Hoffman's wife. The bastard deserved to have that happen, at least.

He wanted to...

He didn't know what he wanted, except to succeed, to be rich, to be famous, to never again have to be torn from sleep by an alarm and stagger off to a day of humiliation and degradation and emasculation at Western Bell. He didn't want to have to endure any more of that at home, either.

Despite himself, a whine escaped him.

"What's going on in there?" It was Marlene, calling from the next room. "Did you break something of mine? Did you spill something on my furniture? Did you hurt my house?"

How foolish could Malcolm have been in those days that he didn't notice her choice of possessive? Not foolish, perhaps: just overly focused on his own misery. Perhaps he did sense, just a bit, on some level, that his marriage would stand or fall on the success of this book, for he tried to make his voice sound bright and cheerful as he said, "Nothing's wrong at all, darling. Just talking aloud. Just planning the sales promotion for my new novel. It's going to be a big one, you know. My breakout book. This is the one that'll finally make us rich. Make us *both* rich. Really, really rich."

"Yeah, right."

Some day, he *would* be rich and famous. Some day, Joe Hoffman, his once-promising career having evaporated, would come crawling to Malcolm, begging for a cover quote for the stupid, dumb, pointless, worthless novel he had just managed to sell to some laughable, insignificant, fly-by-night publisher, a cover quote from the great, famous, brilliant, universally admired Malcolm Erskine, the winner of the Pulitzer Prize and the Nobel Prize and all the available genre prizes, a cover quote that would resurrect Hoffman's career and give him a faint chance of rising out of the gutter again, and the illustrious Malcolm Erskine would put his hand on the bowing and scraping man's head in benediction and he would smile and he would fill his lungs and he would shout until all his breath was gone: "Noooooooooooooooooooooo!"

After he received Marlene's six messages on SAM, Malcolm realized he would have to leave work early and find a place to stay.

By coincidence, the previous day, he had seen a TO RENT sign next to an apartment building near work. Perhaps if he went there right away, it would still be available. However, his work group was scheduled for a warm, collegial meeting that afternoon with Milo

Grossbuck, the Big Guy of Western Bell, and Malcolm knew he dare not miss it because now he needed his paycheck more than ever.

The meeting was scheduled to start at 3:30. Malcolm, held up by listening to Marlene's six installments of hatred, almost didn't make it. He burst into the conference room panting and sweating and quickly took his seat.

His coworkers didn't notice. Some of them, the ones who were disorganized enough to also be almost late and wise enough to know that it was important to be present and on time, were also sweating and panting. The rest were too excited by the thought of this intimate meeting with one of America's great titans of industry to notice anyone else's panting and sweating.

Despite what he had told Jackjackjack, Malcolm didn't really work in the New Ways to Get Money from the Widows and Orphans Office. The proper name of his group was the Zombie Programmers Department. It was true that they were a part of the Every Penny Counts Squeeze 'Em Dry Division within the central billing office, so perhaps Malcolm's exaggeration was excusable.

Back in the early days of his marriage, when he had naively expected sympathy from Marlene, he had described his work as the providing of brain-dead programs for brain-dead users. Marlene had looked him up and down with a sarcastic smile, and he had never repeated the phrase to her. Now he looked around at his fellow zombie programmers and wondered if his eyes were as dead as theirs.

The room was large and was filled with long, narrow tables with chairs lined up on one side of each table, all facing toward the wall opposite the door through which Malcolm had entered. That far wall held a white board, and there was a projector behind Malcolm aimed at the white board. The room was used for classes and presentations more than for conferences.

Malcolm had been in here before. On one of those occasions, he had noticed something interesting.

Near the whiteboard was another door. It had a small pane of glass in it, but the hallway or room beyond was dark, so one couldn't see through the glass. That door was locked, as Malcolm had discovered when he had tried to get out that way in hopes of avoiding the crowd leaving through the main door.

However, during a previous meeting of his work group with a high company official, Malcolm, idly watching the dark pane of glass while trying to stay awake, had noticed a face, dimly lit through the pane of glass by the overhead fluorescents of the conference room.

Intrigued, he had watched.

The face peered through the glass, then looked down at something, then looked through the glass again, then looked down again. The action was repeated a few times, and then the face disappeared.

Taking names, Malcolm realized.

The almost invisible face might be creepy, but there was nothing supernatural about it or what the person on the other side of the door was doing. It was some lackey checking off names on a piece of paper, probably attached to a clipboard below the level of the window.

After that particular meeting, the few fellow zombie programmers who had not bothered to attend had disappeared.

Now Malcolm looked around and wondered who was missing today. How soon would they disappear? They would be dismissed into the outer darkness of the non–Western Bell universe, lost and wailing souls, drifting aimlessly and hopelessly over the blasted terrain that everyone in Western Bell knew the outside world consisted of. They would never know what they had done wrong, whom they had offended, what unwritten rule of Western Bell behavior they had transgressed.

Better them than me, Malcolm thought.

Every employee kicked out, in these increasingly bad Big Gypper days, was one fewer employee who would have to be laid off.

A minion bounded into the room from the door behind Malcolm and leaped and skipped to the front of the room. He had all the manic cheerfulness of JackJackJack. It might even have been the same man. Malcolm couldn't be sure.

The minion shouted, "Hi, everyone!"

"Hi!" most of them shouted back.

"So how are you all today? Is everyone doing great?"

"Yes! We're all doing great!"

"Well, that's just great! So okay, as you know, we're here today to meet with our fearless leader, the Big Guy of our wonderful company, the greatest telephone company in the history of the entire world, Western Bell Telephone and Telegraph!"

Lots of cheering and stamping of feet.

"Great! Okay, so the Big Buck is meeting with every work group in the company so that he can really get to know everyone and really be your buddy because we're all coworkers here and all doors are open and everyone is part of the same team! Yee hah!"

The crowd shouted, "Yee hah!"

It was the new company yell, inaugurated only days before and intended to typify the rugged Western cowboy independence and vigor and energy and competitiveness of the typical Western Bell employee.

"Kim chee," Malcolm said, a few seconds later.

His immediate neighbors frowned at him, and he cursed inwardly and strove for better self–control.

"Okay, so, right, as you probably know, the Big Buck has just returned from a relaxing three months at the Big Guy Institute, which is, you know, like a special place the government runs where big executives can relax and meet together and change their attitudes about various things when what they've been doing makes the government see that they probably need to make those changes, and now he's back here to take the reins of the greatest telephone company in the history of the entire world again and talk to all of us about what he's learned and how he sees the future." He drew a breath. "Yee hah!"

"Yee hah!"

Malcolm managed to join in on the second syllable this time.

Then to his surprise the locked door to the dark regions opened and Milo Grossbuck himself swaggered in.

Grossbuck was tall, somewhat overweight, somewhere in his fifties, bald, and he smirked. His tie cost more than Malcolm had earned in any given month in his life thus far. Grossbuck's suit cost many times as much as his tie. He had coined the nickname Big Buck all by himself and he insisted that everyone use it.

"Hello, everyone!" His voice was enormous. He smiled, and Malcolm was sure for an instant that Grossbuck's teeth were long and yellowish gray and filed to points, but that was surely an illusion.

"Hello, Big Buck!"

A couple of members of the crowd, even more enthusiastic than the rest, called out, "Yee hah!"

Grossbuck frowned. "I'd like to start out with an important announcement," he boomed. "Since I got back from the Big Guy Institute, I've been meeting with the senior management team about a lot of things. Refrigerators are cold places. That's important. Yarrow. About changes we want to make. About new directions for the future."

Uh oh, Malcolm thought.

Some of his coworkers stirred uneasily.

"These are difficult times for all of us," Grossbuck said. "Tough economy. Tough world. Tough competition. Tough, tough, tough. Beedle. Whichness. Goom. But we can handle it. Why?" His smirk became a grin. "Because we're the best! Bring on the competition! Eat our dust!"

There were a couple of scattered yee hahs.

Grossbuck frowned again but continued. "So, yes, we are going to have to rein in a little bit, be more careful with our resources, even watch those pennies, clean out your refrigerators, moldy food in the back, tune up your cars, work even harder and longer to ensure the continued success and strength and growth of this company we all love. Bep. Bep. This great telecommunications corporation that has been so good to all of us. Spleeble. It's a monument. A monument to the greatness of free enterprise and the power of faith. Bow your heads for a moment. Thank you, Lord, for American free enterprise. Tegtegteg. So, well, okay, we won't all be making the great trek into the future together. There'll be an announcement about that aspect of things."

The uneasy stirring grew.

"But the big thing I wanted to tell you about is that we're broadening our scope. Don't mope. Keep up the hope. On the ropes. We're more than just a regional Western company now. We want to assert our new identity and make sure the world knows we're here and we're strong and lean and mean and tough and we can do everything. That's why, effective today, we're changing our name to Western Bell Universal Telecommunications Incorporated. Greeg! The new company cry is," he drew a huge breath into his big torso and bellowed, "Uni! Versal! Uni! Versal! Come on, everybody! Do it with me! Uni! Versal!"

With growing enthusiasm, the gang joined in. "Uni! Versal! Uni! Versal!" Their unease was forgotten.

Malcolm shouted along with the others, although the second time he said, "Virgin! Vestal!" and no one seemed to notice.

"So, yes, well, as you were just told, I spent the last few months at the Big Guy Institute brainstorming with a whole bunch of other big guys from all over corporate America. Geniuses. Brilliant. Real movers and shakers, titans of industry, captains of this great ship we call our free–market economy. Oh, sure, we spent a certain amount of time playing golf and tennis and just walking around and getting some exercise every day during the assigned hours, but then, after dinner at those fucking long tables, we all sat down and talked about what we had all been doing and why we were all there and our wonderful country and the greatness of our way of life and how God loves free enterprise, and we kind of planned out the future. Poop. Did that every evening until it was lights out and they told us we had to go to bed. Bananas. Prunes. You guys and your future and what to do about you and how to take care of you. That's what we planned. And the government. And the media. And just everything. Minnywinny."

He paused in deep thought for a while and then nodded. "Oh, yeah. Oh, yeah. See, people, when you're in charge of the ship, when you're the captain, when it's all on your shoulders, it's like this, see. Murgle. Blither blather."

Malcolm shook his head. "What?" he said.

The coworker to his right, an attractive young woman named Jeannie who worked in a cubicle near his, shushed him. Her eyes were glued to Grossbuck's red, sweating face.

Malcolm whispered to her, "But he's not making any sense. He's speaking nonsense words."

"Gabargle, gabargle, gabargle!" Grossbuck shouted. "Meenie oodie oodie! Snicker whacker. It's like, oh, I don't know, wilga woolgy."

"He's incoherent," Malcolm said.

"Oh, hush."

"We have to refrigerator notebook magazine newspaper radio television control and conglomerate."

A few people said tentatively, "Uni! Versal!"

"All together! All together! Repeat, repeat, repeat, and then eventually everyone agrees!"

The enthusiasm was growing. "Uni! Versal! Uni! Versal!"

Grossbuck grinned approvingly, and again Malcolm thought he saw those ugly pointed teeth. He ignored that and said in a low voice to Jeannie, "He's a blithering idiot. He can't string words together to make a meaningful sentence."

"You don't get it," Jeannie said. She was annoyed. Her voice was also low, but the tone was hostile. "His brain is working so fast that his words can't keep up with his thoughts. He's thinking brilliant business-management thoughts all the time. Corporate leaders like him are the true heroes and intellectuals and mental giants of our age."

A woman seated on Jeannie's other side had apparently been listening to their conversation. Now she joined in. "He's so powerful and impressive!"

Jeannie nodded. "He really turns me on."

Good God, Malcolm thought. Good God, Good God, Good God, Good God! Won't some godlike alien save me? Teach me to blither like the Big Buck? Make women look at me the way Jeannie's looking at that horrifying creature?

Maybe there really are wonderful, noble races out there in space, Malcolm thought, just like in my fiction. And equally horrifying, evil, monstrous ones. Maybe Grossbuck is actually one of the evil ones, stationed here to control us. No, to destroy us! To destroy any human being who shows real intelligence and soul.

Marlene's one of them, too.

"Religious bathtubs," the Big Buck blared. "Radio station. We bought one. We have to get our message out. Deregulation. Bring on the competition. If your faucet's dripping, you should probably replace the washer. Fix the leak. Control the flow. That's gotta be our philosophy. Thank you."

Cries of "Uni! Versal!" Loud applause.

The minion who had originally introduced Grossbuck stepped to the front again. “Okay, so listen everybody. The Big Buck has to get back to the 55th floor now and think a lot for all of us. Before he goes, he wants to shake everyone’s hand and say hello and get to know each and every one of you.”

Oh, boy, Malcolm thought.

His fellow workers moaned a simultaneous orgasmic “Oooh!”

“Except for anyone whose first or last name begins with a W,” the minion said. “Those people need to proceed immediately to Room B, right next door, where a group of managers and security guards want to explain some things to you. The rest of you, please line up in an orderly manner and walk past the Big Buck and shake his hand and say hello at the rate of one employee per three seconds.” He clapped his hands, a sudden, startling, cracking sound. “Move it!”

The cattle lined up obediently on one side of the room and began to shuffle forward at the rate of one employee every three seconds.

Except for the handful whose first or last names began with W. They went obediently through the door at the back of the room and then into the adjoining conference room, Room B, where a gang of managers backed up by large, well–armed security men explained a few things to them. They were then handed their personal belongings, which had been brought there in sealed cardboard boxes, and were escorted from the building via a rear door giving onto a filthy, stinking, dark alley infested with rats, drunks, and roving bands of hungry, armed gang members. The faucet had been leaking quite a bit lately.

Malcolm, meanwhile, had been shuffling forward with the non–Ws. He had contemplated leaving with the W group and then splitting from them outside the door, but something, some instinct born of years of working at Western Bell, had told him that that might not be safe. So instead he had fallen obediently in line behind Jeannie. Now, gloomily, he moved a step, paused, moved a step again, meanwhile staring longingly at Jeannie's back.

When they reached the front of the room, Jeannie gripped Grossbuck's extended hand tightly, stared up at him adoringly, and said, "Do you need a trophy wife, Big," she breathed rapidly, "Buck?"

Grossbuck looked her up and down admiringly and chuckled. It was a sound that turned Malcolm's stomach and raised the hackles on the back of his neck and made him wish the damned Commies would finally start World War Three at that very moment and put these people out of his misery. "Call my secretary," Grossbuck told Jeannie, "and make an appointment."

Jeannie passed on, stars in her eyes, and it was Malcolm's turn. He shook Grossbuck's repellent paw as the great man looked through him.

"Malcolm Erskine." He thought he should say his name.

"Uh huh."

"I hate you. I hate my job. I hate my life."

"Of course you do."

Malcolm froze in horror, then realized that what he had said aloud was, "I admire you greatly, sir, and I feel honored to work for this company."

Some day, you'll be in a book, Malcolm thought. Some day, all of this will be in a book.

Malcolm would be in the book, too. Except that in the fictional version he would behave heroically. With a single, mighty blow, he would vanquish the evil alien invader, the Grossout, and rescue from his slimy tentacular grip the gorgeous, black-haired Jennya, who would fling her arms—

The apartment!

Malcolm looked at his watch and was surprised to see that it was only 4:30. He had been sure it would be midnight.

He rushed from the conference room and back to his desk, shut down his computer, flung his possessions into his briefcase, and sprinted for the elevator. He ran from the building and then ran the five blocks to the apartment building.

Thanks to the dismal economy, the apartment was still unrented. And so, only hours after listening to Marlene's enthusiastic farewell message, Malcolm had a place to live. It was furnished, it was near downtown, it was cheap, and it was immediately available. It was also tinier than anything he had lived in since his student days.

The next day, he called in sick, took the bus to what had been his home, betting that Marlene would be at work (she was), and broke in. He loaded a large part of his personal possessions, including his computer, into what had once been his car and drove downtown. The car was legally Marlene's, just like everything else. She had always preferred to get a ride to work rather than driving herself, partly because it was her nature to have other people do the difficult or tedious stuff and partly because she liked to spend the commuting time telling one or more of her friends how worthless Malcolm was and how she deserved far better. Malcolm didn't know about the last part, of course, although he had guessed that that was what she did during the commute. Because of all this, he had bet—correctly again—that the car would be at the house.

After unloading the car at his apartment, he drove back to his former house, left the car parked where it had been before, and then took the bus back downtown and walked to his apartment.

Then he settled down in his new home and began to write.

He began a new short story, titled "Sleeping in the Devil's Bed," about a fearsome monster from another world, accidentally brought back to Earth by an expedition of hardy space explorers. The creature is called a Marlinga, but the explorers think it is a human woman, the lone survivor of a crashed alien space ship.

That the theme and style of his story were more appropriate to the pulp magazines of the 1930s than to any literary market of his own time didn't bother him. He wasn't writing for art. He was writing for release.

It took him two weeks to complete the story, which turned out to be quite long—too long to sell anywhere he knew of.

In the story, the monster is finally exposed as an alien female from a species whose females first mate with their males and then devour them. The creature's outward appearance is that of an attractive human woman—very attractive, especially in panties—but under that shell it is little more than poison glands and ravening appetite. Its downfall comes when it tries to seduce a seemingly mild-mannered science-fiction writer who divines its true nature just in time and dispatches it in a grisly scene involving a small, dull hatchet and a paring knife.

Just before this scene, the alien monster also threatens the life of the writer's next-door neighbor, a young woman of stunning, exotic beauty, with shoulder-length black hair and olive skin. In slaughtering the monster, the writer also saves this young woman's life, and she demonstrates her gratitude appropriately, in a scene Malcolm described in almost as much loving detail as he had the monster's bloody death.

In the final scene, the heroic writer is shown explaining everything to a close friend of his. They are together in a bar, and the friend has just bought the writer ten beers in celebration. "Best of all," the writer is saying, "I already owned the hatchet and the paring knife, so cutting off this relationship, as you might say, didn't cost me one red cent. I'll sure miss one thing, though."

"What's that?"

"Well, when it all started, before the creature showed her true nature, the dame sure was good in bed."

Malcolm hesitated over those last few lines for quite a while. Somehow, they seemed to strike a false note. But then he shrugged away his doubts. What the hell, he thought. It's better than anything Joe Hoffman ever wrote.

And just to prove to the world how true that was, that very evening, at work, after all his fellow workers had gone home, he printed out the entire story on the office laser printer, and then he made numerous photocopies of it (WARNING: THESE MACHINES ARE TO BE USED FOR WESTERN BELL UNIVERSAL TELECOMMUNICATIONS OFFICIAL BUSINESS ONLY. ANY PERSONAL USE CONSTITUTES A VIOLATION OF THE WESTERN BELL UNIVERSAL TELECOMMUNICATIONS CODE OF BUSINESS CONDUCT AND IS GROUNDS FOR TERMINATION) and mailed the copies out to the other members of the writers' workshop for their critique.

Take that, Hoffman, he thought happily as he sealed the copies in large envelopes from the supply room, stamped them on the postage meter in the mail room, and dropped them in the sack some anonymous company gofer would pick up in the morning and deliver to the Post Office.

Three weeks passed before the writers' workshop met, and during that time, Malcolm did not reread the story his fellow writers would be critiquing. On Saturday morning, as he was eating breakfast preparatory to leaving for the workshop meeting, he decided to skim "Sleeping in the Devil's Bed" quickly to refresh his memory of it, and immediately he realized what an awful mistake he had made.

Why, this is crap! he thought.

This isn't how I normally write, he assured himself, feeling the bony fingers of despair latching onto his soul. I'm better than this.

He hoped that was true.

Years before, he had complained (all right: whined) to Marlene that there must be a cabal of New York editors who met in an underground cave lit by flickering candles where they agreed to reject anything written by Malcolm Erskine. How else explain his lack of success?

"Bullshit," Marlene had said scornfully. "Don't kid yourself. There's no cabal and no secret agreement. They reject your stuff because they read it and see that it's all crap."

Had he been fooling himself all these years? Was his writing, in fact, all crap? No: consider the good reviews his books had received. They had also received some bad reviews, but there was no point in paying attention to those.

Oh, well, Malcolm thought, might as well put a good face on it and bear it.

Which turned out to be hard to do.

Joe Hoffman, of course, led off the critiquing round. "I do think, Malcolm, that I've read this story a few times in collections of old works from the pulp magazines. And I'm forced to say—am, in fact, unable to refrain from saying—that the old pulpers did a better job of it than you did in the current opus."

Why, Malcolm wondered, can't this guy speak English? Why does he always produce those long, carefully thought out sentences and deliberate archaisms? Does that come along with success? Will I start talking that way, some day? Will I, one must wonder, ever have reason to do so—which is to say, will I ever be as successful as he? Christ, now I'm thinking the way he talks!

"I'm not really sure that a detailed analysis of this story would be too terribly productive," Hoffman went on. "Suffice it to say that I choose to dismiss it as a minor Erskine effort—a *jeu d'esprit,* one might say."

If one were inclined to say such pretentious things, Malcolm thought. Prick.

"However," Hoffman continued, "I must object to the details of one scene. On page 28—" *riffle, riffle* as all the others flipped through their copies of the story to find the offending scene "—where you describe the unsuccessful attempt by the lesser science–fiction writer trained in the martial arts to fend off the attack by the Marlinga, the details of the physical encounter are utterly improbable. I feel that I can speak authoritatively on this subject since, as you may know, *I* am a science–fiction writer trained in the martial arts, and I can assure you, Malcolm, that the physical movements you've described are quite unbelievable."

And he *looked* just like you, too, before the Marlinga got him, Malcolm thought. Of *course* I know about your martial arts training, you jerk. You mention it every chance you get. Why don't *you* ever submit anything to this workshop, Hoffman? Afraid to give me a chance at your stuff in public?

Larry Lefkowitz, a younger member of the group, chimed in next. Malcolm had noticed before that Lefkowitz almost always spoke right after Hoffman, whose protégé he seemed to have become. "As you know, Malcolm, and as I have urged upon you before, I feel that the goal of the writer must always be truth, that is, the presentation of the truth to the masses, whether they want to hear it or not."

When, Malcolm wondered, had this child started sounding like Hoffman? And what made the boy feel he had the right to lecture his elders and betters? And why was Malcolm sitting here taking this? And how severe would the legal penalties be if he strangled the kid?

"I, of course," Lefkowitz continued, "am putting *my* efforts into a novel that I know will change the world. Unlike you, I'm not concentrating on mere entertainment. However, that's your choice, and under the terms of the workshop, it's my duty to help you write better entertainment. Or at least to improve your chances of attaining some degree of commercial success. That said, given the nature of the sub–genre you have chosen to write in, I'm willing to accept the silly

tough–guy *patois* used by your protagonist, but other than that I do wonder why you don't strive for more originality and inventiveness in these rip–roaring action–adventure tales of yours. What I want to know most of all is, why, in everything you write, do you always have your hero ending up with a beautiful young woman with black hair and olive skin and almond–shaped eyes?"

"I do not!" Malcolm protested.

"Yes, you do. It's in every one of your novels, and now it's even in this short story. L–o–o–o–n–g short story."

Everyone laughed.

Malcolm gritted his teeth. "Maybe it's wish fulfillment, okay? You have yours. I have mine. It's my fantasy world and my protagonist, so I'll have him end up with whatever kind of girl I want him to."

"Which is to say, a beautiful young woman with black hair and olive skin and almond–shaped eyes." This from Gloria Samson, whom Malcolm had always found attractive before today. Now she launched into an attack on his story that made it sound like the worst waste of paper and ink she had ever read.

"It's not that bad," Malcolm said weakly.

"I think it is," Gloria said.

Bitch, Malcolm thought. Hormones out of whack, or what? He said nothing, though.

"Trés bourgeois," Lefkowitz sneered.

"One thing I have to say," Joe Hoffman added, "is that although we're all sympathetic regarding your marital problems—"

How the hell did he know already? Malcolm wondered.

"Not all of us," Gloria Samson muttered.

"I'm surprised Marlene hung around this long," someone else said.

"—I think you should maintain a more objective attitude toward them," Hoffman concluded. "I don't think you should convert Marlene into the central monster in your story."

Good God! Malcolm thought. It's true! The story really is all about Marlene the Malignant. It's not about some outer–space monster at all!

How humiliating to have to have Joe Hoffman point that out to him.

More than ever, he felt like an outsider in the group. Maybe I really wasn't cut out to be a science–fiction writer, Malcolm thought gloomily. Maybe I ought to try something else, some other field. Maybe non–fiction.

It was one year later that the inspiration to write *Business Secrets from the Stars* struck.

For a moment, Malcolm was moved to submit the manuscript for the book to the workshop as he wrote it, but then wisdom prevailed. For one thing, the members of the workshop, so dedicated to trying to produce serious fiction, would never understand such a book as it was meant to be understood. For another, one of them might understand the book and its potential all too well and steal the idea. Malcolm was not the fastest writer in the world, and he could easily imagine one of the other workshop members staying up for seventy–two hours straight and producing his book before he did.

Malcolm trusted no one. Once, he had trusted Marlene. That, he was determined, would be his last mistake of that sort.

But he knew almost from the start, from the opening words of *Business Secrets from the Stars,* that the book would be his ticket to the top. And so he was able to sit quietly at the meetings of the writers' workshop and feel a superior certainty when comparing himself to his Piketonian fellows. He could see now that they were stuck in place, getting nowhere, repeating themselves, churning out hackneyed work in a genre with a diminishing readership. Their focus was narrow and seemed, with each monthly meeting, to be getting narrower.

Even the ones who did try to break out into the mainstream didn't know how to go about doing so.

They just don't get it, Malcolm thought. They don't understand how the world works.

Larry Lefkowitz, for example. He had finally stopped writing science fiction stories that were thinly disguised political lectures. Now he was working on a long, mainstream novel that was a thinly disguised—but l-o-o-o-o-ng—political lecture. It started with a brief scene depicting rabblerousers in pre-Revolutionary France singing, *"A la lanterne, les aristos!"* Then it leaped to contemporary America, where the sinister ruling class of plutocrats had instructed all the power companies to install exceedingly high lampposts. The book's tentative title was *The Second American Revolution,* and the rabblerousing slogan of its heroes was, "Lower the lampposts!"

Malcolm was astonished at how seriously his fellow workshoppers took all of this. When it was his turn to comment on the chapters they had all read for this month's workshop, Malcolm said, "I think you should make the parallel clearer. Have them shout 'Lower the lampposts!' in French."

Lefkowitz looked surprised, then interested. "I like that! Thanks, Malcolm. I'll do it."

Malcolm could hardly keep his face straight. The book was doomed anyway, but just in case it had had a chance, that touch of wackiness would kill it for sure.

Although the whole lamppost conspiracy thing is kind of clever, Malcolm thought. I wonder if I could use that somehow in *Business Secrets from the Stars.* He pondered the idea for a while but then gave up on it.

Why should he borrow anything from any of these people, anyway? They were insignificant compared to what he would soon be.

Of course, none of them had yet realized that Malcolm was

destined to be the biggest literary and media star that Piketon had ever produced or probably ever would. So to outward appearances he remained a lesser figure in the gatherings, and Joe Hoffman remained the star. That didn't bother Malcolm quite as much as it once had.

Enjoy your chieftainship, you prick, Malcolm thought with calm inner joy. It won't last.

He looked around the room at the others. *They* were stuck on Earth. *He* was on his way to the stars.

CHAPTER FOUR

Ah, spawn of my spawn, starspawnspawn, be always aware, always alert, always on the watch for the Enemy. It may come in a pleasant guise—for example, a pretty good job with decent benefits. It may even appear in the form of a beautiful woman of considerable desirability and unusual skills. But the Enemy's true mission is always to sap your strength, to feast upon your vital juices, and to leave you a drained husk. Do not be deceived, O Earthian hero! Do not become a meal for a Black Widow spider! Yours is a higher destiny!

—Business Secrets from the Stars, through the mouth of Malcolm Erskine, from the channeled spirit of Lukas of Aldebaran, who had scars of his own.

When Marlene and Malcolm first met, she was a receptionist at Western Bell, working at the front desk of the office where Malcolm had just been hired as a programmer. Marlene was small, lean, lively, animated, extremely pretty, with dark-brown hair which she wore at about chin length. At his first sight of her, Malcolm felt as though he'd been, if not quite punched in the stomach, at least slapped there.

On their first date, they talked and talked and discovered an instant compatibility in almost everything—music, movies, books, plays, food and drink, dislike for various fellow employees. He told her all about his writing dreams and the small but promising success he had had at that point. She, misled by the absurd portrait of the writer's life depicted in Hollywood movies, assumed he would soon be rich and, not too many years later, would die of cirrhosis of the liver, leaving whomever he had married a very rich widow.

On their second date, Marlene showed Malcolm that what he had always thought was sex was in fact a pale substitute for the real thing. Marlene was the real thing.

That night, he asked himself, How can I let this get away from me?

By morning, the question had changed. Can I, he asked himself, survive a steady diet of this?

Not to worry, Malcolm.

The supply of rapture diminished quickly after their wedding, which took place three months after that second date. He had been in no physical danger from Marlene, after all.

Psychological danger was a different matter entirely.

After marriage, Marlene disclosed an ambitious facet to her personality that had been well hidden before. Their combined salaries provided a comfortable life for a childless young couple, with a reasonable ration of luxuries, but Marlene wanted much, much more.

First she signed up for one of the programs under which Western Bell paid for college courses taken by its employees.

These programs covered business courses only. Malcolm had once tried to get the company to pay for an art appreciation course he was interested in. The attempt had brought him some very angry interoffice mail from someone who officed on a very high floor. Even those employees who wanted to take business courses usually had trouble getting approval for time off and getting the company to pay the tuition and buy the books. The programs existed on paper to make

Western Bell look good, not to do its employees any good.

But Marlene was very good at getting other people to do things for her, and she had no problem getting the company to pay the tuition for her courses.

In a very few years, she had completed her degree in accounting and had quit Western Bell for a nicely paid job working for the largest commercial enterprise in the state, First Arapahoe Savings and Extortion. The youngish couple's circumstances should have improved considerably because of Marlene's higher salary, but she preferred to spend most of the extra income on herself and save the rest of it in a savings account with only her name on it. Major improvements in their lifestyle, she explained not very patiently, would have to come from increases in Malcolm's earnings.

And speaking of which, "Why aren't you doing something to advance yourself?" Marlene asked frequently. "You could take some courses, like I did, something useful, and either move up the ladder at Western, or else come over to First, like me."

And then Malcolm made his second biggest mistake since marrying Marlene, the biggest having been the marriage itself. One of the times she said this to him—the last time, in fact—he sneered and replied, "Oh, sure, something really fascinating, like a bookkeeping course. Gag. And then I could move up to some really brain–dead job, like Assistant Comptroller, or something."

Marlene narrowed her little eyes and pursed her little mouth. Only the day before, she had said something admiring about Fred Seicht, Assistant Comptroller at First Arapahoe Savings and Extortion. "A damned sight more useful than art appreciation, anyway," she said in what he should have recognized by now as a dangerous tone.

"Right. Sure. I guess an Assistant Comptroller would be more interested in how much a painting could be sold for than in what the artist was trying to say, right?"

"Right, because the artist was probably saying, 'How the hell am I going to pay this month's rent if I don't sell this crummy painting?' And that reminds me, what the hell do you think you're doing buying yourself a computer to do your stupid writing on?"

"I can write faster and more easily on a computer. I explained that to you. There's no comparison between using a computer and using a typewriter."

"Oh, yeah, I understand that, all right. What I'm wondering is why *you* need a computer. It'd make a difference to a *real* writer. I can see that. But not to *you."*

Through gritted teeth, Malcolm said, "Writing's my real future, not moving up the yuppie ladder at First Arapahoe or Western Bell, or anywhere else. I'm a writer, first and foremost. Some day, I'll be making my living at it."

Marlene snorted. "When pigs have wings. So you've had one story published in one of those crummy science-fiction magazines you buy, which is another big waste of money, although not as big as a computer. What they paid you for that dumb story didn't even cover the cost of the postage you spent on sending it to the other magazines that rejected it first."

She knew that because Malcolm had told her. It would not have been true if he had sent the story to the science-fiction magazines first, instead of wasting time and stamps sending it to *Harper's, The New Yorker, The Atlantic, Esquire, Playboy,* and so on. Always start at the top, Malcolm believed. The ones at the top always rejected everything of his, after which he sent his stories where they belonged, to the magazines that specialized in the sort of fiction he wrote. Unfortunately, they always rejected his stories, too.

Except for "Time's Razor," which one of them bought. Marlene was not impressed. One hundred dollars seemed to Malcolm to be a large amount of money for a short story. To Marlene, it was insignificant. After she had said so often enough, Malcolm found himself beginning to think of it as pretty insignificant, too.

Marlene never read any of his work before he submitted it. When he asked her to, just so he could get her opinion of it, she refused. However, he had sold "Time's Razor" before they started dating, so she did read it in its published form—after sneering at the cover of the magazine it was published in.

"Mildly entertaining," she pronounced. "Very mildly." Then she flipped through a few pages to another short story in the same issue. "I read this one, too. 'Morphometasis.' It's a Kafka parody by some guy named—" naturally "—Joe Hoffman. Really good. Now, that guy can *write!*"

Thank you so very much, companion of my bosom.

Malcolm snatched the magazine back and returned it to its place of honor, which was an otherwise empty shelf of the wooden bookcase in his study, the shelf destined to hold the published works of Malcolm Erskine—at least, until the hoped-for time when the published works outgrew that shelf and required a second shelf. And a third...

Even when that magazine was joined by another containing a Malcolm Erskine story (and no Joe Hoffman story in that issue), and then by a novel, and then by a second novel, and then by a third—all paperback, admittedly, but two of them resulting in some lukewarm praise from a couple of reviewers in obscure Sunday newspapers—Marlene was not impressed.

"When you can get enough money from one of those things to buy me a new car," she had said, *"then* I'll be impressed. Or a new house. Or when I see your name on the bestseller lists, maybe then. But not because of this." And she gestured in a dismissing sort of way toward the bookshelf with the two magazines and the three paperback books neatly standing on the left-hand side of it. With that gesture, the five publications seemed to shrink in Malcolm's eyes, and what loomed was the amount of empty space on the shelf.

It didn't help that the second magazine was the sleazy men's publication which embarrassed even Malcolm. Nor did it help when Marlene finally met Joe Hoffman and she immediately told Malcolm that Hoffman was not only what a writer should be but what a man should be, too.

Later, in the grungy little apartment to which the divorce had reduced him, Malcolm was limited to using his bedroom as his study as well, and there was room for only one bookcase, a small put–it–together–yourself thing of scratched and dented and rusted metal that he had picked up at a thrift store. It sagged and leaned and swayed dangerously, and it was completely inadequate to his needs. Nonetheless, he still reserved one shelf for nothing but the published works of Malcolm Erskine, and the smallness of the bookcase made the collection of those works look, if not more impressive than they had looked in the large, sturdy wooden bookcase in what had been his home, then at least less unimpressive. Or so he told himself.

Less unimpressive, Malcolm repeated to himself. The story of my life. From unimpressive to less unimpressive. Ever on the upward path, until, eventually, in the fullness of time and the glory of my fulfillment, I'll become really, truly, seriously not unimpressive at all.

At least now that he was living on his own he could watch Felicia Finewine as much as he wanted to.

She was a television journalist who came as close to being Malcolm's dream girl as any television journalist ever had. Sometimes she read the news, sometimes she interviewed celebrities, sometimes she reported from interesting places and said interesting things about them. Malcolm didn't care what she did. He had watched her fervently for years, although during his marriage to Marlene he had only done so when Ms. Maleficent was out of the house.

Felicia was on tonight, interviewing some celebrity who didn't deserve to be in the same room as her. Malcolm deserved to be there. Malcolm deserved even more than that. For now, he'd have to be content with watching her.

Every now and then, Malcolm went through a phase where he tried to convince himself that Felicia Finewine and all the other desirable women on television weren't real, that they were actually nothing but digital constructs, simulations, created by super-secret, immensely advanced computers programmed by sadists who were, he had to admit, far better programmers than he would ever be. Such women couldn't exist in the real world, couldn't breathe and walk and talk and—oh, most terribly painful thought of all!—condescend to have sex with mortal men none of whom was named Malcolm Erskine.

But even when he did manage to come close to convincing himself that that was true, it didn't lessen his anguish at the knowledge that no such woman would ever condescend to have sex with him. Not as he was now, anyway.

If Felicia Finewine was real—as of course he knew she was—then he could keep dreaming that some day he would achieve a level of celebrity sufficient to attract her interest and that then...then...then...

He never grew tired of those fantasies. He did grow tired of the fact that they remained fantasies.

It was another reason to keep working at his writing, though.

He turned on the television and sat impatiently, drumming his fingers on the arm of his broken-down couch, squirming in his seat, enduring the last ten minutes of some endless, pointless program about the nasty doings of the recently installed President Longlegs. Malcolm hated politics at the best of times. It had nothing to do with him. As far as he could see, it had nothing to do with any real people. It existed mainly to provide employment to political commentators and, right now, to delay the appearance on his television screen of the glorious Felicia.

At last the dreary political nonsense came to an end, and then the string of commercials following that was over, and there she was, Felicia Finewine.

Oh, Felicia! Oh, that hair! Oh, that dusky skin! Oh, that mouth! Oh, those dark eyes! Oh, those luscious, round, full, perfect vowels!

Felicia smiled widely at the camera, and Malcolm's heart skipped a beat. "Before I begin tonight's program," she said, her voice filling him with warmth and happiness, "I'd like to inject a personal note." She held up her left hand to display a monstrous diamond in a jewel-encrusted ring on her third finger. "I just got engaged today!" She giggled. "To a really wonderful guy. He's a big time pro athlete, and he's really," she blushed and looked down at the floor, "really big."

Malcolm's heart skipped three beats. Oh, Felicia! Oh, no! How could you do this to me? Why couldn't you wait till I managed to get famous? You were going to interview me and fall in love with me and fling your arms around me and—

And then he noticed who tonight's guest was, the interviewee, sitting in the other armchair, his foul knees almost touching Felicia's exquisite ones, his eyes fixed on her chest, his hands clutching the chair's arms fiercely, almost as fiercely as Malcolm clutched the arm of his couch: Milo Grossbuck! The evil alien invader from a nauseating star system!

"Tonight's guest," Felicia said brightly, "is a true titan of American industry, Mr. Milo Grossbuck, the Big Guy of Western Bell Universal Telecommunications Incorporated, one of our premier companies. Or, as he's more widely known in the rough-and-tumble, shoot-from-the-hip, wild-and-wooly world of telecommunications in the Western states, Big," she paused for a moment and breathed twice rapidly, "Buck."

"But you can call me Big," Grossbuck said oilily.

Felicia laughed charmingly, as she always did, although for once

Malcolm saw no charm in it. Malcolm, in fact, ground his teeth.

"But tonight," Felicia said, "we asked you to come here, not to talk about the telecommunications industry that you serve so well, fascinating though that subject is. Tonight, you're here to talk about your new book."

"What?" Malcolm shrieked.

"Yes, that's right, Felicious. Felicia. First, this is a good opportunity. I have an announcement. In keeping with our evolving nature, we're changing our name."

Felicia looked confused. "From Grossbuck?"

"No, no!" Grossbuck boomed out a hearty laugh and slapped his knee. Then he slapped Felicia's knee.

Malcolm ground his teeth.

A book!

A knee touch!

A nuclear explosion! Now!

"Not my name. My company's name. As of the first of next month, we'll be known as Western Magna Comm." He pronounced the name as though it portended a shaking of the earth.

"Jesus Christ," Malcolm groaned. "And the new company cheer will be Magna! Bull!"

"We even have a company cheer to go along with that," Grossbuck said. "Wingledoog."

"Of course," Felicia said. "That's very exciting."

"We're gonna be leaner. Meaner. Keener. Neener, neener. Geep. We've also acquired a controlling interest in a couple of major newspapers, including one in our home city of Piketon. Get our word out. Sides, sides. Stories have 'em. We'll get ours out there."

"Now, your book," Felicia said, holding up a thick tome with a gold and black cover with raised silver lettering that caught the studio lights and made Malcolm weep, "is called, *The Big Buck Speaks:*

Straight Talk from a Titan of Industry."

Grossbuck repeated happily after her, "A titan of industry."

"I understand this book is full of hard-hitting straight talk," Felicia said. "Strong, penetrating advice." She paused. "That we should all take in. Big," breathe, breathe, "Buck."

"That's right, that's right," Grossbuck said, nodding. "Real advice for real Americans. About the Founding Fathers. Capitalists. Christians. Strong men. Real men. Intelligent, thoughtful, educated, but not wimps. Like me. Played football. Ovoids. Pigskin. Get Big Government off the playing field. Netch. Bring on the competition. Best team grinds the other guys into the dirt." He pounded the arm of his chair with his soft fist. "That's natural law."

"Wow! I mean, we'll have to break for a commercial now, folks, but then we'll be right back with the Big," pant, pant, "Buck."

Malcolm could bear no more. He wept as he turned off the television set.

Oh, Felicia, Felicia! I've been so faithful to you for all these years! How could you! With him! And you're even engaged! I spurn you, I renounce you, you are nothing to me from this moment forward!

Oh, don't be silly, he told himself. You'd lick her shoes if she asked you to. Which she never will. Not if you never become famous and she never has any idea who you are.

You'll never get famous working for Western Magma or Magna or whatever the hell it is this week, he told himself. It'll only happen through writing.

And at least you've still got your computer.

Marlene had expressed no interest in the machine, no resentment, even, that he had broken into the house and removed it. Of course she had known right away who had done that.

His desk, along with all the other furniture of what had been his study, was still in the house—what had been his house. Or possibly

Marlene had sold it. Or possibly she had given it away. He was sure she would do that rather than let him have it. He was surprised that she hadn't tried to get the computer back so she could do the same with it, just to spite him.

What he didn't realize was that Marlene felt that letting Malcolm keep the computer was far crueler than keeping it from him. She imagined that every time he saw its blank screen staring accusingly at him, saying, "Fill me with words, you worthless piece of scum!" or its keyboard crying out, "Beat on me, shithead, punish me with your inadequate creative ejaculate!" he would be filled with self-hatred at his auctorial inadequacy.

How could she have known that he would, in fact, use it to write his one and only bestseller?

The first chapter of which he completed on a pleasant late Saturday afternoon in October, in the full flood of Indian Summer.

For once, the apartment was not an oven. Malcolm had opened the tiny window in the living room, at the front of the apartment, and the equally tiny window in the kitchen, at the rear, and for once air actually moved through his tomb.

Malcolm finished describing the conversation in which Lukas of Aldebaran, Malcolm's interstellar contact *via* the spirit plane, explains to him the three great principles on which the Andromeda Corporation operated in ancient times:

> *And then Lukas spoke to me further, mind to mind, as follows:*
>
> *Know, O Earthian cousin, that we believe that no customer of ours ever buys anything from us, but rather that we, the Andromeda Corporation, must sell our goods to him. It is in the nature of the cosmos itself that we must be proactive rather than reactive or retroactive, forward looking instead of backward looking, aggressive*

> *rather than regressive. We like to say, "Better a neutron star than a black hole."*
>
> *Know further, O Earthian cousin of mine, that none who works for the Andromeda Corporation is limited in the heights to which he, she, it, or they may attain. He or she or it or they is or are the only entity or entities, the only sentient outcropping or outcroppings of the Cosmic All, manifesting itself or themselves at this point in consciousness time, who can determine how high up the ladder of corporate success he or she or it or they will climb.*

Malcolm pondered that paragraph for a while, wondering if he ought to rework it for clarity. In the end, he decided that the murkier his prose was, the better the book's chances in this New Age. But he did decide to end the chapter with something he thought was rather snappy.

> *Or as we, your cosmic cousins, like to say, "Better to provide your own rocket thrust than to rely on a gravity assist from a passive massive object."*
>
> *And finally, O Earthian descendant of my own ancestors, stardust of my stardust, sharer of the same radiant energy which vitalizes me, know that the socioeconomic system you call "capitalism" is woven into the very woof and warp of the spacetime continuum, the fabric of the cosmos, the cloth of existence. Your holy book, the Bible, tells you so, and that is because it was written by prophets who were attuned to the Infinite All itself. The same is true of other holy books of your world, and the holy books of many, many other worlds, too. Thus you are working in perfect concert and smooth*

harmony with both Science and Spirit when you make all the money you can and think about making money all the time you're awake and dream about it all night. Or as we, the very flesh of your flesh, prefer to put it, "It's not fusion that powers the stars, or gravity that shapes the galaxies, or genetic drift that brings about the species, it's competition!"

And then Lukas's wonderful spirit voice faded from my mind, and I awoke from my channeling trance to the cold, pure wind of the high mountains. Snow–clad peaks marched away before me, blue–tinged by the atmosphere, darkening in the twilight, to the very edge of the world where the sun was setting in scarlet splendor!

Malcolm hesitated. Was "scarlet splendor" overdoing it? Was the closing exclamation mark a little too much? Then he reread the whole chapter and decided that it was all perfect as it stood. Sometimes it was best to overdo things. His long–dead cosmic cousins of the Andromeda Corporation had probably had some favorite saying on this very subject, but he was too tired just then to try to make it up.

This channeling stuff was hard work, very taxing on the imagination. He wondered how the other fakes managed to keep it up. Probably, he decided, by keeping their attention focused on the obscene sums of money they earned from it.

I think, he told himself, I will reward myself with a real dinner, cooked by someone else, eaten on dishes that someone else will wash. No beans tonight. Tonight it will be...

He thought for a while, mentally cataloguing his favorite restaurants and comparing the cost of a meal at each one to the balance left in his wallet.

Greek! he decided, delighted at his choice. Gyros and souvlaki on pita bread with feta cheese and onions and lemon soup and all kinds of other stuff! Washed down with immense quantities of beer! Yes! I deserve it!

And his favorite of all the Greek restaurants in Piketon was within walking distance, which was a very important consideration in these his carless days.

The joint was rocking that afternoon.

The restaurant—built on utterly flat ground but called The Acropolis anyway—consisted of three separate eating areas. To be more accurate, it had one eating area, one drinking area, and one baking area.

The first was the main dining room, which was large, light, and airy, and one of Malcolm's favorite places.

The second was the large bar area through which customers entered the restaurant. It contained a bar of prodigious length and three pool tables. All four were heavily populated today. The noise was deafening, the air was thick with cigarette smoke, and Malcolm decided not to bother with beer because he felt drunk just from breathing the alcohol vapor as he passed through the room.

He was led to a table in the dining room. He waved away the menu, ordered the pile of Greek food he had planned on, and then called the waitress back and urged her to bring him a beer as quickly as possible and to keep replacing each bottle with a new, full one as soon as he had emptied it. This sudden need resulted from his having looked through the glass-paneled door that formed one wall of the dining room, out into the third eating area, the sunny patio.

One of the few topics on which Marlene and he had remained in agreement even during the long period of fights and disagreements, the disintegration of their marriage, was that The Acropolis's patio was unbearably hot except during winter, when it was closed because it was unbearably cold. They had always referred to it as "the baking area," and they had joined in scorn and condemnation of the local yuppies who sat out there working on their tans, catching some rays, or in Marlene's words "Riding that melanoma express." But now he could see Marlene herself out there, dressed in her best yuppie clothing and sharing a sunny table with a man of the same subcultural persuasion.

The man was tall, dark, and handsome. His face was unwrinkled and unsagging, and his shoulders were broad. Presumably because of the sunlight, he had taken off his suit jacket and rolled his sleeves fashionably half way up his forearms, which Malcolm could therefore see were well muscled, with the prominent veins of an athlete. The man was grinning, his eyes were shining, and he was speaking animatedly while he leaned familiarly toward Marlene. She was responding—laughing, smiling, writhing, panting, licking her whiskers and twitching her ears and tail with eager anticipation. Malcolm did not need to be told that her companion was Fred Seicht, Assistant Comptroller at First Arapahoe Savings and Extortion.

Malcolm's first reaction was to order the steady stream of beer.

His second reaction was a flood of blind, unthinking hatred toward Marlene combined with a desire to deal an unimaginably horrible death to her male companion.

His third reaction was the realization that Marlene was indeed an enormously desirable woman.

He had known that once, when they'd first met and in the early days of their marriage, but his appreciation of her great sexuality and high libido had faded when faced, day after day and year after year, with her even more impressive bitchiness. Now he forgot the bitchiness and remembered only the lovely, firm, small body, the litheness and liveliness, the enthusiasm and eagerness. And the skills.

"Oh, Marlene!" he moaned and stood up and lunged and grabbed the first beer from the tray of the approaching and startled waitress and sat down and tilted his head back and choked and spluttered the beer down as fast as he could. It ran out of the corners of his mouth and mingled with the tears streaming down his cheeks. When Malcolm put the bottle down on the table, it was empty.

"Another, sir?" the waitress asked timidly, keeping her distance.

"Yes! Yes! That's what I said—keep 'em coming. Oh, Marlene! Sob."

His food came, the glorious Greek feast he had been looking forward to all the way from his apartment to the restaurant, his reward for his new literary diligence and an advance celebration of anticipated success, and it was tasteless and pointless. He stuffed huge quantities into his mouth, chewed them without pleasure, and swallowed them with the help of much beer, which had also lost all taste or ability to give him pleasure.

"Oh, Marlene," he moaned whenever he wasn't actually swallowing.

The waitress stayed far away, except to bring him the requested steady supply of fresh beer. The other customers finished hurriedly and left. Soon the dining room was deserted except for the miserable and moaning and increasingly drunk Malcolm Erskine.

There were quite a few customers on the patio, but Malcolm could only see Marlene and Fred Seicht. By now, they had finished their lunch and were holding hands and touching each other repeatedly. He had no doubt that they would continue the mutual exploration with even less restraint later. Perhaps—final insult—they would consummate the dinner, have their dessert, in Malcolm's very own ex-bed in his very own ex-house.

"Oh, Marlene!"

Marlene and her assistant comptroller stood to leave, and Marlene turned and noticed her ex–husband. Seicht put his hand on her buttocks. She smirked at Malcolm as they passed his table on the way out.

Malcolm's misery turned back to rage.

The bitch! Stupid, worthless, mindless...*stupid* little bitch! He'd show her! Once *Business Secrets from the Stars* hit the stands, he'd be rich and famous, worth far more than any assistant comptroller and far better known, and then she'd be sorry!

He imagined Marlene looking at his picture in *People* magazine.

"Malcolm Erskine was the most famous of the celebrities who showed up for the premiere of the movie version of his latest novel, *Sins, Sex, and Software.* He was accompanied by his social secretary, the stunningly, exotically beautiful young woman with shoulder–length black hair and olive skin shown here hanging on his arm and his every word and staring up at him adoringly."

Suddenly, the food and drink acquired taste again. Only a few bites were left on his plate, only a few sips in the current bottle. Malcolm savored them for a long time, chewing slowly and rolling the beer over his tongue. Then he paid, heaved himself to his feet, and headed for home, walking with surprising steadiness.

Back at his apartment, he stayed up all night hunched over his keyboard, watching the glowing words of New–Age nonsense springing into existence in orderly lines on his monitor. By morning, he had finished the second chapter of his masterpiece.

Take that, Marlene!

He rewarded himself by going to bed.

CHAPTER FIVE

My cosmic child, these are the true laws of nature, which I shall present to you in the form of bullet points, for this is proper among beings of our intellectual prowess:

- ***The Basic Law of Nature***

Greed and acquisition are at the heart of everything. The more you want, the more you strive to acquire what you deserve to have. The more you acquire, the more you want. This great natural cycle is the driving engine of all progress and all morality. So it was in our day, so it is in yours, and so it shall always be, everywhere in the Universe.

- ***The Marketplace and its Heroes***

From this cycle are derived the laws of the holy marketplace, which are as real and predictable and perfect as those of your fine fellow Newton himself. Learn those marketplace laws and live those marketplace laws and never cease to preach them. Clearly, those who understand and live the laws of the marketplace are men of prudence, high intellect, and powerful virility.

- ***The Role of Government***

Government is an evil device that functions only to protect the weak and foolish from the proper workings of natural law. Government should always minimize the damage resulting from its evil presence by never interfering with you in any way. On rare occasions, however, through no fault of your own, you may find your enterprises in a perilous condition. Your corporations, despite their moral superiority and entrepreneurial puissance, may require propping up in order to survive. At such times, government finds its true—indeed, its only—function: to suck treasure from the pockets of the unworthy and heap it upon you, so that the great engines of productivity may once again hum.

—From a mind–to–mind slide show by Lukas of Aldebaran, as imagined by Malcolm Erskine and reproduced in Business Secrets from the Stars.

By the time Malcolm finished the manuscript of *Business Secrets from the Stars,* he and Judith Tillen had parted professional ways.

Malcolm's marriage had lasted ten years, his first agent had lasted three years, and his second agent had lasted six months.

This is not a good track record, Malcolm told himself. I'd better not get married again.

He assured himself that he also didn't need an agent again. He would market his new book by himself.

First, though, he had to print it. All he had so far was a collection of magnetic domains on a hard drive spinning away in his computer.

In those ancient days, O Fellow Starspawn, laser printers were very expensive and could only be afforded by largish companies or—gnash your teeth at this thought, as Malcolm so often did—very successful writers. Therefore, Malcolm habitually used the laser printer at work. This time, though, he was reluctant to do that. For one thing, it seemed inappropriate for the author of the book that would soon dominate the best-seller lists to have to print it a few pages at a time, all the while looking over his shoulder nervously in case he was caught breaking a company rule. It was not dignified. For another and more important thing, he had the feeling that the frequent mysterious disappearance of dozens or hundreds of sheets of laser printer paper and the mysteriously frequent need to replace the printer's toner cartridge were already being traced to him as the logical suspect.

What he needed was a laser printer of his very own, in his very own cramped apartment, next to his very own personal computer. No, what he needed was the money to buy such a printer.

The very day that thought came to him, a fortuitous letter came, too.

When he first saw the long envelope with the name "Marlene Erskine" imprinted in the upper left-hand corner, along with his own ex-address, he almost threw it away without opening it. He was sure it did not contain an eloquent plea for him to return to her. A complaint connected with alimony payments would have come from a lawyer. Nothing else was of interest to him. Fortunately, he decided to open it and read the sheet inside.

It was a page torn from *Extortion Extracts,* the internal newsletter of First Arapahoe Savings and Extortion. Circled in red, just in case Malcolm might have missed it, was an announcement in the middle of the page.

> *Marlene Erskine has been promoted to First Administrative Executive Assistant Playpal to Assistant Comptroller Fred Seicht. Along with her increased*

responsibilities and higher salary, Ms. Erskine cited the chance to work even more closely with Mr. Seicht, a man, in her words, "with large talents and an admirably hard–driving style." Ms. Erskine, who is a great favorite with all the guys here at Extortion Extracts, also informed us that she expects to be able to use her annual raise for scandalous self–indulgence since her basic living expenses are fortunately being covered by her schmuck of an ex–husband.

At the bottom was a printed note from the new playpal herself.

Dearest Malcolm:

Isn't this great? I know you're so proud and pleased for me. Fred even equipped your ex–study with a new, powerful computer and laser printer so that on days I want to sleep in, I can still do all the important spreadsheeting and word processing that go with my job and print them out snazzily and then go back to bed.

Bed is so much more important and attractive to me now than it used to be.

The printed words were followed by Marlene's signature, which he noted was considerably larger and more ornate than it used to be.

A postscript was added at the very end.

The company's also bought me a new BMW, so I'm leaving your old scrap pile parked at the curb with the key in the ignition. You can have it, if you want. If you don't, I'm sure someone will take care of it real soon.

Malcolm looked carefully at the individual letters. Crisp, clean, even, lovely. What editor could fail to be impressed by a manuscript printed so beautifully?

He checked his watch. Seven p.m. Two hours until full dark. Three hours until Marlene went to bed. Allow two more to be sure she would be very deeply asleep. She had always insisted on her full "beauty sleep," as she called it. He had to admit that it seemed to do the job for her.

Night fell at last—a cool, crisp, cloudless, moonless night. Time passed, and the lights went out in the surrounding buildings. By midnight, except for the streetlights and the occasional car passing on the major street two blocks away, the city slept.

All but Malcolm Erskine.

Malcolm slipped out of his apartment building into the darkness. He was dressed as those bent on dangerous nighttime missions always dress, according to the movies: black pants, black socks, black shoes, black sweater, black woolen cap. Or as close as he could come to that ideal. In fact, he wore blue jeans, navy blue socks, and blue running shoes with, unfortunately, white swirly things on them. His sweater was a very dark red, but it was the darkest sweater he had, and it looked close enough to black at night. He did, though, have on a truly black woolen cap. It was making his head sweat and itch.

He had thought about painting dark blotches under his eyes, as movie characters always did, but he had nothing with which to do the painting. Anyway, he had never understood why that was supposed to help.

And he didn't want to be too conspicuous. He was going to have to travel by bus and foot to get to his ex-house and ex–, and apparently present, car. For that matter, if some passing auto thief had already noticed the key in the ignition and stolen the car, he would have to return to his apartment by foot and bus, empty handed. That might well have happened. According to the date stamp on the envelope, two days had passed since Marlene had mailed the letter, and presumably his old car had been sitting by the curb invitingly during that time.

It was twelve-twenty in the morning by the time Malcolm reached downtown Piketon. He walked briskly along dark, deserted streets that he was used to seeing sunlit and crowded.

He passed occasional groups of two or three young men lurking at street corners. He recognized some of them as the shuffling, deferential panhandlers who approached him during the day. Now they stood straight, and there was nothing deferential in their stares. Police cars cruised by, but not often enough for Malcolm's taste—even though he was also nervous about arousing the suspicions of the cruising police. He snatched the cap from his head and crumpled it up in his hand. His head felt a lot better.

At last he reached the bus stop he wanted, and at last a bus arrived, the nighttime version of the bus he had been wont to take home, when he had had a real home. By now, it was after one a.m. Malcolm, as he climbed aboard the bus, was wide awake, every nerve ajangle.

He looked around surreptitiously at his fellow passengers. These were not the suited, briefcase-carrying types who inhabited the bus in the daytime. Instead, there were one pale young white woman with a sleeping baby and a black eye, one old black man muttering to himself, one young white man staring into space and wearing a bitter expression. And, of course, Malcolm Erskine, shadow in the night.

Each of the other three was dressed too lightly for the chill night and in shabby clothes. Maybe, thought Malcolm, my own problems are not really the worst ones in the world. Then he thought about Marlene and Fred Seicht and Joe Hoffman, and he decided that yes, they really were.

During the day, this bus would have taken him to within a couple of blocks of his former home. But the route was abbreviated after dark, and he found himself with two miles to walk. Thus it was close to two-thirty when he finally came within sight of the house that now belonged exclusively to Marlene. He was footsore and exhausted, but his dented Honda parked by the curb acted as a tonic. The most worrisome element in his scheme was no longer a worry.

With a spring in his step, he climbed the fence and crept across the lawn to the back of the house. Fortunately, the last barking dog in the neighborhood had died of old age two years earlier, and the dogs that still lived in the area were much too sensible to let a prowler disturb their sleep.

One of the living room's large windows faced the back yard. The window's lock had never worked properly. This was how he had entered the house when he had snatched his computer. If you jiggled the window in its frame a few times, the latch would fall open. Malcolm had noticed this at an early date, but he had never mentioned it to Marlene, because then she would have insisted that he repair it, and that would have involved physical effort. How foresightful of me, Malcolm congratulated himself.

Within minutes, he was inside the house, and he had made scarcely a sound.

Not that utter silence was necessary. Marlene always was a sound sleeper, he reminded himself. Especially when I was interested in something other than sleeping.

He crept slowly up the stairs, avoiding the creaky places he remembered. He navigated by touch, surprising himself at how easy it was to do so, how well he remembered every detail of the layout of the house.

His ex-study had been a bedroom when they had moved in, and its door faced that of the master bedroom, where Marlene even now was no doubt dreaming sweet dreams of money and power.

He navigated carefully through the study by touch. His fingers found the new computer and laser printer. Feeling around gently, careful not to knock anything over, he also determined that this was not his old, second-hand metal desk, but a much thicker, heavier one of wood. An expensive wood, he had no doubt. Still operating entirely by feel, he took out the small screwdriver he had brought with him and set about disconnecting the printer from the computer.

A sound from the bedroom!

Malcolm froze in place, holding his breath.

A man's voice mumbled, "Friendly takeover."

Marlene, also mumbling, said, "Risky investment."

Malcolm ground his teeth.

More mumbling, this time too indistinct for Malcolm to make out any words. Then began the rhythmic creaking of bed springs that he had hoped he wouldn't hear.

"Fred, Fred, Fred, Fred!" Marlene called out. "Oh, Fred, you're so adequate!"

Seicht gasped, "Credit–debit, credit–debit, credit–debit."

Marlene, shrieking: "Bottom line! Oh! Yes! Bottom l–i–i–i–i–ne!"

Seicht, grunting: "Injection of fresh capital."

A series of happy grunts and groans and moans and mumbles, kisses and giggles, and then silence.

Malcolm waited until he was sure they were both asleep again and the red glow of fury had disappeared from the world. He flexed the hand that had been trying to choke the screwdriver to death, and then he set about his task again. He wished it were possible to take the desk, too. Hell, to take the house and leave Marlene and Seicht to wake up in a vacant lot, surrounded by interested neighbors.

By five o'clock, he was home, the laser printer was set up, and his manuscript was printing at a steady rate of one page every five seconds. By the time Malcolm had finished shaving and showering, with regular stops to refill the printer's paper tray, he had a complete copy of *Business Secrets from the Stars,* printed so beautifully that just to look at it was a pleasure.

He fixed himself a pot of coffee. He stared at the stack of crisp white pages that he hoped held his future success. He sipped his coffee. He breathed in the brisk, clean morning air blowing in the kitchen window. He even savored the rising traffic sounds, for soon, he was sure, he would be moving to a much more expensive, much quieter neighborhood.

It is a far, far better place I go to than I have ever been, he thought.

And you ain't coming with me, Marlene.

Malcolm didn't want to send any publisher a proposal—an outline and a few chapters—for *Business Secrets from the Stars.* No proposal could do his brilliant idea justice. Editors and marketeers had to see the whole thing to understand properly what a gold mine his gimmick was. So he scoured a few reference books and newsletters he subscribed to and came up with a fairly short list of publishers willing to look at complete unsolicited manuscripts.

He decided to be brave and aggressive and start with the most respected and feared of those on the list.

But for an instant his spirit failed him. When the fresh and beautiful pile of pages was properly rubber banded and cover lettered and sealed within a neatly addressed padded envelope, ready to go out into the world and make its intellectual daddy's fortune for him, that daddy had a moment of doubt. He couldn't help remembering the last manuscript he had sent out in just this way, with the very same high hopes.

That had been *Mired in the Midlist,* his grand comic novel about the wacky adventures of a failed writer trying to revive his career. The book had started out as a serious, grim mainstream novel, but he had decided it would be more entertaining as a comedy and had rewritten it accordingly. He had sent it to Judith Tillen, and she had replied quickly by letter explaining that the book was unamusing and unsalable and she was no longer his agent.

Her letter said, in part, "All humor proceeds from pain. Reading this manuscript, I can feel your pain. I can also see why I've had such limited success placing your work. You would probably be doing your career a great favor if you were to deal with an agent who was more in tune with your writing and more enthusiastic about marketing it."

As she wrote that, she was thinking that Malcolm was a clueless twit as well as a talentless one and that she was far better off without him and that she was sure she'd never hear of him or anything he wrote again. After she sealed the letter, for some reason, she wasn't sure why, she had an overwhelming urge to scour the city for a real Southern–style pecan pie.

Malcolm read her letter a few times. Circumlocuitousness tended to confuse him. One thing he had to say for Marlene: she never beat around the bush. He kept hoping he was misunderstanding Judith's letter and that she really meant that she was enthusiastic about his writing and was eager to keep representing him.

Finally, he had no doubt left. Yes, she was dropping him. His agent was showing him the door.

And why? Because all humor proceeds from pain.

He said aloud, "All humor proceeds from pain? Jesus, Tillen, I thought it proceeded from the desire to make people laugh. So, well, fuck you. Some publisher will like this book. It'll make me rich and famous. Then you'll come crawling back." He indulged for a few minutes in the inevitable fantasy of crawling agents and pleading editors. Then he decided to reread the manuscript of *Mired in the Midlist* to cheer himself up.

He discovered that it was dreck.

Why hadn't he seen this before? Preferably before he mailed it to Judith Tillen?

The book was clumsy and sophomoric and completely unfunny. And embarrassing. The protagonist, Martin Everwrite, was transparently Malcolm himself, although better looking and far more successful sexually.

Malcolm read it all the way through, cringing at every page, and then he destroyed the manuscript. He would never try humor again. It proceeded from pain, and sometimes the pain was a bit too much.

So his hesitation when he was about to mail out the manuscript for *Business Secrets from the Stars* was understandable. But he stiffened his spine and took the bulky envelope to the Post Office.

The package came back to him almost by return mail. Attached to the manuscript was an angry letter which said in part, "Despite the current popularity of the belief that Hollywood actors are equipped to tell the rest of us how best to live our lives, we at Stuffy Press refuse to cater to that idea. Consequently, we will not be publishing any books claiming to explain how Hollywood stars run their businesses."

This seemed to indicate some very personal sort of disillusionment with Hollywood on the part of the editor who had written the rejection letter. Perhaps it was evidence of a failed attempt at a movie career as an actor or screenwriter, a failure which still rankled badly. It was certainly evidence that no one had read the manuscript past its title.

This was disturbing but still not enough to make Malcolm think of changing the title. He sent the manuscript out again.

Not quite as quickly as Stuffy, but not much more slowly, Bandwagon Books returned the manuscript of *Business Secrets from the Stars* with a rather longer and much angrier letter, the gist of which was that channeling and the ancient and cosmic wisdom it brought to a needy human race were deserving of reverence and certainly not of parody.

Damn, Malcolm thought. They saw through me.

But he hit paydirt on his third try. Mammon House didn't waste time on a letter. They called him at work. The editor introduced himself as Jim Emich and said, "This is great stuff! Our marketing people are going apeshit over it."

"All over it?" Malcolm muttered. "Hope it's still legible."

"What?"

"Nothing. Never mind. So I guess this must mean we're talking really big money here, right? Like maybe seven digits for the advance?" Millions, Malcolm thought. They gave themselves away with all that enthusiasm. I'll get millions out of them, just like the big–time writers. I've made it at last!

There was a long silence on the other end of the line. Then Emich's voice returned, sounding weaker and less self–assured. "Well, no, Mr. Erskine. More in the four–digit range."

Thousands, Malcolm told himself, coming back to Earth. I'll get thousands out of this. Just like all of my other books. "I'll think about it. I'll get back to you."

"Very soon, I hope," Emich urged him. "We really want to get going on this, get the cover design started, the brochures. We want to have a complete presentation ready in time for the ABA convention."

Oh? thought Malcolm. Really? The American Booksellers Association? Complete presentation? Brochures, eagerness, and he's in a hurry?

"Seventy–five thousand, payable in full on signing of the contract," Malcolm said firmly, but with his heart in his mouth. "That's my requirement, not subject to negotiation."

Emich, who, despite his mention of four figures, had been authorized to pay considerably more, hesitated for the sake of appearances and then agreed.

Malcolm hung up, leaped to his feet, bounded down the hall to the elevator, and left for the day.

For once, he left the building not feeling gloomy because he knew he would have to return the following morning. This time, he fairly floated through the revolving doors, glorying in the certainty that some morning, not too far away, he would be coming in only to empty his desk and leave the place forever.

Outside, in the air of freedom, Malcolm turned around to look back at the looming gray high-rise that housed the headquarters of the telephone company. Its top scraped the sky. Its bottom extended an unknown number of levels below ground. In between were the drones and workers and queen bees and, Malcolm had always suspected, vast, hidden safes filled with cash squeezed from the ratepayers of Arapahoe. He had been one of the drones, but it was to a far greater, plusher dronehood that fate now called him.

It was time to get out, anyway. The computer biz was changing, rushing forward at an ever-increasing pace. It was harder and harder to keep up professionally. At times Malcolm felt like a man running down hill, going faster and faster in a desperate attempt to keep from falling on his face. His legs were giving out.

Farewell! he caroled silently. Farewell to my career in telephony! Western Bell, you'll have to survive without my negligible contribution!

The star-dwelling Merskeenians had come through for him. "Know this, O Starspawn," as Lukas might have put it. "It is better to be on a free trajectory, in control of one's own targeting, than to be in a captive orbit about a baleful star."

"I'm off to better things," Malcolm would tell Jim Leiter and all his coworkers, successful or otherwise, on his last day. "Got a better offer from the Andromeda Corporation." They would understand that reference once his book came out.

This would be a fine time to take a drive through Redland Heights and admire the mansions and engage in a game of fantasy real-estate shopping. Redland Heights was one of Piketon's oldest and most exclusive neighborhoods, a suburb of immense lawns, immense trees, immense cars, and immense houses. For years, Malcolm had dreamed about living there some day. He wished he could drive there now in his own immense and immensely expensive car, but that luxury awaited him in the future. For the time being, he would have to settle for his old Honda.

Unfortunately, his normally reliable Honda had been making the sort of odd noises one expects to hear only from an old American car, so he had taken it to be serviced a couple of days earlier, and now he would have to take a bus to the garage where he had left it.

It was a greasy, dusty, dirty garage, inhabited by subliterates in oil-stained uniforms who never laughed at his clever jokes and instead, he was sure, secretly laughed at his lack of knowledge about cars. Some day, he would have a servant who would drive his car to a garage for servicing and would pick it up again. A clean, airy garage owned by a fawning fan of Erskine books who would clean and polish the car without extra charge and would feel privileged at having the opportunity to do so.

Or maybe Malcolm would employ his own topnotch mechanic to take care of his fleet of beautiful luxury cars.

That was the life Malcolm deserved. That's what Lukas would have told him.

He ran into Larry Lefkowitz on the way to the bus stop. His first impulse was to avoid the man, but today's great change in his life had changed his attitude in many ways.

"Larry!" Malcolm said warmly, loudly. "Missed you at the last couple of workshops. I didn't know you worked downtown."

Lefkowitz, an inch shorter than Malcolm, nonetheless tilted his head back and looked down his nose at him. "I don't. I don't work at all any more. My wife supports me because she believes in my work. I'm here doing research." He gestured at the few office workers strolling along the sidewalk. "Examining these creatures." His lip curled. "I want to be accurate, show them for what they are. Before they're strung up. Before the revolution."

"Oh, is that still on its way? The revolution?"

Larry looked outraged. "Of course it is! But I'm talking about what happens in my novel. When my book comes out, it will probably be what starts the real revolution."

Malcolm knew which novel Lefkowitz was talking about. The usual one. The one he had been working on for years and years. It kept getting longer. Judging from the chapters he occasionally presented at the workshop, it also kept getting sillier. "Ah, *The Second American Revolution."* What an original title, Malcolm thought, and he barely stifled a giggle.

"I'm thinking of changing the title," Lefkowitz said. "I'm thinking of calling it *Baissez les Lanternes!"* At Malcolm's blank stare, Lefkowitz said, *"Lower the Lampposts!* In French. That was your idea."

"Oh, right. I guess you must have liked the idea a lot, then."

"Well, yes." Lefkowitz looked uncomfortable.

He's going to spend his whole life writing and rewriting this garbage book, Malcolm realized. The manuscript will end up thousands of pages long. And with a French title, too! No one's going to read it. No one's going to *publish* it. He's going to die bitter and unknown and unrecognized and filled at last with a realization of his own worthlessness.

Malcolm actually felt slightly sorry for the fool. A nice gesture wouldn't hurt. "Tell you what. When you have a publisher lined up, let me know. I'll be happy to give you a cover quote." A painless offer to make, given that there would never be a publisher.

Horror filled Lefkowitz's face for an instant, and then he took control of his expression again. "Uh, thanks. I'll let you know. I'll, um, have my editor send the manuscript to you. Gotta go."

Oh, encourage the kid, Malcolm told himself. Before Lefkowitz could leave, Malcolm said, "Or you could send it to me now and I'll give you a quote based on what you already have. That will probably help you sell the book, you know."

"Right. Right. Thanks. Um, I want to sell it on its own merits. Um, well..." He waved limply and rushed away.

Twit, Malcolm thought. Untalented drudge. Feet stuck to the ground, just like the rest of them.

Then he remembered what the twit had said about his wife supporting him because she believed in his work. If not for today's telephone call, all of Malcolm's old gloom would have returned. As it was, he was able to force himself to shrug and wish Lefkowitz the best and only wonder for a moment what Mrs. Lefkowitz looked like.

During the bus ride to the garage, Malcolm stared out the window next to him dreamily and did mental sums. He owed slightly over fifteen thousand dollars on the house and five hundred on the car. So he would now be able to pay those loans off, and pay the taxes, and still have enough left to live on for at least a year—a year during which he could write his fingers to the bone, working to capitalize on whatever success *Business Secrets from the Stars* achieved.

His idyllic fantasy was interrupted when a young woman got on and sat down next to him. Malcolm glanced idly at her and then looked more carefully. Dusky skin. Black hair that lightly brushed her shoulders. Malcolm's breathing and heart rate sped up.

Hi, I'm about to become a famous, bestselling author. Would you like to come home with me and spend the night? Or would you rather go out to dinner first?

While he tried to devise a more promising opening line, she reached into her purse and pulled out a thick hardcover novel and quickly became absorbed in it. He read the title, *Elephantus,* and turned back to the window, grinding his teeth.

His dentist had once warned him that his teeth had odd gouges on the biting surfaces. Mysterious, his dentist had said. It was no mystery to Malcolm.

Elephantus was Joe Hoffman's latest. It was some sort of absurd thriller about a pack of mutant miniature elephants devastating a fictional Rocky Mountain city until a brave hero defeated them and won the fair maiden. No doubt Hoffman imagined himself as the hero, the prick. What need did he have for such fantasies, with that wife of his? And girls like this one reading his book with fascination. Lots of other people were reading it in fascination, too, apparently. The idiotic book was a goddamned bestseller.

Malcolm stopped grinding his teeth and clenched his jaw so hard that his jaw muscles ached.

Mutant elephants!

Malcolm snorted in disgust.

The young woman glanced at him in annoyance and then returned immediately to the oh-so-fascinating bestseller by the oh-so-wonderful Hoffman.

A made-up city in a made-up state!

Malcolm snorted again.

What a moron Hoffman was! At least when Malcolm set any part of his fiction on Earth, he used real cities. Usually famous ones he had never visited, on the assumption that editors and readers would find those more interesting than dreary Piketon. But that was what libraries were for, he thought self-righteously. That's how you came up with realistic depictions of places you hadn't actually seen. Real writers did real research. What would Joe Hoffman know about any of that, though? He was fake on every level.

"Fake," Malcolm muttered.

This time, the young woman didn't even grace him with an annoyed glance. She was so immersed in the wonderful Hoffman's wonderful novel that she hadn't heard Malcolm at all.

Maybe Hoffman's afraid to use a real setting, Malcolm thought. That was probably it. He was afraid he'd insult some real person and get in trouble, or he just didn't trust himself to depict a place readers might actually know. They'd catch on to his ineptitude right away.

Malcolm had always suspected that Hoffman didn't want to take any real literary chances. He didn't have the kind of intellectual courage Malcolm had.

That's because I'm a real writer and he isn't, Malcolm thought. And once *Business Secrets from the Stars* comes out and I hit the big time, everyone in town will know it.

He felt better now. He smiled condescendingly at the foolish young woman. She just needed educating.

Sensing his stare, she looked up at him. At first annoyed, she relented and gave him a friendly smile. "Are you a Hoffman fan, too? He's the greatest science-fiction writer there ever was, isn't he? And this whole idea of a made-up city in a made-up state? Brilliant! That's so much harder than setting a story in a real place and time, you know. Any hack can do that."

With an effort, Malcolm kept smiling. "I wouldn't say I'm a fan, exactly. But I am a friend of his. I'm a science-fiction writer, too. Hoff—Joe admires my work a lot."

The brief moment of friendliness fled from her face, replaced by a you-need-a-better-pickup-line look of scorn. "Yeah, right," she said, and returned her attention to the astonishingly wonderful novel by the best science-fiction writer the world had ever known.

Malcolm stared at her silky black hair for a while, longing to stroke it, and willing himself to neither grind nor clench his teeth.

It's okay, he told himself. Calm down. It's all right. Your time will come. Very soon. This vision of desirability will see your book and your picture displayed prominently in some downtown bookstore, and she'll remember this conversation, and she'll be filled with bitter regret. And maybe some day after she sees that display, you'll have reason to ride the bus with all these plebeians again. She'll board that bus. She'll sit down next to you again. She'll apologize for her behavior today. She'll...

He closed his eyes.

She sat down beside him. "Oh, it *is* you!" she breathed. "I was afraid to hope. I was sure I'd never see you again. You're so wonderful! There never was a writer as wonderful as you. How can I apologize for my behavior last time? I'll do anything."

So they continued together to his magnificent new house in one of the city's ritziest neighborhoods—Redland Heights, perhaps—where the bus detoured in order to deliver them to Malcolm's front door, and then they made sweet and passionate love all night, and the dusky-skinned, almond-eyed, black-haired former maiden pledged to love him and all his books for ever and ever and ever.

And Malcolm opened his eyes, and lo! the seat was empty and she was gone and it was as if she had never been. Which in practical terms might as well have been the case.

Sometimes he wondered where his fascination—almost obsession—with a certain physical type of woman had come from. He couldn't trace it to anything. Just some genetic quirk, he supposed.

Marlene had certainly caught on to it and used it against him. She had been quite aware of his reaction to her. He had assumed she felt something similar toward him, or at least—or perhaps even preferably—a powerful attraction to his deep soul and high intellect.

If only someone had punched him in the gut for real at that moment of first meeting. Maybe that would have broken the spell in time. Now all he had left was silly fantasies about girls like the one on the bus. Would he ever touch such hair again? Would he ever touch a body like Marlene's again?

"Moan," he moaned.

Nonetheless, Malcolm felt better for the fantasy. For once, he thought, it wasn't based entirely on dreamy, boyish sexual imaginings. For once, thanks to today's telephone call, there was a chance that that fantasy or one much like it would come to pass.

His improved mood sustained him while he paid the oil-stained bill at the garage and endured the snickering—to his face, for they didn't even bother to do it behind his back any more—as he pored over the bill and tried to figure out what they had done to his car or claimed to have done to it.

He handed over a distressingly large percentage of his checking account balance and then soothed his soul with a drive through Redland Heights.

For once, when he finally reached home Malcolm didn't see the smallness and shabbiness and general dreariness of his apartment. He accepted it as temporary and he thought about the future.

Marlene had the house, and Malcolm was paying the mortgage on that. He was also required to make the payments on the car, but at least now he had possession of that. He suspected that Marlene was now earning more than he was, but he couldn't prove it. Not that it mattered. The divorce settlement didn't take her earnings into account at all.

Malcolm had once read one of those silly books that advise married couples to argue in order to keep their marriages stable and secure, and he had taken the book seriously, concluding from it that his and Marlene's marriage must be the exemplar of stability. The reality had so astonished him that he had not read the fine print in the divorce settlement—in particular, the lines which decreed that his financial obligations to his ex-wife were not dependent on any changes in her own financial situation. Under that legal agreement, Marlene could win the state lottery and become a multimillionaire, she could remarry, and this time to a vastly wealthy man, she could be elected President of the United States, and Malcolm would still have to keep making the monthly payments on what had been his house and would still have to provide her with a substantial amount of money every month to pay for utilities, groceries, clothes, and entertainment.

Marlene, obviously, had not been so stunned as Malcolm at the unraveling of their marriage. But then, the unraveling had come as no surprise to Marlene.

Fortunately, Marlene had never had any faith in his literary career, and so she had not bothered asking, in the divorce agreement, for some share of his future literary earnings. Once he'd paid off the house and car, all she had coming from him was that monthly stipend, and as his income increased from writing, that stipend would seem smaller with every royalty check.

Tomorrow he would begin the search for a new place to live, something more suited to his new future.

CHAPTER SIX

And so in the course of time, *Business Secrets from the Stars* appeared on the shelves.

At first, the number of shelves and the number of bookstores were both disturbingly low.

Malcolm began to get the sick feeling that once again his high hopes had been foolish and that once again a book of his would appear on the shelves and then disappear again soon after, leaving little trace of itself behind and leaving Malcolm's miserable life fundamentally unchanged.

At Mammon House, Jim Emich congratulated himself on having held Malcolm to such a low advance. Even so, Emich worried that his enthusiasm for the book, expressed in the quarterly marketing meetings, had been excessive and that its failure might tar or possibly even terminate his career. He began to rehearse excuses blaming Malcolm for the book's failure.

Then Malcolm had the brilliant idea of sending a copy by interoffice mail to Milo Grossbuck. On the blank page facing the title page, Malcolm wrote a long, effusive, exquisitely insincere message praising the Big Buck for his brilliant leadership, reminding him of their one meeting and telling BB that it had made an indelible impression on Malcolm, and thanking the Great Corporate Leader Guy for his years of inspiration, without which Malcolm could never have produced this small, humble, but he hoped somewhat useful manual for business success.

Like all great corporate leaders, the Big Buck had as much of the sucker in him as the people he regularly gulled and beguiled.

He read Malcolm's book. First he was floored. Then he was lifted up.

Far more important, he bought copies of it and sent it to every fellow corporate Big Guy he knew. Then he bought many more copies and distributed them to all of Western Bell's uncountable horde of vice presidents. The other corporate Big Guys, also floored and then uplifted, did the same within their own kingdoms.

Business Secrets from the Stars began to appear on business bestseller lists.

Malcolm breathed a sigh of relief. It was also a sigh of surprise at his having for once displayed some kind of marketing cleverness.

Jim Emich stood tall and set his sights higher. Before, he had hoped only to keep his inadequate paycheck coming in regularly. Now he began to think about his own imprint. A James Emich Book. He liked the sound of that.

Mammon House employed a publicist who tried hard to get Malcolm on the daytime television talk shows. The television networks seemed much less impressed by the possibilities of Malcolm's book than Mammon House and the corporate Big Guys and displayed little interest in him. The best the publicist was able to do was book Malcolm on William Buckley's show, where the normal focus was on issues of politics, religion, social policy, and vocabulary size.

Malcolm tried to prepare by reading a dictionary. He soon found himself skimming. He gave up on that idea.

Then he learned that he would not be given the opportunity to shine in isolated splendor but would be sharing the stage with some sort of religious figure. Malcolm decided to arm himself for what he was sure would be a confrontation by reading the Bible. He soon gave up on that, too.

He had never been self–disciplined about research.

The religious guest turned out to be the increasingly famous cleric Father Jerry O'Halloran (born Milton Goldberg, but later converted). He was a public theologian in the sense that he authored columns and books and hoped some day to be the host of his own weekly television show. He would call it "The O'Halloran Hour," or possibly "Listen to Your Father Jerry," and sure and it would be a corker, begorrah and *alevei.* For the moment, he was content to appear on the shows of other faithful sons of the Church.

Like Buckley, Father Jerry had been given a copy of *Business Secrets.* Unlike Buckley and the networks, Father Jerry understood the book's commercial potential. He also saw the potential it held for him. Destroying Malcolm Erskine, humiliating him, blasting him to smithereens just as Erskine was about to attain fame and success, would bring Father Jerry to the attention of the publishing industry, would increase the chances of his selling some kind of religious pap of his own, and would quite possibly bring "The O'Halloran Hour" closer to reality.

As he sat in the studio awaiting the moment of epiphany when the red light on the camera went on, Malcolm looked at the host of the program, who was sliding further and further down in his swivel chair and reading his copious notes. Then Malcolm looked at his fellow guest, who was adjusting his sinister black suit and white collar and filing his long yellow–gray teeth to nicely sharpened points. Malcolm sensed a trap, a setup, a veritable yawning pit opening before his hasty feet. Vultures were circling. Jackals were gathering. His very own tender flesh was the anticipated feast.

The red light turned on.

Buckley began.

First he licked his lips a few times with a whirling, circular motion of his tongue, then he adjusted himself in his chair and slid down a bit further, and finally he said, "One often hears that, ah–ah, *culpam poena premit comes,* as Horace so wisely said, putting it in Latin as was his wont. In this age of social displosion, it comes as no surprise to encounter a variety of protreptic that attracts numerous adherents with, yet, little—or perhaps even nothing—in the way of nidification. Such, I make so bold as to declare, is the case with the philosophy espoused by the lesser of my two guests, Mr. Malcolm Erskine."

Malcolm nodded, feeling and looking ill.

A few ironic cheers arose from the small studio audience, followed by laughter.

Father O'Halloran looked ever smugger. He could scarcely contain his glee. How his sainted mother would have *kvelled,* were she only still alive. Too bad she had suffered a fatal heart attack when he told her he was converting to Catholicism and joining the priesthood.

"My far more eminent guest," Buckley continued, "is Father Jerry O'Halloran, well known for his great work on behalf of the only true faith. In short, my *landsmann.* How they hanging, Jerry?"

"Circumspectly, Bill."

The two Catholics—the born and the made—laughed comfortably together.

Malcolm's feeling of being in a trap increased. What made it worse—more galling, anyway—was the knowledge that he had walked into this trap of his own free will, even with eagerness. He gritted his teeth and tried to gather his courage. Gird thou thy loins, said he to himself. Peril awaits, and only the most charlatanish can hope to win through alive.

Buckley returned to the feast. "Mr. Erskine's, er, doctrines are so well saponified that I need scarcely deadle them to so pilocarpine an audience. Mr. Erskine, would you care to comment?"

Malcolm frowned in deep thought for a few moments, then said, "I could of course simply gandopate, Mr. Buckley—but not, as you so wisely put it, before so pilocarpine an audience. Hence I'll not be the one to suggest that you write a novel in which you kill your favorite protagonist and call the novel *Blackford Croaks.* However, I will philmonderize slightly, if I may—at least to the extent of actual maxmendorization—by suggesting that 'social displosion' is entirely too slemorous a term for the utterly enlogillobous processes to which I have addressed myself in my book."

"Hmm," Buckley said, pausing to consider Malcolm's response. "That's certainly, ah–ah, a vagotropic view. But surely you can't deny, Mr. Erskine, that, ah–ah, you have maginated on an innocent public a granophyre of truly rhadamanthine proportions?"

"Nonsense!" Malcolm said, his face reddening. "Really, Mr. Buckley!"

"If I may interject a fatuous word or two," said Father O'Halloran soothingly, "I'd like to point out that Holy Scripture has something to say about this very subject. For example, in the book of Harold, chapter five, verses one through four, Jesus himself says, 'Yea, verily, say no more, lest ye say more than a man should say. For I say unto you that my father says, Go and say more unto the gentiles and say less unto the Jews. Say, brethren, would ye gainsay the sayings of the Lord your God? So he said, and thus saying, said no more.'"

Malcolm sneered. "Oh, sure, you can quote the New Testament all you want, but what about the Old, eh? What about Moishe 1:8, eh? 'If what you're doing makes you very happy, then you better stop doing it.' Remember that one, Father O?"

O'Halloran winced and grabbed his head with both hands. "Feh! You're giving me such a headache, you *mamser!* Okay, okay. Here's another one from the New Testament. I know this one'll shut you up. Book of Millicent, chapter ninety–nine, verses thirteen through one hundred twenty–one: 'Then the Lord spake unto Millicent, saying, Prove thou that thou lovest me, daughter. And Millicent spake unto the Lord saying, No, no, a thousand times no, and get your damned hands off me.' Well?"

"Hmph. Second book of Shecky, last verse: *'Nu?'*"

"Oy, vey!" groaned the priest.

Ding! First round awarded by the judges to Malcolm Erskine by a score of five to three.

By fadeout, the audience was similarly divided. This was quite an improvement from their feelings when the hour had begun. Malcolm was holding his own.

This at least was how Malcolm remembered his appearance on the Buckley show. More accurately, this was how he told the story in the autobiography he published many decades later, that book, intended to be his second great bestseller, which almost no one read.

Ah, fellow spawnspawn, truth is a slippery thing! We make our own realities. Who is to say what really happened during those endless minutes before the camera? Did Buckley really retreat from the field of verbal sparring when faced with Malcolm's mighty vocabulary? Did Father Jerry really run away, have a sex–change operation, and enter a nunnery? In the great flux of oscillating quantum reality, in this cosmos in which the be–all becomes the end–all and then seemingly instantaneously switches back again, might it not be that Malcolm really did conquer the enemy and win the hearts of the television viewers? Is reality so solid and immutable that we can assert without any doubts that in fact the version of his appearance related by those who laughed at his bumbling incoherence was true then and will always be true? A thousand years from now—no, a mere hundred years from now—will it be their scornful account or Malcolm's self-laudatory one that posterity reads and treasures?

Probably neither.

What history does record is that this one television appearance did not lead to any others. Those with the power to determine who will reap the benefits of being guests on television shows did not seem to feel, from having watched Malcolm's battle with Jerry and Bill, that he would appeal to the viewers of the shows for which they handled the bookings.

Nonetheless, Malcolm's book continued to sell well enough and his fame to spread far enough that competitors appeared quickly.

"...The Tonight Show, starring Johnny Carson and Johnny's very special guest, Shirley MacLaine. And now, heeeere's Johnny!"

The monologue: topical jokes, varied audience reaction ranging from uncontrollable laughter to groans, the host watching the audience and staring half sideways into the camera with his self-deprecating, conspiratorial half-smile.

The commercial.

The guest.

"Well, have you read this new book?" Johnny holds up a copy of *Business Secrets from the Stars* for the camera, then reads from the back cover copy. "'An astonishing new revelation for our times. Learn from our long-dead cosmic cousins how to best manage your career or business. Channeling's most important breakthrough, revealed to you by the greatest channeler in history and his stellar spirit guide.' Sounds like big competition for you, Shirley."

The guest crosses her legs and her gown slides apart slightly at the slit, revealing a pleasing glimpse of her still attractive dancer's gams.

Not bad, thinks Malcolm Erskine, watching his new monster color television screen from his new monster water bed in his new monster condominium in one of downtown Piketon's most monstrously expensive high-rises. Pull your dress up a bit and tell us all what you think about my book.

"Yes, Johnny, I have read it, and no, I don't see it as competition at all. You see, I think Mr. Erskine is working toward the same high goal that many of us are: the raising of human consciousness to a higher plane."

"Right," Malcolm says to the screen, "the raising of my standard of living to a higher plane."

"So, Shirley, you really think that what Erskine talks about in this book is true? That he really was contacted by an alien intelligence? That he's really, er, channeling a being who was one of the vice presidents of an alien business corporation tens of thousands of years ago?" The inimitable half-smile is back.

"I *know* it's true, Johnny. As you know, I've traveled extensively on the astral plane myself, and while there I've encountered a great range of wonderful beings from many different eras and planes, including some from other parts of our own universe, not to mention many from entirely other universes. Anyway, you see, that's why I know that Malcolm Erskine's spirit contact, Lukas of Aldebaran, is real. I've met him on the astral plane. Some years ago, on that plane, Lukas and I had a truly heavenly love affair. He's a very beautiful being, physically very much like us, but spiritually of course far more developed, more evolved."

The half-smile has changed to open-mouthed wonder. "An affair? On the astral plane?"

"Oh, certainly. Did you think that travelers on the higher planes limit themselves to speaking? We can touch, too, you know, while we're there. Anyway, Lukas taught me so much while we were together. He told me many, many things that Mr. Erskine doesn't even talk about. I guess Lukas didn't think Erskine was ready for all the illumination he had to offer. My next book will describe the affair in great detail, and also the revelations Lukas blessed me with."

"Your next best-seller, I'm sure, Shirley."

Modest, slightly smug smile. "I've got my fingers crossed."

Malcolm frowned. He pressed the ON/OFF switch on his remote control and watched the big screen click from glaring color to blankness, the Tonight Show setting and Malcolm's fellow-traveler fading away.

He supposed he should be glad that his book was so successful that the other purveyors of New Age nonsense saw it as a threat or as a new bandwagon they needed to jump on. Still, it bothered him. This was *his* inspiration! No one else should be allowed to benefit from it!

He even felt betrayed that this particular bandwagon jumper was an actress he had once fantasized about, back in the days before his almond-eyed invention had expelled all other fantasy objects.

Jeez, he thought, why don't you have an affair with me, instead? Here, on this plane.

Here on this strange, tricky plane, so filled with the unexpected and disturbing.

It was a good thing, he thought, that he'd already made his own triumphal television appearance. He was still the first name in the public's mind with the newest gimmick. So he hoped, anyway.

The closing years of the presidency of the Great Confabulator were strange ones.

For a brief moment, the American public seemed to wake up and ask itself what it had done. How, they asked themselves, could we have put this dolt in charge of the Big Red Button of Destruction? Did someone dose the national water supply with hallucinogenic mushrooms? Are mind–bending waves being broadcast from all of our television sets? What else could explain that we elected this senile nincompoop in preference to a far better man and then reelected him in a landslide over another far better man? What has happened to America? they wept.

Then they went back to watching television.

But the strangeness persisted. Even after the Grand Enormity had wandered away from office, grinning and winking and waving his white cowboy hat to imaginary crowds, and had been succeeded by his Vice President, Daddy Longlegs, who had ascended to the Presidency by defeating a far better man in his turn, even then the strangeness persisted.

Not that Malcolm minded. He was riding that strangeness to wealth and fame. He no longer needed to heave himself out of bed in the morning, groaning and filled with self–pity, when the alarm went off. Instead, he slept till he awoke naturally, and then he lay in bed for a long time, dreamily, comfortably, groaning and feeling sorry for himself. Malcolm could always find a reason to feel sorry for himself.

For a moment, thinking about the High Defribillator led Malcolm to think about Steve Golden, whom he hadn't seen in a couple of years. Steve had transferred to another work group and they had lost touch. Malcolm had heard through the corporate grapevine that later Steve had been laid off.

Malcolm imagined Steve fulminating about the meandering farewell speech from the Great Fog Machine or the latest addled one from President Longlegs, and he chuckled.

He guessed Steve hadn't managed to get published, or he would surely have heard about it. Ah, well. Very sad and all too common. Malcolm returned to thinking about himself.

A remarkable variety of charlatans flourished during those strange days. The number of them was high even by historical American standards.

One of the more successful was Atlantica. Based in, of course, California, she was a con artist of great wealth and wide influence. For more information about Atlantica, let's listen in on Oprah as, with slightly overdone wide–eyed credulousness, she introduces the hot psychic of the month to her audience, on an episode of Oprah's show that Malcolm somehow managed to miss:

"Attie, as her followers call her, is the channel for an ancient Atlantean warrior. Presidents have been known to consult her so that her spirit guide, Mellabenth, can advise them on international affairs. Her mass audiences are attended by enormous crowds, who pay large sums to hear Mellabenth speak through her. Can I call you At?"

Laughter from the audience.

Oprah's guest was a slight, rather pretty blonde woman in her thirties, dressed in what might have been white pajamas with long, wide sleeves. At this familiarity, she began to tremble slightly, and spittle appeared at the corners of her mouth. She no longer seemed so slight. Oprah drew back, and the audience's laughter grew nervous, uncertain. Finally, Atlantica managed to get herself back under control. "You may call me Miss Atlantica," she said coldly.

"Right, right. Of course, Miss Atlantica. Now, we've wanted to have you on the show for a long time so you could tell us about your fascinating work channeling Mellabenth from Atlantis and the consulting with presidents, and so on, but today, I'd like to ask you about this new book that's just come out about—"

"The Andromeda Corporation," Atlantica said scornfully. "Yes, yes, everyone asks me about it. I haven't read it, but I know all about it. Mellabenth gave me a summary. It's a con game. Mellabenth told me that, too."

"It's selling very well, so I understand."

"A con game!" Atlantica shouted. "That guy—what's his name? The author? I said, *what's his name?"*

"Malcolm Erskine," Oprah said quickly, moving still further away.

Atlantica waved her hand. "Right, him. Anyway, you know he's not really a channeler. It's all made up. If he's a channeler, I'd like to see him do this."

The trembling returned, and so did the spittle—much more of it, this time, long strings of drool looping from the corners of her mouth down to her chest. Oprah turned pale and her audience turned green. Again, Atlantica seemed to grow in size. She frowned deeply, then opened her mouth and spoke in a voice two octaves deeper than her normal tone, a husky growl that could only have come from the massive chest of a long-dead warrior king of ancient Atlantis. "Aye, I say to you that Malcolm Erskine is conducting a scam."

Instantly, Atlantica returned to normal size and facial expression. Calmly, she wiped the drool away with her copious sleeves. "See?" she said smugly.

"Er, yes. But, you know, Miss Atlantica, even though I've only read the first couple of chapters of *Business Secrets,* I found it very interesting. Especially the second chapter, where Erskine talks about the origins of mankind and how we're related to the star-people, the, um, Merskeenians, who built the Andromeda Corporation."

Oprah turned to her audience. "See, apparently our ancestors evolved somewhere out in interstellar space, on another world. Then, about thirty thousand years ago, they were attacked by a terribly evil race of catlike creatures, all females and very human looking, called the Marlinga. Our ancestors were rescued only because of the incredible bravery of a man named M'lersk. They became refugees, traveling in space, and eventually ending up on Earth, in Atlantis, where M'lersk became the father of a race of kings. Some of the other people, though, other Merskeenians, they stayed behind and managed to fight the Marlinga and defeat them, and they're the ones who built the civilization Malcolm Erskine is in contact with. Claims to be in contact with, I mean," she added hastily, having noticed a faint trembling beginning again in her guest.

"Hmph," Atlantica said. "Yes, I know all about that. Mellabenth summarized that, too. After all, Mellabenth and Lukas were both in corporeal form at coincident points in our own plane of existence at very much the same time. Mellabenth says that there is an essential truth to that story, as indeed there always is to all stories, even yours." She said this to Oprah. She turned to the audience. "And yours. But the with–all is not the be–all. Nor is the other."

Tune in tomorrow, when Oprah's very special guest will be a man who married a parking meter.

Malcolm didn't see the man–who–married–a–parking–meter show either because he was in the air, headed west, accompanied by a very large Secret Service man.

It was an interesting day, and it started early.

Malcolm was still asleep when the pounding on his condominium door began. The racket shattered his dream of a stunningly, exotically beautiful young woman with shoulder–length black hair, olive skin, and, of course, almond–shaped eyes.

Malcolm awoke halfway and stared around him wildly, sweating, panting, terrified. It was the Marlingas! They'd come for him, come to tear him to shreds with their talons and teeth, to castrate him, to demean him, to drive him crazy before they killed him and took away all his possessions!

No, he realized, waking the rest of the way, it was just a loud knocking at the door.

Malcolm rolled out of bed and staggered around, finding his slippers and robe. The exquisitely expensive liqueurs and wines and brandies he'd never been able to afford before seemed to cause a sleep fully as uneasy and a hangover fully as fierce as their cheap cousins, especially when mixed in the stomach.

He found slippers, robe, and finally, after a panicky search, the door, and opened it.

Standing in the opening was a suited, gimlet–eyed young man eight feet in height and six feet across the shoulders. He looked tough, mean, and ready to do violence. Before Malcolm could tell him he must have the wrong address—sorry, no Mafiosi on this floor—and slam the door, the young man said, *basso profundo,* "Mr. Malcolm Erskine?"

There seemed no reason to deny it. "That's me. Malcolm Erskine. I write books."

"Yes, sir. I know that, sir. That's why I'm here, sir."

Well, well! There was a definite tone of respect, almost of subservience, in the large man's voice. Malcolm drew himself up and said condescendingly, "What can I do for you, young man?"

The young man reached into his inside jacket pocket, looked up and down the hallway quickly, and then drew out a wallet, which he flipped open to show Malcolm, briefly, an ID card with a governmental eagle on it. "Zip Muchley, sir. Secret Service. What you can do for me, sir, is accompany me to the West Coast. California."

Didn't the Secret Service have any agents who were stunningly, exotically beautiful young women with shoulder–length black hair and olive skin whom Malcolm could wittily offer to follow anywhere? "Now?"

Zip Muchley nodded. "Now, sir."

"Why?"

"Sort of a personal services deal, sir. Someone wants to get some advice from your, er, spirit guide. One on one, like."

"Are you joking? And I'm supposed to go to the Fruitcake State just for that? Who is this person?"

Zip looked up and down the hallway again, then bent at the waist and leaned down, so that his mouth was close to Malcolm's ear, and then he whispered the still potent name.

Malcolm's eyes widened and filled with dollar signs. The magic endorsement! "I haven't shaved or showered or eaten breakfast or any of that. And it's an hour earlier out there. Won't my client still be asleep?"

Zip hesitated. At last, he said reluctantly, "Yes, sir, he will. For quite a while, yet, in fact. But not his wife. She never sleeps. And she's the one who really wants to see you."

"Grumble, grumble," Malcolm grumbled, for the sake of appearance.

"Oh, and I should tell you, sir, that you'll be able to shower and shave and eat on the plane. It's very well equipped."

Yeah, Malcolm thought. I'll bet. Thanks to my tax dollars. "Okay, er, Zip. Let me at least get dressed, and I'll be ready to go. By the way, you have a remarkable voice. Ever thought of going into opera?"

Zip frowned. "'Opera,' sir? What's that?"

The airplane Malcolm was taken to was indeed the famous airliner with the famous seal on its famous tail assembly. That was perhaps why it was parked far out at the end of a runway at an Air Force base outside Piketon. It was too famous to be flown into Piketon International Airport without arousing the local press from their wonted slumber. Had it been sent all this way just to ferry Malcolm Erskine the fifteen hundred miles to Southern California? A personal favor, he assumed, from the incumbent to his predecessor. Your tax dollars at work.

But Malcolm had to admit that the airplane's well appointed bathroom with shower and new–just–for–him electric razor and new–

just–for–him electric toothbrush, all installed with the help of his tax dollars, were pleasant to use, and the breakfast that his tax dollars provided for him afterward, while simple, was very tasty.

He was digesting the last of the smoked pork chops with the help of a cup of coffee as they passed over the Grand Canyon. If, he wondered, looking down into the shadowed chasm, he could drop Marlene into it from this altitude, would he be able to see the dust raised by the impact? It was a fantasy that went well with hot coffee and the aftertaste of smoked pork chop.

Zip Muchley had been by his side all along, except during his shower, during which the Secret Service man had waited patiently just outside the bathroom. He was an extremely large hovering presence and impossible to ignore. Was he there to prevent an attack upon his charge or an escape by him? Under the circumstances, either was unlikely.

Malcolm turned from contemplation of the canyon, now sliding out of sight behind them. "Are you married, Zip?"

Muchley looked from side to side, up and down the passenger cabin, which was empty except for them and the lone steward who had served Malcolm his breakfast and who now waited patiently beside the door to the cockpit, certainly well out of earshot. Satisfied, Muchley said in a low voice, "Yes, sir."

"Happily?"

Muchley smiled suddenly, unexpectedly. "Very, sir."

"Children?"

The smile disappeared. "Five, sir."

"You, um, have pictures of them, I suppose?"

Muchley shook his head. "Not one, sir."

"Too bad," Malcolm said. Thank God, he thought.

"I do have a picture of my wife, though, sir," Muchley said, smiling again in soft, reflective pleasure.

Is she exotically beautiful with shoulder-length black hair and olive skin? "I'd love to see that."

Muchley took out the same wallet he had flipped open earlier to show Malcolm his ID card. This time, he opened it so that a picture encased in plastic showed instead. It was of a blonde bimbo who looked no more than sixteen. Not Malcolm's type, if he had had the luxury of being choosy, but certainly not bad. "Very pretty, Muchley. Congratulations."

"That was taken before she had any of the kids," Muchley said sadly. "She's...changed a bit since then. But she's a terrific gal," he added quickly. "Woman, I mean. A wonderful woman. Just like the great lady we're going to see." His tone had turned reverent at the end.

"You really respect her, do you? The great lady we're going to see, I mean."

"Oh, yes, sir! Finest First Lady in the history of the United States, sir."

"Hmm. I voted for the other First Lady, myself."

Muchley was confused. "But—but then why did you agree to make this trip, Mr. Erskine?"

Malcolm smiled. "Can't hurt the sales of the book, can it?"

Suddenly, Zip Muchley lost his charming little-boy earnestness and assumed in its place a focused seriousness that was altogether more unsettling. He leaned forward, narrowed his already narrow eyes, lowered the pitch of his already low-pitched voice, frowned, and said, "You're not allowed to mention anything about any of this to anyone. No publicity at all. Not a word." He glared at Malcolm, waiting for his response.

Malcolm laughed nervously. "Airplanes are so cold at these altitudes, aren't they?" He held up his hands. "You bet. Whatever you say, Zip. Zip, Zip. Not a word."

Muchley leaned back again, but he kept glaring at Malcolm.

Malcolm sighed and wondered why he had always had such an amazing ability to transform pleasant conversations into emotional cliffs. He turned his attention to the window, to the flat, brown landscape below, and tried to watch for the Hoover Dam and the Salton Sea, wondering if he'd be able to see them from this altitude.

They landed at another Air Force base, this one in southern California, and then they were helicoptered into the mountains, ending up at a helicopter landing strip on private land. A black limousine was waiting for them, bearing small U.S. flags on its fenders. Malcolm wondered if that was legal when transporting a private citizen. He shrugged and climbed in. Probably this whole trip was illegal. Probably there was a regulation somewhere against spending money to transport a private citizen on the presidential jet for private purposes. But power tends to be abused, and absolute power tends to be abused absolutely. Power's siren song: Use me, abuse me. Oh, that feels so good! President Longlegs seemed at least as susceptible to that song as any other President.

As long as he was the beneficiary of that abuse, Malcolm would play along. He was already thinking ahead, planning ways in which he could benefit from this odd experience despite Muchley's warning.

The limousine took him and Zip to a rambling ranch house, Hollywood rustic outside and in. His two hosts were waiting to greet him: the woman aging but still fashionable, a hard, strong person; the man tall, prunishly wrinkled, affable, expectant. They greeted Zip first, using his first name. The Secret Service man licked the great lady's shoes and the great man's cowboy boots and rolled over onto his back for his tummy rub, his tail thumping madly against the entranceway's stone floor.

Then the great lady and the great man turned their attention to Malcolm, calling him "Mr. Erskine" and looking genuinely awe struck.

Malcolm smiled condescendingly and greeted both of them by

their first names. "Hi, Gone. Hi, Fancy."

Zip was scandalized, the great lady looked disturbed, but the great man chuckled and said, "There you go again!"

At first, the conversation was general, dealing with Malcolm's supposed conversations with Lukas of Aldebaran. The great lady wanted details, partly because of curiosity, Malcolm gathered, but partly to reassure herself that it had all really happened. This put Malcolm in a fairly uncomfortable position, because of course it had not happened. He had to invent new details quickly in answer to each of her questions.

What sort of clothing did Lukas' wife wear to big state occasions?

"Robes," Malcolm said immediately. "Purple, I believe. With gold earrings. Long robes. Kind of like a bathrobe."

The great lady frowned in disapproval. "Well," she said uncertainly, "I suppose if that was the approved style of the time, she had no choice. What about her coloring, though? Her hair, her skin."

"Oh, you know, Fancy, just like yours. Um, she colored her hair a lot, and Lukas said she'd had a facelift or two."

"Fascinating! Now, about her shoes—"

"Say," her husband broke in, "did I ever tell you about the welfare queen who had a whole floor of a fancy hotel in New York City and fifty-four kids and expensive liquor and everything?"

"Why, no, not that I recall." Saved by the bell, Malcolm thought.

Fancy said sharply, "Shut up, Gone."

With a sunny smile, he did so.

She turned back to Malcolm. "Let's forget about Lady Lukas' shoes for now. I'd like you to tell me more about the enemy race. What was the name, again?"

"Oh, the Marlingas. Yes, the Marlingas. Unimaginably evil, destructive, greedy, nasty little creatures." He felt on safer ground with this topic. He felt he could invent malicious details about the Marlingas for as long as his hostess wanted. A deeper question was why he was here, but he was prepared to play along for a while. "Capable of appearing to be human, though, even deceptively attractively human. They looked particularly good in, uh—" Panties, he had almost said. "Human clothing. Merskeenian clothing, that is. But they were evil, terrible, the Marlingas."

"Malingerers!" Gone cried out. "Sitting there in their Temple of Gloom! But I got them off everyone's back, didn't I?"

Fancy gave Malcolm an apologetic look and said to her husband, "I'm not going to tell you again. I want you to behave yourself and sit quietly, or I'm just going to have to give you another shot, and you don't like those, do you?"

Gone's lower lip trembled. "No, Mommy."

"All right, then." Fancy turned back to Malcolm, looking quite satisfied with herself. "Please continue."

Malcolm did so for some time, describing Marlene's soul. This was a description of an individual Marlinga, he explained, but they were all identical, every member of the race—their souls, their bodies, even their possessions. Which, he added, they held in common, having stolen them from real human beings.

"Collectivists!" Fancy said with a shiver.

"Communists!" her husband cried.

"Acquisitivists," Malcolm corrected them.

He was about to continue, for the terrible nature of the Marlingas was a topic of which he never tired, but Gone seemed to be suffering some sort of negative effects from his loud yell. Malcolm noticed him bending over, turning his head to one side, and hitting it on the back with the heel of his hand.

"Are you okay?" Malcolm asked.

Gone managed a chuckle. His voice was muffled but still understandable. "Oh, don't mind me. Little problem from falling off a horse and getting shot in the head. Or maybe it was the other way 'round. Anyway, got to drain the extra fluid every now and then." He kept pounding on the back of his head.

"Gone," Fancy said warningly. "I've warned you to do that in the bathroom."

"Almost got it, dear." Suddenly, a spurt of dark, old blood shot from the side of his head and splattered on the carpeted floor. "There. Much better."

Fancy turned red with anger. She stood up and called out a couple of names. Two men appeared, the first one immense and the second even bigger. They dwarfed Zip Muchley, who looked peeved at being dwarfed. It was probably a rare experience for him, Malcolm thought. Fancy gestured imperiously toward her husband, and the two giants stepped over to him, grasped an arm apiece, and carried him off, his heels dragging on the carpet, his eyes swiveling from side to side in confused alarm.

Fancy called out after them, "Give him everything that's left in the little blue bottle. Intravenous."

The giants nodded, and they disappeared around a corner with their famous burden. The last word Malcolm heard from the ex-president was a long, drawn-out "Mommy-y-y!" that was suddenly cut off. A door slammed.

"Now we can talk without interruption," Fancy told Malcolm. "Zip, go outside and walk in the rose garden, would you? It's right outside the back door."

"Yes, ma'am." Zip stood up. "I remember. Just scream if you need protection." He marched away in the same direction the two giants had taken. On the way, he paused to give Malcolm a don't-try-any-funny-business-you-little-creep look, then continued.

"He's so devoted to us," Fancy said.

Malcolm was amazed that he had never before realized what a

dangerous place the world is.

"Okay, Erskine," Fancy said, "let's get down to brass tacks. What I really need is some direct advice from your spirit guide, Lukas. In fact, I'd prefer to talk directly to him. I've always hated dealing with underlings."

"Let's say 'middlemen,' shall we? Anyway, Lukas speaks to me, not through me. I'm not that kind of channeler."

"Hmph. You probably just need a shot of the right stuff in your system. Do you wonders. Look what it did for my husband for eight years."

She seemed to be about to raise her voice again, and Malcolm envisioned her calling for the two giants and giving them instructions concerning *his* blood chemistry.

"I'll give it a try," Malcolm said quickly. "Ask me a question, any question."

"That's more like it. All right, then. Get me Lukas of Aldebaran."

On line two, ma'am, Malcolm thought, wondering what he ought to do next. He could run for the front door, but even assuming he could outdistance the various goons the house seemed filled with, what would he do once he got outside? He was somewhere in the middle of nowhere, and all the transportation was under the control of others. Clearly, it was time for Lukas of Aldebaran to speak.

Malcolm closed his eyes, squeezed his mouth into a thin line, and exerted force as though he were sitting on the toilet. He could feel his face growing red. Not too much, he told himself. You don't want a hernia or a stroke. He opened his eyes wide and staring, and then he opened his mouth and spoke in a raspy, husky voice that he imagined was appropriate for a stellar corporate executive who had died 30,000 years before. "Who calls? Who wishes to speak to me? Who disturbs my rest? And why didn't you go through my answering service?"

"That's me," Malcolm added in his normal voice.

"Shut up, Erskine. Lukas, I am the wife of a man who was until recently the most powerful man in our world. But now he's nobody, and he'll never have that power back again. I miss that power, Lukas, and I want it back. How should I go about doing that?"

Oh, my God, Malcolm thought, and he again considered a dash for the door. "Among my people," he said, assuming again the husky, rasping voice, "we had a saying that applies in this case: 'Let George do it.'"

Fancy's face began to grow red, even redder than Malcolm's had been.

"Of course, that is a loose translation," Malcolm added quickly. "I chose a human name at random, so as not to confuse you with the unfamiliar sounds of our names. Perhaps a more accurate translation would be: 'Things take time.'"

But Fancy's face grew even redder. "How much time do you think I've got?" she snarled.

That was a good point, Malcolm had to admit. "All right, all right. Here's one of my all–time old Aldebaranian favorites: 'It is often most successful to be the successor to the successor.'"

"What the hell is that supposed to mean?"

Malcolm had no idea. For a scary moment, it really had seemed that someone else was speaking through his mouth. He supposed that his unconscious or subconscious or preconscious or one of those things had been suggesting a way out. But now he had to interpret it with his plain old conscious. One thing was certainly clear to Malcolm, and that was that he couldn't continue with the medium act. It was too great a mental strain, and it was hurting his throat.

"Hello?" he said in his normal voice. "Hello? Gee, I'm sorry, Fancy, we seem to have lost the connection. I think there's a lot of etheric interference around right now. Something to do with that big solar flare I was just reading about, I suppose."

"But what am I going to do?" Fancy wailed. "All I've got from your damned Lukas is something oracular that I can't make any sense out of."

"It is often most successful to be the successor to the successor," Malcolm repeated thoughtfully. "Let's think about this for a moment. We all know who the successor to your husband is: Daddy Longlegs. Now who's *his* successor?"

"How the hell am I supposed to know? Whoever wins the election after the next one, of course."

"Mm. Could be the current Vice President, Junior Partridge, right? It so often is."

Fancy shuddered. "And people thought that *Gone* had the IQ of a garbanzo bean."

A split pea in Malcolm's opinion. But no one could say that about the IQ of Malcolm Erskine, whom inspiration had just struck. "Now, let's just suppose that when the next election comes up, the handsome boy Vice President is seen as a major liability. The president might decide to turn to someone else, someone with a place in the public's manipulable heart."

"Gone?" Fancy said uncertainly. "Isn't that unconstitutional?"

"I don't know. But, anyway, that wasn't what I meant. You know, the Democrats might try something underhanded again, a running mate with some kind of group appeal."

"You mean someone who isn't white?" Fancy cried.

"Possibly. I didn't think of that. I was thinking they might try a woman again. So what's a good response to that?"

"Yes!" she shrieked. "Yes! You've done it! You're wonderful!"

Zip Muchley stuck his head around the door and asked if everything was okay.

Fancy waved him away. "Yes, yes. Go back to the rose garden, Zip. Cut a couple for your wife."

"Sure. Thanks." He disappeared, muttering, "Sounded like she was coming, or something."

Fancy had already forgotten him. She was nodding, saying, "Right. Right. So all I have to do between now and the nominating convention is somehow get the young wimp to step aside so that the old wimp will start looking around for a replacement. And I'll make sure the word gets out that it should be a woman, because of my inside info about the Democrat ticket. Preferably me. And then..." She smiled. "Successor to the successor."

"I'm sure you can take care of the rest easily," Malcolm told her, wondering if he would end up having to leave the country in a few years. "Do you think I could, um, get back home now?"

"Yes, yes, of course." Her eyes filled with dreams of near–future glory, the once and future queen shouted for Zip, who came back into the room at a run, one hand holding two yellow roses, the other against his mouth because he was sucking at a deep thorn puncture on his index finger.

"Yeth, ma'am?"

Fancy jerked her head Malcolm's way. "Take Mr. Erskine back home. Then I have another job for you. Mr. Erskine, I might want you back here at a moment's notice for more consultation. And in just a few years, I might be wanting you regularly in...Well, you know where. Otherwise, mum's the word. Got that?"

"Yes'm," Malcolm muttered.

Success was having some very unforeseen complications.

CHAPTER SEVEN

Each of us has a god or goddess within him or her or it or them, and we are each the descendants of star kings and queens, and so we have each inherited the great powers of those ancients and can use them to shape our own reality. Everything is plastic. Shape the universe as you will. Never say die.

—Lukas of Aldebaran, as reliably reported by Malcolm Erskine in Business Secrets from the Stars

The most he could make out of the entire experience was to bill himself, in subsequent advertising for his book, as a "respected consultant to former presidents and their wives." Even that made him uneasy. He kept expecting the two giants from the California retirement retreat to show up at his doorway and remove his limbs. But they didn't, and for all he knew, the blurb did increase the already staggering sales. Money, Malcolm thought. Lots more money. Other than sex and eternal youth, what else is there?

His mind was taken off the whole subject when he received a fan letter from an overnight millionaire.

He was receiving a flood of letters now from all over the world. Most of them were passed on to him by Mammon House. Some of them were addressed to the house Marlene now owned and were sent on by her in an obviously conciliatory act. Isn't money wonderful?

Some of the letters were bizarre ramblings. Most of those were written by hand and few of them were entirely legible. Some were typed surprisingly well, fooling him for the first few few words into thinking that they were sane letters from sane people. And many were indeed quite sane, written by earnest seekers after wealth who were following the absurd principles in Malcolm's book and who owned their own typewriters or computers to write their letters on.

This one, he could see, was one of the last variety. It certainly held his attention all the way through.

> *Dear Mr. Erskine:*
>
> *In one week, by applying your enlightened knowledge, I made one million dollars. In the second week, two million. Last week, it was ten million. Mr. Erskine, I bless you nightly in my prayers. I owe all my success to you. I only wish I could think of some way to repay you.*

Malcolm glanced quickly at the signature at the bottom of the page. Nope: a man. Too bad.

Then he checked the name again. Jimmy Flicker. Why, he knew that name. He had been seeing it lately in the business section of the *Chronicle.* This was a rapidly up-and-coming young fellow who was being touted as very likely to become Piketon's next billionaire, joining the current two, Norris Marvins and Ed Hite. If Flicker's earnings continued to increase at the rate his letter claimed, that should happen in only a few months.

And he owes it all to me, huh?

Surely Flicker had been speaking figuratively. But just in case Flicker was a literal kinda guy, Malcolm called the number on the letterhead. Never pass up a chance to get some of someone else's money, he reasoned.

Malcolm and Jimmy Flicker had dinner together at a very expensive and exclusive restaurant in one of the downtown towers, so expensive that Malcolm felt guilty eating there despite his swollen bank account and certainty of huge royalty checks in the near future, and so exclusive that it never advertised itself and had no sign outside to announce its presence, depending entirely on the word of mouth of its wealthy clientele.

The dining room was small and occupied by only about a half dozen customers. At first Malcolm wondered how the owners could afford to pay the rent and the presumably high salaries of the help, who outnumbered the diners by perhaps five to one. Then he glanced at the prices on the elegantly lettered menu in front of him and knew the answer.

It was fortunate that Jimmy Flicker was paying. How much had Flicker made since he'd written his letter to Malcolm? Another twenty million? Keep eating in places like this, my boy, Malcolm thought, and you'll need every penny of it.

Above the elegant, subdued clinking of the elegant, subdued, obscenely expensive silverware, Jimmy Flicker said somewhat too loudly, "Save some room for the ice cream, sir. It's really great. You know, Mr. Erskine, sir, I was really blown away that you called me up. I just wrote you that fan letter because I was so grateful to you for putting me where I am today. I've tried Shirley MacLaine's stuff, and it never worked. But when you said, 'Each of us has a god or goddess within them, and we're each the descendants of star kings and queens, and so we have each inherited the great powers of those ancients and can use them to shape our own reality. Never say die.' Well, you know, when I read that, it just about blew me away. I nearly lost it."

Malcolm winced. Had he really written that drivel? Money, he reminded himself. Think of nothing but the money. Ethics are worth little when you're poor. "Call me Malcolm, and I'll call you Jimmy. All right?"

Handsome young Jimmy Flicker shook his head, laughing in amazement. "It's true, what I've read: the great ones are always modest!" The plain, non-prescription lenses of his glasses flashed in the subdued, elegant, should-have-been-brighter light, his red tie glowed against his pale blue shirt, and his expensive gray suit impressed the subdued, elegant, condescending-only-to-Malcolm waiters. His razor-cut hair was, of course, perfect. "I'm over here going, like, 'Wow, this is just blowing me away,' and you're over there just being like an ordinary guy."

And I'm, Malcolm thought, over here going, like, you're a twit.

Malcolm picked up the fine goblet—no one would ever have called it simply a glass—and sipped some water. "Yes, Jimmy, I am indeed just an ordinary guy. I was merely lucky enough to be in the right place at the right time when the spirit of Lukas was searching space and time for a mind to pour his wisdom into."

"Wow," Jimmy said.

Someone else wrote this guy's letter for him, Malcolm decided. Some secretary he pays a pittance to.

"Yes," Malcolm said reminiscently, "when Lukas first contacted me, up there on that mountaintop, well, Jimmy, I tell you, it really blew me away. It was awesome. It was incredible. I just about lost it. I was going, like, 'Hey, *what* is going *on?'* You see what I mean?"

Jimmy nodded enthusiastically and put down his utensils, his main course unfinished. Saving room for the ice cream. "That is so true. Yes, sir, I *do* know what you mean."

In that case, thought Malcolm, I'm glad I don't. "So, Jimmy, you said you had an idea about my spreading my word a bit further?"

"Right on, Mr. Erskine. I'd like to see you go for it." The stupid little puppy had suddenly become a narrow-faced shark. His success and his future billionaireness no longer seemed so mysterious to Malcolm. "Seminars, Mr. Erskine. Workshops. Look, your deal with Mammon is probably ten percent royalties for the first ten thousand copies, twelve and a half percent up to, let's say, twenty-five thousand copies, and then fifteen percent for all copies above twenty-five thousand. Close enough?"

"Uh...Oh, yes. Close enough." In fact, exactly what Malcolm's contract with Mammon House specified. This kid was good!

"Okay. Now, the cover price is $21.95, so that means you get $21,950 for the first ten thousand copies, then another, um, $41,156.25 for the next fifteen thousand copies, and then you're up into the fifteen percent bracket." Suddenly he fixed Malcolm with a penetrating stare. "What's your deal with your agent? Ten percent? Fifteen?"

"Zero. No agent."

Flicker—he wasn't a Jimmy any more—nodded vigorously. "Good. Great. So just suppose you sell fifty, no, one hundred thousand copies in hardcover. That's, let's see..." He stared into space, a spreadsheet filling his eyes. He muttered. Numbers appeared in the spreadsheet's cells. He jerked and twitched, and then finally he said, "$310,043.75. Plus, of course, whatever kind of paperback rights deal you can pull off, out of which Mammon House gets their cut, and plus also stuff like foreign rights and magazine excerpts, out of all of which Mammon House also gets their cut. Which I'm betting is fifty percent. Right?"

Malcolm sighed and nodded. He should have tried to bargain Mammon down on subsidiary rights. They might have been willing to settle for twenty-five percent. But he hadn't thought of it until after he'd signed the contract. "Yes, you're right."

"So I figure you'll be pretty lucky to end up with a million, and two million seems kind of unlikely, don't you think?"

Malcolm did think. He hadn't thought about it in quite this detail before now. He'd just assumed he'd end up a millionaire from this one book. Well, in a strictly numerical sense he probably would, but compared to the kind of money Jimmy Flicker was already making, it didn't seem so very impressive any more.

"And that's before taxes," Flicker reminded him, twisting the knife. He waved his hand. "Although I can put you on to a good guy in that department. He'll save you all that he can. But you'll still end up with peanuts."

Before this evening, one million dollars would not have seemed like peanuts to Malcolm. Jimmy Flicker and this restaurant made it seem so now. "Oh, well. There goes the castle in Spain."

Jimmy stared at him in amazement. "Spain? Jesus, Mr. Erskine, why would you want a castle in Spain anyway?" He shook his head. Then he looked up, ready to order dessert.

A waiter appeared immediately.

Jimmy ordered ice cream and coffee for both of them, a combination the thought of which made Malcolm's stomach churn. He had always hated hot and cold combinations. In fact, he had always hated ice cream. Not that he'd be able to afford much of it, on his measly million dollars.

"Anyway," Jimmy Flicker said, "now think about this. Let's say you gave a seminar, teaching your business secrets—sorry, the Merskeenians' business secrets. Let's say you limited the group size to, oh, one hundred people per session, and let's say you charged each person one thousand dollars to attend. We'd make it a one-day session. That should be enough, don't you think?"

Five minutes would be enough for me to say everything I know about business, Malcolm thought. Or want to know. "A thousand dollars? A hundred people?" He shook his head. "I can't imagine that many people paying that much just to listen to me talk."

Flicker laughed. "Hey, Mr. Erskine, haven't you been paying attention to what's going on these days? All kinds of people are giving these seminars, charging anywhere from five hundred to a thousand dollars per day, and they're packing them in! And I doubt if a single one of them is anywhere near as famous as you are now."

"Really?"

"Oh, sure. Now. See, that's $100,000 dollars gross just for one day's lecturing. Ten sessions, and you've probably already grossed more than you will from your book *in toto."*

So that's why Shirley MacLaine does it! This had been a very enlightening dinner, after all. "But that's gross, right?"

Flicker waved his hand. "There'll be expenses, of course: rent, slides, fancy signs, advertising, coffee and doughnuts for the attendees, money for the people who assist you and set the thing up, some kind of nice handout, all of that stuff. Ten dollars an attendee, maybe. Twenty, at the most. Peanuts. Anyway, you can see how it wouldn't even take you a month to *net* the first million, and then you're really on your way. It just keeps on growing by word of mouth, even without any advertising. You'd have to do a bit of traveling around the country, but you'd be pulling down ten million a year, net, easy. Five, if you want to take more time off, only do it for part of the year. Anyway, you can see that that's where the real money is."

Malcolm was too dazzled by dollar signs to respond right away.

"Oh, and another thing," Jimmy Flicker added. "Every time you give a lecture like that, you're setting up another bunch of people to buy your next book."

"My next book?" Malcolm said, coming suddenly down to earth. *Sex, Sins, and Software?* Would the kind of people who would come to the kind of seminar Flicker was proposing be likely to buy such a book? Probably not.

"Sure. Of course. Your next collection of wisdom from Lukas of Aldebaran. There's got to be a lot more of that great stuff floating around out there in the space–time continuum, just waiting to help businesspersons, and you're obviously the natural antenna for the messages. Why, you've *got* to write more books, Mr. Erskine! People need to hear what you have to say."

The thought, Malcolm thought, just blows me away. I'm, like, aghast.

It had been hard enough to come up with one book's worth of the gibberish. How on Earth could he come with another? Malcolm foresaw a long and boring course of study in the ways of the masters—Shirley MacLaine, Alan Watts, etc. If they had done it, so could he.

"Seminars, seminars," Malcolm muttered. The only seminars he had ever given, if those could be called seminars, had been training sessions for software he had written, and those had been straightforward—merely a matter of leading through the operation of his latest program a roomful of computer illiterates, terrified that if they touched the keyboards in front of them they would start World War Three or at the least damage the computer. He had had real information to convey, and he had always been the world's leading expert on the subject at hand. In a Business Secrets from the Stars seminar, the information would all be invented, fictive facts for foolish fellows, malarkey for marketeers, shit for shitheads.

Rich shitheads! He must not allow himself to lose sight of that. Shitheads who could afford the five hundred to a thousand dollars Flicker had mentioned. And as the inventor of the money-making nonsense, Malcolm reminded himself, he would still be the world's leading expert on the subject. In fact, the world's only expert—excluding, of course, the ectoplasmic Lukas of Aldebaran, who scarcely counted.

"Yes," Jimmy Flicker said enthusiastically, "seminars. Big money, big time, Mr. Erskine, sir. What do you say?"

"What do *you* say? I mean, why are you so interested?" In other words, Malcolm was going, like, what's in it for you, and why are you so blown away, and why are you losing it so totally?

"I've got an organization that can handle all the work," Jimmy said modestly. "Great bunch of people, now that I had the dead wood murdered. The ones who're still with me, well, they really know their stuff."

Malcolm had paused with his coffee half way to his mouth. "Cough. Choke. Murdered?"

Jimmy waved his hand. "I call it cosmic outplacement. Cheaper'n laying them off. Anyway, we could set you up real easy, get you going nationwide, making the big bucks. I'll take twenty percent off the top, that's before expenses. But you'll still be making real money."

Oh, what the hell, Malcolm told himself. They probably deserved to be murdered. "Ready any time, Jimmy, my lad." This was all so much more exciting than programming. He could really begin to live now, as long as no one murdered *him.*

"So it's a deal?" Jimmy Flicker asked.

Would it have put a damper on Malcolm's cynical happiness if he could have observed a drama that had taken place that morning in that rambling ranch house in California? Since he would not have seen any connection to the happiness of Malcolm Erskine, probably not.

The Vice President of the United States had been invited to the ranch house where Gone and Fancy lived, respectively, in mindless and bitter retirement. The veep's advisors had been enthusiastic and had packed his bags with picture books and his special Peter Cottontail jammies and had sent him on his way in the care of the ever reliable

Zip Muchley.

The advisors knew that nothing of any substance would take place out there on the West Coast—the idea of consultations between Gone and Junior was too detached from reality to even be amusing—but they also knew that they could say that such consultations had taken place, and that would give their boy the imprimatur they wanted. Surrounded by the glowing nimbus of that blessing, Junior would be irreplaceable as Daddy Longlegs' running mate, and he would contribute to the Longlegs reelection landslide.

The glow would still be there, they were sure, four years later, making Junior the only possible choice for the party's presidential nomination at the end of Daddy Longlegs' second term. Then on to the first Junior administration! Which would mean that for eight years, those advisers would rule the country.

Oh, it was a good time to be alive!

Junior might not have entirely agreed at the moment.

He had arrived the night before. He had met with Gone, which meant that they had been placed in facing chairs and had spent half an hour staring at each other, neither having anything to say. Finally, Junior had said, "You're really old." At that point, both he and Gone had been taken away and put to bed.

The next morning, Junior had another meeting. This time, it was with Fancy. It was a breakfast meeting.

"Eat up," she snapped. "Stop playing with your food."

Junior smacked his spoon repeatedly onto his oatmeal, spraying drops of milk on the tablecloth. "I hate this stuff. Always hated it. When I'm president, ain't never gonna have oatmeal in the White House."

Fancy sighed. Gone was bad enough, but this kid—! She tried adopting a wheedling tone instead of the commanding one that had so far accomplished nothing. "Look, I'm eating it." She forced herself to choke down a mouthful of oatmeal from her own bowl. "Mmm! Boy, that's good!"

Junior looked skeptical and made no move to eat.

"God damn—Okay, okay. Forget the fucking oatmeal." Fancy took a few moments to calm herself.

"Want I should punch him in the kidney, ma'am?" Zip Muchley asked.

Fancy looked at Zip standing behind Junior's chair and imagined with some pleasure the Vice President squirming on the floor and trying to scream. But, no. For now, anyway, she needed him alive and unbruised—and certainly not with internal ruptures. "Thanks, Zip. Not right now." She forced a smile. "So, Junior, what *would* you like for breakfast?"

Junior's face lit up. "Anything?"

"Within reason, anything you want."

"Oh, boy! Kellogg's Frosted Flakes, because Tony the Tiger says they're grrreat, and a fried egg on toast, sunny side up, but I don't want the white part runny because I hate it when the white part's runny. And a glass of milk. Really cold."

"Zip, get it for him."

"Remember what I said about the white part!"

Zip left, muttering about kidneys.

Zip returned a while later with the new breakfast, and Junior dug in happily, saying, "Yum!" and "Oh, boy!"

When he was finished, and Zip had wiped the egg yolk off Junior's face and the milk from the cereal off his red power tie, the dialogue resumed.

"Okay," Fancy said. "As I told you before, all you have to do is tell the President that you think he'd be a safer bet for reelection with me as his running mate. We'll get you back in as a senator, so you can still be almost as important as you are now. How about that?"

Junior's lower lip pushed out. He shook his head. "Don't wanna be senator again. Wanna be veep."

This went on for a few more minutes. Junior refused to budge. He started noisily blowing bubbles in the milk in his glass.

Finally, Zip looked at Fancy and raised his eyebrows questioningly. Fancy said, "Hmm," and thought about political consequences.

Zip took the Vice President back to his bedroom to wait for Fancy's decision. After what he had been put through, Zip was hoping she would choose the kidney option.

Fancy sat at the table and weighed matters.

Successor to the successor. She had it straight from the magnificent Lukas of Aldebaran himself. Of course she had actually heard it from Lukas's spokesman, Malcolm Erskine, who had turned out to be rather less impressive than she had expected. But spokesmen were often a disappointment. What counted was the phrase itself and the unimpeachable—a word she loved—authority behind it. Therefore, it was ordained that she become the successor to Longlegs. In practical political terms, that meant she had to become the Vice President during his second term. Otherwise that horrifying boy would continue as Vice President and would end up as the successor to Gone's successor.

Fancy shuddered at the thought. Surely to prevent that a ruptured kidney was justified!

But would that work? The kid was young, at least for a politician, and seemed to be healthy. A cover story would be necessary.

Alcoholism! Of course. She could see it now.

Fancy wasn't given to fantasies the way Malcolm was. Hers was a cold, hard world of facts and action and cause and effect. The strong won and the weak lost. "You snooze, you lose," she would sometimes say, when she wasn't saying something equally trite or consulting psychics. She didn't see a contradiction there because she was convinced that psychics had real powers and that what they dealt with was just as much a part of the physical world as anything scientists spent their time working with. Easier to understand, too.

This, however, was a moment for pleasant fantasizing. She closed her eyes and smiled at the vision.

The sudden death of the Vice President from kidney failure would be announced on the first day of the Republican nominating convention. Right after the opening ceremonies, Daddy Longlegs would make a wonderful speech about his gallant young partner. The floor of the convention center would be awash in tears. Daddy would be nominated by acclaim to run again. Fancy, Daddy's choice for running mate, would also be nominated by acclaim. Then there would be an electoral landslide victory for the Republican ticket.

And then, and then...

And then, unknown to her, a fleet of black helicopters with special silenced high–tech rotors landed nearby and disgorged a team of deadly ninja killers who would have instantly disabled all the guards posted in and around the building if there had been any. There weren't any because Zip Muchley knew he needed only himself.

When the ninjas burst into the bedroom where Zip was guarding the Vice President, the huge agent chuckled. "You guys have been watching too many movies," he told them.

He stood, sighed, stretched. His muscles bulged even through his Official Issue Secret Service Suit. The ninjas paused and backed away just a tiny bit.

"You could leave now," Zip said. "So I won't have to kill you." Not that he'd mind. Displacement. He'd heard that word somewhere, and he thought it probably applied to this situation.

Someone new entered the room. The ninjas fell back respectfully, making way for the newcomer, who was dressed in ordinary casual clothing instead of a silly ninja outfit.

"Agent Weng!" Zip said in surprise. "I thought you had gone private."

"I did," Weng said. "These are my boys. I'm just doing this as a side contract. Sort of like a favor."

Zip sighed. "I'm sorry it was you." He looked down at Weng from his great height. "I wouldn't want to have to hurt you."

"Think you could?"

"I've always wondered which one of us was better. Anyway," he gestured at the Vice President, and a look of displeasure passed over his face, "I'm supposed to protect him with my life. I guess."

"We're not going to hurt him," Weng said. "Just take him back home. Helicopters outside. Small jet nearby."

"I get to ride in a helicopter?" the Vice President said excitedly. "I like helicopters."

The adults tried to ignore him.

Annoyed, the Vice President reached out and touched one of the many sharp metal weapons dangling from the belt around the nearest ninja's middle.

"Ow!" He stuck the bleeding tip of his finger in his mouth.

"Careful, kid," Weng said. "You'll need all your fingers to wave at the adoring crowds." Weng turned back to Zip with raised eyebrows. "This is normal?"

"All the time," Zip said. "All the darned time. You have no idea."

"And you're going to defend him with your life?"

"Oh, heck. Get the little sucker out of my sight."

"Sucker?"

Zip looked at the floor. "You know I don't use bad language, Weng."

Weng laughed and reached up to pat Zip on the shoulder. "A fixed point in a changing universe. Okay, boys, let's move out."

Zip followed them from the house and watched the fleet of

helicopters rise into the sky and zoom silently away over the hills, carrying Junior back home.

Finally, he turned back to the house. He threw back his shoulders and drew a deep breath. Time to tell Fancy that he had been overpowered and that Junior had been rescued. This was the scary part.

Outwardly, Fancy took Junior's rescue far better than Zip had feared she would. She understood both Zip's limitations and his value to her. Perhaps she had given him too large a responsibility.

Perhaps she should hedge her bets.

At about the time Malcolm and Jimmy Flicker were being served their coffee, Fancy made a telephone call to a run-down location elsewhere in Southern California.

Few calls came in to the twenty-four-hour line these days, but it was manned around the clock, anyway, in smiling hopefulness. The chipper chippy doing receptionist duty on the second shift answered brightly, "Thank you for calling Brothers and Sisters of Jesus! How may we help you grow closer to Him Whom we all love and Who loves us daily, hourly, minutely, not to mention minutely, no matter what we do or how we behave or whether or not we forget Him, for His love—"

"Can it and put me through to Brother Harry."

Dampened, the chippy said, "I'll see if he's still in, ma'am. It *is* late in the day, and Brother Harry's usually left by now. Who shall I say is calling?"

The caller told her. The chippy passed it on. Brother Harry came on the line quickly, smiling widely with his voice.

"Fancy, babe! Hey, it's been a long time!"

His voice was mellow yellow. His persona was from a more honestly psychedelic time.

"At least your little girlfriend calls me 'ma'am.' You could learn from that."

"Fellow sibling of Jesus, Fancy, not girlfriend. We don't have any of that girlfriend and boyfriend shit here. We're all just brothers and sisters, both to each other and to Him Who—"

"Jesus H. Christ, will you stow it!" his caller shrieked at him, displaying again that neat turn for outdated slang which made her calls such a burden to all her old friends. "Harry, just listen to me. You know about this man Malcolm Erskine, don't you?"

Harry repeated the name a time or two. "Nope. Don't believe I've ever met the gentleman."

"Business Secrets from the Stars."

"Oh. Oh, yes. That bastard." Mellow yellow had become sour lemon. "Yeah, we know all about him. The times, they are achangin'. Turn, turn. To everything there is a season. It's all just dust ablowin' in the wind. Just more proof of the same thing, darlin'."

"Oh, spare me the pop music philosophizing. I haven't given up on being on top, and neither should you. So you're going to have to do something about Malcolm Erskine."

"'Do something,' huh? Meaning?"

"Whack. Off. Terminate with extreme prejudice. Fit with cement overshoes. You know what I mean."

"Yeah. You mean 'do away with.' We gave up that kind of shit around 1970, Fancy. The guys I used to use all retired to somewhere in South America. Well, except for two I know. I'm kinda reluctant to use them. Anyway, why're you so eager to see me do something to this cat?"

"Because he's been using Gone and me in his publicity, that's why! And it's got to stop."

"Oh, yeah, the consultant-to-ex-presidents stuff. Well, well. And now you want me to take care of your problem for you. Well, Fancy, you know what I always used to say back in the old days: What's in it for me?"

There was a long hesitation. Finally, Fancy said, "You might get to be the first official White House mystic guru during the administration of the first woman president."

For quite a while, Brother Harry held the telephone without speaking, his mouth hanging open. Finally he said, "Wow! You always did think big, didn't you?"

"So you'll do it?"

"Well, see, I told you that I'm not sure about the couple of translators I still have contact with."

"Translators? What the hell's the matter with you? I'm talking about hit men!"

"Translators to a higher plane, sister in Jesus. They're very religious guys. That's how they describe their profession."

"Jesus Christ!"

"Exactly. Anyway, problem with these two guys is, they're old. They're really dedicated professionals, and they really believe in their work and in Jesus, but they move pretty slowly nowadays, and they kinda have trouble remembering who the target is supposed to be, and once you get them started, it's sometimes kinda hard to stop them, if you should happen to change your mind."

Fancy thought for a while. Finally she said, "Old isn't bad. Rev 'em up."

"If you're sure you want this."

"I'm sure. Is it a deal?"

Malcolm, too, was thinking big at that very moment, inflamed by Jimmy Flicker's casual multiplication of millions. Malcolm and Harry said, "It's a deal," at the same instant.

CHAPTER EIGHT

Bend as the reed, star child. As the willow! Appear to yield, to give, in order that you may ultimately conquer. Your victory will be all the sweeter, and your enemy's back all the more exposed.

—Lukas of Aldebaran

It was the afternoon of the Sunday on which *Business Secrets from the Stars* reached Number Five on the *New York Times* bestseller list. Malcolm had just hung up after agreeing to be interviewed on a local talk radio show when the telephone rang again. Johnny Carson already? Malcolm asked himself. Hope it doesn't conflict with the local show I just agreed to be on. If it did, the local boys would be out of luck.

"Hello!" he said, his voice forceful, masculine, intelligent, deep, and resonant (good for electronic reproduction), and yet at the same time witty, charming, and seductive—in short, the type of voice any famous television talk show host in his right mind would invite back repeatedly.

"Malcolm? Is that you?" It was a voice of honey and roses, musical tones that induced fantasies of love and delight, of scented gardens and cool, moonlit nights, romance and passion, Paradise on Earth, old

Hollywood musicals.

"Uh, who is this?"

"It's me. Marlene."

Marlene! The bitch! The malignant melanoma in the form of a woman!

Instantly, Malcolm's voice became thin, weak, high-pitched, scarcely audible. "What is it?"

"I just wanted to congratulate you, Malcolm. You finally did it, didn't you?"

Did what? Malcolm wondered. Made love to a beautiful young woman with olive skin and shoulder-length black hair and adoring almond-shaped eyes who would love him and cherish him and stay with him? "What're you talking about?"

"Your book, of course. *Business Secrets from the Stars.* I just saw that it's on the bestseller lists. Of course, I'm not surprised. I always knew you'd make it. You've got such drive and determination and talent."

Malcolm stood frozen in place, his mouth hanging open. He must be trapped in a science-fiction plot, an alternate history, a parallel universe in which Marlene Erskine nee Harridan was a sweet, loving woman, a firm supporter of her husband, and a believer in his talents and his future. But that didn't really happen outside the books he read and wrote.

"I'm sorry," Malcolm said, "I guess I must have misunderstood you. I thought you said your name was Marlene, and I assumed you were my ex-wife."

"I *did* say my name was Marlene, and I *am* your ex-wife. Malcolm, are you all right? You don't sound well. Perhaps I ought to come over and fix you supper. I bet you're not eating right."

Malcolm had been standing. Now he sat down. This conversation was more than he had strength for at the moment. Perhaps he was imagining the voice on the telephone. After all, wasn't this every wronged man's dream, the one in which the woman who has done the wronging comes crawling back begging for forgiveness and sex?

All this just because of one best-selling book and the resulting promise of riches and fame? So that's really all it takes, Malcolm thought in wonder.

His voice began to reassume some degree of baritone timbre. "Actually, ex-darling, I've been eating very well. Lots of money for fancy meals, after all."

"Y-e-s-s. I suppose that's true. And how well have you been sleeping?"

Malcolm boomed out a rich, hearty laugh, an outburst of life and vitality from a man of immense potency, virility, and sexual success. "Well, Marlene, the truth is that the little darlings won't allow me much time for sleep. Chuckle, chuckle."

Liar, liar, pants on fire! The truth, Marlene? The truth is that I sleep like a baby—I keep waking up crying for a breast. But Marlene would, he hoped, believe what he had said, and he could imagine her twisting on the hook of her jealousy.

Instead of twisting, she said, "That's great, Malcolm. I'm really glad for you. I guess you don't even miss my special tongue technique now."

Malcolm smothered a groan. Marlene's special tongue technique! Even if his lovely little darlings had been real, they probably wouldn't have been able to match her astonishing skill in certain areas.

Oh, that mouth! Oh, that tongue! His penis stiffened and his spine wilted.

"Malcolm? You there?"

"Uh, yeah, mostly."

"You know, I've missed practicing my special technique on you. You were always so appreciative. Not like—Anyway, I guess you don't even think about me any more."

Malcolm licked his lips and swallowed spit and pride. "Say, Marlene, I don't suppose you'd like to have dinner together, would you? It'd be good to see you again. Talk about things, and so on. We could go somewhere nice."

"Oh, Malcolm, I'd love that! I really think we should still be friends. Come on over and pick me up. I'll be ready."

Belatedly, Malcolm remembered that it had always been the sound of triumph in her voice when she had won a point against him that he had hated the most.

Morning's light brought momentary confusion. On the one hand, the light was streaming in through the wide windows that led to the balcony of Malcolm's downtown condominium. On the other hand, the delectable little body sleeping in a catlike ball beside him was surely Marlene.

Oh, yes, that's right, he thought, remembering. It was indeed Marlene, and she was indeed here with him, and she had indeed treated him to quite an extended session of her special tongue technique during the night. Rather like old times. In fact, rather better than old times.

Malcolm smiled smugly and stretched and felt like a hell of a guy. Dinner the previous evening at the Ile de France had been extravagantly expensive, thanks to Marlene ordering a very expensive wine and the most expensive appetizer and entree and dessert and after–dinner cordial on the menu, but he was Malcolm Moneybags now, he could afford it, and it had certainly been worth the cost. Yes, indeed.

He slid over against Marlene's smooth, slender, firm back and put his arm over her and began to fondle her breasts.

Marlene awoke with a smile and a murmured "Mmm!" She turned toward him, flung her arms around his neck, burrowed her face into his neck, and whispered, "What you need now is a business manager. Someone to handle all your money for you."

M&M together again at last—Marlene Harridan and Malcolm Patsy.

Malcolm stiffened, but not the part of him that Marlene had depended upon to argue on her behalf. Then he relaxed and said, quite calmly and with great self–control, "I plan to be my own business manager, but I might need a bookkeeper on a part–time basis some time in the future. I could probably manage a few bucks an hour for a competent human calculator."

Marlene leaped out of bed. She stood barefooted on the luxurious rug Malcolm had bought only two days before and glared down at him, her face growing redder by the second. Finally she shrieked, "You cheap bastard! Fuck you!"

"You already did, my ex–dear. And so skillfully, too."

"Shithead!"

Marlene had never been very original in her choice of pejoratives, but the vigor she put into their utterance had always been unexceptionable.

"Does this mean our date is over?" Malcolm asked.

Marlene growled, "Fuckface," and stalked over to the chair where she had piled her clothing the day before. She dressed with her back to Malcolm, regaining self–control as she did so. "Call me a cab," she said.

Malcolm actually almost said to her, "All right, you're a cab," but he found the self–discipline not to.

He used the telephone on the small table beside the bed, and then he lay in bed watching Marlene finish dressing and apply a new coat of makeup.

She had always hated the very idea of dressing and making herself up in the morning without showering first. No doubt she was too angry with him now to use his shower and would go home and use his ex–

shower instead. She brushed her hair quickly and vigorously and completed the transformation from tongue-technique expert to maddeningly fetching but simultaneously repellent yuppie. "How do I look?" she asked, smug and in control again.

"Like a gorgeous, sexy woman—"

Marlene glowed at him.

"—who's overdressed and over made up."

Marlene glared at him. "Asshole."

She stamped over to the bedroom door. "I'll wait for the cab downstairs in the lobby. Don't bother getting up to show me out."

As she slammed the front door theatrically shut behind her, Malcolm asked himself if he had actually, finally won one against Mistress Malefica. It seemed that he had. It seemed, also, that he had had to divorce her to do so.

Curious how adept she was at assuming the appropriate persona—sweet or sexy or dependent or strong or whatever combination seemed most likely to get her what she wanted. After his rejection of her business-manager suggestion, though, she had, along with her clothes and makeup, put on her true aspect—Marlene the Malevolent. He could easily imagine her as the evil adversary in a superhero comic book.

Dressed in a skin-tight costume decorated with lightning bolts—and very dangerously desirable she looks in it, too—Writerman's most dangerous foe, Marlene the Malevolent, menaces the stunningly, exotically beautiful young woman with shoulder-length black hair and olive skin who is the guest star of this month's issue.

But wait! Who's that knocking politely at the beautiful young woman's front door?

Why, it's Writerman, Malcolm the Magnificent! Strange seed of even stranger parents, he has come to Earth to fight for truth, justice, and an improvement in grammatical usage. "Begone, foul creature!" he cries. "This innocent young lovely is under *my* protection now!"

"A curse on you and all your efforts! May true literary success elude you forever!" Marlene the Malevolent shrieks, knowing just where the sensitive nerve endings are. Spinning about (thus allowing Writerman a last view and a rogue memory of the firmness of her athletic little backside), she leaps through the conveniently open window and flaps away into the night, having become a bat.

"Oh, Malcolm, my hero!" sobs the exotic young beauty.

In the last panel, we see them clinching, panting with eagerness, leaving to our overheated imaginations what will happen in the subsequent panels, the ones no one will draw for us.

Now that Malcolm thought about it, Marlene's special tongue technique wasn't all that wonderful, really. He must have magnified it in his imagination through some strange effect of sexual deprivation. Surely his exotically beautiful dream girl with the olive skin and the shoulder-length black hair and the almond-shaped eyes would be able to do a far better job of it.

In the meantime, two old men were wandering around Portland, Oregon prayerfully whacking men named Malcolm. They knew the name of the city began with a P.

Learn! How to get people to do what you want!

Learn! How to change people's behavior! Without their even knowing what you're doing!

Learn! How to deal with "difficult" people—people who "just can't cut it"—people who "don't have what it takes"—or even people who're just "hard to deal with!"

Learn! How to Present Yourself—Powerfully, with Polish and Prestige!

Yes! In this exclusive, powerful one–day workshop, you too can learn all of these things AND EVEN MORE! from the only man in the world who channels the wisdom of the ancient Merskeenians, Malcolm Erskine, author of the phenomenal best–seller, Business Secrets from the Stars.

Space is limited. Sign up now.

Or, as the star–dwelling Merskeenians themselves might have put it:

"Know this important wisdom, O sharer of heavy atoms from the very same supernova that that we ourselves derived from in far–ancient times: Every entity or entities wants or want something desperately, even if he or she or it or they doesn't or don't even know it. And if you, our cosmic cousin, are able to convince him or her or it or them that *you* can provide that thing or feeling or wish, fulfill that gaping need, then you will most surely have him or her or it or them by the short hairs and/or tendrils."

And looking over the scrubbed little faces of all the little boys and girls who had each paid one thousand dollars to attend his powerful one–day workshop, Malcolm thought that that was what he most surely had them all by.

One particular girl had hair the color of the hair of the woman of Malcolm's dreams. True, it was fashionably short and had been assaulted by a hairdresser rather than hanging softly, wonderfully to her shoulders. True, this girl was tall—taller than Malcolm—rather than short, and only pretty rather than exotically beautiful, and her skin was creamy, her cheeks rosy, rather than blessed with the olive tones of the skin of Malcolm's dusky dream woman. The latter, presumably, derived from the mystic and erotic East, whereas the young woman seated in the front row at his seminar no doubt traced her roots to somewhere much closer to Scandinavia. But life, Malcolm reminded himself, is a series of compromises.

In her favor, this real female had the dewy lips and unlined face that bespeak the tight skin and high body fluid levels of youth, and her shining eyes followed him in adoration as he stalked about the front of the room spewing gibberish.

When, in his pre–*Business Secrets* days, had a woman looked at him adoringly? Pondering the question, Malcolm was forced to admit that the answer was "Never."

Wisely, he began to direct his extempore silliness more and more at the young woman and to color it more and more with whatever *double entendres* he could devise.

He noticed, though, as the day wore on, that she seemed to be distressed about something. A hint of a frown began to disfigure her pretty brow. It grew, changing from a hint to a chasm. She raised her hand, waving it to catch Malcolm's attention.

Malcolm pointed at her. "I'm sorry. Your name...?"

"Tracy Smith."

Oh, my God, Malcolm thought. His dream girl wouldn't be named "Tracy" or any other two–syllable American female name ending with a long "e" sound. Compromises, he reminded himself. "Yes, Tracy, what is it?"

"I don't understand something."

Tracy's voice was low in pitch and a bit husky. Rather pleasant, Malcolm decided.

"All the names you've mentioned," Tracy continued, "I mean, like, the executives and all, and the heroes of the wars against the Marlingas—they're all men. Didn't these Merskeenians have equal employment opportunity and stuff, since they were so enlightened?"

Malcolm cursed himself. How could he have forgotten to pay lip service to that particular current business cliché? He had thought he'd covered them all.

Inspiration struck. Malcolm was not a hack writer for nothing.

Remembering Larry Lefkowitz, Malcolm tilted his head back so that he was looking down his nose at Tracy. Fortunately, he had trimmed the hair in his nostrils that very morning.

"Have I said that the Merskeenian heroes were all men, my dear young lady?" My dear, delectable young lady.

"Well, gee, no," Tracy stammered, "but, but, you know, you went 'Lukas' and 'Paulus' and 'Henricus' and all like that, so it's pretty clear, isn't it?" She had started defensively, but she ended on the offense.

Malcolm turned to the rest of the class. The women, he noted, were waiting with interest for his answer. The men were staring into space and waiting it out. "Here you see the unfortunate result of an ethnocentric upbringing," he said. "You know, now that it's so vital for us to compete with the Japanese and the Koreans and the Taiwanese and...and whoever, it's particularly essential that we not fall into the trap of thinking that other cultures must mirror our own. What is a man's name here may be a woman's name somewhere else. That's especially true of the Merskeenians, who were *so equal,* so dedicated to *equal employment opportunities* and *non-discriminatory hiring practices* and *equal pay for equal work,* that they even," he paused, his face red, glaring about the room as if challenging anyone to dispute with him, "subscribed to *equal naming conventions* for their children!"

Tracy looked properly ashamed. Malcolm felt that it was necessary to drive the point home still further, though. "Why, I well remember Lukas saying to me, 'Suppose, O fellow product of the Big Bang, that you were called upon to do business in the far land of South Korea. Think what a dreadful and costly error you would commit were you to assume that, just because Kim is a girl's name in the land of your nativity, it must needs be the same in the land in which you are doing business! Should you address the President of that wondrous land of almond-eyed, black-haired women as "Honey," what further prospects would you have of racking up significant sales?' How right Lukas was! President Kim, Prime Minister Kim, Speaker of the House Kim, Waiter and Waitress Kim—Christ, they're all named Kim! Get the point, Tracy?"

Tracy nodded, abashed.

However, at the back of the room was a student with almond eyes and black hair and olive skin and of the wrong sex. He was hesitantly raising his hand, wearing an expression which said clearly that he hated to contradict an authority figure but felt he had no choice when faced with so egregious an error.

What now? Malcolm wondered. Oh, shit. Kim's a surname, not a first name. "Well," Malcolm said loudly, "let's move along. Time's awastin'. Tracy, stay behind after the session's over, if you can. You at the back. Get your hand down."

At the end of the day, as the starry-eyed kids filed out, a few stayed behind.

Some were enthusiastic young men and women with a sharp glint in their eyes that belied their apparent naiveté and revealed that their sights were set on vice-presidencies of the supernumerary corporations that already paid them more than any honest assembly-line worker earned. These, Malcolm was able to take care of quickly with appropriate manufactured Merskeenianisms.

"Send not to ask upon whose face you must tread, because the great wheel turns and treads equally upon all, from the lowest to the highest, and so you might as well get yours while you can." Or, "It is written that the lowest shall be highest and the highest, lowest, so just make sure you end up on the right side of the equation." Or his favorite, "Always sit with your back to the wall." Wild Bill Hickock, one of Malcolm's boyhood heroes, ignored that advice, and just consider, O

Big Bang Buddy, what happened to him.

Two stayers–behind were different. One was the unfortunately male Oriental troublemaker, and the other was Tracy.

With exaggerated facial gestures, Malcolm tried to say wordlessly to Tracy, "Wait a minute, interesting sweetie, while I deal with this jerk." She seemed to understand. He turned to the man and said, "Mr. Kim, I presume?"

The Oriental man seemed confused. "No, Otsinuga. You have been to Korea, sir?"

Only in my wet dreams. "No. But if you're about to tell me that 'Kim' is a surname, rather than a first name, I already know that. It was just an illustration."

Otsinuga nodded. "Ah. I understand. I lived in Korea as a child, but because of what you said, I was afraid I had become confused about Korean names." He nodded happily, all confusion fled, and left.

Malcolm stared after him, mouth agape. What was this fatal power he now possessed, this aura of interstellar omniscience? Were so many people so hungry for illumination, guidance, and certainty that they would accept virtually any silliness if some charlatan in a business suit asserted it, even if it contradicted their own direct experience? More important, was there any limit to the number of dollars Malcolm Erskine could extract from them by seeming to be able to answer their needs?

"Oh, Mr. Erskine," Tracy breathed in hormonally heated admiration. "It must be so wonderful to have a brilliant alien being enter you at night!"

Malcolm turned from contemplating Mr. Otsinuga's back, looked up at her, and grinned from ear to ear.

Two days later, looking forward to another night of being entangled in Tracy's long arms and legs and nearly suffocated by her large mouth and long tongue, Malcolm received from her instead the following note:

> *My new job came through! Thanks to you! Like Lukas says, I made my own reality and went for it and visualized success, and now a man named Mr. Nostra has hired me to be Director of Marketing at his headquarters office in Sicily.*
>
> *I'll be back on business about once a month, so maybe we can get together then and have some good times again. Etc., etc., etc.*
>
> *Have a good one.*
>
> *Tracy*

Malcolm sighed heavily at the loss and consoled himself with the knowledge that there were others. Many others, in fact. Lining up after every *Business Secrets from the Stars* seminar, in fact. Every one of them young and gorgeous, in fact.

So what if they lacked brains? What need had he, confidant of star–dwelling Merskeenians, of women with brains?

CHAPTER NINE

Spawn of my spawn, beware the terrible currents flowing beneath the placid surface of your world. Deep inside the Earth, all is fluid, changing, plastic. Great rivers of molten rock, vast convection currents, rise and fall, bearing upon them the continents that seem to you so solid. This fearsome magma shapes your world and your lives. Who can say what effects it has upon each of you, upon your nature and your life? Who knows what vapors it secretly releases into your atmosphere? Placate this terrible power, for it may burst forth without warning and destroy everything.

—Lukas of Aldebaran, explaining matters he wasn't entirely sure Malcolm Erskine could handle.

When Malcolm was an iddle widdle boy, he read a nauseating children's story about an iddle widdle boy whose doting grandfather lived with the family and was the iddle widdle boy's bestest friend ever. So Malcolm decided that his Grandpa Tibbs would become his own bestest friend. He was sure that his Grampie—the boy in the story had called his grandfather Grampie—would be happy to take on the role.

At that time, Malcolm's paternal grandfather, Tibbs Erskine, had not yet been transported kicking and screaming in a straitjacket to a very special kind of nursing home. He was still living upstairs in the attic, which had been converted to a suite of rooms that would have been quite pleasant if not for the rats, barn owls, and poisonous spiders. All of those steered clear of Tibbs, though, so he found the attic satisfactory.

He had shown no interest at all in his grandson, just as he had never shown any interest in his own son beyond demanding that the poor man provide him with shelter and food. After a long and satisfying life spent making a large number of relatives, business associates, and strangers miserable, Tibbs wanted to spend his twilight years in peace in his attic, sitting at the huge metal desk he had somehow stolen from his last employer, writing page after page of a mysterious manuscript no one was ever allowed to look at, and drinking large quantities of vodka, to which he had become addicted while stationed at the American embassy in Moscow before World War II.

He certainly had no interest in his pestiferous little grandson.

Malcolm was too young to understand the complicated ways of adults. Indeed, that was something he was to have trouble with throughout his life. So, convinced that life must imitate the saccharine book he had just finished reading, he climbed the almost endless flights of creaking wooden stairs toward the attic.

Golly, it sure was a long way up to where Grandpa Tibbs lived! Why, he must be practically in Heaven! Long and difficult though the climb was for Malcolm's short, chubby, unexercised little legs, it seemed more worthwhile the more he thought about his grandpapa's probable semi–divinity. Not only would Malcolm be gaining a new bestest friend, he'd be practically acquiring a guardian angel!

Life was pretty goddamned fucking amazing, little Malcolm

thought, using a coupling of adjectives he didn't understand but had heard his father use when referring to Grandpa Tibbs, so he knew they must be good ones.

Once he finally reached the tippety top of the flight of stairs, Malcolm stopped to catch his breath. He leaned against the banister and breathed and breathed and breathed for the longest time, for he was a very lazy child who never did anything physically that he didn't absolutely have to, and so he was close to passing out from lack of breath and the immense altitude.

Finally, when his heart had stopped hammering away and returned to its normal soft, squishy regularity, he opened the attic door without knocking and stepped inside.

The attic stank.

It made Malcolm sad to think that his grandpappy had to live in a place that stank.

There was Grandpa Tibbs, leaning over his big gray metal desk, writing away steadily with his right hand, his pen making a scratching sound, and holding a large glass of water in his left hand. From time to time, he took a sip from the glass. He was tall and slender, with thinning gray hair that had not been washed in ever, ever, ever so long, a brown, seamed face, a long white beard with odd stains on it, and bony, strong–looking hands with long, yellow nails. His eyes were brilliant blue, and so were the pajamas, slippers, and robe he wore.

This was just as Malcolm had overheard his father describing the scene to his mother, and that gave Malcolm a warm, secure feeling, even though he hadn't understood everything else his father had said and he wasn't sure all of it was nice.

But how nice Grandpa Tibbs looked!

Or so Malcolm was able to convince himself.

Malcolm walked forward until he was standing right next to his grandpapa's leg. He stared up the old man for a while in fascination, intrigued by his concentration. Writing must sure be fun and interesting!

"Hi, Grandpa Tibbs," Malcolm shrieked.

Tibbs leaped to his feet and skittered away. Papers flew every which way. "Jesus fucking Christ!" His voice was hoarse and rough. When he spoke, it sounded like stones rubbing against each other. "Who the shit are you?"

"I'm Malcolm. You're my grandpapa."

Tibbs relaxed and gathered up his papers, shuffling them carefully into order and putting them back atop the large pile on his desk. He sat down again. "Oh, right. Go away. Close the door behind you. Little fucker."

"Watcha doin'?"

"Writing. Get lost."

"Watcha writin'?"

"My memoirs. Piss off."

"Watsa mem...?" Malcolm trailed off without trying to finish the word.

"Holy shit," Grandpa Tibbs said. He put down his pen and glass with a sigh of resignation and twisted in his chair until he was facing his grandson.

This Tibbs looming over him suddenly didn't look so sweet and lovable. Malcolm backed up a step.

"You're as annoying as your goddamned father was at your age. At any age. He still is. Look a bit like him. Your older brother and sister were like that, too. Kept bothering me. Brats."

Malcolm frowned in puzzlement. "I don't gots no older brother 'n' sister."

"You gots your father's mastery of grammar, though," Tibbs said, mimicking Malcolm's childish voice. Then his tone changed to a snarl. "Never could pound any of it into his thick head. Anyway, you used to have an older brother and sister."

"Where'd they go?"

Tibbs leaned forward. His lips drew back in what might have been a grin, but it revealed his long, yellowish gray teeth, all of them pointed as though they had been filed. "I ate them."

For a fraction of a second, Malcolm held his ground.

Then he turned and fled, all the way down, down, down the immensely long flight of stairs, crying and yelling the whole way, falling and banging himself, getting up again, running down the stairs again on his weak, plump little legs, tears running down his face, blood leaking from his nose from one of the falls on the way, terror filling his heart.

Behind him, Gramps laughed and slammed the door shut.

Malcolm's parents met him at the bottom of the stairs and hurried him away to another part of the house, where they comforted him and petted him and bullied him until he finally managed to calm down.

He described what had happened to him in tedious detail, but they assured him he had imagined it all. Why, Grandpa Tibbs wasn't even in the house right now. And of course Malcolm had never had an older brother and sister whom his grandfather had eaten. What a silly idea! Here, have some ice cream.

After a great deal of petting and bullying and ice cream, which he suddenly decided he hated, Malcolm was able to convince himself that he had indeed imagined the whole thing.

As the years passed, and Grandpa Tibbs kept to his attic retreat, presumably adding to the pile of pages that constituted his memoirs and downing a steady stream of vodka, and as Malcolm entered and endured a painful adolescence and horrific high-school experience, the incident began to seem like a dream.

It took on realistic contours only on the rare occasions when Tibbs left his attic for one reason or another and encountered

Malcolm, at which time Gramps would grin ferociously at his grandson and snap his fearsome teeth together and tell Malcolm that he was worthless and would never amount to anything, just like his father. Once or twice he varied things by muttering in that hoarse voice that cleanliness was next to godliness. Tibbs was always accompanied by a ghastly stench that Malcolm finally realized came from him, not from the attic.

There were two other times when the memory seemed real and not a dream. That was when Malcolm acquired a puppy, which disappeared after a couple of days, and then later a kitten, which disappeared after one day.

"Ran away," his parents said, looking uncomfortable and refusing to meet his eyes.

Could it be?

No, impossible.

When Malcolm was thirteen, he had a friend. He had never had one before. Billy was as weird as he was, as socially inept, and just as interested in science fiction, fantasy, and horror. Billy, too, talked about writing and selling the stuff some day. Although neither of them knew it, Billy was considerably more talented than Malcolm and might well have had a respectable literary career had he not disappeared.

He came over one day to see Malcolm at a time when neither Malcolm nor his parents were at home. The front door was open, so Billy walked in, as he had become accustomed to doing. Looking for Malcolm, and curious about the grandfather Malcolm had once told him about, Billy climbed the stairs and entered the Tibbs attic. He was never seen again.

The next day, Malcolm's father, his face grim and pale, arranged to have Grandpa Tibbs taken away to what he told Malcolm was a nursing home.

Years later, Malcolm received a letter from home saying that dear old Grampsy had passed on to a better world. The letter didn't tell him that Grampsy had died in a hail of bullets during an escape attempt from the nursing home, or that the body had been immediately cremated, or that Malcolm's parents, on hearing the news, cheered and hugged each other and made plans for a big evening out.

Nor did Malcolm watch his father ascend the stairs and bring down the reams of Grampsy's memoirs and sit down at the kitchen table to skim them. He didn't watch his father's face turn paler and paler as he read until it matched the newer sheets of paper in color. He didn't watch his father refuse to let his mother read any of it. He didn't see his father haul the piles of paper covered with grandpapa's lovely script out to the driveway and light them all in a giant bonfire and dance clumsily around it.

More years later, after Malcolm had started trying to sell his fiction professionally, he remembered those memoirs and wondered what had happened to them. He wondered if they might have contained some anecdotes from his grandfather's career that he could have stolen and used in a story or a novel. Then he decided that whatever his grandfather had been scrawling so laboriously for so many years had probably been boring and pointless and worthless, and he dismissed it all from his mind.

Preoccupied as he was with himself, Malcolm rarely paid attention to politics. This was an unfortunate habit, albeit only one of many that characterized the confidant of the star-dwelling Merskeenians. Malcolm might have argued that the events he invented for those imagined beings in their ancient time and faraway place had a great impact on his bank account and were therefore more important than real events.

Daddy Longlegs had succeeded to his father's estate, had made much money in the oil business, and had entered politics. In time, as we know, he would become Vice President of the United States, and later, on a doleful day, President.

Alas, he and Grammy had never been able to have human children bearing their own DNA. In a way, that didn't matter, for they had come to think of the three little brothers as their very own human children. This had happened at an early point, perhaps on that August day when they had taken the three simians to church in their three little suits and Reverend Gregory had declared them cute little monkeys.

Earlier, Grammy had said she would raise them as though they were her own children, but the truth was that, until Gregory conferred his blessing upon them, she had begun to be increasingly bothered by their hairiness, their waddling walk, and their habit of climbing the drapes and, from a height where she couldn't reach them, urinating and defecating on her new carpets.

She had sometimes been on the verge of condemning them as dirty, filthy, hairy apes and requesting that Daddy have them put down or at the very least put out—sent away to some traveling circus, perhaps. But Gregory had changed all that. So she schooled her heart and her mind and learned to keep newspapers spread over the carpets and in time she did indeed come to love the three brothers as though they had been her own and as though they had been human. After all, she couldn't deny that they certainly were cute little monkeys.

Perhaps Daddy neglected the boys a bit. He was a very busy man. He flung himself into his official duties when he served as Vice President under the Great Confibulator.

Not that Daddy cared for all of those duties. Some of them he considered beneath him. For example, he had to chair the meetings of the group working on the Teeny Tiny Robot Soldiers Undertaking. Also the group working on the Fiendishly Fine Wire Initiative. And those weird biologists from the Suddenly Severe Tummy Virus Breeding Program. Not to mention the Wishful Thinking Anti–Missile Shield, and the Booby Trapped Eggs team, and those *El Movimiento para Envenenar la Barba de Fidel Castro* people. He hated all of them. Beneath him. Wacky. Silly. Small. He wanted to concentrate on the big, important stuff.

Like the National Cathedral.

Ah, the National Cathedral! That was something worth spending his time on.

Daddy had been charged by President Gone Away with finally completing the construction of the National Cathedral in Washington. This stunningly un-Constitutional undertaking had started many decades earlier and had moved along in fits and starts under a succession of Presidents, all of whom had ignored the whirling sounds emanating from the graves of the Founding Fathers.

There had been occasional opposition from the living, too, but the opposition had been waning for years, and finally Daddy sensed that victory was at hand. Even so, a small gang of fiendish Democrats who wanted to put a stop to the construction refused to budge. Daddy made a list of their names and where they lived and he bided his time.

Shortly after Daddy was sworn in as President, a couple of those awful Democrats wandered away into the Virginia wilderness one day and were eaten by orangutans. The surviving opponents quickly changed their minds, and the necessary funds for the completion of the Cathedral were appropriated. The remaining work was rushed through. A grand opening ceremony was held. Daddy was finally able to relax and enjoy himself a bit with his mistress.

Daddy's determination to have the Cathedral finished didn't stem from his religious devotion, which wasn't particularly strong.

He was able to get Reverend Gregory installed as the Cathedral's Director, and although the building was supposed to be a home for people of all faiths, in practice the services held there were predominantly those of the Church of the Moneyed Classes and were presided over by Reverend Gregory.

And fine services they were. Fine sermons, too. Daddy didn't attend very often, but when he did, he was able to stay awake at least halfway through. Usually.

Gregory liked to start his sermons off with a bang. Often, he'd step up to the lectern, stand silently for a while looking at the great crowd filling the immense space, and then suddenly he'd yell, "USA! USA! Number One! Number One! Jesus wants you to remember that."

That part would keep Daddy awake and smiling. After that, Gregory would tend to get theological, and that's when Daddy's eyelids would start getting heavy.

Gregory didn't care. He was in his element. Let Daddy sleep. Gregory preached on.

"On this beautiful day, in this magnificent house of God, in this fine city, in this great country, the greatest country ever in the history of the world, let us give thanks that we are Americans and not pansy–ass Europeans or something even worse. How God has blessed us! I think he deserves a healthy round of applause. Don't you?"

Applause.

"We have wealth. We have power. We have riches and abundance and glory and might and missiles and bombs and really great television shows. Most important of all, the people here in this really admirable building have lots and lots of money. Money, my dear friends, is a sign of God's blessing. Those who possess money are being rewarded for doing God's will. Those who don't have money—well, obviously God has turned his face from them. Money is the visible form in this world of God's blessing, and it will be transformed for the wealthy into God's eternal spiritual blessing once you pass from this world into the next.

"Therefore, God wants you to accumulate as much of his blessing here on Earth as you possibly can, so that you will be able to exchange it for a vast amount of his spiritual blessing once you are gathered to his bosom. As Jesus told us, it is easier for a camel to pass through the eye of a needle than for a poor man to enter the Kingdom of Heaven."

His audience nodded in happy agreement. Unlike Daddy, most of them didn't find the theological sections of Reverend Gregory's sermon to be tedious or difficult to understand at all. That was part of the man's genius, they agreed—his ability to make even the most complex and subtle theological concepts simple and easy enough for anyone to understand.

Sometimes—rarely—Reverend Gregory would feel in a prophetic mood and would talk about trials and tribulations, the Antichrist and the Second Coming, the End Times and the Millennium. His audience didn't care as much for these sermons as they did for the ones about the blessedness of the rich and their forthcoming rewards in Heaven, but Gregory had a soft spot for what he thought of as his Hell on Earth sermons. He could raise his voice a lot more and shake his finger sternly at the congregation and talk about blood and death and vast destruction and mighty armies clashing in the Middle East. It was a lot more fun. He hated to reach the end of such a sermon—namely, all the namby-pamby stuff about the syrupy-sweet peaceful and loving eternal kingdom of Jesus being established on Earth—but it was necessary to end with that, something upbeat, another promise to his audience of eternal good times which, he would assure them, they had earned.

There was good stuff along the way, though, before he got to the syrupy part. "Every knee shall bow! And America will be seated at the right hand of God, designated to rule the Earth in his name, to be his enforcers. That's what we were chosen for. City on the Hill? No! Army of God in a fortress on the hilltop! We earned it by throwing off the yoke of British monarchy and fighting for our independence. Our forefathers were strong and brave and macho and hairy chested!" He waved his soft fist in the air, and his heavy jowls wobbled.

"They weren't going to take orders from some effete old king over in England! No, they wanted to rule themselves! Free, independent, democratic, strong men. And in the day that is coming, we will be rewarded by being foremost of those who bow their heads and accept Jesus as their lord and master. When that glorious day comes, don't you dare look the Lord in the eye! You will meet your Maker on your knees, like a true free, proud American Christian. Tremble in fear and be humble and contrite before Jesus your lord, because you are Americans! The best, the greatest, the most stupendously wonderful nation there ever was or ever will be."

Zowie!

So let Daddy sleep. Reverend Gregory had a fine, powerful voice, and he seemed able to keep other people awake and listening to what he said. That was what counted—both to Gregory and to Daddy.

Daddy was already planning ahead to his reelection campaign. When that time came, at least once a week Gregory would use the National Cathedral's pulpit to deliver a sermon supporting Daddy. That was the whole point.

Occasionally, Grammy complained about Daddy's neglect of the boys. She didn't understand just how far ahead Daddy was planning and how much of his attention that absorbed. He felt his own future was assured, so now he was putting his efforts into building careers for the boys.

He envisioned a life in politics for all of them, after an appropriate amount of time spent in the oil business. That's how the Longlegs men did it. After some oil time, the boys would go into politics locally, although not at too low a level. Governorships, maybe. Then—and he smiled whenever he envisioned this—one after the other, they would become President.

Daddy decided to introduce the boys to the American public

during a ceremony where everyone would be feeling happy, full of good cheer, and not thinking too deeply about politics. The event he had chosen was the lighting of the national Christmas tree, the first time he would be overseeing this grand national ceremony.

Christmas! An enormous Christmas tree! His boys beginning their journey to world domination! No wonder he was feeling cheerful as he crunched across the thin layer of snow covering the lawn in front of the White House. The sky was clear, the sun was bright, albeit low in the sky and weak, and the air was crisp and clean and cold. Ahead, the tree and the hand-picked crowd and the hand-picked reporters waited. Grammy and the boys were right behind him. It was a good day to be alive.

Until the reporter waylaid him halfway across the lawn.

At first Daddy suspected nothing. He thought the reporter and the cameraman hovering behind him were two of the hand picked, so he smiled graciously at them.

"Mr. President," the reporter said, thrusting his microphone forward, "how do you feel on this lovely afternoon?"

"Grand day," Daddy said. "Good day to be alive. Good folks. Good country. Fine tree. Looking forward to it."

"As you know, sir, questions have been raised about the constitutionality of this ceremony."

"What? Who?"

"Various people, sir. They wonder if it's appropriate for the President, in his official capacity, to be participating in a ritual associated with one particular religious sect."

"Christianity!" Daddy said, scandalized. "Not a sect! Christianity!"

"Yes, sir. The Christian sect. The national Christmas tree, the National Cathedral—what about citizens who aren't Christians? For that matter, what about Americans who are atheists?"

"Atheists! Not Americans. You can't call them Americans.

Shouldn't be allowed to vote. One nation under God. Says so in the Constitution."

"No, it doesn't."

"Declaration of Independence."

"No, sir. Not in there, either."

The reporter would have said more, but Daddy had finally gestured to his Secret Service agents, who descended upon the two men in a swarm, rushed them into waiting cars, and drove them away to a forest in Pennsylvania, where both men committed suicide with well–placed shots to the back of the head.

"Atheists," Daddy muttered. "Rubbish. Not real citizens. Christian nation. Bastard. Hurt my feelings." He shrugged. "But I'm okay. I'm a Longlegs. Don't cry for me, Argentina. Boys, you got that? Understand my point?"

The three J kids weren't paying attention, though. Their eyes were fixed in wonder on the towering California redwood, one of the last of the remaining giants, that had been cut down and then transported in many stages by helicopter to the White House lawn, where it had been bolted back together and propped up to serve as the national Christmas Tree. They were too stunned and delighted to make any sounds at all.

It towered above all the other trees and even above the White House itself. In the bright lights, its trunk glowed a dark red. The deep, twisting vertical grooves in its bark were pools of shadow, hints of mystery. Dying, it sang (to those who listened) of a faraway misty forest, damp, chilly air, dim light, the sound of dripping water, the smell of moist earth, the deep, spongy forest floor, layer upon layer of life, plant life, animal life, insect life—above all, life.

Jibber thought it would be a really neat thing to climb.

"This way, boys!" Daddy said. He strode toward the podium on the lawn where he would make his perfunctory remarks before throwing the cross–shaped switch that would light up the great tree and remove another brick or two from poor old Thos. Jefferson's wall. Not noticing that his three boys weren't behind him, Daddy ascended the podium and grinned happily at the reporters and television cameras. He was at the top of the world! This was where he belonged!

There was a pause while a group of aging men with expanding middles, wearing rough approximations to Revolutionary War army uniforms, trudged into view. It was the Capital Chapter of the National Musket Association. Grim–faced, determined, patriotic, the group marched in ragged order to the base of the immense tree. There they halted, executed an almost acceptable about face, and stopped, facing Daddy, their muskets resting against their right shoulders at varying angles approximating the vertical.

The chapter president waddled forward and positioned himself in front of them. "Musketeers!" he cried. "Present arms!"

Daddy watched the confusing, disorganized display with a smile frozen on his face.

Why were these ancient fools doing this? Why weren't they in some rest home, watching the tree–lighting ceremony on television? Why did he have to endure this? He was the President of the United States! The leader of the free world! The most important man in existence! He didn't have to eat broccoli, and he shouldn't have to be subjected to this.

For a while, the Musketeers bumped into each other, dropped their weapons, spilled powder and musket balls onto the White House lawn, and in various ways provided great entertainment for their fellow citizens.

Malcolm, who had nothing better to do, was watching all of this on television, and for a few minutes, the Musketeers made him feel less sorry for himself. For that he felt grateful to the Musketeers, whom he normally considered a great scab on the body politic and a suppurating lesion in the national psyche.

The Musketeers finally got themselves sufficiently organized and ready to fire a musket volley in honor of Daddy, the White House, the nation, the Revolution, Christmas, Jesus, Santa Claus, gunpowder, and their dwindling testosterone. They stood stiffly, holding their muskets pointing at a forty–five degree angle, and pulled their triggers almost simultaneously.

The muskets belched flame and smoke and dirt and the occasional ramrod. Daddy and everyone else ducked. Musket balls pinged against the White House walls and bounced away and rolled across the lawns. Remarkably, casualties were identical to those suffered by the British forces at the hands of the Minutemen at the Battle of Lexington Green, when the Shot Heard Round the World began the American Revolution. Which is to say, there were no casualties.

Emulating the Minutemen they idolized, but fortunately in much more organized and less panicky fashion and far more slowly than the Minutemen retreating from Lexington on that glorious occasion, the Musketeers marched away out of view of the television cameras and their puzzled fellow citizens.

Malcolm put his umpteenth beer aside and stood up and saluted the television screen.

When the muskets had roared and the smoke had billowed across the lawn, the three simian brothers had scuttled for cover. Jibber had led the pack. He had been feeling jumpy all day. That morning, Tess had waggled her star–spangled behind at him again. She was determined to do her androidal duty as it had been programmed into her. Jibber had been keeping watch for her out of the corner of his eye ever since then. Any sudden movement, especially if it involved a star, alarmed him.

Now, as the sound died away and the smoke broke and dissipated in the light breeze, the three brothers appeared again. They looked around cautiously at first. When it became clear that there was no danger, they grew bolder.

Evading the Secret Service men by scampering between their legs, the three began to circulate in the crowd, charming one and all. Jibber gibbered adorably, Jebber made eyes at the pretty women and happily let them pet him, and Jabber picked pockets quickly and efficiently.

The Secret Service men were closing in—warily, for the little boys had big simian teeth and had used them on members of the SS before. Resignedly, Jebber and Jabber let themselves be corralled. But Jibber's attention had returned to the un-Constitutional enormity of the national Christmas tree. Waddling rapidly away from his would-be captors, whom the crowd delightedly and deliberately interfered with, Jibber made his way to the base of the dying redwood and stood leaning against its trunk, staring up at the branches draped with lights stretching away up into the twilight sky.

A Secret Service man broke from the crowd. His clothes were torn, his hair was rumpled, his face was scratched. "I've got you now, you little shit!" he shrieked, instantly destroying his career, and flung himself through the air at Jibber.

Jibber squeaked and leaped at the tree.

There were no branches this low down, but the bark, rough even in its natural state and severely gouged by the equipment that had been used to extract it from among its dwindling band of brothers and then transport it across the continent, provided adequate handholds for the little creature's small, strong fingers. Up he scrambled, looking more like a large spider or perhaps a robot than the son of the actual, for sure, goddamitall President of the United States.

He stopped halfway up, panting from a combination of exertion—he hadn't done this kind of climbing for a long time, after all—lingering fear of Secret Service men and muskets, and exhilaration. Mostly from exhilaration.

As he recovered his breath, he began to smell insects. These were different from any insects he had smelled before. They were aliens, natives of a very different place, doomed creatures snatched from one of the world's most beautiful places and brought to one of its most treacherous. Being insects, they didn't see things in those terms. Being Jibber, Jibber didn't either.

He poked a finger cautiously into one of the bark's deep cracks, speared something interesting with his fingernail, and pulled it out to examine it.

He looked at the thing, wriggling helplessly against the monkey spike sticking through its body. He sniffed it and the juices oozing from its grotesque wound and spreading over his fingernail.

He put his finger in his mouth, sucked the little critter off, and tumbled it around with his tongue. He maneuvered it over to the right side of his jaw and then squeezed it slowly between his molars.

The crackling and popping feeling and the brief desperate scrabbling of its tiny feet against his tongue were a new delight. This insect was deliciously different from any insects he remembered from Africa or had eaten in Texas or Washington! This tree was certainly a fine thing, but the insect was even better. Wherever the tree had come from—and of course understanding geography was far beyond Jibber's mental capacity—he wanted to go there. How he would feast!

He became aware again of the crowd below him. He looked out over them. They were staring up at him in amazement. Instinct told him to forget about the insects for now and concentrate on going up, to the heights where lions and leopards and humans wouldn't be able to follow him. He gibbered at the upturned faces for a few seconds and then turned his own gaze upward again and resumed climbing.

Watching from across the lawn, Daddy was torn between feelings of paternal delight and vicarious pleasure at the exploits of his little boy, and fury at the little bastard.

Thank God we were able to keep him from being sent to Viet Nam, he thought. What would have happened once he'd seen those damned jungles over there? We'd probably never have seen him again. Or maybe he'd have shown up some day in black pajamas. You never know with these boys.

Meanwhile, Jibber, climbing ever more rapidly as he fell back into the swing of his original lifestyle, had reached the very tippity top of the tree!

Except that it wasn't the real, original top, for that had been sliced off and the trunk had then been shaped and prepped and a large star inserted into it. This decoration would become the star of the evening when Daddy threw a switch. It would become a light unto the nations. It would be as if God had reached down one mighty, lengthy finger from Heaven to demonstrate to the world that America was his favorite nation, the divinely chosen Number One.

Daddy wanted to delay the lighting ceremony until Jibber could be brought safely down. However, various political aides muttered worriedly to him about the evening television news schedules and the suddenly bored and increasingly restive crowd.

Damn bullies, Daddy thought. People been bullying me all my life. Never get to do just what I want to do.

He pulled the switch.

Nothing happened.

Unfortunately, while climbing, Jibber had once or twice pulled himself up by the electrical wire that circled the mighty tree trunk and was meant to carry electrical current to the star. With the last such yank, as he was pulling himself onto the tree's flattened top, he had managed to pull the wire loose from the star.

"Now what?" Daddy asked the Universe.

Quick checks were made and it was determined that there was no problem with the power supply or the electric wire leading to the tree.

Clearly, the problem must be somewhere above the ground, somewhere up there.

"Up there," Daddy said, pointing. "Someone's going to have to go up there and find the problem and fix it." Looking up, he could see the fake star silhouetted against the real ones. And then he saw something else that made his heart skip a beat. Another silhouette suddenly appeared next to the star, the unmistakable shape of his darling little boy, the hellspawn idiot.

"Good God," Daddy said. He pointed again. "Damned good thing there isn't any current. Someone's got to go up there and get him down."

He looked around at the sturdy yeomen of the Secret Service, all of whom looked at the ground or gazed into the general distance.

"Hmph," Daddy said dismissively. "Need a helicopter. Do it myself. Used to be a flyboy in the old days, you know."

Shamed by the courage or at least bravado of the creaking antique, a couple of SS boys reluctantly offered to do the flying and rescuing themselves. Fortunately, helicopters are abundant in and around the White House, for the nation never knows when it will be necessary to whisk the president to some trouble spot to perform a deed of diplomatic derring-do, or when it will be necessary to snatch him away from danger. Within minutes, the two Secret Service men were lifting off—*wop, wop, wop*—and heading toward the top of the tree.

They circled around the top. They turned the craft's spotlight on and focused it on the small flat space where Jibber stood gripping the star in sudden terror. He stared openmouthed at the monstrous insect that was about to pounce on him.

The two men in the helicopter wondered what their next step should be.

"I say we just shoot the little fucker off there," one of them said.

"Easy target." He held up his hands as though he were aiming a rifle. "Pow, pow, pow! Blast him to smithereens."

"Tempting," the other man agreed. "But incriminating. We'd be the obvious suspects. Maybe I could swing in low and blow him off with the downdraft. Look like an accident. We were doing our best. Following procedure. Couldn't be helped. You know the drill."

"Good idea! Let's give it a try."

The moved down toward the frozen first son. The manmade wind blasted at Jibber, pushing him away from the star, toward the edge. But his fingers squeezed even more tightly.

Suddenly, part of him did unfreeze. Two parts, actually. Fore and aft. Terror emptied his bowels and his bladder simultaneously. Such was the force of his evacuation that his trousers burst apart and liquids and solids covered his legs and the ground in an instant.

They also covered the base of the star, at precisely the point where the wire had been pulled away. The fluids completed the broken circuit. The national star burst into life.

Jibber howled and flung himself backward, flying off the small platform and landing on one of the higher branches, to which he clung with arms and legs and hands and feet and teeth.

At the base of the star, the fluids and solids Jibber had left behind sizzled and sparked and danced in the powerful current, shooting off the tree like the dastardly rockets of the dastardly British in 1814.

The humans watching below were entranced.

"Ooh!"

They pointed at the brilliant sparks.

"Aah!"

One of these little Jibber–produced Congreves flew into the helicopter and hit the pilot in the eyes.

"Shit!" the Secret Service man shrieked accurately. He clawed at his face and the helicopter spun around and went up and down and flipped over and plummeted to the ground, fortunately avoiding the crowd.

The two Secret Service men were later buried in Arlington National Cemetery with full honors.

Jibber eventually made his way down the tree under his own power.

The full story of the incident was detailed to the nation by various television news services later that evening and repeatedly for the next few days.

The story they told was not entirely accurate in every detail, however. According to the media, the national Christmas tree had been sabotaged by Iraqi agents. These infiltrators shot down the helicopter dispatched to stop them and undo their evil. The day was saved by Jibber Longlegs, who single–handedly undid the sabotage, enabling the star to shine properly, after which he subdued the Iraqis and ate them, which was why there were no bodies to display.

"Plus," the newsreaders all added, "on top of all of that, he sure is a cute little monkey."

Watching one of those broadcasts, Malcolm found himself wishing that he were a cute little monkey. Or at least that someone would find him cute in any sense. He could hear Grandpa Tibbs sneering and snarling that he was worthless and would never amount to anything.

Thank God Marlene had never met Grandpa Tibbs. Malcolm shuddered at the thought of two such evil forces cooperating, creating between them something so terrible, so destructive to what there was of Malcolm's ego, that the fabric of reality might have been rent by it. He could not imagine a greater evil than those two acting together. Nothing so terrible had ever been seen in the world or ever would be.

In the meantime, two old guys were wandering around Portland, Maine religiously offing men named Malcolm.

P. P. Something beginning with P.

The Longlegs presidency drifted along.

A reporter got wind of the existence of Daddy's mistress and tried to dig up all the juicy details. The reporter was abducted by aliens. The mistress was sold to Longlegs family business partners in the Middle East.

The three brothers never stopped looking like miniature apes, but as the years passed they became increasingly human in the ways that counted.

Jabber never lost the gift of the gab. He went into business, specializing in crooked deals, underhanded negotiations, and skimming millions from the government. In this, he was of course no different from countless businessmen with parents who were outwardly human. And that was fine with him. Unlike his two simian siblings, he had no wish to stand out. All he wanted to do was get disgustingly rich, and if he managed to destroy some companies and lives along the way, that was just icing on the cake.

Jibber and Jebber both went into politics, gladdening Daddy's heart. Carefully guided every day by legions of Daddy's family retainers, the two monkeyboys did well. In time, both were elected governors of large states.

Jebber had never lost the habit of covering up his face and then spreading his fingers and peeking out. The voters in his state were enchanted by the gesture. It reassured them that he could quite literally see no evil. That seemed a good reason to vote for him.

Jibber had kept up his habit of gibbering meaninglessly. The voters in his state were convinced that it must all mean something, and so they voted for him. Besides, he was such a cute little monkey.

This was all occasionally disheartening to the more intelligent and worthy human beings both brothers had defeated, but they kept reminding themselves that "democracy" derives ultimately from an ancient word which means "rule by fools."

Occasionally, the three brothers still gathered at the family estate to pick lice out of each other's hair. Photographers were not allowed on the property at such times.

CHAPTER TEN

My dear spawn, at this point, something so awful happened to America that Lukas must talk to you about it directly instead of working through the medium of Malcolm Erskine for fear that Malcolm's very sanity might be blasted to isolated, wandering engrams by the shocking details.

A dreadful period began that was thereafter referred to in the Longlegs family only as The Interregnum.

To put it briefly, Daddy was defeated in his bid for reelection.

Not only that, he was defeated by a parvenu. Not only that, the parvenu was a highly intelligent man who had been a Rhodes scholar, whereas Daddy, in the words of his own daddy, was not the swiftest yacht in the harbor. Not only that, the parvenu was a genuine Southerner, whereas Daddy was a secret New Englander who only pretended to be a rugged son of the sweltering South. Not only that, the Southerner spoke English in complete, lengthy, well constructed sentences, whereas Daddy's short utterances were frequently difficult to parse, and indeed sometimes made no sense at all. Not only that, the Southerner's wife was relatively pretty. Not only that, four years later the Southerner was reelected.

And worse was to come.

Charitable though I, Lukas of Aldebaran, star-dwelling Merskeenian, want to be to all the deeds of my Earthian descendants, I must admit that Daddy's tenure in office had been a disaster. By the end of that tenure, the nation's unemployment rate was approaching 95%, the nation's debt was a number that made even a Merskeenian, used to dealing with truly astronomical figures, blanch, and the national Disgruntlement Index, more popularly known as the How Much Does The President Stink Index, was the highest it had ever been since measurements began.

But after eight years of the presidency of the Southern parvenu, all of this had been reversed. Jobs were being created, money was being made and spent, national harmony was increasing, a mood of peacefulness and hope permeated the country from sea to shining sea and was spreading beyond, and the aforementioned index had plunged.

Something had to be done.

Numerous Republicans vied for the party's nomination, for the chance to attack the Democrats' certain nominee, the Southerner's Vice President, Tom Moore. There was much consulting in smoke-filled rooms. Deals and throats were cut. Characters were assassinated. Fancy was told to go suck an egg.

Fancy? Gone's wife, the former First Lady, the gray eminence, the power behind the throne, she of the stiff smile and stiff back?

Yes, that Fancy. Gone was far too gone to run by now, even if the 22nd Amendment hadn't forbidden it. So Fancy saw herself as the savior of the nation and the party. Who else could win back the White House for the Republican Party but the near-widow of the near-dead Great Combobulator?

Of course she would have preferred to have my imprimatur, as delivered through Malcolm. She decided to forego that because Malcolm's powers of communication had suddenly deteriorated. He could tell her nothing of any use, and when pressed by her, he grew fearful and babbled. This made Fancy so angry that she had Zip

Muchley remove Malcolm to a special location where he was held incommunicado in a damp basement, chained to a wall. Fancy planned to keep him there until after her inauguration, after which she would have him tortured with hot pokers. Not because he possessed information anyone wanted or anything of that sort, but simply because her former admiration for Malcolm had changed to a deep, cold hatred and she wanted to hear him scream. For now, she visited him daily to hear him whimper.

"My athlete's foot has flared up because of the dampness," he would whine. "And it itches horribly. And I can't reach it."

Fancy would laugh and say, "The hot pokers will make you forget all about your athlete's foot."

"Why me?" Malcolm said. "Why, why, why, why, why?"

"You told me that Lukas said I would be the successor to Gone's successor. I based all my plans and hopes on what you claimed Lukas predicted. Obviously you were incompetent or lying, because that obnoxious fellow and his horrid wife got into the White House after Gone's successor, instead of me. I don't believe you really speak for Lukas of Aldebaran at all."

"Oh. Oh, wait. I misheard. I think he actually said the successor to the successor's successor. I missed one successor. It must have been that solar flare again. It interfered with my reception."

Fancy laughed bitterly. The sharp, high-pitched sound was absorbed by the damp walls and the sodden, moldy straw on the floor. Only the sound of dripping water remained.

And Malcolm's moaning.

"Marlene," he moaned.

Stunned by what he had just heard himself say, he stopped making any sound at all. Marlene? If Marlene were here, she would laugh along with Fancy, but happily, not bitterly.

After a while, Malcolm began moaning again, but wordlessly.

Fancy nodded in satisfaction and climbed up the slimy stone steps. She was a bit unsettled that Malcolm's new version of Lukas of Aldebaran's prediction, even though it was obviously something he had come up with on the spur of the moment in an attempt to save his skin, matched so closely the plan she was actually pursuing. Could he be telling the truth? Could he truly be channeling that wondrous stardwelling being, just as he claimed? It was a question she would have to devote some thought to.

But if he *was* telling the truth after all, then she had no excuse to hold him prisoner, let alone watch him being tortured with hot pokers later on. However, she enjoyed having him imprisoned in that basement. She would enjoy watching him be tortured even more. It was all good practice.

So she was presented with a moral dilemma, and she hated those.

She told herself that she didn't have to think about it now. For now, she had to spend some time in some smoke–filled rooms to make sure that the prediction really did come true, whether Lukas of Aldebaran had in fact uttered it or not.

So Fancy marched into a very important smoke–filled room, interrupting a very important smoke–filled meeting.

She looked around in disgust. Giant bodyguards stepped forward threateningly. Fancy gestured, and Zip Muchley loomed up, and the bodyguards retreated, bowing low in fear and admiration. Another gesture from Fancy, and Zip moved around the room opening windows. The bodyguards were all the more impressed, because these windows were solid parts of the wall and were not designed to be opened.

After the air had cleared a bit, Fancy said, "I'm your candidate, boys."

"But you're a girl!" one of the fat cats said.

Zip didn't need a gesture from Fancy. He picked the man up and threw him through the now-open window. Fortunately for the fat cat, they were on the ground floor and the man was well padded. He picked himself up painfully, turned toward the building's front door, then thought better of it and limped away.

One of the other fat cats held up both hands placatingly. "Now, just listen to me, Fancy, and hold your gorill—your man there at bay. Even if you get a majority of the votes in this room, that doesn't mean you can get a majority of the delegate votes at the national convention. Because, well, after all, he was right: you're a girl."

Zip growled and pawed the ground. Fancy ground her teeth, but she gestured to him to hold off. "Bribery," she said. "Vote rigging."

The fat cat nodded. "Sure. Of course. We always do that. You know that. But will it be enough? This is a very conservative crowd we're dealing with. Much more so than in the past, thanks to the lasting effect of the work done within the party by your wonderful husband, long may the gods bless his name and strew rose petals before him."

The other fat cats and their bodyguards bowed their heads in silent reverence for a moment.

"But that very conservatism," the fat cat continued, "means that this isn't yet the year for a female candidate. Some day, no doubt. Not this year."

Fancy hesitated for a long time, but in the end she realized that the man was probably right. She glared around the room. "I'll be back!"

She turned and left. Zip glared around the room, too, and then he followed his mistress.

They went back to the damp basement and tormented Malcolm for a few more hours.

It wasn't time for the hot pokers yet. Fancy had decided to wait for Inauguration Day for its symbolism, even though it would be someone else's Inauguration Day.

While Fancy was tormenting Malcolm, Daddy Longlegs was conferring with party fat cats himself and having a much more successful time of it than Fancy was.

He didn't suggest himself as a candidate for President, of course. They would have laughed at him if he had, given that he had been in the White House and had been defeated. He was a loser in their eyes and in the eyes of the rest of the world.

In fact, Daddy yearned to be back in power. He wanted to squash the parvenu who had defeated him. Since the parvenu had served his full two terms and wouldn't be running again, Daddy would have settled for squashing Tom Moore as the next best thing. Daddy knew that would never happen. The nation had voted him out once and would be unlikely to vote him back in. The bitter truth was that no one had ever liked Daddy.

Most of all, he didn't suggest himself as the candidate precisely because the men in those smoke–filled rooms would laugh at him. He'd be back in South Africa, on that hunting trip after the war, or back in his own daddy's company and the company of his daddy's friends. He'd be back among powerful men with powerful voices who were laughing at him, diminishing him, reducing him to impotent boyhood. He wouldn't be able to stand that.

So he suggested Jibber instead.

At first, they laughed at that idea, too.

"Oh, come on!" one of the fat cats said. "This is ridiculous. The kid looks like a chimp, and he doesn't even speak English. You may be able to get away with that kind of crap in Texas. Everyone knows the whole state is filled with kooks and wackos who vote straight Republican no matter what. But now you're talking about the United States of America. We're going to be facing a guy with brains. We don't have anyone like that in our party, so we're going to have to go for cute. Is that kid of yours cute? Is he even American?"

"Of course he's American!" Daddy said. He was scandalized. Well, all right, strictly speaking that kid of his was South African, not American, more strictly speaking South West African, and most strictly speaking he wasn't even Daddy's kid. But there was a paper trail on record now that proved beyond doubt that Jibber and his two brothers had been born in Texas, had gone to school there from pre-school through college, had learned to drive there, and had even performed valiant military service in the Texas National Guard during the Vietnam War.

He kept arguing and wheedling, but the fat cats were reluctant. Finally, Daddy flew back home to Texas, picked up Jibber, and then flew back East again with him.

Daddy and Jibber went back to the smoke-filled room he had left hours before. Nothing had changed. The same men were there, or perhaps they had been replaced with other men who looked just like them. That was immaterial. Great powerbrokers are as interchangeable as lowly peasants. It's not who they are, their individual identities, that counts. What counts is the role they play in the great Cosmic Ferris Wheel of Corruption, the amusing Sideshow of Pretending That All Votes Count Equally, the Three-Ring Circus of Plutocratic Privilege, and the sinister zoo in which the hungry Lions and Tigers of Aristocratic Greed roam freely and the gates are locked so that the rest of us can't get out. And what exactly is that role? Well, spawn, you'll never know, so it's best that you not worry your little head about it.

Jibber leaped up on the fat cats' immense, fabulously expensive conference table and capered from one end to the other. His special miniature cowboy boots clippity-clopped on the wood like the sound of a horse moseying along in the great wide-open spaces of the mythical Old West. His special little silver spurs scratched the highly polished surface, leaving marks like the brands leathery old cowpokes make on leathery cows in Western movies. His special small cowboy hat, pulled low over his brow, made him look almost human. He turned somersaults for the nice men and then pulled his little silver six-guns from their little leather holsters and fired into the air—*Blam! Blam! Blam!*—as though he were shooting down a dozen lily-livered, hoss-stealin' varmints.

Don't worry, everyone! They're only cap guns!

Then he struck a pose, legs naturally bowed, hands on hips, eyes slitted into a squint as though he were looking for mysterious meanings or possibly more varmints in some distant mountain range, and he gibbered briefly.

"My God," the fat cats all said simultaneously, "he sure is a cute little monkey!"

Oh, of course there was the formality of a series of primary elections and state party caucuses to get through. Jibber breezed through all of that. He made a few speeches—which is to say, long sequences of meaningless gibbering—and repeated various parts of the cowboy routine that had won over the party fat cats.

"What a cute little monkey!" everyone said. "Why, you know, maybe he really should be the Republican candidate for President of these stupendous United States! How can the Democrats compete against this?"

But Mr. Umbral still had some doubts. He felt the ticket needed balance. Not the geographical balance political parties usually strive for in their presidential tickets, but species balance. Just in case anyone was so rude and unwise as to raise questions about the humanity of the candidate at the top of the ticket, Umbral felt that an undoubted human being should be chosen as running mate. Moreover, some voters might think that Jibber seemed, well, less than entirely mature.

Oh, the little cowboy hat and boots and six guns were a wonderful touch, no doubt, and perfectly suited to push the appropriate buttons of the great American electorate. But still it might be wise to balance that with a vice-presidential candidate who exuded a simulation of wisdom, experience, age, and, to use a then-popular word that had absolutely no meaning in the real world but that all newspaper journalists felt they had to write at least twice a day, *gravitas.*

Mr. Umbral knew just the man for the job. He had the family retainers bring back a loyal family servant who had been deactivated long ago, Howard Phillips Moon, and bring him up to date. Properly prepared and coached by Umbral, the bald, vacant-eyed old Moon looked perfect for the part.

"Doesn't speak well," Daddy said doubtfully. "Doesn't move much. What we used to call a stiff."

"That's the *gravitas,"* Mr. Umbral said. "Don't worry. I'll throw a few dog biscuits to a few of our favorite reporters, and Moon will be seen as perfect."

And so in the fullness of time and the strangeness of politics, Jibber Longlegs became the official Presidential candidate of the Republican Party and Howard Phillips Moon became the official Vice Presidential candidate.

Jibber's acceptance speech consisted of a few seconds of gibbering followed by squinting into the distance from under the rim of his cowboy hat, firing his little cap guns, clomping around on the podium in his little cowboy boots, and finally turning a very nice somersault.

Moon wasn't able to be present at the convention site. Instead, he was shown on the giant television screens nodding gravely to the delirious crowd.

Now the ticket was in place, and all Jibber had to do to enter victoriously the White House his father had been forced to leave so ignominiously was get past Tom Moore.

Moore was a man of high intelligence, deep thoughts, impeccable personal behavior, and admirable history. Clearly, the best way to defeat him was to deny all of this and call him names.

At his very first campaign appearance after winning his own party's nomination, when Moore introduced himself—"Hello, I'm Tom Moore, and I'm running for President"—shouts arose from agitators planted in the crowd: "Liar!" "No, you're not!" "Wimp!" "Coward!" "Balding man!"

Moore appeared puzzled but pressed on. "Eight years ago," he droned, for the sad truth was that he did have a tendency to drone a bit in those days, although to his credit he never gibbered, "when we came into office, the country was in terrible shape. But look at us now."

"Liar!" "Adulterer!" "Whoremaster!" "Murderer" "Thief!" "Child abuser!" "Communist!" "Shapechanger!" "Balding man!"

Behind the shouting protesters, other hired troublemakers held up signs, waving them to catch the attention of the television cameras. The signs bore pictures of Jibber in his adorable little cowboy outfit. Underneath the photo were the words CUTE LITTLE MONKEY.

That evening, local and national news reported on Moore's campaign appearance, and their reports were remarkably similar. A pretty newsreader, probably either male or female, reported with a sneer that the shifty, cowardly, shady, draft-dodging, balding Vice President had incoherently babbled a bunch of lies and nonsense and that Governor Jibber Longlegs sure was a cute little monkey.

When Jibber made his first campaign appearance, he stood on the podium, struck his little cowboy pose, and gibbered for a while. The crowds went mad. The press reported with awe that he was not just a cute little monkey but a remarkably intelligent and perceptive and wise one as well.

This pattern was repeated throughout the campaign.

During the televised debates between the two candidates, Moore spoke cogently and in depth on various issues, Jibber gibbered and posed, and the press reported happily that the governor had blown the Vice President out of the water.

Judging by the slow creep in the polls toward Moore, none of this was quite enough. So when it leaked out that Bip and Bop had robbed a bank and had then used the money to buy vast amounts of alcoholic beverages at a liquor store and had then nabbed a police car and crashed it into a lamppost and had then passed out in a pool of their own vomit in full view of a television news crew interviewing Wallace "Ten Ton" Tenhut, the middlequarterthudpacker of the Piketon Ponies professional football team, who were in Washington for a scheduled humiliation at the hands of the local professional football team, the Longlegs political cabal got very worried indeed.

But of course the police looked the other way and the press did its part to help.

Had Malcolm been free to watch television news instead of whining piteously in a damp basement, he would have seen film of Ten Ton helping to clean the unconscious girls off, his meaty hands lingering just a tad too long on their jail-bait bodies. He would have seen the anchorman smiling approvingly at the whole escapade and opining that, while Jibber was a straight-shooting Christian, pure of heart and mind, the twins—the Terrible Twins, he called them roguishly—reflected the essential real ordinary guyness in Jibber's genes. Wasn't this a whole lot better than the boring, intellectual, nerdy child of the current and soon to be ex-President?

Concluded the newsie, "You can bet those cute little kids will be grounded for a few days for this escapade, chuckle, chuckle!"

In fact, Mr. Umbral chained Bip and Bop in a damp basement of his own for a week and scourged them with whips and told them he was considering following his own long-ago advice to Rehoboam and scourging them with scorpions.

But the amused public knew nothing about that basement or

those chains. All the public heard was the carefully constructed spin emanating from the press office of the Longlegs campaign. Daddy and Mr. Umbral and the rest of them were sure their spin would do the trick.

And yet, despite all of this, Moore won the election.

No, I shouldn't say that. In my Merskeenian way, influenced by my great distance in time and space, I, Lukas of Aldebaran, feel that Moore really did win because so many more Americans voted for him than voted for Jibber. But it appears that the noble Founding Fathers of your great Republic had some other system in mind. In the days of your nation's spittle-dribbling infancy, those otherwise sensible fellows imposed upon you something called the Electoral College, a weird and bizarre institution that, more than two hundred years later, enabled the Longlegs family retainers, and evil minions of theirs strategically planted in supreme positions of judicial power years before, to so manipulate matters in the state of which Jebber was governor that despite losing the election Jibber was declared the victor and President Elect.

I am so unable to understand what happened that I must resort to ellipsis and metaphor, to star-spanning mysticism, to cosmic circumlocution.

Let me try it this way, then.

Rlen, the dark and evil queen of the Marlingas, swept over your land, waving her wand of terror and confusion. All the lightness and happiness and goodness leaked away and you were flung into a strange alternate history, a deviation from your true path, a dimension of falseness and pretense and hubris and self-deception. Those freedoms of yours that the world once admired, yes, even they began to fade. In this sinister alternate world, your prosperity and joy could not survive, and so they turned gray and brittle and vanished. The very particles of time—chronons, we Merskeenians call them—of which the prosperous years had been composed fled screaming to the real world from this terrible alternate one, leaving you bereft of all you thought you once had. It was as though the preceding eight years had not even happened. Your light was stolen from you, and the old darkness was followed by the new. The world fell backward eight years through time and reverted to the day after Daddy Longlegs had left the White House!

And Rlen flew away, cackling, into the cold spaces between the galaxies. As I watched her go, leaving your world a shattered ember, I was filled with the uncontrollable hatred that any proper Merskeenian feels toward her and all the Marlingas, even though I had to admit, watching her sinister cape flutter upward in the terrifying winds of hyperspace, that she certainly did look awfully good in tights.

On the bright side, you now had cell phones, laptop computers, and broadband to the home, and Malcolm was back in his house without a scratch on him and with only the vaguest hint of a memory that something terrible had happened.

In the meantime, utterly untouched by everything, two old men were wandering around Paducah, Kentucky terminating guys named Malcolm with extreme prejudice and copious hallelujahs. They were wearing out, but they pressed on because they were pros.

CHAPTER ELEVEN

O hero-cousin, beware of the dangers that swim beneath the surface of seemingly placid waters! Those dangers are real. They are hungry. Your flesh is their food. Strike first! Get them before they get you. Kill! Eviscerate! Squash, mash, pulp, disgustify, convert into scarlet paste!

—Lukas of Aldebaran, as quoted in a section Malcolm later decided to cut from the manuscript.

Just what kind of piranhas swam in the seemingly placid waters into which he had plunged so joyfully began to become clear to Malcolm during his appearance on a radio talk show in Piketon late on a Friday night.

Until Jack called, Malcolm had been wondering if being a guest on this show was not a waste of time. Now that he was already a name on a national level, how much good could this small-time stuff do him? He answered the callers mechanically, hardly hearing their questions, letting his unconscious handle them while he daydreamed about wealth and fame and power and the requisitely olive-skinned, almond-eyed, black-haired, and beautiful young woman.

Oh, that ideal, that girl of his dreams! He had been yearning for her for years. He had never met her. He was no longer convinced that he ever would. He feared he would go to his grave, old and shrunken and trembling and drooling, without finding her. Or worse, that she would be the nurse in attendance at his deathbed, repelled by him as he gargled off this mortal coil.

How long before you start going downhill? he sometimes asked himself.

You never will, he answered. You'll never be over the hill because you were never up it. You emerged from puberty already on the downslope.

Then Jack said "Anti–Christ," and Malcolm stopped daydreaming and started paying attention.

"Come again?" Malcolm said.

"The Anti–Christ," Jack, the caller, repeated. "That's what the Pastor said it was. Last Sunday, during his sermon."

Such a normal voice, Jack's was. Not husky or grating or cold and deadly. Just an ordinary, everyday voice, the voice of the fellow sitting next to you on the bus or driving the car behind yours on the freeway or aiming the rifle through your living–room window.

Hank Singer, the show's host and a very friendly, easy–going fellow, was looking worried. He raised his eyebrows inquiringly at Malcolm, and Malcolm understood the gesture as asking whether he wanted Jack cut off.

Malcolm shook his head. Instinct warned him that he ought to get some more information from Jack.

"The Pastor?" he repeated. "Which pastor is that, Jack?"

"The Pastor!" Jack said, clearly scandalized. "Pastor O'Hair."

"Oh, him." That kook, that fellow charlatan. O'Hair was a Piketon institution who had outgrown the city. His stature had diminished a bit in recent years, but even so his radio and television programs were broadcast worldwide and his inspirational books were frequent residents on the bestseller lists. Malcolm had been aware of the latter fact, for it always caused him tooth-grinding chagrin, and he occasionally hit upon the man's television or radio broadcasts while exploring along the dial. But he had never paid any real attention to the man himself. He had always had the impression that O'Hair was evangelistic white bread, not to be compared with, say, Jimmy Earl and his Children of God organization. "Anti-Christ" scarcely seemed a term one would expect to hear from the Wonder Bread of the pulpit.

"Now just who is the Anti-Christ in, uh, the Pastor's view, Jack? Not me, surely." Malcolm laughed easily, condescendingly.

"No, of course not!" Jack said scornfully. "You? What a laugh! No, man, the Pastor said that this voice you hear, this guy from outer space, that's all really just a demon, an evil spirit, maybe even the Evil One Himself. You ain't hearing no spirit channel, or whatever you call it. You're listening to the voice of the Devil, Charlie, the sulphurous breath of the bottomless pit."

Not bad, Malcolm thought. I'll have to steal that line some time. "How too terribly clever of Pastor O'Hair," Malcolm said, feeling very witty. "And just how does he claim to know this about Lukas of Aldebaran and the star-dwelling Merskeenians?"

"Because he's a man of God, and you're just a poor, blind dupe," Jack said. "Anyway, the clues're there, if you pay attention. Just look at the name: Lukas—Lucifer! Aldebaran—Devil! Don't you get it?"

Yes, Malcolm got it, and he was suddenly cursing himself for not having foreseen this little twist. He could have named his made-up space critter anything he wanted to—Arthur, or Btspflk—but instead he had chosen a name calculated to cause him trouble. A little voice in his head—the voice of experience, rather than that of a star-dwelling Merskeenian—told him that he had created a situation with nasty potential. He was becoming aware of the piranhas, sensing their multitudinous teeth.

Malcolm cleared his throat. "Well, Jack, all I can tell you—and any other follower of Pastor O'Hair who's listening in tonight—is that when I first heard the voice of Lukas of Aldebaran, speaking inside my mind up there high in the mountains, I just knew he had nothing to do with the Devil and that he's only interested in our good. Lukas is a mortal, Jack, just like us, and he wants to be our friend."

"Oh, your soul is snared already!" Jack said in a voice echoing with genuine sadness. "I can see that the Old Enemy has you in his clutches and it's too late to save you. Well, we good Christians're just going to have to do what we can to save the world *from* you. Have a nice weekend." Click. Buzz.

Malcolm stopped for a few drinks after the show. He needed something to stop the shaking that had suddenly afflicted his hands.

The radio studio was downtown in a shiny new high-rise. The bar was on the ground floor of the same building. From the bar, Malcolm walked the two blocks to another shiny new high-rise in which his new condominium was located. The pleasure he had felt every time he returned to this new home since moving was missing this evening.

The panhandlers just added to his distress. Where had they all come from? And not just panhandlers. Drunks, too. And people, apparently sober, dressed in dirty clothing, with long, unwashed hair, sitting on the sidewalk, leaning against buildings, holding cardboard signs saying they were homeless. He remembered when you only saw such people in certain parts of the city, like the area around the Mexican restaurant he used to go to for lunch.

Come to think of it, that restaurant was closed now. Everything in that block was closed.

He pushed past the people loitering in front his building, trying not to look at them, and let himself in the front door, making sure it closed and locked properly behind him and that no one had followed him in.

He had not been home since morning. He extracted the day's mail from the lobby-side opening of his mailbox and then went to the elevator and pressed the button.

As Malcolm was waiting for the elevator, the front door opened behind him. He spun around in panic. But it was a fellow condominium owner, not one of the homeless people. The newcomer also took care that the door locked behind him.

What Malcolm was really worried about was not that a homeless vagrant would use the opportunity to get in. They were disturbing people, but he was pretty sure they were harmless. What frightened him was the thought that the person squeezing in behind one of the building's legitimate residents might be Jack, the scary caller to the radio program. Although, for all he knew, Jack might be posing as one of the vagrants outside. Then it occurred to him that this neighbor could in fact be Jack. How would Malcolm know?

He shivered uneasily and edged away from his neighbor, a stolid, beefy, middleaged man, as the latter joined him by the elevator door.

I really don't know much about this guy, Malcolm thought. He looks normal enough, but he could be a cold, heartless killer. Or some other kind of kook.

"Getting terrible, isn't it?" the man said. He shook his head. "What are those people doing around here? We don't want them here. The city government should do something about it. The government's as worthless as the bums outside the door. Homeless! Yeah, sure. How can they be homeless? That's ridiculous. There are lots of vacancies right here in this building. More all the time. Why don't they get a job? Then they could buy a place to live, like us. Lazy losers, that's all they are."

"Well," Malcolm said, "I kind of have the feeling that there aren't a lot of jobs to get right now."

"Bull. There's lots of work if you're aggressive and go out and get it. I'm doing all right. What are you, some kind of Democrat or something?"

Malcolm considered saying, "At least I'm not *trés bourgeois,"* but he lacked the courage. Instead, he smiled noncommittally and kept his thoughts to himself. As they rode up together in the elevator, Malcolm made a point of looking through the accumulation of envelopes, avoiding further conversation.

The other man got off the elevator at the twentieth floor, giving Malcom a hard stare through narrowed, suspicious eyes as he left.

After the elevator door had closed again, Malcolm took a few deep breaths and tried to relax. Then he started looking through his mail again. He hadn't been paying attention to the envelopes the first time through. He'd been watching his fellow passenger from the corner of his eye, half expecting the man to cast aside his cloak of middle-class normalcy and reveal himself as a raving maniac.

The amount of mail Malcolm received had increased greatly with his increasing success. Many people in the publishing business now wanted to be his friends. There was a time when Malcolm would have cut off a finger or possibly even two to gain such friends. (The pinkie: not a major finger for a writer.) Now their pleading tones filled him with contempt—and, on the positive side, helped him forget about Jack and the other kooks whose existence Jack's existence implied.

What's this? Malcolm thought with rising excitement as the elevator rose toward his fortieth-floor apartment. One of the envelopes bore for its return address the word "Lucasfilm" and an address in California.

George Lucas! He must want to buy the movie rights to one of my novels!

Malcolm tried to rip open the envelope with hands which were now trembling from excitement rather than fear.

Sir:

> *Be advised that your use of the name "Lukas" in your book Business Secrets from the Stars constitutes an illegal use of a trademark registered in the name of our company, Lucasfilm Enterprises, and you are hereby ordered to cease and desist immediately. Production and distribution of your book must halt immediately, and all copies already distributed must be immediately recalled and destroyed. Failure to comply...*

Malcolm groaned and rested his feverish brow against the cool metal of the elevator wall. Why, he wondered, doesn't anyone love me? Where was his dream girl who would take his soul and his life and his sex organs into her capable hands and make everything right? Why wasn't success bringing happiness? Why, what, who, when, and where? "Mommy," he whimpered, "they're beating on me again."

When he was small and other boys had indeed beaten him, Mommy had clutched him to her immense bosom, smothering him and making him forget his misery by replacing it with the desperate need to breathe. He had hated big breasts ever since. His dream girl had small, firm ones.

So did Marlene.

The elevator stopped, Malcolm got off, walked down the hallway to his apartment, entered, locked the door behind him, fixed himself a mightily powerful drink, guzzled down half of it, and almost dialed his ex-telephone-number and begged his ex-wife to come downtown and comfort him.

Fortunately, he caught himself in time.

She would set conditions. She might even want them in writing.

He finished his drink. The drink had restored a bit of his courage and self-confidence, so he fixed and quickly drank another just like it.

I'll manage, he told himself. I'm the descendant and confidant of a star-dwelling Merskeenian. Nothing can stand in my way. I deserve another drink.

Meanwhile, meetings were being held, machinations were being finely machined, and malevolence was maturing. The piranhas were gathering, licking their lips, sharpening their teeth, exciting their appetites with happy imaginings of the rending of flesh. Malcolm's flesh. Boy, were they hungry.

One of those meetings was being held at an idyllic retreat high in the Rockies in Arapahoe, far from highways and population centers. It was, in fact, almost like the location Malcolm had invented for his book, the mountaintop where Lukas of Aldebaran had supposedly spoken to him, mind to mind. At Starland in the Rockies, however, the minds were using their mouths and English words to communicate with each other, and those words were not pretty.

Nor were most of the people.

Present were Carol O'Hair of the city of Piketon, known to his well and frequently fleeced flock as "The Pastor," his wife, Elizabeth "Bess" Walters O'Hair, known to the Pastor's staff by epithets not suitable for repetition, the Very Reverend Jimmy Earl, founder and head of the Children of God, televangelist nonpareil, and Shirley, Jimmy Earl's virtual right hand, his most trusted employee, his confidante and coconspirator and head operative. She was young, she was beautiful, and she had been born without a heart—Jimmy Earl's kind of woman.

Jimmy Earl was talking and everyone else was listening. "Now, Carol, you're just not listening to me. Or else you're just not understanding me."

"We understand perfectly well, Jimmy," Bess Walters said. "We just—"

"Shut up," Jimmy Earl said. Bess looked outraged and amazed. Shirley snickered. Jimmy Earl continued. "I'm telling you, Carol, I keep telling you, we can't just let this guy keep on with this crap. It's dangerous. He's got to be stopped, and Piketon is supposed to be your area of operations."

"And Carol keeps telling you, Jimmy," Bess said, "that you're exaggerating the danger. This Erskine is just one of many. There's lots of New Age con men around. Always have been. They come and they go. We should ignore them. In the end, they're just a passing fad."

Jimmy Earl pretended to ignore her. Instead, he spoke directly to the Pastor.

"First of all, Carol, none of us can afford to ignore these New Age con games because we've made the New Age stuff one of our main bogeymen. Secondly, we especially can't afford to ignore any con man who's got a pitch that rivals ours. The number of sheep is finite, and if these New Age fellas fleece them too well, what's left for us?"

Carol, wispy and uncertain at the best of times, looked even more wispy and uncertain. "But, Jimmy, we all know they're false prophets, and that the voices they hear are of Satan, not God. All we really have to do is occasionally remind our flocks of that, and—Is something wrong?"

Jimmy Earl's pudgy body was shaking, his pudgy cheeks were quivering, his oily hair was standing up on his pudgy scalp, and his pudgy brows had drawn together in a fat frown. His chipmunk face turned dangerously red, and then he burst out, "Jesus God Almighty, man! Don't start believing your own spiel, or you're dead in this game!"

"Sorry," Carol muttered, while the others stared at him with varying degrees of contempt.

Oh, how Carol missed the good old days—not so very long ago—when he had been a power himself in the electronic land of televangelism, when the services held in the Lifeway Temple and the weekly Hour of Power program had been carried on radio and television stations across this broad and fertile land of ours and verily even into other lands, even those of the heathens.

Now the dominant forces in the business had narrowed down to a few, among whom Jimmy Earl was the most powerful and widely heard and seen, and Carol O'Hair now found himself in a position much like that of Malcolm Erskine before the publication of *Business Secrets from the Stars.* That is, he was a mid–list televangelist. From a man of political as well as religious importance whose influence had reached far beyond the borders of the state of Arapahoe, he had become little more than another cog in the Reverend Jimmy Earl's money–making machine.

Now that he thought about it, Carol realized that he missed even more the earliest days, before he had become a big name. He missed his youth, when he had believed what he preached. He couldn't deny the suspicion that never in his life had Jimmy Earl believed a single word of his own sermons.

What am I doing here with these people, Carol wondered. Plotting to destroy a man, for God's sake!

He reminded himself that Malcolm Erskine was a man who deserved destruction. He had to keep remembering that.

"Now, then," Jimmy Earl said, his blubbery face relaxing into the smooth, genial blandness so familiar to his electronic flock (fifty million strong, so Jimmy Earl's public relations man claimed). "Here's how I'm going to take care of this guy. First, the softening up. That comes from you, Carol. I want you to keep up the sermons where you say that Erskine is really listening to a demonic spirit, or maybe even to the Devil himself. Keep on with the pitch that Erskine is at best a dupe, some sort of herald of the Antichrist, at worst the Antichrist himself. Stir up the hicks in your town. We want a certain number of frightening phone calls and letters to Erskine and newspapers and radio stations and so on. But keep it under control. We don't want any real violence, because that would reflect back on you.

"When I think he's softened up enough, I'll give him a call myself and suggest that maybe he ought to make some kind of public retraction of all his shit and apologize to all the Godly people of America he's insulted," quivering cheeks becoming a mottled red again, "with his anti–Christian," breathing speeding up, "anti-family—"

"Reverend Jimmy," Shirley said quietly.

The redness faded, and Jimmy's breathing slowed. Again he smiled with otherworldly emotionlessness. "Thank you, Shirley. Anyway, I'll suggest to the man that he ought to quit while he's got a head."

"Well, I don't know," O'Hair said, frowning. "It hasn't worked so far, and I know he's had a threat or two already. Either the fellow doesn't frighten all that easily, or else there's just too much money in it for him to give up. Or it could be that he actually believes everything he says." His voice trailed away for a moment, and he sighed deeply. "Maybe we ought to just—" He had intended to say, "forget about it all and leave him alone." But then he looked at the rapacious faces around him and looked at the floor and said nothing. These were scary people, and his own beloved helpmeet was one of the scariest.

"If he doesn't," Jimmy Earl said, "we go to Plan B."

Bess O'Hair glared at him. "Oh, Jesus, you sound like a fifties B movie."

"Whatever *that* is," Shirley said, emphasizing to the assembled company that, unlike Bess, she was not old enough to remember fifties B movies.

Glares, hisses, snarls. Carol O'Hair looked terrified. Jimmy Earl looked smug. Finally, Reverend Jimmy interrupted the feline confrontation. "Shirley, tell the folks about Plan B." To the O'Hairs, he said, "Plan B was Shirley's invention. Ain't she great?"

Shirley explained Plan B. Carol O'Hair paled, giving his normally pale skin a ghostly look. Bess O'Hair nodded with reluctant respect. Had Malcolm Erskine been a fly on the wall, he would have fainted.

Another wall on which Malcolm should have been a fly was that of Jimmy Flicker's office at the new headquarters, in downtown Piketon, of his new corporation, MegaFlicker. In fact, though, to have heard anything, Malcolm would have had to be a fly with extraordinary hearing, since the office was immense and Jimmy's absurdly large desk was in the very center of it and thus so far from the walls that a conversation held in normal tones at the desk would have been inaudible at any of the walls. But if he *had* been a fly on that wall, endowed with preternatural hearing, and had he recovered from the earlier fainting spell resulting from overhearing the conversation between the men of God and their female lieutenants, he would have fainted again.

Jimmy Flicker's lieutenant was male, middleaged, exceedingly tall, stupendously broad across the shoulders, expressionless of face, and murderous of mind. His name was Mongo. He liked to tell his victims his name because he liked to see the bewilderment it engendered and because he was amused by the knowledge that they would never get the chance to pass his name along to anyone—the police, for example. His official title at MegaFlicker was "Director of Cosmic Outplacement."

Coincidentally, Mongo had been an astronomy buff since boyhood and thought it would have been very nifty if Malcolm Erskine really had been in communication across time and space with an ancient star dweller who could pass on good info about the true nature of the universe. Although even in that case, he suspected, Malcolm's purple prose would have made the telling of those cosmic truths unreadable.

"There's another one just hit the stands," Mongo said. His voice was appropriately deep, but it was soft and mild rather than properly menacing. Mongo had never felt any need to develop a menacing tone or way of speaking. That was because, other than telling outplacees his name, he never bothered with preliminary verbal threats or game playing. He preferred to get to the actual bloodshed right away.

"So what's this one called?" Jimmy's jacket hung on a stand beside his desk. He snapped his red suspenders irritably, a nervous habit he had been unable to break.

"Management Secrets from Ancient Empires. Very serious stuff, it looks like. Written by a real history professor, and it really does tell all about how various ancient societies were governed."

Jimmy waved his hand in dismissal. "Bull crap. We can ignore that one. No one will go for that. It's another non-starter."

Fortunately, so far there had been no serious threat to the sales dominance of Malcolm's book. The previous week had seen the publication of *The Stars and Your Business—an Astrological Guide.* Yet another, as Jimmy Flicker liked to say, non-starter. The competition, up to this point, had consisted of obvious repackaging jobs—books written before Malcolm's great success, and now reissued with new covers and usually new titles to try to cash in on his hit idea. It had not worked yet, and both Malcolm's book and his seminars continued to reign supreme.

Next, Jimmy supposed, would come the quickie jobs, books dashed off in a matter of days or weeks which came closer in tone and fundamental ideas to Malcolm's. It seemed likely to Jimmy that none of those would hit the big time, either.

But even as he sat there listening to Mongo report on the latest contender for Malcolm's title, Jimmy Flicker knew that someone, somewhere was writing the book that would become the new champion. Of this he was quite sure. Things don't stand still in the business world. It was Malcolm's book that had taught him that! Nor do good ideas remain unstolen for long.

And when that new champion ascended to the top of the heap,

where would Jimmy Flicker's investment in Malcolm Erskine and his seminars be? Nowhere, that's where. Losing value quickly, that's where.

The very thought of one of his investments decreasing in value was enough to make Jimmy go like, "Wow! I'm losing it!" More precisely, it made him queasy. If the investment were actually to decrease, Jimmy would be blown away. More precisely, he would throw up. Given the cost of the carpet in his office, that was unthinkable. Can't happen, Jimmy Flicker thought. Mustn't happen. No, wait, that's not the way Lukas of Aldebaran would think! Lukas would say: "Starseed of my starseed, you *cannot allow it to happen!"*

Energetically, like a star-dwelling Merskeenian, Jimmy Flicker jumped to his feet. "Yes!" he cried. "No, I won't!"

Mongo was used to this sort of behavior on his employer's part. He awaited his orders calmly.

"Mongo, go and see Erskine and tell him I'm going like, he's gotta produce a new bestseller and protect my investment in him. Quickly."

"Or?"

"Or I'll lose it completely. I'll find someone else to do the job instead, and Erskine will be cosmically outplaced."

"Aah." Mongo smiled happily. He loved performing cosmic outplacement on ineffective employees of MegaFlicker. In fact, under whatever circumstances, he simply loved performing cosmic outplacement.

In South Carolina, at the bottom of a sea of humidity, atop a low ridge overlooking the more conventional sea, surrounded by acres of startlingly green lawns and shaded by immense oaks, a complex of linked, low, white buildings housed the international headquarters of the Children of God. Central to the complex were the television studios from which the Very Reverend Jimmy Earl broadcast his message of hope, love, and greed to an addicted world; the mail room where an army of clerks and machines processed the flood of contributions that came in daily from the addicts; the sumptuous living quarters where Jimmy Earl indulged in his cheerfully debauched lifestyle; and one of the biggest and most secure safes in private hands in the world.

Not so central physically, but very important indeed, were the offices of COG's Security Division. One office in particular, although small and unpretentiously furnished and decorated, was the most important place in the Security Division and possibly the second most important place within COG headquarters. This was the office of the aforementioned Shirley, whose official title was Reverend's Right Hand but whose job in reality was Chief of Security and Inventor and Perpetrator of Useful Evil Deeds.

At the moment, the wall of this office was yet another one to which Malcolm Fly should have been attached by his sticky feet. He would have needed those sticky feet to stay attached, for the scene in this office would also have caused him to faint.

Shirley was in her office discussing Malcolm Erskine with a rather tall, very pretty, fairly young woman. Shirley began by asking her about certain aspects of the World's Greatest Channeler's personality.

"He's not a bad guy, really," Shirley's operative said thoughtfully. "Easily manipulated, of course, and not all that bright. And desperate for love and comfort, which is what made him so easy a mark. And sex, obviously."

Shirley nodded. "Nothing unusual so far."

"Well, yeah, I guess there's nothing really unusual about him, when you come right down to it. In any sense, I mean. Actually, I kinda think that underneath all the fakiness and smarm, there's a nice guy hiding in there. Well, somewhere, anyway."

"We're working the intimidation angle right now. Think that'll do the trick?"

The operative thought that over for a few moments, then shook her head. "Malcolm's no hero, that's for sure. In fact, he's a physical coward. But his greed is in control. In my opinion, he's not going to give up the channeling scam for anything."

"Hmm. We'll see about that. Next step is to make an offer, something that's lucrative enough for him but still gets him out of our hair. What about that?"

"It'd have to be one hell of an offer, wouldn't it? I mean, look at those photocopies I gave you." She was referring to photocopies of various financial records of Malcolm's. "How can you match those numbers?"

"Could be a problem. If he refuses our offer, we'll have to go to Plan B."

The other woman's eyes widened. "Oh, I hope not! The poor man!"

"Well, we'll see what happens. All right, I've got your written report, so that should supply me with any other details I need. Good job."

The other woman blushed. Praise from Shirley was rare and to be treasured.

"And if I need more info from you, I'll call you," Shirley added. "Enjoy that liaison job with our foreign associates. That's a good step up the ladder. Why, one day, you'll probably be back here trying to take my job away from me!"

The two women looked at each with unsmiling eyes while they both laughed heartily at Shirley's very small joke.

CHAPTER TWELVE

Oh, my fellow cosmic ray, brother spawn of the same mother stars, companion traveler through the great void, blah, blah, blah, gibber, gibber, gibber...

—Lukas of Aldebaran, as quoted verbatim in Business Secrets from the Stars

The White House was in crisis.

No one on the outside knew anything about it. That was the way it was with the Jibber administration. When they took over the government, the Jibber team assured the nation that the adults were now in charge, that honor and dignity now reigned supreme, and that the business of the Executive Branch would henceforth be conducted in a calm, methodical, carefully planned manner. Crises and unanticipated events were a thing of the past. Since it was essential, as every member of the administration team agreed, to preserve the illusion that all of this was true, those crises that did arise were kept from the ken of the outside world. No matter what frenzy and despair might fill the private offices inside the White House, the façade of unflappability was always carefully maintained. Because of the complete absence of competence, maintaining the illusion of complete competence was imperative.

And so no one knew that Jibber, frustrated and bored by being confined to the White House, furious at never being allowed to take off his little cowboy boots even though they had started to pinch, completely unmollified by being told that he was a cute little monkey and really, really, really the President of the United States to boot, an office and role he didn't understand anyway, had reverted to the ways of his primitive youth.

How he yearned for the vast savanna of southern Africa! The veld called to him with its siren song.

He didn't know of the old Great White Hunter proverb, that Africa is like a lion, and once it gets its claws into you it will never let you go, it will always draw you back. He would have appreciated the sentiment.

Well, except for the part about the lion. As a tiny little simian, he had spent a lot of time in the highest branches of the trees, shivering, as lions roared below or, even more terrifying, as leopards climbed toward him, testing the branches, finally giving up only when they climbed high enough that the branches could no longer hold their weight.

Anyway, when the lions and leopards weren't around, Africa was a wonderful place. Oh, and the cheetahs. And the baboons. And the snakes. And the hyenas. And the humans. Well, anyway, when all of those weren't around, it was a great place to be a little arboreal simian of an undescribed species. As long as an adequate number of females of your own species were hanging around, and they usually had been, for they also seemed to think that Jibber was a cute little monkey.

But now, here on this cold continent, how sadly different his life was.

It hadn't struck Jibber until now. He had been, he thought, happy for years, playing son to Daddy and Grammy. Being made a governor, even though he didn't really understand what that meant, had been fun enough for a while. The same applied to being made President. That had been briefly amusing.

But Jibber had a very short attention span, and now he was bored. He missed Africa, he missed the trees, he missed those vigorous little females of his unknown species.

Especially today.

The morning had started with deceptive calm. Jibber was in the Oval Office, curled up on the white leather couch at one end of the room, dreaming of Africa, while Daddy and Mr. Umbral and various aides and Cabinet secretaries gathered around the giant desk that was supposed to be Jibber's and stared at the mounds of crackling parchment that made up the original Constitution of the United States. They had requisitioned the document from the National Archives so that they could try to make some sense out of it. They had been doing this for the past two days, and none of them was yet able to make head or tails of its archaic language and obsolete concepts.

Bip and Bop, now grown into juvenile delinquents, stood nearby smoking and glaring in resentment at the adults who refused to let them out of their sight. They were also discussing in low tones whether Jibber was hairy all over and speculating about how interesting certain activities might be.

In the middle of all of this, Tess entered the room.

Jibber awoke immediately. It was the smell of machine oil that roused him.

Jibber's repeated refusals to mate with Tess after that first disastrous attempt had played havoc with her programming and internal mechanisms. She advanced toward him with a fanatical robotic glint in her eyes. Her face almost had an expression. Planting herself in front of the couch, she stared down at the shivering little simian, who shrank away into a corner as if hoping the leather would swallow him and hide him. Oblivious to the gang around the desk, Tess pulled up her skirt, pulled down her panties, spun around, and bent over, shoving her star–signaled banger in Jibber's face.

Jibber screamed and made it from the couch to the drapes in one leap and from there to the chandelier in another. As usual when alarmed, he emptied his bowels and bladder.

"Gross!" Bip said.

Bop said, "He's not a cute little monkey now!"

They giggled.

Daddy sighed and gestured to a Secret Service man. "Clean this up." He pointed at the soiled Constitution.

"Um, sir, the ink," the Secret Service man said. "I think we'd better get some kind of expert in here."

"You got a handkerchief?"

The man nodded.

"Use it. Just wipe it off. Doesn't matter if the ink smears. No one's read it in years."

Bip said, "When you gonna house train the little bastard, Grandaddy?"

Mr. Umbral said to her, in his cold, dangerous voice, "At least with him it comes out of the proper end. He doesn't spend his time getting drunk and throwing up all over Washington."

The twins subsided and began to move quietly toward an exit.

Daddy looked up at the chandelier thoughtfully. "Does okay if he's not startled. That's the problem." He looked at Tess. "Yep, there it is. Done her job. Liability."

Daddy looked at Mr. Umbral. A communication seemed to pass between them. High frequency. Encrypted. Burst messaging. Very cool top–secret CIA, NSA stuff.

"In the meantime," said Mr. Umbral, "a nice lice–picking would probably do wonders to calm him down." He snapped his fingers. "Lackey! Bring in the lice–pickers."

A lackey saluted and rushed from the room. He returned moments later, followed by four humble men.

The four humble men knew what their duty was and needed no instructions.

Jibber recognized them immediately. Gibbering with delight, he leaped from the chandelier to the drapes to the floor, and in another leap into the midst of the party of lice-pickers. When he landed on the floor, he hit the middle of one of the puddles of his own feces and urine, which splashed in all directions, but he was so delighted by the prospect of a session of lice-picking that he ignored that. He would have ignored it in any case. He always did.

The lice-pickers grimaced at the smell as he landed among them, but they quickly schooled their faces to neutrality and surrounded the crouching simian and began to comb through his fur, picking out lice and dirt and anything else they found. With determination if not happiness, they bent to their task. It was a position made easier by their lack of vertebrae.

Jibber sat rocking slowly back and forth, gibbering quietly, happy as a cute little monkey resting safely high in a tree in the warm southern African sun. As the Senate and House Democratic leaders and whips scrupulously did their job, Jibber let himself imagine that he really was back on the endless veld, safe with his mindless, irresponsible, hedonistic little friends, far, far away from all of this painful complexity. Oh, if only he could be back there, in that paradise of simplicity, that uncomplicated world! No more cowboy boots, no more playacting, no more Tess, no more Bip and Bop. No more pretending to be a man.

Later that day, the First Lady left Washington on a previously unannounced trip to visit her supposed parents back home in Texas. As the tastefully decorated special Prima Donna Boeing 757 zoomed along somewhere over the desolate outback territories of Missouri, the pilot said, "Whoa! What was that? Like a flash of light, or maybe a streak."

The copilot joked, "Maybe they're testing the Wishful Thinking Missile Defense System out here."

The pilot glared at him. "That's not funny."

According to the report Malcolm watched that evening on one of the cable television news networks, this was what happened next:

"A loud buzzing drone filled the air, and a formation of Japanese Zeros dove out of the sun! The Boeing 757 pilot struggled manfully to evade the nimble and surprisingly fast Zeros, but the large plane lacked the necessary maneuverability, and despite the Boeing's powerful jet engines, it proved impossible to outrun the fiendishly ingenious enemy. Bullets pounded into and through the 757, quickly killing everyone on board and smashing control surfaces and fuel lines. The great doomed aircraft struggled valiantly to keep flying, demonstrating its heroic American spirit, but alas the fight was hopeless. Soon, its nose tilted downward and it roared toward the ground, defiant to the end. The Zeros followed it down until they saw it plow into farmland and explode into a million zillion quadrillion pieces. The Zeros circled the smoking wreckage in an evil, triumphal aerial dance and then climbed back up into the sky and vanished again.

"We should mention that the company that distributed the fuel used by the Boeing 757 is owned by this network's parent company."

The news broadcast didn't mention that the Japanese government made repeated, urgent offers to send aviation experts of its own to the crash site to help reconstruct the incident, but those offers were refused.

Jibber was shown on television gibbering. The news anchors described his comments as simple, straightforward, from the heart, deeply moving, and quite poetic. His speech, they said, would no doubt be printed in schoolbooks and studied by America's kiddies for generations to come. Such manly eloquence at a time of such sadness and national tragedy could only increase the public's already fervent love for their leader and boost his poll ratings all the more.

Besides which, they pointed out, he sure was a cute little monkey.

When puberty struck, Malcolm, like most boys, first noticed girls in a painfully intense way and then, with just as intense a pain, noticed that they were not noticing him. As is also the case with most pubescent boys, the fantasy world Malcolm spent much of his time in changed at this point from a series of unlikely good vs. evil adventures to a series of unlikely sexual encounters.

As the years passed, the female actors in his sexual fantasies changed from either fuzzily generic sexpots or clones of specific girls at school to that ideal that would never cease to obsess him: the petite, olive-skinned, almond-eyed beauty with shoulder-length black hair.

In the meantime, his relationships with actual flesh-and-blood girls and then women were always much less satisfying than the ones he imagined with his dream girl. Marlene, at least at the beginning, had been the rare exception. But of course that relationship had been an illusion, in its own way as unreal as his dreams. Ultimately worse, really. His dream girl would never have treated him the way Marlene did!

Early on, Malcolm had learned, again like most boys, that in the eyes of those females to whom boys are most attracted, the male population is divided into the tiny percentage of the worthy and the vast numbers of the unworthy. Malcolm had spent his post-puberty life as one of the unworthy, a category from which he had come to believe he would never escape.

This was a field of endeavor in which there was no such thing as upward mobility. One did not work or even claw one's way up the ladder, for sadly there was no ladder. Like any Medieval peasant, one was doomed to remain in the scummy station in life into which one was born. Or perhaps a better analogy would be to say that the gods chose to smile upon the few and to frown upon the many, and there was no reason or even predictability about their choices. It was much like the way they smiled upon some writers and sneered at the rest. The few smiled upon were blessed with lives of erotic or writerly fulfillment, and the great numbers of divinely spurned were condemned to lives of erotic or writerly frustration. Or both, in Malcolm's case.

Pretty girls, he learned early, were not pleased when he approached them. It wasn't just that they didn't want to go out with him. They didn't even want to speak to him. They didn't want him to speak to them. They didn't want him to look at them. They shuddered when they sensed his longing stare. Eeeuuw! Eyeball licks from the unworthy! I've got his optic juice on me!

Malcolm would sigh and retreat to the welcoming arms of his dusky dream girl.

Then Marlene came along and, for a short time, made him stop thinking about his dream girl. Then Marlene revealed her true nature, and he needed his dream girl all the more. Then he hit it big with *Business Secrets from the Stars* and even bigger with his seminars, and suddenly women were flinging themselves into his bed. He didn't need his dream girl! He didn't need Marlene! This was one of his oldest fantasies come to life!

And then, astonishingly, even this began to pall.

True, the young women from his seminars who fell happily into his bed were all slender and firm and flexible and enthusiastic, possessed of all the enviable physical traits of youth and wonderfully willing to ignore Malcolm's own lack of the same. True, they varied as to physical type: today a blonde, rosy cheeked and open, and tomorrow a brunette, dark eyed and mysterious; today a tall, aggressive athlete, and tomorrow a tiny, clinging, delicate flower. Oh, how he rejoiced in them all! And yet, once past their youth and firmness and enthusiasm, once no longer enticed, intrigued by the very fact of their differentness, he was forced to admit to himself that they were all the same: bimbos. They were lovely shells encasing minds with intelligence quotients barely above room temperature.

After all, had they been intelligent, they would never have paid good money to attend anything so nonsensical as a *Business Secrets from the Stars* seminar.

The day came when an exceptionally beautiful young woman in one of his seminars offered herself to him, and Malcolm told her he could not fit her into his schedule—and the truth was that he had just realized that he would rather finish the novel he was currently reading than couple with the enticing creature.

I'm getting old! he cried inwardly.

No, I'm getting bored.

Marlene the Maleficent, Malcolm misses you. Evil and self-seeking and amoral you may be, but you are no bimbo, and you are never boring.

Fortunately for Malcolm's peace of mind, just at the point where he had recognized how essentially empty his sex-filled life had become, how bored he was with sexual adventures for the experiencing of which other men would have sacrificed various limbs, he was distracted by being invited—at last!—to appear on a nationally televised talk show.

The host, Johnny Aggressive, was a former boxer. He seemed unable to sit. He spent much of every show on his feet, moving about, bobbing and weaving, as though he were still in the ring, still avoiding his opponent's fists, still looking constantly for an opening, for a chance to land a killing blow.

Malcolm thought he was obnoxious, but he would have suffered through a couple of hours with a far more obnoxious host for a publicity opportunity like this.

There was an additional inducement that Malcolm was reluctant to admit even to himself because it seemed so silly. Johnny A., as his fans called him, was married to Felicia Finewine.

Maybe, Malcolm hoped when he was invited to be one of Johnny's sparring partners, just maybe—oh, God, please!—the otherworldly newsgal would be visiting her husband's show and would pass through the Green Room while Malcolm was there.

But she wasn't and she didn't, and so nervously Malcolm drank half the bottle of cheap, free Green Room champagne and staggered out into the terrifyingly bright lights.

SCENE: Five people sit on ordinary chairs on a stage. From left to right, they are:

Brother Harry. Bearded, mellow, stuck somewhere between middle age and old age, twinkly–eyed founder and head of Brothers and Sisters of Jesus, or BASOJ. His graying hair is long and unrestrained, flowing Jesus–like to his shoulders. His beard, also graying, is also rather Jesus–like. "Be cool! Be mellow!" That, in the stated philosophy of BASOJ, is the essence of the word of Jesus Christ. Jesus wants all his brothers and sisters to lay back, to kick back, to commit similar linguistic atrocities. Life can be beautiful, bro'. You just don't know. Go with the flow. Vo–de–oh–do. BASOJ is headquartered in Southern California. What a surprise! Brother Harry wears flowing, loose–fitting robes. The robes have visible patches. Things have not been the same for BASOJ since the young generation it once appealed to became not so young and their attention turned from the ERA to

IRAs. Brother Harry is beginning to look past or through Heaven to the infinite realms beyond. He thinks Malcolm has come up with an interesting gimmick. Too bad about those hit men.

The Very Reverend Jimmy Earl. No twinkle in *this* eye. Average height, average looks, blessed with an astonishing abundance of non-graying hair, pudgy in body and face, frowning browed. He's a Christian of the crusading sort. Jimmy Earl envisions evil being destroyed by the sword, not, like Brother Harry, by the mantra. Actually, Reverend Jimmy was born and reared in Southern California himself, but he knew enough about America's unquestioning acceptance of regional stereotypes to found his religio-political pressure group in South Carolina and to adopt a very genuine-sounding South Carolinian accent. His organization is the Children of God, or COG. It is of the anal-retentive fundamentalist, or ARF, persuasion. In the privacy of his thoughts, and of course he would never say this aloud, he sneeringly calls his movement Christian Repetitionism. His suit is very expensive.

Malcolm Erskine. Brilliant channeler of star-dwelling Merskeenians, prophet of a New Age, best-selling author, conductor of expensive and fully booked seminars, herald of innovations in business techniques, suddenly woozy victim of cheap champagne, spineless wimp who is trying to move his chair away from that of Jimmy Earl and toward

Cal Shegitz. Handsome astronomer, exemplar of the public scientist, professional Brilliant Intellectual Guy, host of documentaries, witness before Congressional committees, author of articles in *Parade* magazine. Off-camera, he is someone Malcolm Erskine admires for his work at undermining pseudo-science. On-camera, he is an enemy for the same reason.

Atlantica. Famous channeler of Mellabenth, an ancient warrior from Atlantis. If Malcolm can't be squelched, Atlantica's name is mud.

Atlantica, too, lives in California. ("The country is on a tilt," Eric Sevareid once said, "and everything loose is sliding toward California.") Atlantica charges astonishing fees to attend one of her channeling sessions. There, a fleecee is granted the unique opportunity to see Atlantica grow in stature, lower in voice pitch, and spew forth meaningless oracularisms. Atlantica lives a very pleasant life of rustic bliss and horses and limousines and antique furniture. She is determined that this Erskine fellow and his absurd Lukas of Aldebaran not be allowed to undermine it. Mellabenth has some ideas about that.

Camera pans audience, showing the tall, muscular, shaven-headed host standing amidst the masses, allying himself with them against the vicious enemies on the stage. Lacking room to dance around, he is bobbing up and down on the balls of his feet. He exudes the barely restrained aggressiveness his audiences love.

Why am I here? wonders Malcolm. Why did I agree to this?

"Today's topic," Johnny shouts, "is channeling ancient beings in order to gain wisdom for today, or advice for living in today's world. Okay, okay." He calms the audience, who snicker and hoot and in general behave quite badly. "Let's give these folks a chance to speak their piece. Then you can ask your questions and tear them into bloody, bleeding, disgusting chunks of PUTRID FLESH!" Regains control of himself, lowers voice. "Our main guest today is Mr. Malcolm Erskine, who has written the bestselling book *Business Secrets from the Stars."*

Malcolm raises his hand unenthusiastically.

"Okay. And we also have with us blah, blah, blah." Johnny introduces the other guests. "Okay. Let's start with Ms. Atlantica. Ms. Atlantica, you also channel an ancient being. However, yours is from ancient Atlantis, the way I understand it. Mellabenth from ancient Atlantis, right?"

Atlantica nods. She is happy. She will absolutely cream this upstart, Erskine. "That's right, Johnny. And Mellabenth has told me to say that Mr. Erskine is clearly a fake, someone simply trying to make a buck off the gullibility of the masses."

Malcolm laughs aloud. "Shocking," he says, shaking his head. "To think that anyone would even think of conning the gullible masses. I just don't know what this world is coming to."

Johnny tries to say something, but Atlantica doesn't give him a chance.

"Oh, yeah? Are you trying to say I'm not really channeling an ancient Atlantean warrior? Well, let's see you do this, buster!" She frowns, concentrates. She begins to grow in height and girth. Her head swells and arteries throb in her neck. Her voice drops in pitch an octave or two. Her eyes widen and glare at Malcolm and the audience. Spittle flying, she growls in a huge, masculine basso, "I say to you, Malcolm Erskine is engaged in a con game. Evil will befall any who heed him!" The special effects disappear, and Atlantica detumesces to her normal small, blonde, rather attractive self. "Can you match that?" she asks smugly.

It didn't work when I tried to do it for Fancy, Malcolm remembers. Maybe I should try again.

Once again, he holds his breath, squeezes as though he were on the toilet and constipated, and makes growling noises.

His head begins to feel like an inflated balloon. The cheap champagne begins to gurgle back up his esophagus. Once again, Malcolm decides that this could have serious medical consequences.

Letting all his blood drain back to its normal places, and then waiting a few more seconds for the champagne to subside, Malcolm assumes a superior look and says, "Lukas of Aldebaran wants me to say that such silliness is beneath him. It is beneath his dignity. He will speak only to me, and I will then pass along his words. He also wishes me to say that he has encountered Mellabenth of Atlantis on the astral plane and he wants everyone here to know that Mellabenth was always a pretentious idiot and has not changed, not even after death. Cheap tricks and special effects are no proof of divine inspiration. If you wish for enlightenment, buy and read the book I have dictated to my dear friend, Malcolm Erskine. If you, Ms. Atlantica, wish to learn to see the truth behind the veil of unknowing, Mr. Erskine will be glad to instruct you on a private basis."

The two contenders retire glowering to their corners, one frustrated, the other sighing deeply in relief.

This isn't so bad, Malcolm tells himself. I can handle it.

"We'll be back in a minute, after this word from our sponsor," says the host. After the red light on the television camera fades away, he addresses his guests. "Dynamite, guys. Good round. Keep it up."

During the commercial, Johnny chats with members of the audience, perhaps preparing for the part of the show in which audience members ask the guests challenging and discomfiting questions. The guests avoid looking at each other, wait out the sixty seconds, wonder why they've let themselves in for this.

Lights, camera, action. The ordeal begins again.

Johnny: "Now I'd like to turn to our guest scientist of the day, Dr. Cal Shegitz, famous brilliant person. Dr. Shegitz, Mr. Erskine, right there on your right, has become, almost overnight, the most famous channeler in America, maybe in the world. He says he's the conduit, if you will, for a being who was an upper-level executive with a star-spanning corporation many thousands of years ago. What do you have to say to that?"

Shegitz focuses his brilliant eyes on Malcolm and fixes him with a brilliant stare. "I just want to ask Mr. Erskine to do one thing for me," he says in his brilliant voice. "Prove it."

You shit, thinks Malcolm. Why aren't you out arresting fake fortune-tellers or something? How'd I ever hurt you?

And yet Malcolm is uncomfortable with this confrontation. In his pre–channeling life, he had often cheered the debunking work of Shegitz and his colleagues. For a moment, Malcolm's conscience manages to struggle back to life.

"Well, Mr. Erskine?" prompts Johnny. "Isn't there something you'd like to say?"

Yes, Mr. A. I'd like to say that I've been in love with your wife for years. Resolutely, Malcolm suppresses his conscience. Think of the bucks, he reminds himself.

"Yes. I'd just like to ask Dr. Shegitz how he and his fellow scientists measure love? Or justice? Or God?"

"Come, now," says Shegitz impatiently. "You're trying to confuse the issue. Those are abstractions, whereas in your book, you make very material claims."

But Malcolm knows he's on a roll, he's got the rationalists on the run, they're wobbly, they're dropping their guard! More accurately, Malcolm has redefined the high ground. Even Atlantica is nodding, supporting him: We hucksters of fuzzy–mindedness must stick together!

Malcolm raises his voice to override the other man's. "Oh, yes, narrow–minded *science* may try to tell you that if you can't measure it, it doesn't exist. Hah! In fact, hah–hah! They laughed at Galileo, they laughed at Einstein, they laughed at Gandhi. Now they laugh at us—at me, at a visionary woman like Atlantica, at...at...at others. But the people whom we help know that what we say is real.

"You see, Doctor," he becomes condescending, "there's a wider reality than you are aware of, a greater universe. You can only measure a small part of the universe, only sense a small section of the whole, because you limit yourself to what your instruments can see. But what of the human mind, eh? What of the greatest instrument of all, the human heart, eh? Why don't you open yourself to the wonders around you instead of limiting yourself to the small, drab, colorless part of reality inside your laboratory?"

Once again, Malcolm has the experience of listening to himself speak, as though another intelligence is in charge of his mouth—and a rather silly intelligence, at that. Remember the bucks, he thinks desperately, fighting his urge to contradict his own words.

Atlantica jumps to Malcolm's defense. The audience separates into warring factions—verbal war, so far, but glares are being exchanged and hands are being clenched into fists. Johnny calls for another commercial and spends the interval calming everyone down.

"We're back!" cries Johnny at the end of the break.

He's looking at a sheet of paper.

"Mr. Erskine, before we continue with our other guests, I'd like you to respond to something I have here. We tried to get a representative of the Church of Scientology on today's show, but that didn't work out. However, the church did send along the following statement, which I have here, and which I'd like you to respond to. I quote. 'The entity Malcolm Erskine claims to be channeling, Lukas of Aldebaran, is quite real. In ancient times, he was the enemy of mankind's ancestral stellar god-kings. Therefore, we wish to warn the public that this entity is a very dangerous one. Anyone paying attention to what the entity says through the mouth of his human stooge, Malcolm Erskine, is risking the onset of a whole raft of very damaging engrams. Warning! If you have spent any time and money reading Malcolm Erskine's book or attending one of his seminars, you are surely already encrusted with engrams, which seriously retard your progress toward cleardom. Go to your nearest Church of Scientology office immediately for help. We hope that Malcolm Erskine will stop listening to that dangerous voice from the past and will himself come to one of our offices for a complete engrammatic analysis before it's too late.'"

"Hmm," Malcolm says. "Well, I'm afraid it's already too late. I'm irreparably saturated with my own form of clearness, which gives me the enviable ability to see through fake religions, and which thus also makes it impossible for me to take Scientology seriously. Perhaps your famous wife might want to interview me, Johnny. I could explain my views in more detail that way."

Malcolm pauses expectantly, but Johnny merely stares—or glares—at him steadily.

Malcolm sighs in defeat and concentrates on the matter at hand. "I must say, though, Johnny, that I can only hope that when *I'm* dead, I'll be able to write science-fiction novels that are even half as commercially successful as those written on the other side of the veil by the most famous Scientologist of them all."

Johnny looks at the reddening faces of engram-free clears in his audience and decides to move along to another adversary.

"Reverend Jimmy Earl, I understand you also think Mr. Erskine actually is channeling a real being, but, like the Church of Scientology, you don't think this being should be trusted?"

Jimmy Earl glares at Johnny because the host has made most of his speech for him. "That's right," he says, opening his mouth the minimum necessary to let the two words out. But then he turns his glare on Malcolm and seems to gain motivation from the way the world's greatest channeler shrinks away from him.

"Although I'd hate to have anyone think I agree with the Scientologists' kooky theology," Jimmy Earl continues, "they're at least partly on the right track. I have no doubt that Erskine is really tuning in on some cosmic voice. But you see, Johnny, the problem is that this voice he hears is actually the voice of the Devil, or at least one of his subordinate demons. In short, a demonic spirit."

Jimmy Earl tries to affect heartiness, warmth, and fatherly concern. It's the sort of pose he does well on the television screen, and those watching the show on television are fooled by it. But Malcolm, sitting so close to him, can feel the man's underlying malevolence as if it were a physical force. Malcolm would have pooh–poohed the idea of a demonic spirit before this encounter. Now he thinks he's sitting next to one.

"You know," Jimmy Earl continues, really getting into the mood, voice getting deeper and louder, face reddening, heart rate increasing, testosterone production rising, "I just hope our friend Malcolm here can pull back in time, before the evil fiend sinks his hooks fully into his soul and drags him kicking and screaming down into the bottomless pit, into the eternal fire that burns and sears and melts forever, without cease or respite." He turns the full force of his hate–filled stare on Malcolm.

Shades of Jack on that call–in radio program in Piketon! Malcolm tries to drive that thought away. It's an unsettling coincidence, this similarity between what a weird, anonymous voice said on the telephone in Piketon and what this frightening preacher and political lobbyist is saying now on television. But of course it *is* only a coincidence. Surely.

"Hey, man," Brother Harry says with a lazy, Southern–Californian chuckle, "chill out, dude. Look, it's like getting two radio stations mixed up, you know? Two signals, I mean. Overlapping. Sometimes it's hard to sort that out, two crossed signals like that, but you can do it if you try.

"Now, Malcolm, he's just encountering a lot of static and everything, and so he's a bit confused. He's picking up some good stuff, see, real information, like maybe from some guys in flying saucers way out there or something, but he's got a lot of noise in there, too, so he's not hearing the words right. The Word, I mean, the Logos. But that doesn't mean he's hearing a message from the Nether Regions, right?" He laughs loudly. "I mean, hey, if that was the case, if everyone who's a bit confused about his inner voice is really listening to the Devil, then we're all in a whole shitload of trouble, right? Hey, Jimmy Earl? You, especially."

At this point, Johnny and a detachment of studio security men have to intervene to prevent a fistfight between the two ministers of Jesus. The brawl spreads quickly into the audience. Fists and blood fly abundantly. The show comes to an abrupt end.

Theological disagreements can be *so* disruptive.

The glow of his televised triumph over his opponents faded as time passed, and once again Malcolm found himself obsessed with the emptiness of his personal life.

Reverend Jimmy Earl would have had a public answer to that problem, Malcolm knew—something about accepting Jesus as his personal savior. Jimmy Earl's private, personal answer to the existential dilemma of human existence was obviously a bit different. It was more along the lines of feed the masses the nonsense they crave and charge them well for it. The first answer was philosophically repellent to Malcolm, and he had already succeeded with his own version of the second without it bringing him real satisfaction.

For a while, Malcolm was able to occupy himself with moving to Redland Heights, where he had bought a mansion that had once belonged to an oil multimillionaire who now lived about eight miles away in a cardboard box under a highway overpass.

One of Malcolm's next-door neighbors, if one can speak of neighbors when the distances between houses are so great, was Pastor Carol O'Hair. Neither man was yet aware of this.

Malcolm's downtown condominium, which once would once have seemed a luxury almost beyond reason, had come to seem cramped. And he had ceased to find living in the center of the city exciting. Instead, he now found it noisy and crowded and frequently scary. He felt that the tranquil spaces and lovely vistas of Redland Heights fit better with his new life as one of the world's most successful authors.

Malcolm had always been organized about his writing but disorganized about everything else in his life. Even though he'd been living in his condominium for a relatively short time, the place was a mess, and as he boxed his belongings for the move, he kept finding items he had forgotten about. One of them was a slip of paper with Steve Golden's number on it.

Wow, Malcolm thought, Steve Golden! He still owes me a bunch of beers on the occasion of my divorce. I could use that right now. Moving is thirsty work.

Somewhat to Malcolm's surprise, the telephone number was still good. Also to his surprise, Steve didn't seem delighted to hear from him.

"I left you a few messages after I was laid off," Steve said, his tone chilly. "I was surprised that you didn't call back."

"Oh, my gosh, I never got them! I wondered what had happened to you." Although, now that he thought about it, he remembered that he had gotten those messages but had erased them. He had intended to call Steve, really he had, but it had slipped his mind in the midst of all the exciting things that had been happening to him. "You know I finally made it, don't you?" he asked, feeling happy all over again.

"Yes. I've seen the book being advertised. Congratulations."

"Thanks. It's really been great. Major lifestyle change. Freedom from worrying about money. Remember how we used to talk about that all the time?"

"I remember."

"Well, it's been even better than we used to imagine. So how're you doing?"

"Well enough. It was rough after I was laid off, but after a while I got hired by a really nice small software company. I like the people, and I like the work."

"There's no security in a small company, Steve. You should try to get back in with one of the big ones."

Steve laughed—a harsh and bitter sound. "You think there's any more security in a big company?"

"Sure. You just have to keep your head down and play the game. Don't get noticed. You know, the way it was at dear old Western Bell."

"That worked for you, did it?"

"Well, obviously! I stayed there as long as I wanted to, and I quit on my own schedule, not on theirs, with my dignity and self-respect intact."

"I see."

Somehow, the conversation hadn't sparked in the old way. Malcolm felt he was making all the effort, and Steve wasn't holding up his end. Malcolm knew what to say to remedy that, though, what topic would get Steve's juices flowing.

"How's your writing going, Steve?"

"I don't write any more. Wasn't worth the time or the effort. I'm a software guy. I'm happier this way."

"Oh. Well, okay." Wait a minute! Politics was a better bet to get Steve going than books. "So what do you think about that guy in the White House?"

"I try not to think about him. Can't do anything about it, anyway. I focus on the people I'm close to and on my work."

"Um, so, how'd you like to go out for a beer? A couple of beers?" Malcolm forced a laugh. "Maybe ten."

"I'll take a rain check on that," Steve said. "I'll call you some time. Bye."

"Oh, right. Okay. Bye." Malcolm hung up, feeling puzzled and hurt. Then it struck him. Golden was jealous! Instead of congratulating his old friend on finally achieving the dream they had both talked about so often, Golden was seething with envy. What a self-centered jerk!

Well, fuck you, Golden, Malcolm thought. I don't need you. I've got that career, literary fame, literary success, money, my new house.

He threw himself back into the task of moving with even greater energy than before, if with no more organization.

Moving his belongings, buying additional furniture for the many large rooms in the new house, and finally simply glorying in possessing the lovely place held his attention for quite a while.

And then, inevitably, the novelty wore off and Malcolm felt empty and bored again.

It's just a phase I'm going through, he told himself. I need even more sex. No, I need the right *kind* of sex. Yeah, that's it! I need...I need...I need Marlene's special tongue technique!

He sobbed aloud, for he knew that it wasn't really the MSTT he missed so much as Marlene's evil, destructive, but always fascinating personality. Where would he ever find her match?

Or could his problem really be that he was no longer writing?

Having admitted to himself that he was burned out on sexual adventure and variety—something he would once never have thought possible—and tired of mouthing nonsense before rooms full of gullible yuppies, he tried to resurrect his erstwhile habit of writing fiction for at least an hour every evening. He was horrified to find that he had been done in by an auctorial version of Gresham's Law. The welter of bad prose he had produced in the form of *Business Secrets from the Stars* had driven from him the ability to produce good prose.

Malcolm's artistic enthusiasm wasn't increased when he made the mistake of showing up, after a long absence, at the old writing workshop. He had expected to be greeted with deference, even awe. He was, after all, the local boy made very, very good. Instead, the reaction was condescension. He thought he detected a trace of contempt.

Worst of all, Larry Lefkowitz was crowing about having sold that damned revolution book, now titled *Lighting the Lamp: a Novel of the Second American Revolution,* to Stuffy Press. Apparently it had also somehow become transformed into a fierce political satire. Malcolm couldn't imagine Lefkowitz writing—or even saying—a single amusing line, but obviously he had been able to fool Stuffy.

"This is the book that will destroy the Jibber administration!" Lefkowitz crowed. "As well as make my literary reputation. And I owe it all to our fearless leader." He nodded toward the paternally beaming Joe Hoffman and laughed, and everyone laughed along with him, except for Malcolm, who of course ground his teeth. "Joe, your literary critiques and your professional advice and your support, and hell, even the title of the book—well, I would have given up long ago if not for you. Thank you, man." He choked up. Everyone choked up, although one member of the group was choking on bile.

And yet, even though Lefkowitz was intolerable and his sudden success was infuriating and the whole Hoffman tribute was inexcusable, Malcolm had to admit that the man had clawed his way to this point by constant effort and refusal to surrender. Being supported by his wife while he wrote full time hadn't hurt, sure, but he had been writing steadily and determinedly even before that. And most of all, most galling and humiliating for Malcolm to admit, Lefkowitz had not compromised his beliefs. He had insisted on being who he really was, on being his real self, on writing what he really thought.

Whereas I, Malcolm admitted, feeling horribly depressed, have become a prostitute.

On the other hand, he rallied, I'm one of the higher paid ones.

On the third hand, I have trouble sleeping with myself.

On the fourth hand—no, wait, it's still the third hand—I don't have anyone else to sleep with right now.

Once again, he wondered what Mrs. Lefkowitz looked like.

Malcolm bought a copy of the Lefkowitz book as soon as it was available. It was good. It was very good indeed. That was the second most depressing thing about it. The most depressing thing was the glowing cover quote from Joe Hoffman.

Lamp zoomed up the fiction bestseller lists. Everyone was talking or writing about it. Larry Lefkowitz was an even bigger local star than Joe Hoffman, who seemed genuinely happy about his protégé's success. Lefkowitz certainly received far more respect in the small social circle of Piketon science-fiction writers than Malcolm did.

So it was scarcely surprising that Malcolm found it hard to drum up much enthusiasm for writing the next business advice scam book. Moreover, silly as the Business Secrets scam was, he still found that it took up a good deal of his time. There were financial records to maintain, tax papers to file, class records and handouts to prepare. Even his almost stream-of-consciousness lectures took a certain amount of forethought. He found even one hour of writing a night difficult to achieve just because of lack of time, entirely apart from the lack of inspiration and artistic self-discipline.

When Mongo showed up at his door, Malcolm was thinking of simply quitting the whole silly business and finding some quiet place to work on being a writer of solid fiction once again. After all, he told himself, I've got enough money. I've made enough from this scam to take care of me for life, as long as I don't overdo it to a monstrous degree.

Mongo changed his mind quickly.

Malcolm had never met Mongo—didn't, in fact, even know the man existed. His existence, however, as he filled the doorway and stared down at Malcolm with a lack of expression, was hard to ignore.

Malcolm looked up at Mongo, and a shiver ran down his spine. It was late evening. Finding this strange, disturbing monster at his front door was not reassuring.

"Yes?" Malcolm said. "Hello? Wrong number?"

Mongo smiled ever so faintly and entered, brushing Malcolm aside. Malcolm thought of leaving the door open so that the neighbors could hear his screams. Then he looked at Mongo again and realized that, if mayhem were intended, he probably wouldn't have time to scream, so he closed the door and followed Mongo into the house. "Yes?" he said again.

"Name's Mongo. I work for Mr. Flicker."

Relief washed over Malcolm. A MegaFlicker messenger boy, that was all. Nothing to worry about. He upbraided himself for his moment of fear. To compensate, and to restore his self–respect, he assumed a lofty, superior tone. "So, you have some sort of message for me from Jimmy?"

Mongo nodded. "Sort of message, yes. Mr. Flicker wants to know when you'll be done with the best–selling sequel to *Business Secrets from the Stars.*"

Malcolm tilted his head back so that he could at least give the appearance of staring down his nose at Mongo. "Sequel! Don't be silly, fellow. One book like that is more than the world needs. I'm thinking of quitting the whole idiocy and going back to being just a writer. A *real* writer, I mean. A writer of real books. Tell Jimmy I'll be in touch with him soon about winding up our relationship."

Mongo snickered so softly that Malcolm wasn't sure he had really heard anything.

"Oh, say," Mongo said, "I don't think you want to tell Mr. Flicker anything like that. I think you want to tell him when your best–selling sequel will be finished and ready to send to your publisher."

It was one of Mongo's greatest talents that he could communicate the idea of a deadly threat without having to put it into words. He had succeeded in communicating it to Malcolm, but Malcolm foolishly decided that he must have misunderstood the man.

"There won't be a sequel," Malcolm said. "Didn't you understand? And I'm dropping this seminar business entirely. I've made enough money to satisfy myself."

"But not enough to satisfy Mr. Flicker. He told me to tell you that if you don't come up with that sequel very soon, before someone produces a book that beats yours out, he'll have to find a substitute for you. He'll have to hire someone to write the sequel."

Malcolm thought about that. "You know, that's not such a bad idea! I could get on with my real life, and someone else could do all the stupid writing stuff, and I'd still be getting lots of royalties out of it. Yes, I like that!"

Mongo shook his head fractionally, less a movement from side to side than a quiver. "Mr. Flicker doesn't operate that way. When he replaces people, that means he doesn't need them any longer. Mr. Flicker doesn't approve of dead wood."

Suddenly, Jimmy Flicker's voice came back to Malcolm: "Great bunch of people, now that I had the dead wood murdered. Cheaper'n laying them off."

Malcolm found he barely had enough breath to ask, "What's your job at MegaFlicker?"

"Director of Cosmic Outplacement." Mongo squeezed his hands into fists casually, then relaxed them again. The crackling of his knuckles filled the room.

"Six months," Malcom croaked. He leaned against a nearby chair—a newly purchased expensive antique—for support.

"What about six months?"

"To write a book. Five months."

"Takes you that long?" Mongo's eyebrows moved microscopically closer together in what might have been the ghost of the suggestion of a frown. "Mr. Flicker won't be happy with that."

"Four months."

The frown became almost visible. "Mr. Flicker's afraid someone else will beat you to the punch way before that."

"Three months, then. Christ Almighty, man, what am I supposed to say?"

"Say 'one month.'"

Malcolm groaned. "One month," he whispered.

"Good. I'll see if I can get Mr. Flicker to go along with that."

"You'll let me know his answer, won't you?"

Mongo looked Malcolm up and down carefully, as if measuring him for some purposes of his own which Malcolm would be much better off knowing nothing about. "One way or another." He vanished.

Malcolm closed the front door, locked it carefully, and then went all over the house, checking that every door and window was properly bolted. He had the feeling that it didn't matter—that Mongo could walk through the wall if he wanted to. Not by any supernatural means, either.

Mongo! he thought. What a name! An absurd name. Is he supposed to be from the planet Mongo, like the guy in Flash Gordon?

No, said a nasty little voice, from the twin planets Fear and Agony.

Marlene Malevolent! Malcolm needs you yet again!

"Uh, hi, Marlene?"

"Ho, ho, ho! Do I sound like her?" Rich, deep, expensive chuckle. Fred Seicht, of course. Had the bastard moved in already, with his designer suits, his designer voice, and his designer dick?

In my bed! Malcolm thought.

Your ex–bed, his nastier self reminded him.

"I mean, could I speak to Marlene, please?" Please! Why in God's name am I saying please? Put down my ex–phone and let me speak to my ex–wife, you shithead!

"And whom shall I say is calling?"

Malcolm ground his teeth and brought himself under control with considerable effort. "Your predecessor, you prick!" he screamed into the receiver. Not just a prick, but a grammatical ignoramus. Knowing that, however, did not make Malcolm feel any better.

"Oh. Okay." Seicht held the receiver away from his mouth and called out, "Sweetheart! It's the teeny weenie!"

Malcolm heard Marlene giggle in the background and he almost hung up. But the moment passed and Marlene's voice came purring over the line. "Hi, there, Tiny Tim. What's up? I already know what's up over here. Giggle, snort, stop that, wait a minute, oh, Fred, not now!"

Could Mongo be any worse than this? Could physical agony resulting in death really be any more awful than the mental torture Marlene was so adept at subjecting him to? After very little thought, Malcolm decided that at the hands of Mongo it probably could, and so he pressed on with his prepared speech.

"I've been thinking, Marlene. I've been thinking about your idea of my hiring you as my business manager. I think you could do a really fine job for me. Hell—" conspiratorial laugh "—I *know* you could, so—"

Marlene interrupted. "Stop trying so hard, Malcolm. You're in some kind of shit, and you're turning to me. Am I right?"

"Well, um..." He sighed. "Well, in a manner of speaking, you're kind of right."

How did she do that? How did she gloat across the telephone line without saying a word or making a sound? What talents this woman had! Even now, after all those years of marriage and divorce and continuing attempts at mutual destruction, he was still learning things about her.

"It'll cost you, sweetie-pie lover-guy," said Madame Malefica.

"Oh, of course. Well, sure, Marlene. I was planning to offer you a good deal. High five figures, benefits to be negotiated."

Marlene chuckled—Seicht's obnoxious chuckle transposed from

bass to treble clef. "Let's start talking six, plus a percentage of the gross."

"Christ, Marlene!"

Her voice turned to honey and rose petals. "And I'll throw in my special tongue technique as part of the deal."

Malcolm was feeling so emasculated at the moment that that offer was less inducement than it would once have been.

Before Malcolm could say anything, Fred Seicht's voice boomed out in the background. "Hey, wait a minute, now! Just what the hell're you talking about to that twit?"

Marlene, her voice so cold it made Malcolm fear he might get frostbite even over the telephone, said, "Shut up, Fred. Go home. I'll call you when I need you again."

Spouting lines that belonged in bad novels—"*You'll* call *me?* When *you* need *me?* Hey, babe, I made you and I can break you!"—Seicht left the house, or so Malcolm deduced from the sound of a slamming door.

"Now then, Malcolm, my dear." It was honey and rose petals again. "Shall I come over there and we can talk terms?"

Oh, my fellow cosmic ray, it is among us a well known truth-statement that an executive of the genuine nova-born class does not hesitate or excessively chew over conflicting options when required to make a decision. Rather he grasps the mightier of the horns of any dilemma and simply dismisses the other. Only thus may the bull of discord be vanquished and contention among subordinates be avoided. Or so Malcolm was told by Lukas of Aldebaran, the star-dwelling Merskeenian, as reported on Page 342 of *Business Secrets from the Stars.*

Well, there is *some* truth to that crap after all, Malcolm thought, making a snap decision with a gusto that would have delighted any onlooking Merskeenian executive, if there had been one looking on. If, for that matter, the Merskeenians had ever existed.

"Tell ya what, babe," he said grandly, "you draw up a contract and bring it over, and I'll probably just sign it with very few changes. How's that sound?" For not only was his need for someone to handle all his business while he tried to grind out a sequel to *Business Secrets from the Stars* that would be acceptable to Jimmy Flicker a desperate one, but also, as he had just realized, employing Marlene and keeping her busy and beholden to him was the perfect way to keep her apart from Fred Seicht.

"Why, Malcolm, how sweet! How about, um, ten tomorrow morning?"

Honey and roses, roses and honey. Malcolm smiled, feeling better than he had since the looming up of Mongo.

Or was that really not honey, but molasses? Certainly there was about Marlene more than a faint hint of sulfur.

In the meantime, two old men read through the very small telephone directory in Pawnee, Oklahoma. There was not a single listing for a man named Malcolm. They looked at each other in something approaching discouragement. Each one thought the other one looked awful, exhausted, close to being translated by Mother Nature. Since both were heavily armed and had killed dozens of men, many of them named Malcolm, neither chose to mention how bad the other looked. Instead, they crossed Pawnee off their list of towns and cities beginning with P and trudged back to their car.

CHAPTER THIRTEEN

Oh, what wonders Marlene worked during her first days on the job! It was enough to make Malcolm wonder why he had ever felt unhappy during their marriage. Suddenly he could remember only the happy times together—the first week of marriage—and the special tongue technique, which had actually improved during their time apart. He wasn't quite as emasculated as he had thought.

If it had not been for the swift approach of the deadline he had negotiated with Mongo, Malcolm would have been happy.

As he sat staring at his blank computer screen trying to squeeze from his equally blank brain more words of Merskeenian wisdom, Marlene was efficiently juggling calls, appointments, bills, letters, appeals for advice or blessings, bookkeeping, and his sexual needs. These were the very details which had been overwhelming him before, although now they seemed insignificant in comparison with Mongo.

Mongo dominated his thoughts, driving out whatever creativity of the *Business Secrets from the Stars* sort Malcolm might otherwise have had left.

"Look, dear," Marlene came into his study to say brightly. "Our net worth is up another zillion dollars."

At another time, Malcolm might have reacted to that word "our." This time, he kept staring at his blank screen and muttered, "Mongo."

Marlene came in to say, again brightly, "I've got your seminars fully booked through the next year, beloved darling. We'll clear at least five googol dollars from the marks."

"Mongo."

Marlene again, brightly again, although perhaps with a growing hint of impatience. "Very good news, oh heartthrob beyond compare. I express-mailed a copy of *Business Secrets from the Stars* to George Lucas, and one of his people just called to say that he read it, loved it, intends to use all of your cosmic principles from now on in running his businesses, and he's instructed his lawyers to keep their hands off you because you are clearly a major manifestation in this time and place of the light side of the Force, or something along those lines."

For a moment, Malcolm's mood lightened. "Gee, that *is* good news!" Then his face sagged and his gloom returned and he sighed and said, "Mongo."

"God damn it, you spineless wimp!" Marlene shouted.

Malcolm tore his eyes from the screen and looked at her, framed in the doorway of his study. The Marlene of sweetness and light, honey and roses who had been living with him for the last few days had vanished, replaced by the Marlene who had been so much more familiar to him for so many years.

"That's you!" she shrieked. "Sit on your ass and let the world push you around, and then whine about your problems. Get moving on it!"

Malcolm shrank back in his chair and whispered, "Mong—Marlene."

"Use your situation! *Use* your problems. Isn't that what writers are supposed to do? Make a book out of the danger you're in!" She spun about and marched away, down the hall to her own office.

Slowly Malcolm straightened. Hmm, he said to himself. She has a point. Stars, stars...*Defense of the Stars, Freedom among the Stars*...Naah. No zing. Wait! Stick with the tried and true! *Business Dangers from the Stars!* Yes!

His fingers scurried about the keyboard and words poured across the screen.

Down the hall, in her sumptuous office, Marlene straightened from her work and concentrated. Her predator's ears quivered, acquired the signal, locked in. Malcolm was typing.

She nodded in satisfaction and retracted her claws. The boy was good for a few more bucks. She wouldn't have to tear his throat out yet.

Heed me now, oh my interstellar beloveds, fellow spawn of the incomparable throbbing heart of a cousin star. When your unmatched efforts and clear moral superiority to the masses and strict adherence to the principles explained in my first channeled book have been rewarded with power, riches, and exalted position, it will happen that the slime, the curs, the worms, the excrement beneath you will look at up your eminence and be consumed with jealousy, and they will try to destroy you and pull you down to their own nauseating level. They might, for example, send large men to inflict pain upon you. Or perhaps the threat will take the form of succubi who will try to drain you of your cosmic life-force by the use of exotic pleasure techniques. Learn, then, how I, Lukas of Aldebaran, and my fellow corporate heroes Paulus and Henricus dealt with such dangers in the long-ago time that is yet coincident with your own time through the vibrational interface of the etheric planes.

But first let me remind you of the deeds of M'Lersk, who rescued your very own ancestors from the dread Marlingas. Oh, what a hero was he! And oh, what unutterably evil creatures were they!

Oh, yeah, Malcolm told himself. Mammon House'll love it. The marks will eat it up. Flicker will call off Mongo. Everything's going to be okay again!

Oh, silly Malcolm.

After one week, Malcolm had one hundred adequate pages done. When inspiration ran dry, he was able to recycle short stories he had written years earlier but never sold, changing the good guys into Merskeenians and the bad guys into Marlingas or rival businessmen. All he had to do was keep up that rate of production, and he would have the life–saving book done by the end of the month Mongo had allowed him. Which meant he had to avoid any interruptions.

Marlene was fending off all such interruptions, whether telephonic or in person, with her usual competence. Not only did this help Malcolm by giving him the time he needed to write *Business Dangers from the Stars,* but it also kept her far too busy to spend any time with Fred Seicht, as Malcolm was sure she had been planning to do. Just call me Malcolm the Arch Manipulator, he told himself. He rather liked the sound of that.

However, after one week, Mongo loomed in to see if Malcolm was producing as promised, and not even Marlene could keep Mongo out.

It was Sunday morning, and Malcolm was sitting before his computer, happily producing nonsense, when chills began running up and down his spine and his hair stood at attention.

"Mongo!" he said. He turned around, and there was Mongo,

reading over his shoulder and nodding.

"Pretty good," Mongo said in his quiet basso. "How many pages?"

"A—a hundred. And fifty. Hundred fifty."

Mongo nodded again. "One hundred pages. Keep it up."

If I can ever get it up again, Malcolm thought.

Mongo turned to Marlene. "I know the way out, ma'am. Next time, don't try to stop me." He left.

Marlene and Malcolm listened intently, holding their breaths. They heard a faint creak from the stairway, then a slight *click* as the front door closed. Then they both breathed again.

For the first time, Malcolm noticed that Marlene was massaging her left shoulder with her right hand.

Alarmed, Malcolm said, "Christ, did he hurt you?"

"Only slightly. If he wanted to, I bet he could *really* hurt a girl."

And now for the first time Malcolm noticed that she was breathing faster than normal, her cheeks were pink, and her eyes were wide and bright.

"Oh, Jesus," he said, "what next? You mean that for all those years, you never told me that you like to have men hurt you?"

Marlene looked at him in scorn. "Not *you,* for God's sake. Get back to the book."

"Pervert."

"Wimp."

Malcolm was trying to come up with something that would hurt, when a large number of clean-cut young men with short haircuts and wearing expensive suits trooped in. Obviously, Mongo had shut the front door but not locked it.

"Christ Almighty!" Malcolm shrieked. "What is this, a fucking convention? I've got work to do!"

The young men looked at Malcolm condescendingly. "Lots of engrams here," one of them said, and the others nodded.

"I have here," the one who had spoken said, bringing from behind his back a small metal box with a light bulb set into its top, "our newest engram–o–meter, which we have specifically designed to help detect the malign presence of Marlingas. The Marlingas who threatened the ancient star–kings who are the ancestors of all of us are still around, as you obviously know. They have evolved to outwardly resemble human beings. By alerting the world to their presence, you, Malcolm Erskine, have done us all a service. The Church of Scientology acknowledges that service and wishes to incorporate your revelation into its own work. You need only modify your seminars and writings to reflect the wisdom revealed by the Founder, and we will be able to absorb you and your organization smoothly and to our mutual benefit." His backup team nodded in unison.

"You mean 'common benefit,'" Malcolm said. "Clearly your box doesn't work. Anyway, I'm not interested. Why should I let you guys in on my game?"

"Because we'll be in on it anyway, with or without you. We've got the manpower and resources to drive you out of business."

"Oh, yeah? Well, *I've* got Mongo."

"Mongo?" The spokesman exchanged a puzzled look with his subordinates.

"The monster you must have passed on the way in."

"Oh." The scientologists all looked unhappy. "Well. Perhaps we'll be going now. Too many engrams here, anyway. I think I'll recommend that all clears stay away from you in case of engram infection. 'Bye, now." They trooped out, down the stairs, and through the front door, looking carefully to left and right as they went.

"My, what a polite bunch of handsome young men," Marlene said. "So healthy and clean cut."

Malcolm glared at her. "Think of them as threats to your income. And lock that damned front door."

"Brothers and Sisters of the Saucer People!" Chirpy, chirpy. "Siblings to all wonderful beings everywhere in God's huge and wonderful Universe! To what galactically enlightened being may I direct your call?"

"Jesus Harvey Christ! You know who I am by now, so just put me through to Harry."

"This is Brother Harry, confidant of star creatures. Please be assured that beautiful beings are on their way in their saucer ships even now to take us all to a better, lovelier place."

"God damn it, Harry."

"Oh. Hello, Fancy."

"Listen, are those two whatever you called them, translators, still on the job?"

"As far as I know. I revved them up and pointed them in the right direction and let them go."

"I've changed my plans. Send out the recall code."

"The what?"

"Jesus, what kind of primitive organization are you running? Call them back. Mission cancelled. No killing."

"Hey, Fancy, girl, mellow out. Like, chill. I told you. Once you turn the key to the ON position with those guys, there's no OFF. They keep going till the job is done or they're dead."

"Oh, shit."

Piketon! That was it! Of course. How could they have forgotten? Thank you, Jesus!

On another Sunday morning, Mongo appeared in Malcolm's study again. This time, Malcolm was sure the front door had been locked. Marlene was apparently in her office, unaware of the presence of the intruder. So Mongo, somehow, had let himself in.

"Well?" Mongo rumbled.

"Two hundred pages," Malcolm said, sweating, babbling. "Okay, actually one hundred ninety eight. But I'm on schedule, see?"

"Mr. Flicker says that some of the your rivals are doing pretty well with seminars and radio shows. Says this book's got to recapture your market share and you've got to get back on the seminar circuit soon as you're done with the book. Also, the word I hear on the street is that some Jesus freak outfit has pointed a couple of hit men in your direction. Professionals. Mr. Flicker says that if you do the job on this book, then I can knock off their hit men. That'll scare off any others. If you don't do the job, we'll just let the guys the freaks hired take care of you for us." He looked Malcolm up and down. "Too bad. I was looking forward to doing that job myself. Cowards are always the most fun."

"But, Mongo, I need protection now! If I get killed by hit men, then I won't be able to finish the book, will I?"

"You'll be dead either way, so why should you care?"

"I think we have a different approach to life, Mongo."

Mongo shook his head. "Nah. It's death we have a different approach to. Keep writing. I'll be checking."

"Two hundred pages!" Malcolm moaned to himself. "Oh, God!" For the truth was that he had been struggling to reach the one-hundred-and-fiftieth page when Mongo appeared. More than going slowly, the book had hardly been going at all during the last couple of days, and he had been despairing once again of finishing by the Mongo-imposed deadline. Now the despair overwhelmed him.

"I've got to have a break!" he screamed. "I've got to get out of here!"

He raced down the stairs and out the front door and into a shrieking blizzard and a temperature of three degrees below zero. In typical Piketon fashion, the seasons had changed almost overnight from high summer to deep winter. Malcolm leaped back into the house, shivering and blue.

Marlene appeared at the top of the stairs. "You idiot. You'll freeze to death if you go outside dressed like that."

"Supposed to be a painless death." That made it seem attractive, a relatively easy way out, compared to the methods of death others seemed to be planning for him.

On the other hand, death in any form was still death. Malcolm didn't know what Mongo had really meant by his cryptic remark, what the immense psycho's approach to death was, but Malcolm did know that, in his own view, death was not a good thing.

He locked the front door. "I think I'll watch television for a little while."

Marlene narrowed her eyes. "How's the book coming?" Her claws extended by half an inch.

"Just passed page two hundred. Right on schedule, see?"

Marlene grunted something and retreated to her office to divert more of Malcolm's money to her Swiss account.

Malcolm went down to the basement level of the house, where he had had a huge room filled with very soft furniture built. It was also equipped with a wet bar, and an immense television screen covered one wall. He mixed himself a drink and flipped on a national cable news channel. They were carrying the Larry Lefkowitz story again, as they had been, it seemed, whenever he turned them on for the last couple of days.

"Oh, Christ," Malcolm said. "He was just some local guy. It's not really a national story, people. Even though he did have a goddamned bestseller. Fiction bestseller." He swallowed his drink and went to the bar to mix another. "Novel. Bestselling novel."

He felt depressed at the death of someone he had known who was younger than he was and pleased that someone who had had so much more success than he had had was dead and guilty that he didn't feel sorry for Larry and Larry's wife, whom Malcolm had never yet met and now probably never would, whatever she looked like. And however much she needs comforting, he thought, and felt really, horribly guilty for thinking such a thing.

The newsreader was a brainless and normally dull, droning, boring young woman, but she repeated the details of this story with an enthusiasm and shining-eyed delight that Malcolm found disturbing. Behind her, the screen displayed a small photo of the body hanging from a streetlight in downtown Piketon.

"In his suicide note," the newsreader said, "the bestselling author spoke of his despair due to the negativity of his life and work. He wrote, 'I am unable to love our leader the way a true American should. This troubles me. I've been laying awake at night worrying about it. I feel so guilty. Can't get it out of my head. Got to put a stop to it. Farewell cruel world.'"

She paused for a moment and shook her head as though awed by Larry's last moment of eloquence. Then she said, "The family has asked that instead of flowers, donations should be made to the local Republican Party organization of your choice."

That lamppost certainly was a high one, Malcolm thought. Who could have imagined that Larry Lefkowitz would have had the strength to climb up that tall, slippery metal pole while carrying a rope, tie one end to the top just behind the light and the other end around his neck, and then jump off? Malcolm shivered at the image and took a large gulp of his drink. What a stupid thing for Lefkowitz to have done. Malcolm couldn't understand it at all. Obviously the kid must have been upset. The grammar in his suicide note was proof enough of that. But what did he have to be upset about? He had success and a happy marriage to a supportive wife.

Unlike me, Malcolm thought, and he swallowed another large

gulp.

The newsreader gave way to an interview with Joe Hoffman. At least this was something new. Malcolm hadn't seen this before.

The voiceover said, "Earlier today, we recorded an interview with Piketon's other famous, brilliant, excellent, topnotch, fascinating, bestselling science-fiction writer, Joe Hoffman, who was widely regarded as having been a mentor to Larry Lefkowitz and indeed to every other science-fiction writer of any importance in the city of Piketon.

"Mr. Hoffman, Larry Lefkowitz often called himself your protégé, and in particular he said that he would never have written *American Lamppost* if not for your encouragement and support and help with the actual writing of the book. You must feel his tragic suicide even more deeply than his millions of fans. It must feel as though your own writing has died, in some sense."

Hoffman smiled nervously at the camera. "Well, you know, Mr. Lefkowitz gave me far too much credit when it came to *Raise the Lantern,* or whatever it was he called that book. I encouraged him to keep writing it because I could tell from the moment I met him that he was a deeply troubled young man, and I thought that actually finishing a novel, even if it never got published, would be good for him psychologically. I thought it might introduce some stability into his life. From what little I read of his manuscript while he was working on it, I wasn't sure it would ever be published, and I certainly didn't agree with the book's political sentiments. Not at all. In fact, I disagreed with his politics vehemently. But anyway, as I said, I thought working on the book would be good for him."

"So you didn't work closely on it with him?"

"No! Oh, no. Not at all. I hardly ever saw the man. Once or twice a year, he would show up at a little writer's workshop we have here in Piketon and show all of us the latest chapters. I think we all found his

writing a bit...Oh, I don't know. Obscure? Is that the word I want? Hard to follow. Except for the political attitudes, which we all found offensive, of course. Bordering on unpatriotic, even. I, especially, felt that way. But we all encouraged him, anyway. For the reasons I gave. Perhaps that was a mistake. Perhaps we should have urged him to just give it all up and concentrate on his regular job."

Good grief, Malcolm thought. Hoffman, were you really that jealous of the guy's success? Or are you just pissed that you don't have a protégé any more? Well, you had your chance to help my career, and you passed that one by, and now I don't need you, you jerk.

Angrily, he hit the PREVIOUS button on the remote control. He didn't remember what channel he had been watching before, but whatever it was, it was bound to be better than trying to endure Joe Hoffman.

It was COG–TV, the cable channel owned by Reverend Jimmy Earl, and Jimmy Earl himself was preaching at the moment.

Malcolm often watched religious cable channels. He thought they provided some of the most entertaining comedy being broadcast. Although Jimmy Earl was a bit less amusing on screen since Malcolm's encounter with him in person.

The real problem with this variety of comedy, however, was that it didn't stay amusing for very long. After a few minutes, Malcolm switched the channel to a local station. It was carrying Pastor Carol O'Hair's weekly show, "Parables from the Pastor."

That palled quickly, too. To amuse himself, Malcolm started pressing the PREVIOUS button and switching back and forth between Jimmy Earl and O'Hair. Only then did he realize how similar the two preachers' messages were that morning. And that both were talking about him.

"This Lukas is a demonic spirit, and this Erskine is under his control," Jimmy Earl said.

"Or possibly consciously in his employ," O'Hair said.

"Maybe, just maybe, this here Lukas of Aldebaran," roared Jimmy Earl with red face and bulging eyes, "is the Devil hisse'f!"

"And we must consider the possibility," O'Hair speculated, "that Mr. Erskine, whether he is merely the dupe of the Evil One or an active and knowing disciple, is here to herald the coming of the Antichrist and the End of Days."

"He must be killed!" Jimmy Earl bellowed. "I call upon all good, true Christians to off the scumball!"

"Those who are true followers of Christ," mused O'Hair, "therefore have as their duty the shortening of Mr. Erskine's time on Earth."

Malcolm watched and listened with his mouth hanging open. He sat through both programs to the end. Then, moving like a zombie, he stood, went upstairs to the front door, took a warm coat from the closet, and stepped out into a brilliant world where the storm had passed and the sun, in a blue sky, shone on a sparkling layer of fresh snow.

Malcolm finished putting on his coat, buttoned it, plunged his hands deep in his pockets, and trudged away through the snow.

A firecracker went off in the distance, and something burned his cheek.

He brushed at the sting and saw blood on his hand.

Another firecracker, and this time snow erupted at his feet.

Malcolm's brain froze in terror, but fortunately his feet started moving. He floundered back through the snow to his front door and made it to safety just as a third bullet shattered a brick in the wall beside the doorway.

CHAPTER FOURTEEN

Ace Detective Lance looked offended. "You got no proof of his involvement, Mr. Erskine. Besides, he's a pillar of the community."

"But O'Hair said in a television sermon that I should be killed, and then someone tried to do it!"

"Could be coincidence. Besides, probably lots of people are saying you should be killed. Goes with being a celeb."

Malcolm sank into one of his many expensive, overstuffed armchairs and put his elbows on his knees and his head in his hands. "And Reverend Jimmy Earl? He said the same thing on TV."

"Outside our jurisdiction. Okay, look, Mr. Erskine. What we got here? We got a guy who's famous. That's you. Then we got person or persons unknown shooting three bullets at the famous guy. Famous guy ducks into house. Shooting over. We recover bullets, find no trace of person or persons. No big deal. Happens two, three times a week in this city. So I'll write up the report, and then we'll file it away, and then some day you'll tell your grandkids about this interesting but minor thing that happened to you."

"If he lives to have any grandkids." That was Marlene's contribution. She didn't seem as upset by the shooting incident as Malcolm was.

Malcolm wondered suddenly what sort of life-insurance policy Erskine Enterprises had taken out on its founder and chief source of income. That was one of the details he had left entirely in Marlene's hands when he hired her.

He remembered something else, though. "I heard there were a couple of hit men after me," he told Ace Detective Lance. "Professionals. Maybe you should look into that angle."

"Who'd you hear that from?"

"Sources."

"Uh huh. Sources. Professional hit men. Right, Mr. Erskine. We'll look into that angle right away."

A uniformed flunky appeared. "Ace Detective Lance, sir?"

Lance turned away from Malcolm with obvious relief. Lance was thirty–one, on the fast track, and he had asked to be assigned to the Erskine shooting because cases involving celebrities usually resulted in useful publicity for him. This Erskine guy, though, was a whining, self–pitying putz who was much more concerned about his own skin than the ace detective's career. "Yes, Officer Flunky?"

"There's a couple of guys outside to see you. They're from the Secret Service."

Lance's eyebrows rose considerably. "No kidding? You checked their IDs?"

Flunky nodded. "You bet, sir."

This was more like it! National recognition for his ability, at last! Maybe he *should* go after Jimmy Earl. Lots of publicity there.

"Bring 'em in."

But the two men who entered, it turned out, were there because of Malcolm and not because of Ace Detective Lance, whom they treated as a nonentity. They brushed aside his fawning and boot licking and repeated offers to help them with their case.

"Yeah, yeah," the taller one said. "Right on, Base Detective. Now, why don't you and your men just leave and go write up your reports, or whatever, and we'll take care of everything here."

The shorter of the two turned his attention to Malcolm. "Sir, you have nothing more to worry about. The Secret Service is here."

"'Are here,' Jerry," the taller Secret Service man said over his shoulder while he watched the crestfallen ace detective of the Piketon Police Department shoo his men out of the house.

"No, Al," the shorter one said, his voice calm but muscles bunching in his jaw, "'is here.' 'Secret Service' is a collective noun."

"Not necessarily, Jerry." Al turned from the door, and his expression gave the lie to the calmness in *his* voice. "You know, before World War One, they used to say, 'the United States *are*', but then, after the war, the usage changed to 'the United States *is.*' However, in Britain, I believe they still say, 'Her Majesty's government *are.*' So you see, it depends on usage, and that can change. Also, I think Fowler explains that it has do with how you intend the noun—as a collective singular, or as a group of individuals acting in concert."

"Bullshit, Al! I don't give a shit about Fowler or Her Majesty or World War One! I'm telling you that modern usage is to treat all U.S. government agency names as collective nouns, which means they take the singular form of the verb!"

"You little asshole!"

By now, the two agents were standing practically nose-to-Adam's-apple. Both faces were red, and veins stood out on both foreheads. Suddenly, a thought struck both simultaneously. They stepped apart and returned to their normal coloring.

"Say," Al said, "this is silly. Why should we be arguing about it when we've got the real authority right here?"

"Yeah," Jerry said. "That's right. Mr. Erskine, you're a genuine professional writer, so you know all about these things. Which one of us is right?"

This is definitely a nightmare, Malcolm thought. I'm actually still back in ninth grade in that old bastard what's-his-name's class and

I'm dreaming all of this. Soon I'll wake up and I'll be sitting behind that sexy little brunette again. Christ, what was *her* name?

"Mr. Erskine?"

"What? Oh, yes, sorry." Reality. The sexy little brunette of long–gone days no doubt was now a mother and no longer sexy. Possibly she was no longer little or brunette, either. "Well, fellows, I have to admit this is not a subject I've ever investigated. You know, I've never written anything about United States government agencies."

"Yeah, say, that's right!" Jerry said. "So how did the Merskeenians say it?"

Malcolm cleared his throat a few times to give himself time to make something up. "Oh, well, actually their language had a special verb form for large collections of individuals acting either as a unit or separately. It didn't really correspond to either the singular or the plural. Now that that's out of the way, what are you fellows here for?"

"To protect you, Mr. Erskine," Al said. "We're going to take you into hiding to protect you against all the people who're out to kill you. You know, kind of like that guy in England who all the Iranians wanted to kill."

"'Whom' all the Iranians wanted to kill," Jerry said immediately.

They turned to Malcolm again in mute appeal.

"Uh, I'm afraid Jerry's right this time, Al. So how are you going to protect me? Lots of armed men surrounding the house all the time, maybe? Armed escorts wherever I go? That could be a bit inconvenient, but I guess I'm willing to put up with it if you are."

Jerry and Al shook their heads. Al said, "No, like I—I mean, *as* I said, Mr. Erskine, sir, we're going to do it the way the Brits protected their guy. We're going to hide you away where no one will ever find you."

A chill ran down Malcolm's spine. "Uh, just where would that be?" Six feet under? "And who told you to do this?"

"Oh, don't you worry, Mr. Erskine, sir. We've been doing this to folks for years, so we know what we're doing. No problems, no pain. I guarantee."

Jerry chimed in, "We can't exactly tell you right out who's behind this, sir, but I *can* tell you that it's a lady you've met before who has played a major role in America's return to pride, self–respect, and standing tall before the world."

"Oh," Malcolm said in relief. "Her."

"'She,'" Jerry corrected. "It's kind of by way of being a personal favor to the lady."

"Wait a minute!" Marlene said. "He can't go into hiding. Erskine Enterprises will lose too much money!"

Jerry and Al turned to her.

"Must be Mrs. Erskine," Jerry said to Al.

"That's it. They said she was staying here," Al said to Jerry.

"Anyway," Jerry said to Al, "the channeler for a great being like Lukas of Aldebaran wouldn't cohabitate with some bimbo he wasn't even married to."

"'Cohabit,' not 'cohabitate,'" Al said.

"Oh, right. That's what I meant."

"If you twits are finished," Marlene said, "I'm the *former* Mrs. Erskine. Remember that. Anyway, we can't afford for Malcolm to go into hiding."

"Can you afford for someone to blow him away?"

Marlene smiled happily while she thought about that image for a moment. "Depends on various things."

"I'll probably be able to do the second book even more quickly in hiding, beloved companion of my days and nights," Malcolm said to her. "Make even more money even faster."

"Okay," Marlene said. "I'll take care of things while you're gone."

"Could be a long time, ma'am," Al said.

"Anyway," Jerry said, "if he's gone, whoever's after him could very well decide to settle for offing you."

"Yeah," Al said. "Kind of a consolation prize, see."

"So we're taking you along," Jerry said.

"Not that we give a shit about you, ma'am," Al said. "Don't get us wrong. It's just that society has a duty to keep great men like Mr. Erskine happy and untroubled."

"I was wondering when society would realize that," Malcolm said.

The four years of carefully controlled public appearances and uncontrolled abuses of power were drawing to a close. Soon it would be time once again to, as the press still put it so quaintly, face the voters.

Various people were thinking about this and making plans.

Every now and then, Gone sparked back to a partial awareness of the world around him. It was as though, Fancy thought, a small group of dying brain cells experienced a final few minutes of life just before sputtering out. It tended to happen when he saw Fancy mentioned on television, which he spent his waking hours watching.

"Look, Mommy," he quavered, pointing in the general direction of the glowing screen. His finger slewed from side to side, but Fancy knew he wanted to draw her attention to whatever was on the television.

He was draped limply on the couch. She was sitting at the large conference table that took up most of the room. She was looking at a sheet of paper and drawing a line in pencil through the names listed on the sheet. One name after the other. A heavy, black line. Sometimes, she pressed so hard that the pencil point broke and she had to sharpen it again by shoving the end of the pencil in the electric pencil sharpener, a machine which calmed her down by giving rise to pleasant, awful fantasies.

"What now?" She looked up.

Felicia Finewine was on the screen. Gone liked her almost as much as Malcolm did, and unlike Marlene, Fancy was willing to indulge her husband in watching the beautiful if stupid newsreader because it kept him quiet.

Fancy hated the woman's hair, though. Why didn't she get it properly styled and permed and shellacked and chiseled?

Then she noticed the picture of Brother Harry hovering seemingly in the air behind Felicia's luscious left shoulder. Fancy ignored the newsreader's faults and concentrated on what she was saying.

"Some kooky guy from a weird saucer cult said today that former First Lady Fancy Away was a member of his organization way back when she was young."

For an instant, Felicia looked surprised at the idea that Fancy had once been young, but then her deeply imbued professionalism reasserted itself, and she schooled her face to neutrality and continued. "The cult is starting a membership drive, and it plans to use the connection with Mrs. Away in its new publicity materials. The kooky guy says that he remembers when Mrs. Away was a real live wire."

That was too much for Felicia, who stopped talking and stared at the teleprompter in disbelief.

"That bastard!" Fancy said.

"Bad word, Mommy!"

"Shut up."

"Okay."

Fancy ground the name "Harry" into the sheet of paper and then drew lines through it over and over, forcing the smashed pencil point deep into the wooden table beneath. "Bastard," she kept muttering.

Fortunately, Gone was too interested in the commercial that had replaced Felicia Finewine to complain again about Fancy's language. He was watching happily as the Western MagnaComm corporate logo changed to the new, even stranger one representing ColossoVerse, the company's new name. A voiceover informed him that more details about the new organization would be forthcoming by way of the company's recently acquired radio network, newspaper chain, and television network, the latter being the one he was watching.

Gone smiled happily. It was all the same to him.

"I'm so bored! This place is driving me nuts! I've got to get out of here!"

How many times had Marlene said that? Malcolm had lost count. Three days had passed in hiding, and she had begun on the afternoon of the first day.

"This place isn't so bad." It was a pleasant enough suburban tract house in Virginia. If not for the humidity, the excess of small life forms, the lack of mountains and winter, and the accents of the locals, Malcolm could have imagined he was back in his ex-house in a middle-class suburb of Piketon. It didn't help that their guardians wouldn't allow Malcolm and Marlene to spend much time outside the house and restricted what outside trips they were allowed to make to short distances and short durations.

"How long will we have to stay here?" she asked.

"Until they feel my life isn't threatened any more. I don't know. Ask Jerry or Al."

Marlene sneered. "Oh, sure, of course you like those two shitheads. They're just like you. What's that you're working on? The second *Business Secrets* book, I hope."

They were in the living room-dining area of the house, and Malcolm was sitting at the table reading through a small pile of manuscript pages. He put his hands down quickly on the pages on the table and spread his fingers, trying to hide as much of it as possible. "Well, um, no, actually it's fiction."

"Christ, Malcolm! You never made any money from your fiction!"

"What do you think *Business Secrets from the Stars* is?"

"You know what I mean. So, what is this? Another novel no one will ever publish?"

Malcolm sighed. The sooner he told her, the sooner the shrieking would be over. "No, it's a couple of short stories Jerry and Al wanted my opinion on."

Understanding dawned. "They're God damned *writers?* They're God damned wannabe *writers?* Oh, Jesus, just what I need, two more of them!"

"What the hell does that mean, 'two more of them'?" Malcolm shouted. "I'm no wannabe, you bitch! I'm the real thing! At least Jerry and Al recognize that, which is more than you ever did."

Now that they were properly warmed up, Mr. and the former Mrs. Erskine happily resumed the kind of energetic dialogue that, during the years of their wedded nightmare, had kept so many of their erstwhile neighbors awake so far into the night.

Under the present circumstances, though, the shrieks and howls and insults instead brought two Secret Service agents running. They separated the contenders just after Marlene had pointed out that the bullet that had grazed Malcolm's cheek had given him only a very small scratch and so it was pretentious of him to still be wearing a bandage over it after three days, and just before she tried to prove her contention that the scratch was surely healed by ripping the bandage off his cheek.

"Jesus, guys," Jerry said in a loud whisper, holding Malcolm back by twisting his hands behind him in an exotic and painful hold he had learned from a certified sadist at the Secret Service training academy, "you want the entire neighborhood to hear you?"

"Yeah," Al gasped, keeping Marlene at bay by dancing around vigorously so as to avoid her kicks and punches, thus diverting her attention from Malcolm, "Jeez...Christ...neighborhood...Ow!"

A *basso profundo* voice interrupted them. "Hey, how're you guys doing?"

Everyone disengaged.

"Zip!"

"Agent Muchley!"

"Sir!"

"Well, hel–l–lo."

"Mr. Erskine, Jerry, Al. Er, Mrs. Erskine."

"He's not available, Marlene," Malcolm told her.

"They're *all* available, dear."

"Agent Muchley coordinated this mission, Mr. Erskine," Jerry said. "You might say he was the *éminence grise* of our little enterprise."

Al shook his head. "That's not the phrase you want, Jerry."

"Five bucks says it is."

"You're on. I'll get my Merriam Webster's," Al said.

"Uh–uh. My Funk and Wagnall's," Jerry said.

"My God!" Marlene said

The two men strolled away together toward the basement they had converted into a study containing two desks and two laptop computers, arguing as they went the pros and cons of using foreign phrases in one's fiction.

Marlene retreated into her peeve.

Zip Muchley beckoned to Malcolm to join him in the kitchen.

"Like a beer, Mr. Erskine, sir?"

Malcolm nodded, and Muchley took two beer bottles from the refrigerator, twisted the caps off both, and handed one to Malcolm.

Malcolm looked closely at the mouth of the bottle. There were no threads in the glass. This was not a screw–top bottle.

Malcolm sipped thoughtfully, wondering how the immense, upright Muchley would do against the immense, evil Mongo, if it should come to that. Jerry and Al, he suspected, would be pretty useless against Jimmy Flicker's Director of Cosmic Outplacement. Muchley, though, might be another matter.

"You ever hear of a guy named Mongo, Zip? A really nasty, dangerous guy?"

Muchley frowned in thought. "Wasn't he the guy in Flash Gordon? Evil Emperor of Outer Space, or something like that?"

"Close enough. Pretty good beer."

"Yeah, I guess, if you like beer. Tell you the truth, though, Mr. Erskine, I normally don't touch alcohol. It reduces fertility and testosterone, it messes up your brain, and it's just not right, morally speaking."

"I hear it can lead to the smoking of marijuana, too."

"Really? Wow! I didn't know that. See? One more reason to stay away from the stuff. I just thought I should have some now so that we could perform some male bonding."

Why don't you go perform some bonding with Marlene? Malcolm thought. I'm sure she'd find the idea more appealing than I do. "That's important to you, is it?"

"Oh, sure. It's one of the reasons we won the Cold War. Real man–to–man bonding, but without any of that pansy kissing the Russians go in for. That's why they lost."

Future historians will be in your debt, Malcolm thought.

"Okay." Muchley put his beer down half finished. He washed his hands carefully in the kitchen sink and dried them for a long time on the towel hanging over the sink.

"There!" he said finally, looking satisfied and relieved. "Now, then, Mr. Erskine, we've got that out of the way, so let's get to what I wanted to tell you about."

Malcolm had finished his own beer. He pointed at the one Muchley had put down. "You want the rest of that? Or a fresh one?"

Muchley shook his head emphatically.

Malcolm took another beer from the refrigerator and opened it the wimpy way, with a bottle opener.

"You see, sir," Muchley said, "I was ordered to keep you safe by a certain great lady you've already met."

"Oh, yes, Jerry explained that to me. Or maybe it was Al."

Muchley looked disappointed. "They didn't tell you why, did they?"

"No."

"Great! I get to do that! See, she knew for sure that there were assassins out there looking for you."

"That's interesting. How did she know that for sure?"

"Oh..." Muchley waved a hand in a gesture signifying vagueness. "She has her sources, which are different from our sources. Anyway, she didn't call me in until she received the results of an opinion poll she had had commissioned, having to do with presidential preference."

Jesus, Malcolm thought. "Showing that a certain great lady would have a good chance at becoming the first woman president?"

"Exactly, sir. But it also showed that she would never win the Republican nomination unless she had committed herself to just the right running mate, someone the younger, more entrepreneurial party members really look up and feel speaks for them."

"I could think of a few names," Malcolm said. "Industrialists, Wall Street jackals. Oh, sorry. They prefer to think of themselves as sharks."

Muchley shook his head. "Only one name does the trick: Malcolm Erskine."

Malcolm choked on his beer. "Holy shit, fuck, and damn!"

Muchley stiffened. "Of course, you'll have to clean up your

language first, sir. Anyway, through the information she's gathered from her own sources, the, uh, the lady we're discussing was able to give us some good leads as to the identity of the hit men, and even who was behind them, so we're pretty confident that we'll be able to track them down quickly. You shouldn't have to be stuck here too much longer. Then we can take you and your, er, lovely wife—"

"Ex–wife!" Marlene shouted from half a house away.

"Ex–wife," Muchley said, lowering his voice almost to inaudibility, "back home and you can go on with your vital work of teaching America the wisdom of the Merskeenians and cleaning up your vocabulary and preparing for your brilliant political future, sir." He straightened suddenly and saluted. "I look forward to serving under you, sir!"

Malcolm raised his bottle to Muchley in response. Honor of the regiment, he thought. God, King, and country. Or Queen, God, and country, as it might soon be.

Two days later, Malcolm was taking a break from his non–labors by watching the news on television. He was paying little attention to the news itself. Rather, he was fantasizing about the anchorwoman. It was Felicia Finewine.

He had already forgiven her for her long–ago betrayal with the ghastly Grossbuck and for being married to Johnny Aggressive. What eyes! What a mouth! Why did she have to hide so much of herself behind that frustrating desk? Since television stations and networks so obviously hired their anchorwomen for their looks anyway, why didn't they do such viewers as Malcolm a favor and dress the anchorwomen in bikinis and show them full length? He wondered if it would do any good to write to them with that suggestion.

He was thinking about such matters more all the time.

On their second day in hiding, Marlene had moved into a separate bedroom, displacing Jerry, who had been forced to share a room with Al. ("But he snores!" Jerry had whined. "Tough shit," Marlene had sympathized.)

And then a couple of news items caught Malcolm's attention enough to shatter his fantasy and convert Felicia Finewine's mouth from an object of erotic speculation to a conduit for vital information.

"In the Rocky Mountain city of Piketon, two bodies were discovered in the Pike River, which flows through that city. The bodies of two elderly white males, their feet encased in cement, were discovered by early-morning joggers on a path that runs beside the river. Since the river is only about a foot deep at that point, the bodies were clearly visible from the knees up. The dead men had been shot in the back of the head, and both have been identified as having links to organized crime on the West Coast. The names of the victims are not being released until police can determine which federal penitentiary next of kin are serving time in.

"Also this morning, a mysterious explosion and fire destroyed the Southern California headquarters of a weirdo cult, a bunch of losers who worshiped flying saucers, the Brothers and Sisters of the Saucer People. Fire department officials report that the building was engulfed in flames when they arrived and that their men could do little. The building is reported to be almost completely destroyed. A number of bodies were found inside the building when firemen were finally able to enter. Apparently, all the members of the bizarro cult had committed mass suicide."

Felicia broke off to smirk at the screen as though to reassure her devoted fans that no one who looked like her would ever do something that dumb and pointless.

She continued. "One of the bodies has been tentatively identified by means of beard-styling records as that of Harold Jaminchkovich, better known as Brother Harry, the self-styled, quote, Enunciator of the New Christian Space Enlightenment, unquote."

Brother Harry! Malcolm thought. Translated to a higher and far mellower plane of being! Maybe I should start channeling *him* now.

Jerry burst into the room. "Hey, guess what, Mr. Erskine, sir! Agent Muchley just called in to say we can take you guys back home now. The danger's over. We've already got you both tickets on a commercial flight to Piketon this evening, so start getting packed, and after dinner, Al and I'll take you over to Dulles and drop you off."

"About fucking time!" Marlene called from somewhere. "Keep it down! I've got some phone calls to make."

CHAPTER FIFTEEN

Malcolm climbed out of the unmarked Secret Service car feeling nervous. Behind him was a stream of cars letting people off or picking them up, in front of him was a row of glass doors leading into the airport, and in between was a broad expanse of concrete filled with arriving and departing passengers, piles of luggage, porters, and electric carts. The number of places a man with a gun could be hiding stunned him.

The weather was chilly, and everyone he could see was wearing some sort of coat or jacket, some of them quite heavy and bulky. Any one of those seeming passengers could be fingering a pistol concealed in a coat pocket, ready to walk up to Malcolm and remove the Devil's agent.

Or the assassin might not even be here. It might be someone quite far away, with a high–powered rifle aimed at the back of Malcolm's head. He spun about quickly, as if to catch sight of the distant killer or at least confuse him.

"Well, come on!" Marlene snapped at him. "I want to get back to Piketon."

"Uh, yeah, right." Malcolm picked up his suitcase. He paused to wave goodbye to Jerry and Al, but they had already driven away. He noticed that Marlene had left her suitcase for him to carry, so he picked it up in the other hand and staggered after her and into the building.

After they had checked their two cases through to Piketon and let the ticket attendant do her mysterious ripping of some illegible pages from the ticket and making cryptic marks on other pages, they found themselves with an hour to wait. Marlene put both tickets and boarding passes in her purse.

"I guess we can go down to the gate," Malcolm said.

"No hurry, now," Marlene said. "I'm curious. Were the stories those guys had you read any good?"

Malcolm thought about whether to tell her the truth.

Al's story wasn't a story. Rather, it was the outline for a novel titled *Nuts to Your Guts*. It was an action-adventure tale about an astonishingly brave, resourceful, and tall Secret Service agent named Hal Stone who, after a series of adventures, half of them sexual and the other half bloodily violent, defeats the secret organization that has been trying to undermine the industrial world. A grateful United States President then rewards Hal with the hand of his beautiful daughter and promotion to head of the Secret Service.

Jerry's was a science-fiction short story called "First Landing." It told about two alien beings fleeing from the destruction of their planet. They seem to be quite human in appearance and behavior, and, if the reader can judge from the occasional arguments they have about proper usage, their native language is English. The male alien, Jerdam, is short by alien standards, but possessed of a mighty intellect and record-setting sexual abilities. The appreciative female alien, Evelyn, has admired and desired him from afar for many years (each year being divided into twelve "mununths") and is delighted to have been the woman Jerdam chose to heroically save from the disaster that has destroyed their race. They land on a verdant planet populated only by placid animals and vigorously set about regenerating their species. Jerdam shortens his name to "Adam," Evelyn shortens hers to "Eve," they name their new world "Earth," and the garden spot they live in they call "Eden."

Reading all of this earnestly written tripe, Malcolm had felt that special surge of joy known only to a moderately successful writer who discovers that a would–be writer is emphatically not a rival to be feared. At the same time, he had grown to like the two Secret Service men during their enforced vacation together in Virginia, while Marlene had clearly disliked them, so he told her, "Rough, but promising. With lots of work and the proper guidance, I think they could both do okay. They'll never reach my level, of course, but pretty soon they'll surpass, say, Joe Hoffman."

He had expected that to elicit at least a scowl, if not an insult, but instead Marlene looked happy.

"I read an interesting magazine article while we were shut up in that stupid house with those two promising authors," she said. "All about trends in popular culture. Seems channeling's on its way out. I think that maybe, real soon, your level won't be so high, Malcolm."

"Worried about your milch cow, my beloved? I think the goose has a few more golden eggs in him."

"Planning a sex change, Malcolm?" She smiled broadly, but not, Malcolm realized, at him. She was looking over his shoulder.

"Hey, Teeny," said a voice from behind him.

It was Fred Seicht.

While Malcolm stared with open mouth, Seicht stepped to Marlene's side and put his arm around her shoulders. "Hi, baby."

Marlene smiled happily up at him, notably unsurprised to see him.

"What?" Malcolm said. "What? What?" Suddenly he was struck by the feeling that the goose had become more important as a source of *pâté de foie gras* than of golden eggs. "Marlene, what the hell are you up to?"

"Cashing in my investment, darling. Hellooo," she added, looking over his shoulder again.

Malcolm saw the look of arousal on her face and the look of awe mingled with fear on Seicht's face, and he felt the prickles in his own neck, and he knew who was standing behind him without needing to turn around. "Hello, Mongo."

"I suppose you're going to come with me quietly and not give me an excuse to mangle you, huh, Erskine?" Mongo said.

He needed an excuse? Malcolm turned around finally. "You know me by now, Mongo. I save my heroism for the appropriate moment."

Mongo seemed to snicker, but then his face relaxed into its normal placidity. He said to Marlene, "Check's in the mail. Now the two of you use those tickets and take that flight to Piketon."

Marlene began to protest that the arrangement had been that Mongo would have the money with him, but Seicht, his face white, yanked her away in the direction of the gate.

"Erskine, your taste in women is all in your mouth."

Actually, Malcolm thought, in her mouth. "As bad as your taste in bosses, Mongo. My month's not up yet."

Mongo actually laughed very slightly. Or perhaps it was merely a heavy breath. "This hasn't got anything to do with that. Let's go see my boss. Sure you don't want to make a run for it? Crowded place, cops all around, and all?"

Malcolm gave him what he hoped was a scornful look and gestured for Mongo to lead the way.

The way led out of the airport and to a waiting limousine with a uniformed driver. The license plates, which Malcolm got just a glimpse of, read CHANNL.

Mongo gestured Malcolm into the back seat ahead of him, then climbed in and said, "Go," to the driver. The car moved smoothly away from airport and out into traffic. The path home receded behind them.

At first, Malcolm tried to remember their route, memorizing

landmarks and highway names and numbers. Since he did not know that part of the country, he hoped he would be able to reconstruct the trip later when talking to the police. Then he noticed that Mongo was watching him with amused tolerance, and he realized that Mongo knew that he would never have the opportunity either to talk to the police or to remember this trip. Malcolm pressed himself back into the seat to try to hide his trembling.

I'm going to die, he thought. Actually and really going to die. And I've never published a really successful novel.

He looked at Mongo, sitting relaxed and comfortable beside him.

And it's going to hurt a lot.

Their destination was a house in a rural setting, surrounded by enormous trees that shielded it from the highway. The day had grown increasingly gray and cold as the light faded, and now, as dark was coming on, it was raining. From a light drizzle, the rain turned to a heavy downpour.

The car pulled up in front of broad, white stone steps leading up to an ornate doorway. Mongo leaped out, yelled, "Come on!" and ran up the steps.

Malcolm got out more slowly. He stood beside the car, looking up at the sky. The blowing rain stung his cheeks and soaked his clothing. Perhaps if he stood like this with his mouth open, he'd drown, as credulous folk believe turkeys do in the rain. Drowning might be a less painful death than the one Mongo was no doubt planning for him.

Mongo, however, was not to be cheated. He returned, grabbed Malcolm's arm, and yanked him up the stairs. "You trying to catch your death?" he shouted at Malcolm. "Jesus, what a lame brain."

Thank God, Malcolm thought, stumbling up the stairs. He's here to protect me, not kill me! Relief overwhelmed him, and he felt like crying.

"I don't want you all fuzzy-minded with a cold virus, or dying of pneumonia," Mongo said as he pulled the door open. "I want all your nerve endings working at peak level."

Inside, the house was elegant, featuring much old, well polished woodwork, antique furniture, and nineteenth-century portraits hanging on the walls.

Mongo stopped in front of a small table of red wood with curved, slender legs.

"See this, Erskine? Genuine eighteenth-century piece. Imported from France before the Revolution. Theirs, I mean, not ours. Look at the workmanship, the delicacy. Beautiful, huh?"

"One of the loveliest tables I've ever seen." Whatever might make Mongo feel more kindly toward him, Malcolm would say it.

"Course, the old stuff gets fragile as the years pass." Mongo picked the table up with one hand and squeezed, and the wood splintered. He dropped the shattered thing, and when it hit the floor, it fell apart into three pieces. "Come on." He strode off down a long, portrait-lined hallway.

Malcolm followed hurriedly. The table, after all, had had a long and full life. What right did it have to complain? Malcolm, on the other hand, was still relatively young, and there was so much he had not yet experienced.

He stifled a sob of pity for himself. I haven't been *that* bad, have I? he asked an uncaring universe. I don't really deserve this, do I?

Mongo led the way to what, in the house's youth, must have been one of many small sitting rooms. In these more degenerate times, it was equipped with a large color television set. And an array of leather straps and whips hung from the walls.

"A torture chamber, Mongo?" Malcolm asked, his amazement temporarily chasing away his fear. "I know editors can get unpleasant when authors miss their deadlines, but this—!"

Mongo looked insulted. "You kidding? You think I'd need any of this shit? Hell, no, it's not for torture. The boss uses it for sex."

It did not fit in with Malcolm's preconceptions about Jimmy Flicker. Lukas of Aldebaran would surely have disapproved. But now that he looked more closely, he noticed an armchair with an improbably large dildo built into its seat, and what might have been a gynecologist's table, complete down to the stirrups, but also with a hole built into it.

But no Jimmy Flicker was to be seen. "Is he tied up, heh, heh?" Malcolm asked.

"Who?"

"The boss."

Mongo exhibited the faintest trace of a smile. *"She's* on her way. You just stay here and wait for her." He turned and left the room.

Earlier, Marlene had made some weak joke about Malcolm's planning to have a sex change operation. Now he began to wonder if Jimmy Flicker had had a sex change operation.

Well, why not?

It would fit in with this alternate universe he seemed to have stepped into, this odd world in which nothing was as it seemed. His placid life as a cynical hack-writer con man had been interrupted by Secret Service men and inept Piketon detectives and madmen firing rifles at him and goons the size of two-story houses and a former president's wife who wanted to be president herself and an ex-wife who had hated him and then seemed to be crazy about him and now had apparently turned him over to a young, amoral entrepreneur—scratch that: all entrepreneurs are amoral—who murdered his subordinates because it was cheaper than laying them off and now had had his sex changed.

And all because Malcolm had dreamed up an ancient stellar spirit who dispensed business advice telepathically.

It wasn't as if I *hurt* anyone, for Christ's sake, Malcolm sulked mentally. I just took their money. But they could all afford it. I'm really just a modern Robin Hood, that's all. Just what does this fucking universe have against me, anyway?

Looking around, he became aware that the room also contained more conventional furniture. Did Julie Flicker, or whatever he called himself now, like to relax in a comfortable armchair while whipping his well–restrained sex slaves? For that matter, how did one get sex slaves? Classified ads in certain magazines? There was a sex magazine in Piketon, the *Piketon Pearl.* Malcolm had sometimes fantasized about answering some of the ads in it, but he had never screwed his courage to quite so unconventional a sticking point. None of the ads had been for sex slaves, though.

"Ah, so! We meet again, Mr. Malcolm Erskine!"

Malcolm would have laughed at the B–movie corniness of the line, had it not been for the fact that the woman speaking those words struck fear to his core. As it was, he stared speechlessly at Atlantica, his face betraying his fear.

She smiled with satisfaction and locked the door behind her.

Malcolm at last regained the power of speech. "I thought you were in California."

"My horses told me they preferred the southeast."

"Oh. Well, okay. And so now *you're* working for Jimmy Flicker, too?" Was Flicker planning to replace him with this charlatan?

Atlantica looked at him in amazement. "What does Flicker have to do with any of this?"

"Are you kidding? What about Mongo? Since he works for Flicker, naturally—"

"Oh, of course. Now I see why you're confused. Mongo doesn't work for Flicker any more. I hired him away. I made him a better offer."

Malcolm wondered what that offer could have been. "He seemed to be a very loyal MegaFlicker employee. I wonder what Jimmy Flicker had to say when Mongo told him he was leaving."

Atlantica smirked. "Flicker tried to say a few things, but by that point no one could understand him. He rode the tiger for a while, but then he released the tail."

"Oracular, Attie. Sounds like something Mellabenth would say."

Atlantica thought about that for a moment. "Does, doesn't it? Thanks, I'll probably use it. In fact, Mellabenth is what I brought you here to talk about."

"Wait a minute! This is going too fast. I've got to sit down." Malcom chose one of the room's normal armchairs and sat down. Briefly, he wondered what Mellabenth would have thought if that ancient Atlantean warrior could have seen Atlantica seating herself upon the dildo that projected from the chair opposite his. The image of her doing so was surprisingly arousing.

Malcolm yanked his mind back to his predicament. "Okay, so what does Mellabenth have to with your hiring away Jimmy Flicker's Director of Cosmic Outplacement and having him kidnap me and bring me here?"

Atlantica was wearing the white robes that seemed to be her standard costume for public appearances. She chose a chair facing Malcolm's—but not the one with the built-in dildo—and sat in it. She placed her hands on the chair's arms and held herself in the air like a gymnast, folding her legs beneath her and then lowering herself onto the chair. The robes fell away to reveal very shapely thighs.

Malcolm felt the stirrings of an erection. Oh, for God's sake, he told himself. Not now!

"As you would know if you had played the game, Erskine, Mellabenth is president of CEA, the Channeled Entities of America. All the entities channeled by serious, established channelers in the United

States and Canada hold regular meetings to coordinate policy."

Malcolm could not come up with a single smart–aleck comment in response to this, not even in the privacy of his thoughts. His brain, in fact, seemed to have stopped working.

"At our last meeting, we all agreed that you were becoming a problem. Some of the channelers talked about hiring a hit man and having you blown away."

Hit man—the magic phrase. Malcolm's brain started working again. "Wait a minute. First, I thought the proper *patois* was 'to off,' not 'to blow away.' Second, who was having this meeting, the channelers or the, er, entities?"

"Well, for Heaven's sake, they have to do everything through their human mediums, of course, so we channelers get together and convey the entities' debate to each other and then back to them. We're sort of like United Nations interpreters, see."

This makes as much sense as anything else I've heard, Malcolm thought. "So they don't have a big meeting room somewhere on a higher plane of existence, with ectoplasmic coffee and doughnuts, and conference calls to other planes?"

Atlantica glared at him. "You're not taking this seriously, are you?"

"It *is* hard."

"Mongo."

Malcolm began taking the conversation seriously.

"All right," Atlantica said, satisfied with his suddenly sober expression. "Anyway, Mellabenth convinced the other entities that blowing you away—or offing you—wasn't really the optimal solution. He pointed out that we needed to bring you into the fold so that you and, um, what's his name?"

"Who? Whose name?"

Atlantica began to swell, her face reddening, pulsing veins standing out on her forehead, foam appearing on her lips.

Malcolm shrank back in his chair.

"Your entity, lout!" Her voice was huskier, deeper. "The being you channel!"

"Lukas! Lukas of Aldebaran!"

Atlantica detumesced. Malcolm breathed again. This woman's pyrotechnics, he realized, were almost as frightening as Mongo's quiet looming. Of course, he admitted to himself, I *am* unusually easy to frighten.

Atlantica continued. "Right. Lukas. Anyway, Mellabenth wants you and Lukas brought into the fold. You'll join our organization, you'll pay your proper percentage of profit into the kitty, just like everyone else, Lukas will announce that he was Mellabenth's subordinate in ancient times when they were both mortal, and you'll swear your personal allegiance to me as president of the channeler's auxiliary of the CEA."

"Well, golly, that sounds simple enough. I just give you all my money and accept you as my boss, and I'm free to go. Of course, if I refuse to go along with all of this, then I get to keep all of my money, and I remain my own boss."

"Mongo."

The ultimate counterargument. Malcolm sighed. "You know, if I do agree to your terms—offer, pardon me—I'll be giving up quite a bit. Money, freedom, a great future."

"You'd also be gaining a few things, and I'm not just talking about your life and health." Atlantica rose from her chair and strode over to stand behind Malcolm's chair. She placed one hand on each shoulder and squeezed hard enough to cause pain. "Ever been tied up by an expert?" she breathed in Malcolm's ear.

So there *are* things Marlene doesn't know! Malcolm thought. Why are beautiful women so fascinated with me?

"I've always loved tying up and controlling and humiliating men like you," Atlantica said. "You know—weak, shallow, insignificant men.

The kind who really deserve to be stepped on and squashed."

The door burst open, splinters of wood flying from the broken frame around the lock.

"Nobody move!" a deep voice roared.

A river of conservatively suited, short-haired, clean-shaven men poured into the room. At their head was Zip Muchley. Jerry and Al were right behind him. All were brandishing immense cannons disguised to look like handguns.

"Are you all right, sir?" Al asked.

When he did not reply immediately, Jerry said anxiously, "Mr. Erskine, sir, are you all right?"

They crowded around his chair, peering down at him, concern writ large on all their faces.

Not as all right as I would have been if you hadn't interrupted. "Yes, I'm fine. No one's harmed me." He stood up and turned toward Atlantica.

She was being held firmly by two large young men, looking dwarfed between them and no longer so dangerous. She glared at Malcolm, at the two who held her, and then at all of the others. "Who the hell are you, and what do you want? We were just having a business discussion!"

Zip Muchley shook his head and said in a stern tone, "We know better, ma'am. You had Mr. Erskine kidnapped and brought here so that you could try to put an end to his important work for world enlightenment and the advancement of the free enterprise system, ma'am. We had a call from an unnamed source giving us all the info, and then when we sneaked in here, we captured a couple of your followers, and when we tortured them, they spilled the beans."

"Tortured?" Malcolm said, feeling queasy.

"Oh, don't worry, Mr. Erskine," Jerry reassured him. "That's just Agency officialese for 'questioned.'"

"Yeah," Al said quickly. "Questioned them. That's all."

"Anyway, ma'am," Zip continued, "you're now under arrest for violation of the Freedom of Channeling Presidential Decree. Trial will be before an Agency administrative judge tomorrow morning, sentencing to follow immediately. You do not have the right to remain silent. Mr. Erskine, sir, we'll be transporting you to California for safekeeping. Uh, you know where. You can stay there and plan strategy with, uh," he looked around, "you know who."

Oh, Christ, Malcolm thought. Out of the frying pan, into the fire. Lukas, how I wish you were real and could help me!

The lights went out.

The room was utterly black. There was much shouting and cursing and the sound of large bodies milling about and stepping on each other's toes, accompanied by much more cursing.

A small, hard hand gripped Malcolm's and yanked. A voice whispered in his ear, "Keep quiet and come along."

Atlantica? Who else could it be? Some of her underlings were free, after all, and had staged a rescue attempt. Malcolm hesitated only for a moment. Of the frightening alternatives facing him, this seemed at the moment to be the least unpleasant. Not that he could have chosen a different alternative, anyway. The hand grasping his had a grip he doubted he could break, and when his invisible rescuer moved, he had no choice but to stumble after.

After a few minutes of zig-zag progress, rebounding from one cursing, shoving Secret Service man to another, Malcolm could tell he was in an open space. Outside the room and in the hallway, he guessed. Still there was no light. The entire house must be in darkness.

The hand pulled him along for some distance. "Step down a few steps," the voice whispered. They went down a half-flight of stairs.

Light came on, temporarily blinding Malcolm.

"How interesting," a voice said. "Step outside to do some

astronomy, and everything goes to hell. Hey, Erskine, open your eyes."

"I don't want to, Mongo. It's nice in here." Nevertheless, he did open his eyes.

Mongo loomed before him, exuding even more menace than usual. He held a very large telescope and tripod easily in one hand and a flashlight in the other. He put the flashlight on the floor, balancing it on its end so that its light splashed on the ceiling. He placed the telescope carefully on the floor and then took off the heavy coat he had been wearing and let it drop over the telescope. Under the coat, he wore a white dress shirt that was stretched to bursting over his huge chest.

They were in a kitchen, a very large one, the sort of place where, in an earlier age, malnourished servants had labored to produce vast meals for their well fed masters. To Malcolm's right, an immense wooden table was littered with dirty plates. In a platter in the center were the remnants of a large ham. Sturdy wooden chairs surrounded the table.

The hand holding his had let go. Malcolm turned to his left, expecting to see Atlantica. Instead, he saw a stunningly, exotically beautiful young woman with shoulder–length black hair and olive skin and almond–shaped eyes.

He grabbed one of the wooden chairs and fell into it. His knees had lost their ability to support him.

Mongo glanced at Malcolm. "You'll keep for a while," Mongo said. He turned to Malcolm's dream girl. "I think I'll kill you first."

CHAPTER SIXTEEN

"But it won't be much fun," Mongo added. He gestured toward Malcolm. "He's such a wimp, I don't know how long I can make him last. And you," he turned back to Malcolm's dream girl, "why, you're so itty bitty and fragile, a real light shot to the heart'll do it instantly."

He moved so quickly that Malcolm couldn't quite follow what had happened. All he was sure of was that Mongo *had* moved, first forward and then back into position again, and that his dream girl had staggered back. But now she was standing normally again, although she was rubbing her chest.

"Pretty good," she said admiringly.

The slightest trace of a frown of puzzlement flickered on Mongo's face. "Interesting," he said. "You're stronger than you look. You a freak with your heart on the right side, or something?"

The dream girl shook her head. "Better than that. I'm a freak with no heart at all. My turn."

This time, Malcolm couldn't follow the action at all. He sensed a flicker of motion, but his dream girl seemed to be where she had been all along. Mongo, however, bent suddenly at the knees and sat down heavily on the floor. The room shook when the giant landed.

Mongo raised his hand halfway to his chest, but then let it fall limply. A red stain spread over his shirt, centered just to the left of the center of his chest.

"Gasp," Mongo said.

He wilted to the floor and lay limply on his back. A pink froth formed on his lips. Blood began to dribble from his slack mouth. He looked up at Malcolm's dream girl with adoration in his glazing eyes. "I love you," he bubbled, and died.

"Usual reaction," said Malcolm's dream girl, dismissing the dead cosmic outplacement director. "Come on, Erskine, the SS men will be here in a few minutes." When Malcolm stared up at her with a look combining total devotion and paralyzing fear and did not move, she snapped, "On your feet! Now!"

Malcolm leaped to his feet and stood at attention.

"Good. Follow me. There's a car waiting out by the highway. Hold my hand. We cut all the outside lights as well. You can call me Shirley."

Another long drive to an unknown destination, the time spent in the back seat of a large car next to a frightening individual.

There were differences, though.

The person next to Malcolm this time was not Mongo, but rather the woman he had fantasized about for years, become flesh. She was perfect. Even in the dim light cast in the back seat by the dashboard and by the reflection through the windows from the headlights, he could see that much easily.

It had not, however, been part of his fantasy that his dream woman would be as much a killer as Mongo, or possibly even more a killer. For that matter, in his fantasies, she had paid attention to him, passionate attention, rather than staring out the window, lost in her own world. And, mysterious daughter of the wondrous East, she had not been named "Shirley."

Malcolm racked his brain for an appropriate topic with which to start a conversation. He really wanted to know whether she was his savior or his abductor, and if the latter, just what the nature was of the frying pan into which he was being forced to jump.

Better to ease into the difficult stuff, he told himself. "So, Shirley," he said heartily, "how do you like our country so far?"

He would not have thought that such dark eyes could emit such freezing cold rays. He shivered and drew back into his corner.

Shirley looked satisfied. "I was born in this country, you twit. And so were my parents and grandparents and great-grandparents, at least. That's as far back as the family records go. Now, tell me something. I suppose I'm the woman you've fantasized about all your life, and you can imagine nothing more heavenly than to be allowed to get into my bed and make worshipful love to me, right?"

Malcolm nodded eagerly. Could it possibly be...?

"Usual reaction," Shirley said. "From now on, don't call me 'Shirley,' call me 'Miss Weng.'"

"Uh, okay, Miss Weng."

Shirley shook her head. "Changed my mind. Don't call me anything. Don't speak to me. Retreat into your fantasies. And don't look at me." She returned her attention to the passing night.

I've read about women like this, Malcolm thought. In fact, I've *written* about women like this.

In his fiction, though, he was always in control. His protagonists, who were always the same ideal, the man he wished he could be, were suave when they should be suave, gentle when they should be gentle, and always, always completely successful with the women he invented for their pleasure. Real women and real life were so much more difficult for Malcolm to deal with. In real life, events, circumstances, and women were always in control and Malcolm never was.

Perhaps it was time to change all of that, to assert himself, to emulate his own fictional creations.

He kept his head pointed forward and swiveled his eyes to the right to get a straining look at Shirley Weng's profile.

Good Heavens, how utterly perfect! His dream girl had always been a bit fuzzy in the details, as dream girls tend to be. This woman was sharp and hard and clear.

What better circumstances to start his new self–assertion than these, and with what better companion to do so than the girl of his dreams incarnate? Then he remembered another very clear detail connected with Shirley Weng: the terrifying Mongo dying with blood bubbling from his mouth and his chest crushed. And he decided that this was not the time, not the place, and not the companion after all.

He turned his own attention to the window beside him. The darkness outside was broken only by occasional highway signs and the lights of towns and cities. The night air was clear, cleaned by the earlier rain. They were apparently on Interstate 95, heading south. Where that put them, and where it meant they were headed, Malcolm didn't know. He knew only that they had started somewhere in Virginia.

In fact, he realized that he couldn't even be sure of that. He knew that the house in which the Secret Service had been hiding him and Marlene was in Virginia. He also knew that Mongo had taken him from Dulles Airport on a relatively short drive, but he had only the fuzziest idea of the geography of the East Coast. Should have paid more attention in grade school, he told himself quite a few years too late.

For that matter, he should have worked harder at his meaningless job for the last few years and given up any idea of writing bestsellers. If he had done that, he'd now be bored but safe back home in Piketon. Just as divorced, of course, but would that have been bad?

Hours passed, and Malcolm kept awaking with a start to realize that he had drifted off to sleep. He glanced carefully to the right again. Shirley was as upright and wide awake as at the start of the ride. She seemed not to need sleep. Malcolm hoped the same was true of their driver.

He tried to keep his back straight, hoping that when he did doze, he'd stay upright himself. It scared him to imagine what Shirley might do to him if he fell over against her.

He dreamed strange dreams of space adventures involving Merskeenians and Marlengas. Shirley was there, too. She appeared not as the prototype of a race, but as an individual being, immensely powerful, huge, a living space battlecruiser, arriving unheralded from the dark intergalactic depths, flying into Merskeenian space to blast to smithereens a strange, pervasive menace called a Mongo. The Merskeenians radioed their thanks to their enigmatic savior and began to plan a monument to her and a farewell ceremony. But she hung around, refusing to offer an explanation as to why she had not yet announced a departure date, becoming a looming menace herself. The Merskeenians began to feel very nervous.

Malcolm awoke feeling eager to get to his computer. This was not bad stuff! He could do something with it, add to the pulpy mythos he was building. Perhaps, after the *Business Secrets from the Stars* episode of his life had passed and he had retired to a mansion somewhere high in the mountains, far from Piketon, he could start churning out a ten— or twelve-volume action-adventure novel about the adventures of Lukas of Aldebaran and his fellow Merskeenians. Drop all the pretense and market it as fiction. There was a ready-made market, after all.

So what happens next? he asked himself. Well, Lukas, with his usual courage, volunteers to fly into space and try to board the Shirley creature and communicate with her man-to-whatever. No, not "board her." Make that "enter her."

Malcolm headed back to dreamland with a smile.

The car decelerated suddenly, jerking Malcolm awake. Fear clutched at him. The driver had fallen asleep! No, they were exiting from the Interstate at last.

The suddenness of it had driven from him the dream he had been having. He had managed to dream of being Lukas entering the amazing Shirley, but he had a vague memory that the results for Lukas had not been pleasurable.

The rising sun sat huge and red on the horizon off to the left. From the raised exit ramp, Malcolm could see a vista of lush growth spreading in all directions, glowing red in the sunlight. Malcolm could imagine he was still in the land of his dreams, that he was on some exotic planet circling Aldebaran, the red giant star. Strange, dense alien plant life covered the surface of this world. What beings moved beneath that cover? Enemies? Friends? What new, happier life awaited him on this world?

Oh, Lukas, Malcolm thought, I wish you were real and your civilization really did exist 30,000 years ago and still did exist and was on its way to rescue me and take me out into space.

The ramp curved to the east and headed almost directly toward the sun. The redness was fading quickly, giving way to a normal, earthly daylight.

The two–lane highway they were now on was much lower, and all Malcolm could see through the window was a wall of trees to either side. Now and then, he caught glimpses of standing water between the trees. Great limbs stretched horizontally from immense trunks. In places, these branches met above the road, creating a tunnel. Grayish, fuzzy strands hung from the branches, sometimes reaching almost to the ground.

"I think I've seen this in a movie," he said, speaking aloud, forgetting the rule about not addressing Shirley Weng.

She seemed willing to forget the rule, too. "I think you should start living real life for a change, Erskine," she said.

He looked at her quickly, almost expecting to see that she had become transformed into Marlene. It was, after all, a very Marlene sort of line. He found himself unable to look away. The light had lost most of its redness by now, but even so the faint rosiness of it on Shirley Weng's astonishing face rendered Malcolm as breathless as Mongo had been at the end. One way or another, he thought, she destroys men's hearts.

"Put your eyes back," Shirley told him. She leaned forward and looked through the front window. "Not much longer," she added. "We're getting close."

"So, where are we going?" Malcom asked. "You haven't told me yet."

"To see the only man who values me for my brains," Shirley said.

Must be a blind eunuch, Malcolm thought. Reflecting that Shirley's low, strong voice was as erotic as the rest of her, he amended that to a blind, deaf eunuch.

The road began to rise. The car turned off onto a side road that climbed for a while and ended in a paved parking lot. Malcolm got out and stretched. He found himself near the edge of a dropoff looking out over the Atlantic Ocean. The parking lot was at the edge of a ridge stretching parallel to the beach below. The rest of the ridge, as far as he could see, was covered by thick lawns of deep green shaded by immense trees like those he had seen to either side of the road leading here, but even larger and not so close together. Their thick branches spread out horizontally, and the same gray, fuzzy strands he had seen earlier hung from them. From the parking lot, a white concrete pathway headed across the lawns in a ruler–straight line toward a low, white building mostly hidden by the trees.

Malcolm thought that he would have found it all quite charming if not for the thick, clammy air and the even heavier atmosphere of menace.

"Come on," Shirley said. "Let's get into the air conditioning." She looked as uncomfortable as Malcolm was beginning to feel.

At least she's not a complete superwoman, he thought.

She hurried along the pathway, Malcolm following, happy for the moment just to watch her walk. His happiness was tempered only by the fear that their destination might be a torture chamber.

Shirley led him to another low, white building adjacent to the one Malcolm had first seen through the trees. There appeared to be a series of such buildings stretching away in various directions, linked by paths and covered walkways. This place, whatever it was, was much bigger than he had at first realized, and Malcolm began to have the impression of a very large, very wealthy organization.

Shirley stopped before a wide, blank door and pressed her thumb against a small plate set in the wall. There was a soft buzz, and the door slid aside. She beckoned him in after her, and the door slid shut again behind them. It sounded heavy. Solid. Unbreakable.

The characterless hallway ahead of them, with doors set in it at regular intervals on each side, and with a row of fluorescent lights overhead bathing it in shadowless white light, could have been a hallway in any of the office buildings of Western Bell or any other giant corporation with too much money and too little taste or character. The overdressed office workers striding purposefully up and down the hallway and into and out of the various side offices could also have been Western Bell employees—although if they had been, they would have been strolling aimlessly.

Colossoverse, he reminded himself. Not Western Bell. Maybe they don't stroll aimlessly now. Maybe all the aimless strollers have been cosmically outplaced since my day.

Shirley, like everyone else he saw, strode purposefully down the hallway. Malcolm, who had never learned to stride with or without purpose, panted behind her, trying to keep up.

She entered an office, beside the door of which was a plaque reading

COG
SECURITY DIVISION

Malcolm paused to read this plaque and try to deduce its meaning.

"Come on, come on!" Shirley snapped.

He followed her down another hallway, this one lined with photographs of smiling men and women. Above each photograph was the title "Employee of the Month: January," "Employee of the Month: February," and so on. Below each photograph was the employee's name: John Smith, Harold Smith, Jane Smith, Mary Smith, and so on down the line.

Malcolm stopped suddenly in front of one of them. The employee's name was Tracy Smith. The smiling face was the very familiar face of that Tracy who had exerted herself in his seminar and then in his bed, which exertion had occurred during the month she was named employee of the month for.

"Come on, come on!"

Shirley was unlocking a door. On it was painted

REVEREND'S RIGHT HAND
SHIRLEY WENG

Malcolm cleared his throat. "I think I'd like to go home now."

Shirley laughed. "Not bad. Try to keep your sense of humor. It'll probably help."

"Oh, I'm quite serious." He turned around and found himself staring at the stomach of a very large man, so large that both Zip Muchley and Mongo would have looked small beside him. Two more of the same size stood to either side. Malcolm had not even heard them coming up behind him.

"Maybe later," he muttered and entered Shirley's office.

It was small and contained only a desk and two chairs, one behind the desk and the other facing it. Both had arms, which seemed unusual to Malcolm, since he knew that it's a standard office intimidation technique for the interviewer to have a chair with arms and the interviewee not to.

Shirley sat in the chair behind the desk and pointed toward the other chair. Malcolm sat in it, telling himself that, as soon as he gathered his wits and strength, he would think further about what to do instead of following her orders.

The three giants had entered behind him. They produced a leather strap apiece, two short and one long. The two with the short straps used them to tie Malcolm's arms to the arms of his chair, and the one with the long strap passed it around his chest, pulling him tight against the chair back.

Oh, I see the reason for the chair having arms, thought Malcolm. This is certainly much more intimidating.

Shirley waved the giants away and came around the desk to check the straps. "Good," she said. "Well done, kids."

The three giants stood around anxiously while she checked their work. At her praise, they all blushed and giggled and shuffled their feet around. "Thank you, Miss Weng!" they said in unison.

"Relax, Malcolm," she told him. "Come on, kids."

Malcolm heard the office door close. He twisted around as far he could to the left and the right. He could see the whole room, that way. He was alone.

Sort of alone.

The only other presence was a large photograph, on the wall to his left, of a jowly man trying to beam down beatifically but managing only a mitigation of his more normal scowl. Malcolm knew that face well. It was that of the Reverend Jimmy Earl, founder and owner of the

Children of God. Malcolm had thought he was already frightened, but now real fear, real panic possessed him.

He had been well aware of Reverend Jimmy Earl's malice hiding behind his beneficent manner that day the two had confronted each other on Johnny Aggressive's television show. He had seen then that this was not a man into whose power he ever wanted to fall. And now he had done just that. Moreover, Tracy's picture outside Shirley's office had made it clear that the Children of God had been watching him, in some sense perhaps manipulating him, for quite a while. Malcolm felt powerless and doomed.

Surviving Mongo should have inured him to anything. Perhaps it would have, were it not for the memory of the dreaded Mongo dispatched so easily and gruesomely by the petite Shirley. What were the truly large Children of God capable of?

The sound of the door opening interrupted these thoughts. Malcolm twisted around to see the Very Reverend Jimmy Earl himself entering the room, with Shirley right behind him.

She closed the door.

"What, no Goliaths this time?" Malcolm asked.

Shirley smiled. "I don't really need them, do I? Just used them for convenience before. I knew you wouldn't struggle against them, so you wouldn't get hurt. If I'd been the one tying you up, you might have struggled."

And I would have gotten badly hurt. Malcolm got the message. Remembering Mongo, he was sure she was right. Would there have been pleasure in the pain, if it had come from so exquisitely beautiful a source? Mongo had seemed to think so, but Mongo had not been normal.

Jimmy Earl took the chair behind the desk, and Shirley perched on the edge of the desk, facing Malcolm and watching him intently. Oddly enough, she was still his dream girl and Malcolm still felt his heart melting when he looked at her. Sick, sick, sick, he told himself, but the lecture had no effect on his feelings.

Jimmy Earl sat down heavily, the chair creaking beneath him. He sighed in relief as the weight left his feet. "A biblical reference, Erskine? I'm surprised."

"Goliath, you mean?" Malcolm said. "Everyone knows that one."

"Still, I'm surprised that you know it. To Hellspawn like you, the Bible is a forbidden book."

I need to get on this guy's good side, Malcolm thought. He must have one. I know what'll work. I'll be informal and friendly. Let's see, he's obviously Southern, and he's got one of those compound names, just like Jimmy Carter—James Earl Carter. And everyone uses that familiar approach: even the TV people call him "Reverend Jimmy Earl." Yeah, worth a try. "You have a lot to learn about us Hellspawn, Jimmy Earl."

Jimmy Earl's naturally red face turned redder. He shook his finger at Malcolm. "Don't you dare call me that! You call me 'Reverend,' you hear?"

That good side might be very hard to find. "Oh. So, read any good books lately, Reverend?"

Jimmy Earl calmed down and leaned back. "Only the Good Book, young man. Something you should do, too. Now, I'm glad you brought up the matter of good books. That's why I've asked you to come here to talk to me."

"Asked me?" Malcolm repeated in amazement.

"Looked voluntary to me," Shirley told him.

Beyond denying, Malcolm realized. And he would still follow her anywhere she asked him to.

"What I wanted," Jimmy Earl went on, "was to explain to you what you're going to write next. I've got very specific plans for your next book."

"I think I've had this conversation before," Malcolm said. "With Jimmy Flicker, in fact." And even before that—before he'd become famous but after he'd had some books published—with people who were convinced they had wonderful ideas for bestselling books and wanted a professional writer, like Malcolm Erskine, to do the trivial part, the actual writing of the book, in exchange for half the book's earnings. In pre–Flicker days, though, there had been no implied threat in those conversations—no Mongos, no Shirleys.

"Irrelevant," Jimmy Earl said with a negligent wave of his hand. "I understand that Flicker's gone to his judgment. Anyway, I'm having a detailed outline prepared, and then you'll write the book to those specifications."

"Rewrite what I've done?" Malcolm cried in despair. "Rewrite the damned thing? Without even a signed contract? I've already written half the book one way, and now you expect a rewrite?"

Jimmy Earl raised his eyebrows. "You think this is your old life and I'm just some worldly publisher?"

Malcolm looked from Jimmy Earl to Shirley and back again. No, this man was much scarier than any worldly publisher, and this was an even more unmanning experience than having a conversation with a hostile editor.

"You got a title yet?" Jimmy Earl asked.

Malcolm sighed. Title, pages already written...What did it matter? He was scarcely a free agent. He wondered if he'd ever be a free agent again—or, for that matter, a live one. "Yes. *Business Dangers from the Stars."*

Jimmy Earl smiled. "I like that! What's the story line and subtext?"

"Subtext!" Malcolm had never in his career written subtext. He was convinced that no one ever did. "Well, I guess the subtext is how to make bunches of money, just like the first book. Basically, it's about protecting your company from attack by business enemies, as communicated by Lukas of Aldebaran based on the experience of the Merskeenians in fighting various interstellar enemies."

Jimmy Earl looked thoughtful. "That's not bad. I know I've got enemies." He chuckled suddenly. "One less, now that that turd Brother Harry's out of the way. Thanks be to Jesus and whoever planted those bombs. Boy, what a fire! Roasted hippie Jesus freak saucer nuts, I tell ya!" He shook, his laughter coming in violent gusts. His face glowed a rosy purple. Tears streamed from his eyes. Shirley yanked a tissue from a box on her desk and handed it to him. He wiped his eyes, blew his nose, thanked her, and said to Malcolm, "Okay. Now. I've got enemies, but the Great Enemy, the Great Opponent—that's the one we've got to worry about."

He leaned forward and transfixed Malcolm with an intense stare. "I guess maybe you won't have to do too much rewriting. Just make it clear that the interstellar enemies your Merskeenians were fighting were really just minions of the Evil One, and it was through the help of Jesus that they won."

"I don't get the point of all this," Malcolm said. "Why do you care what I write?"

"Because you're taking business away from me!" Jimmy Earl roared, half rising from the chair, his face reddening again.

"Reverend."

"Thanks, Shirley." He sat down and gave himself a moment to calm down, then continued. "I tried getting rid of you before by preaching that the voice you've been hearing is actually the Devil's voice and you need to be eliminated for the good of Christianity. Well, that didn't work out. I'm glad it didn't. I realize now that you're more useful alive. I don't just want to stop losing members of my flock to your New Age crap. I want to keep my flock and add your marks to it. That's what all this is about.

"See, I could preach a sermon claiming that you're just

misunderstanding the messages you're getting. Oh, I could say something like, um...Yeah, okay, here it is." His voice became larger, more resonant, more suited to a great cathedral or a great television audience. "The voice you're hearing in your head is really an angel speaking to you, trying to tell you about something that happened long ago out in space, but you're such a secular, worldly man, so misled by the godless ideas rife in our society today, that you misinterpreted that voice as belonging to some kind of spirit being. Then some shit about channeling, New Age, danger to family values and what made America great. Then I'd say, the angel's really trying to turn you around, bring you back to Jesus, to the faith of your fathers, and show you how God and the Devil were fighting for souls even back then. You just thought it was all about saving a big corporation.

"But if I do say all of that, the people who listen to me will be the ones who always listen to me. I can't reach your audience, and they're the ones with the real money. You can reach them. You can bring them to Jesus and the Reverend Jimmy Earl."

"But if God was fighting the Devil through the medium of the Merskeenians 30,000 years ago," Malcolm pointed out, "then that was 25,000 years before the earth and mankind were created, right? So God created some other human race long before he created us. That sounds like someone else's theology, not yours."

Jimmy Earl grinned at him. "Good boy, Erskine. But you know that that kind of shit only matters with my usual audience, not with yours. Gotta tailor the message to the audience, right? You obviously have that technique down pat. And of course so do I. Trouble is, my technique doesn't work for your audience, and what I'm afraid of is, some time in the not very distant future, my audience is going to start diminishing, but yours is going to keep growing."

"So what this amounts to," Malcolm said, "is that you want to take over my business because it has more, uh, growth potential than yours."

"Yes!" Jimmy Earl smacked the desk, making pens and pencils dance and making Malcolm jerk in his seat. He would have jumped out of it if not for the straps holding him firmly in place.

"But I want you to do the actual writing," Jimmy Earl continued, "because you've got a real skill with it. Maybe you need better production and marketing, but we've got the capability for that right here, in our headquarters."

For the first time in a long time, Malcolm felt he had some bargaining strength. "Well, now, JE, let's talk about this. First tell the most beautiful killer in the world to untie me."

Shirley laughed. "What a silver tongue!" she said in a mocking tone. "What woman can resist you?"

Without waiting for orders from Jimmy Earl, she slipped off the desk and stepped over to Malcolm's chair and began untying him. The message was twofold and clear: First, there's at least one woman—Shirley Weng—you cannot have, and she's the one you obviously want the most. Second, the straps were for initial intimidation. By now, you realize that they're not really necessary.

Deflated only slightly, Malcolm stood up, then leaned on the desk so that he could look down on Jimmy Earl. "What you've admitted, Jimmy, is that you don't have anyone in your organization, including you, who can do what I do. You need me for the sake of your future survival. However, I don't need you, do I? So I guess I'll be leaving now. Miss Weng, would you be so kind as to drive me to the nearest airport?" He headed for the door, delighted with his own bravado.

"Guess it really is time for Plan B, Shirley," Jimmy Earl said with patently false sadness.

Malcolm stopped at the door and turned around. "That's where you declare bankruptcy before your whole ministry fades away?"

Jimmy Earl giggled. "No, that's Plan C. Plan B is where we offer you the chance to become a subsidiary of the Children of God, and if you turn the offer down, we take you waterskiing in the Atlantic Ocean. On cement waterskis."

"Oh."

"So maybe you might want to weigh the pros and cons a bit longer. We've got a real nice suite set up for you to do the weighing in. One of the Goliaths is right outside the door. He'll show you the way."

Malcolm tried to think of a courageous exit line, but even if he had been able to come up with one, his mouth had become too dry with fear for him to be able to utter it. So he settled for a glare, instead, and stalked out of the room. In the hallway, a monstrous hand landed on his shoulder and steered him away. He didn't bother trying to turn around to see the monstrous hand's owner. He was sure that when you've seen one killer Goliath, you've seen them all.

When Malcolm had been led away, Jimmy Earl said to Shirley, "I have to zip up to Washington and meet with that creepy little guy."

Shirley shivered. It took a lot to make her shiver. "It's really necessary?"

"Gotta keep all the options covered. And that's a major option."

"Be careful, Reverend."

"Don't worry. I've dealt with creepier guys." He paused than said, "Actually, I guess I haven't. Anyway, I don't know how that'll work out, and as I said, I want to keep all the options covered. That brings us back to your spineless little friend, Erskine. You know I'm not going to let that much money and the future of my organization slip away that easily."

"Easily is right. You've softened Plan B considerably."

Jimmy Earl shrugged. "Well, you know, disemboweling him while he's roasting over an open fire would have been very satisfying, but in the end it wouldn't have done us any more good than the quick cement waterski solution. What I really need is him alive and unharmed and cooperating willingly. Which is why I've actually decided to follow what I'm calling Plan A Point Five."

"Plan A Point Five?" Shirley stared at his smiling face. "Oh, Reverend. No."

"Yep. I can't think of anything that would do a better job of keeping a guy like that under my control than letting him have sex with the girl of his dreams."

"Jesus Christ," Shirley muttered.

"Tsk, tsk, profanity," Reverend Jimmy Earl said with an avuncular chuckle.

CHAPTER SEVENTEEN

O, tall trail rider! O, metaphorical cowboy silhouetted heroically against the purple–red sky of sunset as your horse passes clippity–clop over the top of a ridge, taking you on your solitary voyage through wastelands and wildernesses that you singlehandedly civilize and make productive! O, noble creator of wealth, mighty mind, great heart! It may happen from time to time on your hero's voyage that you will find yourself isolated and surrounded by relentless and heartless enemies, with your glorious six guns completely out of bullets. In that day of peril, you must remember that your destiny is both mighty and long term. The loss will be the world's if you let yourself be destroyed. How shall a man make profits if he has lost his head? Therefore, adopt the guise of thine enemy. Become as one of him. Hide your hero's light under a bushel. You will live to fight another day. In the meantime, hold onto your hat. Hold onto your head.

—Lukas of Aldebaran, Merskeenian pragmatist

In Los Angeles, Gloria Pacifica was putting on her usual act. Gloria had taken over the channeling of the one–time Atlantean warrior Mellabenth after the mysterious disappearance of Mellabenth's first channeler, the famous Atlantica. Not much had changed, really. Gloria looked a lot like Atlantica, and the act was very much the same.

So there Gloria was, doing her shtick before an auditorium full of entranced and well fleeced sheep, when something went very wrong.

The first stages progressed as usual. She swelled, foamed at the mouth, spat, gave forth oracular pronouncements in a deep, male voice. But the swelling didn't stop. Her eyes bulged, her torso ballooned, her voice changed to a very feminine shriek, and Gloria Pacifica exploded.

The audience awoke from its trance and ran screaming for the exits. Once they were outside the building, quite a few regained their presence of mind sufficiently to return to the ticket office and insist on a refund. Then the ones who had been in the first few rows hurried home and showered vigorously.

Fortunately for television news organizations, the auditorium had been supplied with video cameras. Gloria, tiring of these live appearances and annoyed with the inherent income limitations enforced by auditorium size, had decided to start selling video recordings of her sessions. She had anticipated high sales. Indeed, the video of her exploding became the highest grossing item on the underground market. The television network news shows began the trend by repeatedly showing the bloodiest part of the explosion on their nightly broadcasts—after, of course, warning their audiences that the upcoming scenes contained graphic matter that might disturb those of a sensitive nature, thus ensuring that no channels would be changed.

While Gloria Pacifica's demise was the most spectacular and the most widely publicized, she was not the only channeler or psychic or astrologer to change planes of existence violently. From California to

New York to Florida to Texas, Malcolm's colleagues died from suspicious fires, unknown but quickly deadly diseases, strokes, heart attacks, drownings, collapsing buildings, exploding eggs, vicious crystals, and in one case apparently from having sex with a prostitute equipped with a poison–injecting device in a most unsuspected place.

The earthbound manifestation of the Channeled Entities of America was being snuffed out of existence.

The credulous were sure that all of these catastrophes were visitations from the astral plane, that spirits long dead were displeased with their earthly mouthpieces. To Malcolm, who knew just how silly the idea of astral spirits was, the string of horrible deaths smacked unsettlingly of James Bond. "Unsettlingly" because he was supposedly under the protection of people who spent a large part of their agency budget inventing James–Bond ways of killing people. When was his turn coming?

Shirley laughed when he finally expressed his fears to her. "Think you'd still be alive if that was the case? Can't you see what's happening? It's your competition that's being eliminated. And if anyone else is bothering you that we don't know about, just tell me."

Malcolm's spirits rose immediately. He had been pinning the blame on the wrong organization. This was better than the little box in front of the Palace of Justice into which informers could slip pieces of papers bearing the names of future headless corpses during the French Revolution!

In Washington, meanwhile, armed troops filled the streets. Since it was Veterans' Day and the troops were the aged survivors of past wars, staggering under the weight of their unloaded rifles, this was not a threat to the Republic.

Someone invited Gone and Fancy to join the Longlegs clan on the reviewing stand, where Mr. and Mrs. Away easily stole the limelight. The Great Encumberer grinned vacuously and waved, while beside him the former First Puppeteer waved, pretended to be enjoying herself, and prompted her husband. The television cameras zoomed in on them and ignored the official President and his relatives.

During breaks in the ceremonies, the television commentators chatted about the truly unusual aspect of this visit by the former President to the present one. Gone and Fancy had been invited to move into the White House, in a guest suite, where their advice, support, and telegenic presences would always be available to the current Chief Executive.

Malcolm, watching all of this on television at his home in Piketon, to which he'd been allowed to return after his whining had worn Shirley down sufficiently, was intrigued. Every now and then, the camera would tear itself away from the beloved faces of the former First Mummy and his wife and pan across the reviewing stand. Always at the side of the present President and his father were Zip Muchley and Jerry and Al.

"My old buddies are sticking close to the wimp and the chimp," Malcolm said to Shirley, who for the moment shared his house, his bed, and his daily decision making.

"Of course," she said. "History's on the move."

"So whose side are you on?"

Shirley grinned at him. "At the moment, yours. Aren't you lucky?"

Malcolm forced a laugh and returned his attention to the television screen. Now the similarities with revolutionary France were making him uneasy.

The parade coverage ended, and a local newscast got underway. The screen filled with the Five's Alive! logo of Channel Five, which in turn gave way to a beaming clone in a suit who said, "Good evening, Piketon! And welcome to the Five's Alive! news at five on Channel Five! We'll be back in a moment with all the news, sports, and weather we think you need to know, after these messages."

Big Bob Buckle in a Hollywood-western cowboy suit speaking in an embarrassing television-western accent, advertising the pickup trucks for sale in his giant lot. "Whadda deal! Whadda steal! Trade in yore raffle, yore dawg, heck, even yore waff. We don' mahnd. We'll deal!"

"First Arapahoe Savings and Extortion, oodles of bucks to lend. You've got a house, right? You've got future earnings from your job, right? You have a firstborn, right? Say, now, those are collateral! Put that house and career and fertility equity to work! Forget all that bunk about the economy. We're here for you. Come in and borrow!"

"ColossoVerse Corporation regrets to announce an increase in rates, recently rubber-stamped by the Arapahoe Public Service Commission, which also rubber-stamped our acquisition of all the cell-phone and cable-television companies serving this area. But because we believe in giving you, our customers, a choice, we're reminding you that you don't have to buy your phone service from us. You can try doing without. Snicker."

"Arapahoe Natural Gas, Electricity, and Radiation Company, here, just to say that the preceding message applies to us, too. Most especially so because we've just been acquired by ColossoVerse Corporation."

Anchorman reappeared, his face somber. "Tragic news in our city today. We go live to Mort out at the Pony Dome. Mort?"

The scene switched to an outside shot of the covered stadium in which Piketon's professional football team wasted time and money, then switched again to show the grim-faced Sports Guy sitting behind a desk. He had removed his jacket, had loosened his tie, and had rolled his sleeves halfway up his forearms to show that he was broadcasting live from the scene of the testosterone display itself. The room's walls were purple—Pony Purple, the team's colors.

"Thanks, Hank. In the worst disaster Piketon has ever experienced in its history, our own Piketon Ponies were defeated today in a National Football League game by the visiting Houston team, who took advantage of prejudiced refereeing, a prejudiced crowd, and prejudicial weather and field conditions. The final score was...high for Houston, low for Piketon."

"How high and how low, Mort?"

Flicker of annoyance. "Very high and very low, Hank. Let's just leave it at that, okay? You can read the paper tomorrow, too, just like everyone else."

Indulgent laugh. "Well, hey, Mort, you know, that's why people watch us in the evening. They want to get the important news right away. So, how high and how low?"

Open anger. "One thousand and three to zero, Hank. Satisfied?"

Hank whistled. "Wow. That sure is high and low, Mort."

Mort grunted something below the level of audibility.

"But at least you got to watch the Ponytails live, right?"

Mort brightened and grunted more enthusiastically at the memory of the Ponies' high-stepping, slutty cheerleaders.

Back to Hank. "In other very important local news, Federal banking officials today concluded a lengthy investigation of a Piketon institution, First Arapahoe Savings and Extortion. First Arapahoe has been placed in receivership. Mr. Fred Seicht, the Assistant Comptroller at First Arapahoe, has been notified that he will be taken into custody as soon as he has had enough time to settle his affairs and transfer his assets to Rio and get the hell out of the country. Seicht, who was not available for comment to your hard-driving investigative reporters at Five's Alive! news, has also been dismissed from his job. His position will be filled by a Ms. Marlene Erskine, formerly Seicht's assistant, who is said to have cooperated fully with Federal officials in their investigation."

The sober expression gave way to a warm, friendly one. "I'd just like to add a personal note, here. Marlene Erskine is a great favorite with all the guys at the station, and we'd all like to wish her the best of luck in her new position. Go for it, Marlene!"

Sober again. "Sad news from Washington. Yesterday, we reported on the passing of Vice President Howard Philips Moon, whose body was found severely decomposed in the master bedroom suite in the vice presidential residence some hours after the suite's refrigeration unit had failed. Now we've been informed of the death of Junior Partridge, who served as Vice President during the Daddy Longlegs administration and was being talked about as a possible running mate for Jibber Longlegs in the upcoming election.

"We're told that Mr. Partridge died from kidney failure. Apparently, Partridge was a secret alcoholic for decades, consuming a minimum of a gallon of high–test every day of his life since his teens. It's a wonder he lasted this long.

"Partridge died in the White House guest suite now being occupied by former President and First Lady Away. Partridge was visiting the former President and First Lady to ask their advice about various foreign policy matters in case he was chosen to run for Vice President again. The announcement about his death and its cause was made by former First Lady Fancy Away, who expressed her and her husband's grief at the loss of so energetic and irrepressible a young man. Mrs. Away said, and I quote, 'He could have been President some day, but it looks like the stars were against it.' Mrs. Away also announced that Mr. Partridge's body was cremated early this morning in order to spare the nation a prolonged and damaging period of mourning."

Anchor Hank, knowing nothing about it, did not report on the turmoil in the residential quarters in the White House, far away from the guest suite now occupied so happily by Fancy and Gone.

Daddy Longlegs was in a panic. To him, the death of the Vice

President wasn't just sad news, it was a disaster.

Daddy had worked it all out. Moon's refrigeration unit was not supposed to have been turned off until Jibber's second term was almost over. At that point, with Moon out of the way, Jebber would be put forward as the logical next Republican presidential candidate. His campaign slogan would be, "Continue the policies of Jibber! Policies that have made our nation feared again all over the world!" Or words to that effect.

It would have worked. Daddy was sure of it. The Longlegs dynasty would have continued without a pause.

But now? It was too soon to bring Jebber into the picture. You couldn't have two brothers running for the nation's top two offices! For all Daddy knew, there might even be a proscription against that in the Constitution. True, the original copy of that document was unreadable, but he believed there were duplicates somewhere. In any case, he was sure it wasn't politically feasible to make Jebber the running mate.

Moon had been a placeholder. He had been a good placeholder. Now Daddy had to come up with a different placeholder.

Turning from news of the deaths of Americans, Hank brightened. "Here's the latest news about the earthquake in Mexico. According to observers in—" frown of concentration "—Kye–yew–dad True–zhee–low, the death toll from yesterday's trembler is at least 3,000."

"Temblor, damn it!" Malcolm shouted. He jumped to his feet, leaped across the room, and switched the set off. "Yeah, go for it, Marlene. Go right down to Kye–yew–dad True–zhee–low and get squished by a falling building."

"Could be arranged," Shirley said.

For just a moment, Malcolm had forgotten her presence. He shivered. "No, thanks. Don't do it on my account. You know, I still don't understand why you *are* doing all of this stuff on my account."

"Don't you remember that meeting Zip took you to in California a few months ago? You prescribed a course of action to a certain great lady, as Zip would say. You told her what path to follow."

"Jesus!" His words, a few phrases invented in desperation, in fear for his life, had led to so many murders and even, perhaps, to a silent coup in Washington? It was hard for Malcolm to believe.

What was even harder to accept was that his conscience was back, revived from seeming death. "I don't want to be responsible for any more of this, Shirley. Lukas just evaporated, and I'm going back to being a novelist."

Shirley looked sad. "Oh, Malcolm, don't start displaying strength and courage and conscience. I really hate that in a man. Haven't you been having a good time with me, especially at night? If you back out, I'll have to go to a great lady for a decision about what to do with you."

"What?" Malcolm said, bewildered. "Not to Jimmy Earl?"

Shirley smiled. "Politics. Bedfellows. Strange."

Malcolm shivered. "Oh." He sighed in defeat. "So, um, what does Lukas have to do next?"

Shirley laughed happily and jumped on him and flung her arms and legs around him and kissed him until he was near suffocation.

"Great!" she said. "That's my spineless guy! I just love it when you're all weak and malleable! Really turns me on. Come on, let's go upstairs for a couple of hours, and then I'll tell you what happens next with Lukas."

That's me, Malcolm thought. Mal. Short for Malleable.

But he went eagerly enough when Shirley, holding his hand tightly, headed for the bedroom.

CHAPTER EIGHTEEN

A boxer must learn to roll with the punches. Johnny Aggressive certainly had.

As Felicia had moved upward, power–bed–wise, Johnny had correspondingly moved from hosting a slightly sleazy television talk show with sparse viewership to being one of the more powerful ranting rightwing loonies on the air. Now he was on both television and radio, the latter a medium he would once have spurned but whose political and remunerative power he had had explained to him by Felicia in words of no more than two syllables. She had also explained why he needed to change his political colors from vaguely populist and sympathetic to the working classes to right wing, angry, and unquestioningly supportive of the plutocracy. To a man who in his youth had fought under a variety of pugilistic pseudonyms, this was easy to understand. Roll with the punches.

So why did Tom Moore choose the Johnny Aggressive Television Hour—"A hard punch in the mouth from the Fist of Truth!"—to make his announcement?

Perhaps it amused him to play Daniel in the lions' den. Perhaps he wanted to make a point of his physical and intellectual courage when compared to the pitiful little critter in the White House. If it was the latter, he had miscalculated, reckoning without the image painted for the public by the media.

In any case, on a Thursday evening, there he was, Tom Moore, The Brain Cell Kid, daring to go fifteen rounds with the cauliflower–eared Fist of Truth himself.

Ding! First round.

Johnny comes out of his corner quickly. Chin tucked, hands up, dodging and weaving, throwing quick testing punches. Brain Cell looks like an easy mark, a glass jaw, but you never know, some people say he's tougher than he looks.

"So you have something to tell the American people, Mr. Former Vice President?" Light hit to the shoulder.

Doesn't shake The Kid. "That's right, Johnny. I know there's been a lot of speculation, and I'm here tonight to put it to rest."

"Speculation?"

"Speculation. Hesitation. Reservation. And from your end of the political spectrum, more than a little misinformation and prevarication."

Uh–oh! That one slipped past Johnny's guard. It's early in the first round, and already The Fist is rocked.

"I'm running for President again," Moore says almost offhandedly.

Johnny dances back, raises his guard, shakes his head, circles the ring, gets his concentration back.

"Come on, Mr. Former Vice President and Already One–Time Loserman! Everyone knows that my side—I mean, the current administration—is made up of men of the highest integrity, whereas you were part of an administration that set records for sleaze and corruption and just general overall un–Americanness!"

There's applause from the audience.

Actually, there is no audience. The applause is canned.

Brain Cell Kid frowns, loses his rhythm for a moment. The canned applause caught him by surprise.

But it's only for a moment. Then he's back in control again, up on the balls of his feet, shoulders up, hands up, eyes on the prize.

"You're not stupid, Johnny. You're better than the people you work for. I respect your intelligence, so I'm asking you to respect mine and that of the listeners."

Oh, that got right through! Johnny can scarcely breathe! "Unggh!" he says.

"Johnny, there was a special counsel appointed with all sorts of investigative powers. He probed and pursued and spent tens upon tens of millions of taxpayer dollars investigating the President I served with, a man I'm proud to call my friend. That special counsel couldn't find any corruption at all. Isn't that true? You're a guy who knows the score, Johnny."

Johnny looks around desperately.

Ding! Time for a commercial!

Saved by the bell.

The metaphorical pugilists are replaced by a very wide man who is bursting out of his expensive suit at the chest and the waist. He has a happy, friendly grin on his round and vapid face. He reads his lines carefully and painfully from the teleprompter, pausing often.

"Hi! Wallace 'Ten Ton' Tenhut here. You know, back when I was a middlequarterthudpacker for the Piketon Ponies, even though I was getting pounded throughout the football season by all those opposing middlesemithudpackers, I never had to worry about medical care for my broken ribs and broken nose and crushed pelvis and crumbled vertebrae, not to mention the softer parts, because the Ponies had really good medical insurance. Even if the doctors hadn't been able to pull me through, I knew that my family would be taken care of. That's because the Ponies also had good life insurance policies for us. And who do you think sold us the policies for health and life insurance? That's right! The company I'm proud to be President of and also spokesman for: American Flag Partial Life and Health Insurance

Company. We can do the same thing for your family that the Ponies did for me! For only pennies a minute, you can have the confidence and security that come from knowing you've provided properly for your family. The President himself backs us on this."

He chuckled. "No, not me! I mean the real President, the big President, the President of the United States! Jibber Longlegs!" He sighed. "What a guy he is. So call the number on your screen now. Or visit our Web site, which is also on your screen. And tell them Ten Ton sent you!"

Wallace Tenhut grins again, briefly allowing a glimpse of long gray–brown teeth that end in points.

Fadeout to a waving American flag.

Extremely rapid voiceover: "Offer void where investigated. Fine print available upon request via postcard to the address flashing at the bottom of the screen. Credit check and physical check–up may be required. Certain medical conditions and causes of death not covered. Sponsored organ–donor program available. American Flag Partial Life and Health Insurance Company is a wholly owned subsidiary of ColossoVerse Corporation."

Ding! Round Two.

The Kid comes out swinging, driving The Fist back against the ropes. The man is giving the paid loudmouth a boxing lesson.

"Let's pick up where we left off when your bosses sprang that out–of–schedule commercial, shall we?" says Moore. It's a left, straight from the shoulder! "Every single member of the current administration has been convicted of at least a dozen major crimes. They're a gang of filthy, wriggling demons from the lowest pits of Hell!"

Left, right! Left, right! Johnny huddles against the ropes, trying to cover up as much of himself as he can, hoping only to stay on his feet until the end of the round, which seems to be an eternity away.

"That's why the Longlegs gang stole the election for that scumball, sleazeball, pile of shit Jibber! So they could pardon those bastards, and they wouldn't all end up breaking rocks, as they deserve!"

"I thought you were polite and mild mannered," Johnny manages to gasp.

The Kid looks surprised and steps back. "You're right. I am. I mean, I used to be. Something has come over me."

Johnny pushes away from the ropes and staggers around the ring. He swings wildly, with more hope than science. "We stole it from you once. We'll do the same thing again."

That was a lucky one. The Kid wasn't paying attention. He had let himself become inner-directed again, caught up in pondering moral imponderables. That wild punch opened the old cut above his left eye and his face is bloody! Now he has to retreat, grinding his glove into his face to try to restore his vision.

This time, The Kid is the one whom the bell saves.

A waving American flag fills the screen. "America the Beautiful" plays softly. A stylized Revolutionary War Minuteman, thrusting out a chin that's almost enough by itself to frighten off the dastardly British, fades into view and merges with the flag. A deep, powerful, awfully manly voice with an angry undertone begins to talk about the evils of government oppression.

"First they came for the landowners," it says, "but I was not a landowner, so I did not speak out. Then they came for the SUV owners, but I was not an SUV owner, so I did not speak out. When they come for the gun owners, will there be anyone left to speak for me? Yes! There will be the National Musket Association! A fraternity of free men, plus a handful of token women, dedicated to protecting your right to keep and bear and fire off musket balls anywhere and everywhere you damned well want to!"

The letters NMA now fade in and join the waving flag, the firm–

jawed Minuteman, and the patriotic music.

The manly voice bellows, "Join the National Musket Association! Become one of us—the few, the proud, the brave, the Musketeers!" More quietly, almost conversationally, the speaker continues, "Remember: Muskets don't kill people. Fuzzy-minded liberal government policies kill people."

And with a *ding!* we're back for Round Three!

The Fist of Truth looks confident now, after the favorable way the second round finished.

But the Brain Cell Kid looks confident, too. Looks like he's recovered completely. He's calm, relaxed, strong, and the split over his left eye has closed already and is scarcely visible.

The Fist takes the offensive. "A popular President, the whole world frightened of us, and an American populace that has completely forgotten its own history. Why are you even bothering, you loser? Why don't you just lie down and get counted out before you even begin? Avoid the humiliation."

"Well, I'll tell you, Johnny." It's a flurry of blows. "The economy is in a shambles, and the people know it."

The Fist dances backward.

"The world doesn't fear us," The Kid says, "it hates us. It knows we've become dangerous and irrational."

The Fist is having trouble with his footwork. "That doesn't matter! We're strong now, thanks to Jibber. No one can touch us. We dominate! We rule!"

The Kid shakes his head slowly and deliberately. The Fist is mesmerized by the movement and drops his guard. "No, we're weak. We talk big, and we bluster and swagger now, but we're overextended. We have no friends. We don't even have allies. The administration doesn't know what it's doing, domestically or in foreign affairs."

The Fist can no longer raise his hands. His arms hang down by his sides. He's defenseless. Gamely, he tries to fight on. "Jibber is...Jibber is..."

"He's a smelly little chimpanzee controlled by a gang of scum–sucking sleazebags."

Poor Johnny! He's down on one knee. Both knees. Hands and knees. Swaying from side to side. Trying not to fall over. He manages to gasp, "Stronger than you."

"Not this time. I'm going to be ruthless, this time."

Johnny, the former Fist, moans and topples onto his side. The referee begins the count. He should have begun it well before this point, but the network is doing everything it can to make Johnny look like the winner, or at least not like the loser.

The Brain Cell Kid retreats to his corner and stands watching calmly. The referee gives as slow a count as he thinks he can get away with, but it isn't slow enough. It's only forty seconds into the third round, but it's all over.

Before the referee can say "Ten!" and hold up The Kid's hand, declaring him the winner, the scene gives way to yet another commercial.

"You know, fellows, some people are saying that if you want to show what a sensitive, caring kind of guy you are, you should drive one of those little pansy cars. You know, the kind that come about up to your belt and have no power or pickup and that you can't take off the road on your huntin' and cowboyin' expeditions. The kind that use some kind of fancy–schmancy girly hybrid fuel stuff, whatever that is, who knows, only brainiac losers understand that stuff. The kind of vehicle that, well, you know, doesn't have any big, heavy rivets. You know the kind of massive, hard rivets I'm talking about. With corners. You can hurt stuff with 'em. You can hit 'em with a big, heavy iron mallet like you carry around in the back of your truck, and they make a big clanging sound."

Image of a big, heavy iron mallet hitting a big, heavy, massive, hard rivet with corners set into the side of a huge, cowboyin', huntin' kinda truck. *Clang!* A really mighty *clang!*

"Yeah. Like that. So buy yourself one of the new GM Ford Crushems. It's an SUV. It's a really big, tough pickup. Go anywhere. Do all your big tough work with it. Yeah, man."

Image of a huge vehicle, front half an SUV, rear half a really big pickup. Fifteen feet high. Three axles. Immense tires. Lotsa metal. Lots and lotsa massive rivets.

"And you know what? Those little pansy cars? They get in your way, you just crush 'em. In your Crushem. Yeah.

"Comes in a ladies' style, too. Get one of those for the little woman. You'll feel safer knowing she's driving that. Not some stupid station wagon made in Japan or somewhere.

"It's your patriotic duty."

Image of a waving American flag. It's remarkably similar to the flag images used during the commercials for the National Musket Assocation and the American Flag Partial Life and Health Insurance Company.

A slightly quieter, less aggressive voice says in a friendly manner, "One year's free membership in the National Musket Association given away with each purchase of a GM Ford Crushem. Offer good through October."

While the commercial was playing, the referee was escorted from the studio, out through a rear entrance, and into a disgusting alley, where he was flung down a manhole into the sewers and the mouths of the waiting albino crocodiles.

The Fist of Truth just barely escaped the same fate.

It turned out that what Lukas was expected to do was become actively involved in Earthly politics.

Malcolm had never bothered inventing political opinions for Lukas—except in a marginal sense during his tense interview with Fancy—because Lukas's purpose was the making of money. Not that Malcolm was really required to invent political opinions for Lukas now. The opinions were fed to him. He was required only to generate purple Merskeenian prose for Lukas to express those opinions in.

This caused one last momentary squiggle from Malcolm's conscience.

Malcolm had many faults, as Marlene had so often pointed out to him. But he also had a few virtues, and among them was his great sympathy for the socioeconomic underclasses. Not that he had often put that sympathy into practice, either with his money or his vote. However, he had long ago vowed that he would never vote for a Republican candidate in any election, no matter how pretty the speeches that candidate made—or, for that matter, in changing times, how pretty the candidate. Now he was being forced to help a particularly despicable gang of Republicans keep control of the government. Without his help, it was just conceivable that they might lose that control.

"Well?" his conscience asked pugnaciously. "Now what, huh?" it persisted, gaining strength and confidence. "Huh, Malcolm? Huh? Huh?"

Shirley explained real life to him. "If you help them get reelected, they won't have to resort to force and bloodshed to stay in power. So by helping them, you'd actually be helping to preserve the Constitution. If you refuse to help them, you'd be helping to destroy the Constitution. Not to mention yourself."

In the face of logic like that, Malcolm's conscience gave up the fight in a huff and went away.

So it was that Malcolm found himself speaking at expensive dinners, addressing groups of Republican Party insiders, many of whom were horrified at the idea of having Fancy as their party's vice-presidential candidate in the upcoming election. But it wasn't Malcolm doing the speechmaking, supposedly; it was Lukas of Aldebaran speaking through Malcom Erskine.

He stood at the head of a long table covered with expensive food and drink and lined on both sides with men with large bellies, dressed in expensive suits, and wearing worried expressions, and said, "O children of the stars, O saviors of your nation, O tall-proud walkers, O mercenary mulcters of the macho morning in America—" puzzled frowns at that one, and Malcolm told himself to exercise some restraint "—know thou now of thy leader's thoughts and mine. Send not to ask for whom the bell tolled: it tolled for Junior."

There was an uneasy stirring at this. Junior had had his fans, and they were still upset at his death and unconvinced about its cause.

"And also for the moon guy."

The grumblings were replaced by nodding of heads. No one had been surprised at the setting of the moon. Few regretted it.

"So now what?" someone called out. "Does Lukas have any advice about who we should choose for the veep candidate?"

"About whom you should choose?" Malcolm said, drawing out the m. "Yes, trail riders. Yes, self-sufficient, self-made followers of the star-born cowboy way. Lukas has some thoughts."

"Stop stalling," Shirley's miniaturized voice whispered in his ear.

"Fancy that. That is what Lukas thinks."

Through the veils of cigar smoke, Malcolm saw confusion on many of the faces already addled by alcohol.

"Fancy Away," Malcolm said. "Wise mother figure, life companion of the Great...of the great one himself. She has offered herself as Jibber's running mate, and Jibber has smiled upon her, and Jibber is a cute little monkey."

"But, hey, say, no way." The speaker was an angry young man

halfway down the table on Malcolm's left. "We owe something to Junior. He did a good job for us back..." He trailed off in confusion. He frowned, trying to remember something. "Well, however many years ago that was. I'm not gonna go along with just forgetting him. He had a wife, too. She's already expressed some interest in the veep slot. If we're gonna go with a female candidate, then we oughta be talking about Mrs. Partridge. She's a lot younger than Fancy, anyway. Fancy's looking pretty bad these days." There were a few tentative nods of agreement from others.

Malcolm leaned forward slightly to get a better view of the man who had spoken. He stared at the man until Shirley's voice whispered, "Okay. Identified. He's dead. Get on with the crap production."

Talk about the evil eye, Malcolm thought.

He continued. "War, as we heroes among the stars learned some thirty thousand of what you call 'years' ago, is not only a matter of attack, but also of defense. And defense requires knowing in advance your enemy's plans. The Marlingas against whom your stellar hero ancestors fought were not only powerful, malicious creatures—" and favorites of all the guys at the station "—but also cunning and devious. When this fearful enemy knew of our defensive plans, they would immediately change their own attack strategy. Thus it is that your enemies have laid secret plans and made secret promises that their own running mate in your forthcoming election will be female—"

A stir ran around the table.

"—and black—"

The stir increased.

"—and homosexual—"

The stir became a rumble of rising voices.

"—and Jewish—"

The party men were rising to their feet and begging Lukas to assure them that it wasn't so.

"—and a homeless street person flag–burning feminist fetus killer!"

Screams and shouts and strong men fainting and pledges of support for the only possible running mate who could preserve control of the White House for the Grand Old Party. The cries of "Fancy! Fancy! Fancy!" became a roar in unison.

This was the way these dinners almost always ended. Usual reaction, said Malcolm to himself.

To a degree, events happened just as in Fancy's vision of...well, however many years earlier it was.

At the Republican convention, Jibber was nominated for reelection by acclaim. He gibbered for a while from the podium. Everyone was assured that he had just delivered one of the most eloquent and stirring acceptance speeches in the history of any American political party. One line of it, the delegates were told, signified his selection of Fancy Away as his running mate.

Fancy was then nominated by acclaim.

The campaign was under way.

But then things got a bit rough.

To the amazement of party officials, Daddy Longlegs, Mr. Umbral, and reporters covering the campaign, the Jibber charm seemed to have worn off.

Oh, he was still a cute little monkey. No one would dream of denying that. And he still did a fine job of playing cowboy and posing in his little boots and hat and squinting into the distance. And he gibbered away quite charmingly on the campaign trail.

And yet, despite all of that, the polls showed Tom Moore, who had won the Democratic nomination fairly easily, first staying even with Jibber and then actually pulling ahead.

Perhaps it was the awful state of the economy. Perhaps it was the occasional outbreaks of armed insurrection here and there and massive forest and brush fires and terrible floods and windstorms and general horrendous weather extremes. Perhaps it was the mounting losses in the large number of almost secret small wars American forces were engaged in all over the world. Perhaps it was the dramatic growth of foreign competitors, such as the European Union, which was rumored to be holding serious talks with both Russia and Canada about those two countries joining up. Perhaps it was the ill-defined feeling on the part of the American public that something had gone wrong, that the country had taken a wrong turn somewhere, that the era of American dominance in the world had already ended, and that it had ended a generation or two earlier than historical forces should have caused it to end.

There were even protests! Against Jibber! How could this be? How could any true American raise his voice against this cute little monkey? And yet some did.

There were few protestors at first—just a handful at each campaign appearance by Jibber. They held up signs with fairly mild messages, like GIVE US BACK OUR BUDGET SURPLUS. Boring, really. Easily ignored by the press. Especially since they were forced to remain within four foot by four foot First Amendment zones, and those were always situated blocks away from the place where Jibber would be putting on his little squinty-eyed tough cowboy act for the rubes.

Ignoring the protestors turned out to be a mistake, though. Even though they were never shown on the evening news, they were emboldened by being allowed to protest at all. They recruited more of their scummy fellows. Their numbers grew. They ignored the First Amendment zones. Their signs began to bear more provocative messages, like UNELECTED FRAUD and JAIL TO THE THIEF and EAT GRUBS AND DIE. Every now and then, and despite the great care taken by cameramen and editors, viewers of nightly television news still caught occasional glimpses of the knaves and their treasonous signs.

Pictures of the protests spread by e-mail and were posted on reprehensible Web pages. The crowds of protesters grew ever larger. Their signs became ever more daring.

It was time for a lesson.

Jibber was scheduled for a performance in Indianapolis, in front of the state capitol. A First Amendment zone was set up a block south, on Maryland Street. This was much closer to the event than previous First Amendment zones. That made it much more likely that the protestors would be seen on the evening news. That was the intent.

This particular First Amendment zone was two feet by two feet. Five hundred protestors showed up and were directed and then forced into the four foot square space by 5,000 heavily armed and armored city police, National Guardsmen, and U.S. Marines.

Now, as a consequence of youth and vegetarianism, the average left-wing protestor is rather slenderer than the average American. According to a number of reputable scientific studies, the four square feet allocated for free speech in Indianapolis on that balmy day could have accommodated a maximum of six such protestors if they all exhaled at the same time. That's not allowing for their signs or their rude gestures. So that left 494 of them outside the First Amendment zone. That is to say, 494 of those wretched, un-American creatures were without any legal grounds for exercising that right of free speech that they childishly thought the Bill of Rights guaranteed to them wherever they were in the United States. Astonishingly, they insisted on exercising that right even though they were clearly not entitled to do so. Who could have imagined such effrontery?

Actually, the Longlegs political advisers could have imagined it and had imagined it and were counting on it and were well prepared for it.

The news cameras arrived. They were directed to nice vantage points.

All of a sudden, helicopters roared in from all directions. They landed on the street and in every available open space and more heavily armed and armored troops emerged from them. Giant vehicles rumbled in along every street and disgorged still more well equipped, uniformed patriots. They were joined by barely restrained packs of slavering dogs and mounted policemen riding powerful and nervous horses whose eyes rolled around in their heads—a visible sign of the unpredictable, murderous stupidity characteristic of the species.

The dangerously outnumbered police and National Guardsmen and Marines were being reinforced just in time! If they had not been, who knows what might have happened in that tense and dangerous situation? Their foe was ruthless, unprincipled, angry, and in all too many cases inadequately shaved and bathed.

There was a moment of misleading calm.

The two mighty armies faced each other across a six-foot no-man's-land of concrete. The breeze stilled. Birdsong ceased. The world held its breath. The future of democracy hung in the balance.

Then the forces of law and order smiled happily, raised their nail-studded clubs, and charged.

The injuries were ferocious. Five policemen suffered rotator cuff tears from swinging their clubs too vigorously. An unknown number of police and military uniforms were so badly stained by blood and brains and various other disgusting stuff that they could not be cleaned and were buried with full honors. A half dozen clubs were actually broken, and one pitiful dog lost a tooth! (But that's okay: he was later given a medal in a touching ceremony attended by a spare Cabinet secretary.)

The un-American enemy did not escape without injuries, you will be glad to know. As the protestors were hauled away so that they could rot deservingly in jail, television viewers who were still paying attention noticed that arms, legs, and not a few necks were bent at very strange angles and in a few cases seemed not to be properly attached.

The lucky six protestors who had arrived first and squeezed into the tiny space where the First Amendment applied were untouched. After all, they had been following the rules. In fact, as the battle progressed, they managed to squeeze so much more closely together that it was possible that another demonstrator might have been able to fit in with them and also enjoy the blessed rights protected by our much admired and imitated Constitution. If any other demonstrator had still been in a position or condition to stand up.

There were no more protests.

But Jibber's poll numbers kept falling and Moore's kept rising anyway.

It was incomprehensible to the Longlegs gang. They simply couldn't understand it.

But of course the reason it was happening didn't matter. What mattered was the danger that Jibber might actually lose the election.

Something had to be done.

First the Longlegs clan tried the obvious and easy approach, the one that had worked so well the first time. Whenever Moore spoke, hired hecklers yelled the usual insults at him: "Nerd boy!" "Smart kid!" "Liarliarliarliarliarliar!" "Bald man!"

Some of those hired hecklers were reporters covering the campaign. During the first two debates between the two candidates, some of those hired hecklers were the panelists asking the candidates the questions.

The National Musket Association did its best to help. They would show up at the edge of the crowd during Moore's appearances and fire their muskets in an attempt to drown out his speeches. This was not very effective, though, because their muskets were of course single–shot muzzleloaders that required much fussing with balls and rags and black powder and ramrods and so on, and the Musketeers were all old, crotchety, arthritic, severely overweight and out of shape, inept would–be warriors. They did distract the crowds' attention from Moore from time to time, but not in the way they intended.

Just as they had four years earlier, the various news channel clone announcers did their best to help.

When Bip and Bop were caught quite literally red–handed after machine–gunning a group of German tourists in front of the Lincoln Memorial and then picking the corpses' pockets because they—Bip and Bop—were fresh out of beer money, the press uncovered a monstrous scandal involving Tom Moore's wife.

The news clones made sure that this scandal dominated the evening news. Mrs. Moore, they reported breathlessly and wide–eyed, had just been issued a parking ticket! She had parked in a no–parking zone! In Washington, D.C., itself, the nation's beloved capital! Why, that was practically in the Oval Office! And her husband had the audacity to ask the voters to let him besmirch that same Oval Office with his presence? Oh, these were evil and declining days, indeed. The great republic was skirting the abyss, and only one cute little monkey could save it.

Mrs. Moore protested that she didn't drive and indeed didn't even have a driver's license.

The press was even more scandalized. This shameless woman, who actually shared a bed with the disgusting Tom Moore, and who knew just what they did there, had not only parked her car illegally practically on the sanctified floor of the Oval Office itself, she had also been driving without a license! Nauseated, the news clones could scarcely force themselves to mention this depravity further, although they would somehow manage to do just that repeatedly for the remainder of the campaign.

But how about those Bip and Bop gals, huh? What a pair of cutups! And so appealing, too, in their charming, free–spirited youthful way. The Toothsome Twins, one male newsreader called them. "I realize that you're a gal, too, Joanie," he said to his partner, "but you gotta admit they're a very attractive pair of young ladies."

"I guess so, Jerry. Now, let's continue with this terrible breaking story about the Moore woman's traffic crimes."

"Uninhibited barely legal twins," Jerry said. "Whoa." He licked his lips. He seemed oblivious to Joanie's constant warning looks and kicks under the desk. "They are of legal age now, aren't they? Bip and Bop?"

"I believe so." Joanie gave up on him and turned toward the camera. "Let's bring our viewers up to date. Earlier this evening, the alleged wife of the alleged Democratic candidate for President was observed illegally parking her car practically on top of the desk of the real, actual, honest–to–God President of the United States, the divinely ordained Jibber Longlegs himself. We're glad to report that the beloved cute little monkey is safe and unhurt. As for the so–called Mrs. Moore, however—"

"Did you see that one shot of Bip?" Jerry asked her. "When she tripped over that dead German guy and her skirt came up to her waist? Man, oh, man..."

"We'll be back right after these messages," Joanie said.

"Hey there! This is Ten Ton Tenhut, former famous jock. I just took on the job of Former Famous Jock Fake Spokesman here at ColossoVerse Corporation. I'm speaking to you from my new office up here on the 55th Floor of our headquarters building in downtown Piketon. The view is great. Hey, look at this!"

He pointed, and the camera swiveled to show a wall covered with the mounted heads of lions and leopards and cheetahs and Cape buffalo and other huge, fearsome beasts.

"I bagged these myself! Got 'em over there in Africa. I was on a hunting safari with former President Daddy Longlegs and our amazing current President, Jibber Longlegs himself. Man, you shoulda seen the way Jibber took care of those lions and stuff. Made me even prouder to be an American than I already was."

There was a certain degree of exaggeration in this account. The slaughter had not taken place in Africa but at Great White Hunter Safari, a game farm in Florida owned by a major donor to the Jebber Longlegs gubernatorial campaign fund.

The farm bought aging lions, tigers, bears, and so on from zoos and traveling circuses. Some of the big cats came from private owners who had bought them as cute cubs. After a few months, owning such pets no longer seemed like such a good idea, and not just because of the rising butcher bill.

At Great White Hunter Safari, the tired, confused, hungry, mostly old animals were drugged to provide an extra margin of safety and chained to posts sunk deep into the ground to provide yet a further margin of safety. Then they were peppered with bullets from a safe distance and from the far side of a deep ditch by manly men who paid a high fee for the privilege. Eventually, despite the poor accuracy of the mighty hunters, the four–legged beasts died, after which their heads were removed and prettied up (colored putty worked well for the many bullet holes) for proud display by two–legged beasts.

Of course Jibber had not been present. No force on Earth would have gotten him that close to those big cats, not even old, drugged, chained–up ones.

Daddy had been there, though, firing away, and whooping and hollering like a television Texan. He was putting some things to rest.

"Anyway," Ten Ton said, "the reason I'm here on your screen right now is just to tell you that we really like you, we think all you guys are great, and we're here for you, everywhere, all the time. We'll have more to tell you in the future about the role you'll be playing in the new ColossoVerse, but for right now, that's all I wanted to say. 'Bye now!"

The newsroom appeared again, with Joanie sitting alone at the desk looking very perky. "Welcome back, everyone! We'll have a five–second recap of international news, followed by the twenty minutes of sports updates that we do every half hour, and then please stay tuned for an hour–long special I'll be hosting titled, 'The Moores: Merely Evil and Depraved, or Actual Pawns of Satan?'"

The glossy magazine inserts in Sunday newspapers across America ran stories about Jibber's astonishing heroism during the Viet Nam War, telling readers how he had flown his jet fighter on solitary support missions, braving fearsome ground fire to help embattled American troops, and how, on two occasions, when that help was not sufficient, he had returned to his base and then led a thrilling charge on horseback, deep into Vietcong–held territory, six–guns blazing, to rescue our gallant lads. Meanwhile, said the magazines, Tom Moore had been hiding stateside, emerging only to spit upon returning American soldiers.

None of this helped.

Moore was pulling further ahead in the polls. Just possibly, the Longlegs–Umbral–inspired propaganda had gone just a tad too far and had thus lost credibility. Scenting victory at last, the Democratic leadership chipped in all their pennies and quarters and purchased an almost complete set of vertebrae.

The situation was perilous. Sterner measures were needed.

Came the third and final presidential debate.

Moore looked calm, confident, even a bit cocky.

Jibber looked nervous. For once, he almost seemed to understand what the human beings he lived with had been talking about.

Secret Service agents were scattered about the auditorium and four of them stood protectively on the stage, one on each side of Jibber, one on each side of Moore. They stared around sternly at the crowd, at the candidates, even at each other. From time to time, they exchanged quick hand signals. It was very impressive.

The candidates gave their opening statements.

Jibber went first. As he had been so carefully trained to do, he clomped out from behind his podium in his little cowboy boots, pushed his little cowboy hat back on his head, stood bowlegged for a few minutes, hands on his hips, squinting at the crowd with his jaw thrust forward, and then gibbered for a few minutes. As he turned and clomped back behind his podium, the Republican half of the audience jumped up from its seats and applauded and shrieked and squealed and stamped its feet. They were joined by the panel of reporters who were there to ask questions of the candidates.

After the crowd and the panel had settled down, it was Tom Moore's turn. He smiled slightly and said, "There you go again."

The Democratic side laughed and cheered.

The moderator spoke angrily into his microphone. "People, we can't have this! You're just taking time from the candidate you support. Please hold your applause till the end of the debate. Unless you're so overcome with patriotism that you can't help applauding our wonderful President. That would be understandable. But don't applaud the other guy. Thank you."

"Thank you," Tom Moore said ironically. "I assume that long interruption won't be counted against my time, and the clock starts now?"

The moderator made a face at him and muttered, "Wise guy."

Moore shifted his attention to the crowd. He seemed straighter, bigger, stronger than four years earlier. He ignored the pitiful little simian and the panelists and spoke directly to the audience in the auditorium and those watching the debate on television.

"Four years ago, unemployment stood at under four per cent. According to the most recent figures, it's now at 99.6 per cent. A budget surplus of 250 billion dollars has been converted to a deficit of five trillion dollars. From the most powerful, wealthiest, and admired nation in the world, we've gone to being poor, weak, despised, and on the verge of civil war."

That was as far as he was allowed to get. The Republican part of the crowd and all of the panel were on their feet screaming insults and shooting rubber bands at him.

Moore stood his ground quietly and stared down the rowdies. When the noise had subsided enough for him to be heard, he said, "Now, I'd like to ask a question of..." He paused for a few seconds and then, with a faint, ironic smile, continued, "...the President."

The two Secret Service men guarding Moore moved close in and raised their hands threateningly, quite close to his head.

Moore turned his head toward Jibber and started to say something.

His head fell off.

The audience watched in silent horror as Moore's head, his expression one of surprise and disapproval, thumped to the floor of the stage. Blood shot in powerful spurts from his cleanly sliced neck. His torso collapsed and twitched for a while and then stopped.

The Secret Service men who had been on the stage leapt off it to avoid the spreading pool of blood.

The audience and the panelists exploded into motion. They ran screaming for the exits.

Hiding behind his podium, Jibber also screamed. As was his wont when he was terrified, which he was so much of the time, he expelled violently all the feces and urine in him. He vomited, to boot. Fortunately for his political career, the podium hid him, and the one television camera whose operator hadn't fled was trained unwaveringly on the two separated pieces of Tom Moore.

Which meant that the camera caught the return of the two Secret Service men who had been standing on either side of Moore. They mounted the stage, treading very carefully. They looked at the body with distaste, looked around to make sure the place was empty, and then, very gingerly, picked up something from the stage floor that the camera and its operator couldn't make out. They put whatever it was in a box, turned to leave, and noticed the camera and its red light and the man standing behind it.

The poor man should have fled with the crowd. As it was, so unhinged was he by the extra few minutes of watching Moore's ghastly body, that he destroyed his camera and the tape it contained and then went to the nearest men's room and drowned himself in a toilet.

That evening, the horrible end of the debate was the only topic on television. Over and over, grim-faced news anchors told America how President Jibber Longlegs had taken charge immediately, calming the crowd, comforting Moore's widow, and assuring everyone within hearing that he would not rest until he had brought to justice the vile evildoers who had in so cowardly a manner struck down the former Vice President and brainiac loser. Jibber's virile anger and manly sorrow were much remarked upon.

Later reports indicated that the villains were a gang of ancient Nazis who had been hiding out in Argentina since the end of World War Two, striving to perfect a death ray. Apparently they had managed to infiltrate the United States, bringing a working version of their hideous device with them. Their intended target, of course, had been the noble Jibber, not the debased Democrat, but they were, understandably, very old Nazis indeed, and their eyesight was terrible.

Jibber's administration issued a stern warning to Argentina, telling the South American nation that if it didn't hand over the Nazis and their frightful machine in twenty-four hours, along with detailed proof that no more such machines or Nazis were present in the country, then the United States would have to take unspecified action and could not be held responsible for the consequences.

Americans went to bed shocked at the loss of the man most of them had intended to vote for in the coming election but heartened and comforted and with renewed confidence in the strong, protective hand of their eloquent President.

Not reported was a diplomatic dispatch received in Washington later that night from Brussels explaining that the Argentine government had begun negotiations with the EU concerning a mutual defense treaty, and in light of that, Brussels strongly advised Washington not to issue any warnings or ultimatums to Buenos Aires. Or to anyone else south of the Rio Grande. Or, for that matter, anywhere else.

Washington's response, also not reported publicly, was couched in the usual diplomatic circumlocutions. It could be accurately translated into conversational American English as, "Oh. Okay."

The vertebrae the Democrats had recently bought and installed crumbled. Perhaps they had been obtained from an unreliable supplier.

The party passed over Moore's running mate and chose for its new Presidential candidate an obscure governor who, it came to light during what was left of the campaign, had belonged to Students for a Democratic Society while in college and whose grandfather, in a nice piece of family generational balance, had been a bigshot in the Ku Klux Klan. His running mate was Moore's original running mate—that same black, female, Jewish homosexual who had once been a homeless street person, had once burned the American flag, and favored abortion on demand. During the campaign, it was disclosed that she had also once been a man, but that seemed anticlimactic.

The election results resembled the outcome of a football game starring the Piketon Ponies on one side and any competent team on the other.

The following spring, only seven months after Jibber's record–setting landslide reelection victory, and only four months after he had been inaugurated for his second term as President and Fancy had been inaugurated for her first term as Vice President, the Longlegs family went sailing together off the New England coast.

Daddy had always loved sailing. It made him feel manly and competent and not like a wimp at all. Grammy hated sailing, but she often went out with Daddy in order, so to speak, not to rock the boat. The three little brothers feared any body of water that was more than a foot across, but they hadn't realized where they were being led until it was too late. Bip and Bop had been carried aboard in an alcoholic haze and handcuffed to their beds below deck, and they still had no idea that they were at sea. Newspapers had been spread in a thick layer over the floor of their cabin in preparation for their awakening.

Mr. Umbral was not aboard, even though he had suggested the sailing trip. "A victory celebration," he had told Daddy. "And it will promote family togetherness. You can get the three boys back into line. They've been acting somewhat too independent lately, don't you think?"

Daddy did indeed think so. He nodded vigorously. "Water," he said. "Fear. Threats. Keep those terrible twins in line, too. If they don't, over they go. Maybe a good idea, anyway. Hate those girls."

But now, far out upon the heaving blue–green breast of the mighty ocean, Daddy was concerned with something else.

Staring down at the wooden planks that formed the deck, Daddy frowned. "What the heck is that?" he said. "Doesn't look right. Tiny, moving things. Eating the deck. Jibber, stop squeezing my hand so hard!"

But then Daddy realized what he was looking at and he understood the sudden yawning chasm at his feet. "Shit!" he shouted. "Mr. U.!"

The President of the United States shrieked in sudden fear, let go of his daddy's hand, leaped away, and scampered to the top of the main mast, spewing feces and urine all the way up.

A giant meteorite crashed into the ocean, vaporizing zillions of gallons of seawater and the sailboat and the entire Longlegs family.

Or so the official account said.

Not a trace of the boat or the bodies of those onboard was ever found. It was as though they had been reduced to their individual molecules and then eaten, as one television newsreader put it imaginatively just before he too disappeared. The caskets at the state funeral were therefore only symbolic, even Jibber's tiny one with the cowboy hat, boots, and toy pistols laid touchingly upon it. A horse was bought from a glue factory, humanely killed, and buried next to Jibber's empty casket in Arlington National Cemetery to symbolize the deep–rooted essential cowboyness of the late President.

Fancy ascended to the presidency immediately.

Together, Zip Muchley and Shirley Weng paid a visit to Malcolm.

Malcolm gibbered like a terrified little simian, but in the end they persuaded him to take on his new assignment.

CHAPTER NINETEEN

O poor, gullible, forever earthbound reader! You ask me—me! a star-dwelling, high-income Merskeenian executive with much better things to do!—if it is true that we make our own reality and that we can be anything that we want to be if only we follow the appropriate set of rules and procedures, such as those outlined in the best-selling business self-help book by Malcolm Erskine. Oh, don't be a twit. Of course not. Reality is reality. It's real, it's there, and if you're smart, you'll do your best to understand exactly what it is and then you'll accept it. However, this much is true: Other people are gullible, and if you can dupe them into believing in the right silly, made-up version of reality, then you can end up being filthy rich and never having to work again. Just like my unscrupulous channeler, Malcolm Erskine.

—Lukas of Aldebaran, coming clean

Fifteen years later, on the day after Fancy's state funeral, Malcolm began writing his autobiography.

No one had expected Fancy to last that long. Certainly no one had believed she would stay in power for that long.

China killed her, finally. Not the country, but dinnerware that arrived with a pattern different from the one she had ordered. She was infuriated. She was explaining to the portrait of Calvin Coolidge how justified her fury was when something burst in her head and she smiled pleasantly at Calvin and became forever as silent as he was reputed to have been.

She was buried in Washington, along with her husband. The memorial tomb had never been finished, and the foreign power in whose steadily expanding territory it was now located had no reason to spend any money on it, although it did briefly consider completing the thing so that it could serve as an offbeat tourist attraction.

Malcolm was now anticipating, without any great pleasure at the prospect, his sixtieth birthday.

He was overly aware of the body parts that no longer worked as well as they once had. He dwelt on this far too much. Lukas! he would often cry in his mind. Lukas of Aldebaran! Old buddy! Bring me the secret of immortality and eternal youth from your magical pharmacopoeia among the stars! Since Lukas was a fictive invention and telepathy was a dream, Malcolm was not surprised that he never received an answer, but in his secret heart he always hoped that some day he would.

"And not a second bestseller in all this time," he grumbled. "Maybe because I never did finish *Business Dangers from the Stars.* Or maybe because in *Sex, Sins, and Software,* only the first chapter had any spice, because there's no sex in software and I couldn't dream up enough sins. You know, I thought at least all the computer programmers in the world would buy that one, which would at least have meant pretty good sales, but it turned out that all of them prefer to read science fiction, and I can't seem to write that stuff any more. And then I thought my book of critical essays on popular novels, *The Unbearable*

Lightness of Inferior Fiction, would be a hit, but I couldn't even get it published."

"Well, now," his next-door neighbor and dearest male friend in all the world said in mild reproof, "some might say that having one smash hit bestseller and being Vice President of the United States and changing history were enough accomplishments for any one man's lifetime."

"Yeah, there is all of that," Malcolm said, smiling a bit smugly. "Although the bestseller was cynical hack work, I was only V.P. for six months, and the change in history was not exactly for the better."

"There were some good things about it," Carol said, and now it was his turn to be smug.

Shortly after Fancy became President, the Rapture occurred. Actually, it was a rather small-scale version of the Rapture, limited to one man and experienced by no one else. That one man was Reverend Gregory. He was enraptured to some other plane of existence, and Carol was nominated by his dear friend Jimmy Earl as a fine replacement. You could say, as Carol once told Malcolm, that both Gregory and he were kicked upstairs, although in very different ways. As a result, Carol was the White House's favorite preacher during the long years of Fancy's ascendancy, thanks to his toadying television sermons from the pulpit of the National Cathedral about God's approval of the administration.

The long years of that ascendancy had ingrained a lot of habits in everyone. Even though he knew that Fancy was definitely dead and gone, Carol looked over his shoulder and scanned the distance for observers before he said, "I'm sure that in your memoirs you'll blow the lid off everything that happened. That'll give you another bestseller."

"I'm certainly not going to write my political memoirs," Malcolm told him. "That's an occupational disease of ex-government officials which just wastes a lot of paper. Besides, as I said, I was veep for only six months, and it was a long time ago. No interest in that. Maybe I'll write a literary memoir instead. Tell the truth about my writing career."

They broke off to make obligatory kitchey-coo sounds over Carol's three-week-old grandchild. Carol's daughter and son-in-law had just come over to proudly show the neighbor what they had produced.

When the smelly little creature was finally removed to have its diaper changed, Malcolm and Carol resumed their conversation.

"I'm more than fifteen years older than you," Carol said, "and I'm too old for this grandfather shit. Anyway, I don't know if you're wise to expect people to rush out and buy a book telling them how you made fools of them. You might earn more resentment than sales."

"This isn't exactly your field of expertise, is it?" Malcolm said with open annoyance.

"What? Fooling people and taking their money and yet having them still love me for it? Are you kidding? Anyway, I bet you have a lot of good anecdotes about your political career that you could make a book out of instead."

Malcolm smiled at some memories. "Yeah. A few." Now *he* looked over his shoulder quickly before continuing, then he said in a low voice, "But I wouldn't want to write 'em down. Too many of the people involved are still alive. Listen to this, Carol. First cabinet meeting after the big reshuffling and restructuring of the government. There I was, sitting at an immense conference table in the White House, wondering what the hell I was doing there..."

Hear, O star-dupe, O one of the uncountably many suckers of the galaxy, one of whom is born every minute on each world that bears self-styled intelligent life, hear what Malcolm Ur-Cynic told his dear friend, Carol Pabulum–Preacher.

There he was, sitting at an immense conference table in the White House, wondering what the hell he was doing there, when Fancy called the meeting to order. Responsibilities of all those present had been radically redefined by the new president by means of presidential decree. The Speaker of the House had informed her that she couldn't do that without congressional approval, and some of her changes might possibly need a constitutional amendment, although he wasn't sure about that and would have to consult with his staff, so she had him taken outside by the Secret Service and shot, after which she specified who was to be the next Speaker, and there was no more trouble. Certainly Malcolm had been frightened enough for all of Washington.

"Secretary of Defense!" Fancy called out. "What's the latest on the Wishful Thinking Missile Defense System?"

"Please, Madam President," the secretary said in a pained voice, "it's the Prayer Shield. We changed the name, remember? Well, we're not doing too badly. We're running into some problems with the new software you mandated, the stuff that will provide real–time horoscopes for all of our officers as part of the fire–no–fire decisionmaking process, so we're gonna need a few billion more dollars and maybe another ten years."

"Dollars are no problem," Fancy snapped. "Time is. Keep on schedule."

"I should add," the Secretary of Defense said with obvious reluctance, "that we're running into a lot of resistance from some of our people. They're not taking the new stuff seriously, so they're not cooperating."

"Take 'em out and shoot 'em."

"Oh. Er, yes, ma'am." The secretary looked at the Secret Service men standing motionlessly behind each chair and chose discretion over valor.

For a moment, Malcolm thought of Jimmy Flicker and how well he would have fit in here. He should have been Vice President, Malcolm thought, not me.

"Secretary of Interior Design! Fall fashions better be on schedule."

"Oh, yes, indeed, Madam President! No delays in my department. No, sirree. I've got my people assembled in the Oval Office for a preview private showing for you, ma'am, as soon as this meeting's over."

Fancy smiled her pleasure at the nervous secretary. "What else?"

"And the new color scheme for the private quarters is also waiting for your approval, ma'am."

"Very good! Keep up the good work, and I'll give you a state of your own.

"Secretary of Separation. I understand you're having a bit of trouble."

"Oh, hell, no, ma'am. Hell, no! Not any more." Jimmy Earl chuckled happily. He was in his element now. This was so much easier than that damned television show. More real power, too. He had done his part to get Fancy in there, and this was his reward, and he was perfectly happy with it. Now that Jefferson's damned wall was finally gone, the main target of his television sermons was gone, anyway, so he would have had a hard time coming up with something to talk about before the cameras.

"You're referring to that little hooraw out there in Colorado, I guess." Coloraduh, he pronounced it. He didn't even have to think about the accent any more. "Yeah, there was a brief uprising by some seculars in Boulder, but it was put down nice and quick and real effectively—" he licked his lips at the memory of the video images he had seen "—by the Fourth Georgia Volunteers. Those fellas moved up from their base in Colorado Springs right smart. Very efficient group.

I'd like to give them some kind of reward and expand their area of responsibility. They're really good boys."

Fancy waved her hand. "Sure. Of course. Whatever you think." She seemed distracted suddenly.

Despite how much she owed to the next Cabinet member, she was reluctant to call on him. He gave everyone the creeps. She could see how the other Cabinet secretaries and assorted underlings had surreptitiously slid their chairs away, putting as much space between him and them as they could. There was no help for it, though. He had named his price, and she would have to put up with him. "Secretary of Security? Any problems?"

Mr. Umbral smirked. He had had to search far and wide, but he had finally found someone capable of doing the refurbishing work. Workmanship had finally returned to the old level, and the newer artisans were as good as those of long ago. At last his sneer was gone and he had full control over his mouth once again. "Of course not, ma'am. All domestic matters are fully under control. I'll say no more in public."

With almost visible relief, Fancy said, "Vice President! Have you squelched this Radio Free Europe crap yet?"

Malcolm sighed. This would make him the only cabinet member so far with bad news, and he could feel the eager monster behind his chair breathing on the back of his neck. "I'm afraid the Europeans are adamant, ma'am. They say they won't stop their broadcasts unless you drop martial law, reinstitute elections, plus a few other demands. Oh, and they said to tell you that the trade sanctions will also remain in place, and they won't lend us any more money, either."

Fancy grew red faced and pounded on the table. "This means war!"

The Secretary of Defense held up a timid hand. "Uh, ma'am? Ma'am? I don't think so, ma'am. See, we buy all our weapons from the

Europeans now, as it is. I mean, the Northern Union."

"Then we'll use the ones we've already got!" Fancy yelled. "Throw everything at 'em!"

"Well, actually, they're kind of too big for that. Have been, ever since Canada and Russia joined their Union. Also, we don't really have anything left to throw. We sold the last of it to some South American country last year to make our interest payments."

"Interest payments!" the president shrieked. "Secretary of Book Cooking! I thought I told you, no more payments to foreigners!"

"That's right, ma'am. I believe the Secretary of Defense was referring to debts incurred by your predecessor."

Fancy calmed down immediately. "Oh. The previous administration. That's okay, then. So when will we be finished with these interest payments?"

With great reluctance, the Secretary of Book Cooking said, "Never, I suspect, ma'am. In fact, they'll probably increase."

"What?" Fancy shrieked. "That doesn't make any sense! If we're making our payments, then eventually we'll pay off the original loan."

"Unfortunately, the original loan and the payments were defined in Euros. Or as they're now called, Newros. At that time, the Euro was somewhere around a dollar and a quarter. Now the exchange rate is just under twenty-five dollars to the Newro and it's getting worse steadily. Takes more dollars than we have just to make our payments. We have to keep getting new loans from them to pay off the old ones. And the new loans are also in Newros, of course. At very unfavorable interest rates. Then there's oil."

He was warming to his task. The Secretary enjoyed immersing himself in the ebb and flow of these figures. He had been an honest accountant in his youth, and now, if he concentrated on the more minute details, he could forget how he had sold out.

"Now that the NU controls all the energy output of Russia and

Canada and the Middle East, and they sell that to us in Newros, too, the payments situation just keeps getting worse every month. Every day!" he added, shaking his head in wonder, almost in delight. He finally became aware of Fancy's narrowed eyes and the pale faces of the rest of the Cabinet and the way they were drawing back from him. "Oh. Er. And as you know, they won't allow us to lean on Venezuela or Mexico or Nigeria or any of those guys. As the Secretary of Defense will explain to you if you ask him." He held his breath, then released it when Fancy's glare switched from him to the Secretary of Defense.

But Fancy deflated. Despite the bluster—hers, and also America's long national tradition of collective swagger—she knew that there was nothing she could really do against the outside world. Better to concentrate on domestic matters.

She didn't want to drop this discussion without demonstrating her contempt for that increasingly powerful rival, though. She sneered. "The Northern Union. What a dumb name! What does that make us—the Confederacy?"

There was a long and awkward silence and much gazing at floor, walls, and ceiling.

"All right, all right," Fancy said. "Let's get on with it. Secretary of Development."

The Secretary of Development was the only one present not wearing a suit. Instead, he always dressed as a forest ranger. It was the uniform of his Department. His khaki outfit was complete with ranger hat, which he wore all the time, even indoors, even at Cabinet meetings.

"The National Forever Majestic Redwoods Forest is in fine shape, ma'am. Sorry, I mean the National Gone Away Forever Majestic Redwoods Forest. I was out there just yesterday. The tree is up to three feet in height already. Looks healthy. Lots of well paved space around it, so we won't have to worry about fires or insects. We're good for a few hundred years!" He laughed a hearty outdoorsman's chuckle that no one joined in on, so he continued quickly.

"I was there to dedicate a plaque. It's the first thing any tourists will see when they enter the forest. It's right in front of the tree, and it says, 'When you've seen one redwood, you've seen them all.' It's really appropriate and really beautiful and impressive, and it just makes your heart swell with pride in this great land of ours."

Fancy didn't seem all that interested. "Fine. Well done." She waved her hand dismissively and moved on to something more interesting. "Secretary of Posterity, what's the latest on the Naming Initiative?"

The Secretary of Posterity jerked straight and blinked a few times. Malcolm realized the man had been dozing and that before that he had probably been drinking. Poor guy, Malcolm thought. He's under even more pressure than the rest of us. Which means he's in more danger.

The Secretary said, "Moving right along, ma'am." He pulled a crumpled sheet of paper from his shirt pocket, flattened it out on the table, and said, "Let's see. Since my last report, we've added 5,100 middle schools, 1,870 high schools, 3,503 city office buildings, 132 junior colleges, and over 15,000 grade schools to the list."

"How about the cowboy museums? You know how important that would have been to Gone."

The Secretary licked his lips. "We have five of those, ma'am."

"Five?" Fancy barked. "That's the same number you had last time."

"I think that may be all there are nowadays, ma'am. They've been shutting down over the years."

"All right, all right. So all these places now have Gone's name on them?"

"Yes, ma'am. The Gone Away South Middle School, the Gone Away North Junior High School, and so on."

"Hmm. Lacks something. No ring to it. Maybe I should have told you to include my name. The Gone and Fancy Away South Middle

School. The Fancy and Gone Away West Senior High School. That sort of thing. Well, I'll think about it. While we're on the subject of schools, remember I told you we needed to throw a bone to the supporters of my predecessor."

"Yes, ma'am! We've got the Jibber Longlegs Memorial Jungle Gym at a middle school in Duluth. Or maybe it was DuBuque. Begins with a D, anyway."

"Good enough. Now. What's the situation with that stupid National Cathedral?"

"Not stupid any more, ma'am!" the Secretary said enthusiastically, relieved to have something good to report. "The bill passed both houses this morning and is already on your desk. As soon as you sign it, the building will become The House of Gone Away Glory! Ma'am!"

Fancy nodded in satisfaction. "Not bad. Although...Gone and Fancy...Oh, never mind. Let's move along. The Rushmore Project. Status?"

"Right on schedule." The Secretary of Posterity was feeling better—and safer—by the minute. "Three of the heads are already gone. Washington, Jefferson, and Lincoln. Those were the easy ones to get at. Demolition on Roosevelt will be getting underway in the morning. They tell me it should be done in a week. Then they'll have to start the refacing and reshaping of the cliff before construction starts. As I told you before, it's going to be tricky because of the shape of the mountain. Getting a single giant head carved in there is going to mean removing an amazing mount of rock."

Fancy glared at him. "I give the orders. You execute them. That's the way it works. The details are up to you. If you can't handle it, there'll be a different kind of execution."

The Secretary froze in his chair, blinking rapidly.

Suddenly Fancy smiled. "But that's okay, because I've changed the plan. Instead of Gone's head in the middle, I've decided I'd like to have

Gone's head on one side and mine on the other. Facing each other. They'll be hollow. Then after I've passed to the higher plane where Lukas of Aldebaran lives," she smiled fondly at Malcolm, who replied with a grimace that he hoped she'd take for a smile, "Gone's and my mortal shells will be placed inside our heads. They'll be," she looked up at the ceiling, "tombs that generations of Americans will visit to pray and light candles before."

The room was silent. The rest of the Cabinet, Malcolm was sure, was as stunned as he was. And probably as terrified.

"Not generations," Fancy said. "Thousands of years."

"But, ma'am," the Secretary of Posterity said, proving Malcolm wrong in the sense that one Cabinet Secretary was not too terrified to speak, or possibly was too tipsy to hold his tongue, "if we change the plans like that, the engineers and designers will have to start all over. It'll put us way behind schedule—months, maybe years!"

Fancy stared at him for a long while. Finally, she said, "Say good night now."

The Secretary of Posterity began to rise from his chair in alarm. Suddenly, a brawny arm encircled his neck. He was yanked up, over the back of his seat, and then dragged from the room choking and trying to breathe. None of the other Cabinet Secretaries or their assistants or Under Secretaries moved. The Vice President certainly didn't.

Fancy patted her stiff helmet of gray hair. "We'll continue. Social Secretary!"

And they continued.

At which point, Malcolm's story ended. There were some things he had never told his friend Carol, and never would tell him, about his brief career just beneath the pinnacle of power.

For example, after the Cabinet meeting he had just described to Carol, as Shirley was escorting Malcolm through a crowd of respectful—indeed, cowed—tourists outside the White House, he said to her, "This is ridiculous. This is terrible. This is awful. I don't belong in the vice presidency any more than...than...than Fancy belongs in the presidency."

"Ssh!" Shirley looked around quickly. "Christ, you idiot, save it for when we're alone. For now, she's still basically fond of you. Something to do with a prophecy from Lukas that came true. Something about a successor."

"Oh, God, that. I told her that Lukas said it was best to be the successor to the successor's successor. In that case, meaning she should strive to be the successor to Gone's successor." He stopped in amazement. "I was right! I mean, Lukas was right! She's the successor to Jibber, and he was the successor to Gone."

They started walking again, but they stared at each other, both frowning in puzzlement.

"Is that right?" Malcolm said. "Something's missing there. Was there someone else?"

Malcolm was scarcely aware of the tourists, but the tourists were very aware of him and Shirley. Despite his title, Malcolm's face wasn't well known. Only Fancy's picture appeared in newspapers, and only her image showed up on the evening news. But the tourists sensed something about these two, and they shuffled away to get out of their path. Perhaps Malcolm and Shirley had an aura of power about them. More likely the aura was Shirley's. The tourists were aware of something, though. It didn't really matter who these two were. Better safe than sorry. Best not to stare at someone whose back was straight. Certainly wisest not to look them in the eye. You never knew.

Foreigners were very rare in American cities nowadays. These tourists were Americans, born and bred. (Naturalized citizens were extremely rare, too.) They were typical Americans, the salt of the Earth, the backbone of America, minutemen at heart all of them, ready to defend against invasion by the evil British, or, to bring matters up to date, the vile and despised Northern Unionists.

They were shuffling about in the very place where, in the summer of 1814, the indescribably treacherous British set fire to the young nation's sacred capital, the flames being watched from a safe distance by President Madison and the city's valiant defenders, who had skedaddled out of way of the cowardly Redcoats. The tourists wore t-shirts emblazoned with the American flag with its sadly diminished star field and pugnacious mottoes such as "These colors don't run!" and "Patriotic pride!" and "Land of the free, home of the brave!" They watched the ground and they watched their thoughts. Back home, they watched their neighbors.

The tourists parted for Malcolm and his dream girl, revealing the glass coffin around which the crowd had been clustered. It contained the onetime Great Discombobulator, now the First Mummy. Gone lay on his back, hands folded across his chest, smiling his famous vacuous smile and staring up into space.

Malcolm's attention was distracted and then riveted. "Did you see his lips move just now?" he whispered to Shirley.

"No, of course not. He's dead." In fact, though, she had not been watching the Great Prune. Instead she had been nervously examining the crowd of tourists for faces she knew from her own agency. As she knew from a recent briefing, undercover agents with recording devices were everywhere.

"Could have sworn they moved. Looked like he was trying to say 'Mommy.'"

"Oh, forget that, damn it!"

By now, they were clear of the tourists, and Shirley relaxed a bit. Behind them, invisible tubing fed another jolt of paralyzer into the First Mummy.

"All right, Malcolm, let me look into it. I'll see if I can get you out of the job in some way that doesn't have anything to do with death or crippling injury."

"Gee, thanks!"

Shirley rubbed her chest and smiled. "That's okay. Life is full of interesting surprises, and some of them are even pleasant."

Too few of them, in the opinion of most of us, and especially in Malcolm's opinion.

On his way into the Cabinet meeting, he had run into the Secretary of Security in the hallway. They had never exchanged anything beyond the briefest of greetings before, and Malcolm wanted to keep it that way. Mr. Umbral gave him the creeps.

Today, though, Mr. Umbral seemed to be in a good mood, and he greeted Malcolm more warmly than he usually did.

Malcolm considered what he knew about the other man's Cabinet department and decided to respond in kind. "Fine day, isn't it, Mr. U.? Shame not to be outside."

Umbral grimaced at the nickname and even glared at Malcolm for a moment, but then his good mood returned. "Always better to be on the inside than on the outside, Mr. Vice President. Especially now. After all this time, I'm finally getting it right. I can tell. I've tried and failed so often, thought I had it each time, found out I was mistaken, that I'd chosen poorly. I didn't understand that you have to meld all the disparate forces together, rather than choose just one of them." He nodded. "Yes, it's working at last."

"How very nice," Malcolm said, having no idea what the man was talking about and not caring. It was undeniably true that a variety of diverse forces had come together to make Malcolm's life miserable, but this creepy fellow had nothing to do with that. "Life takes unexpected turns," he said, not knowing what else to say.

Mr. Umbral looked him up and down with interest. "That's quite true. I worked with your grandfather long ago. I don't suppose he mentioned that?"

Malcolm was unable to think of anything to say in response to that.

"No, I suppose not. Old Tibbs always knew when to say nothing. One of our best. One of the absolute best." He looked at Malcolm carefully again, as though trying to assay his genes.

"Well," Malcolm said, "we shouldn't keep the President waiting, should we?" He gestured for Mr. Umbral to precede him into the room.

"No, I don't think you should," Mr. Umbral said. He smiled at Malcolm again, briefly showing the pointed tips of his brown teeth, and passed through the doorway.

I'm in an alternate universe, Malcolm thought. And it's the wrong one.

"I think it was during that Cabinet meeting," Malcolm said, "that I finally admitted to myself just how much I did not belong there. Finally Shirley said she'd see what she could do to get me out."

"And I guess she succeeded, then?" Carol asked.

"Took her a few months, but she did. Basically, she made a deal with her SS buddies."

"Almost cost me my job, too."

The two men turned around at the voice. A stunningly, exotically beautiful woman had come up behind them. She had shoulder-length black hair with a very few gray strands in it, olive skin with only a few wrinkles, and almond-shaped black eyes that betrayed an inner cynicism. Those minute signs of age, to Malcolm's occasional annoyance, made her not less attractive but—maddeningly—all the more irresistibly sexy.

Carol squeezed his lips into a thin line to keep himself from drooling visibly. Ah, lucky Malcolm!

"The deal," Shirley explained to Carol, "was that I'd be personally responsible for Malcolm from that point on and I'd make sure he didn't do anything to embarrass the President. Fancy hated the deal, but she couldn't budge Zip or the others. I was one person they weren't going to eliminate for her."

"It helped," Malcolm added, "that Fancy got distracted around then. That was when she was planning the commando raid into Brussels to kidnap the wife of the President of the Northern Union and bring her to Washington for trial and execution."

"Jesus!" Carol said. "I never even knew anything about that! Trial on what charges?"

"Oh, I don't know. Maybe for being too young and slender and good looking and having too much fashion sense. Fortunately, Fancy was dissuaded."

"Malcolm," Carol said, "you've done and seen so much, you simply have to write your memoirs. Record everything for future historians."

Malcolm said vaguely, "My debt to the world, huh?" Then he looked around nervously. Then he laughed at himself. There was no reason to be nervous. All the dangerous people were dead. Well, except for Shirley.

"And then our second civil war broke out," Shirley said, "and *everyone* got distracted. Old news. Malcolm, did you see that Jerry and Al's new science–fiction spy thriller reached Number One on the New York Times bestseller list?"

"No, dear, I didn't see that, and I'd really rather not talk about it."

"Well, then, did you hear the news about your ex–wife?"

"She went on a hike in the mountains and got eaten by a bear?" Malcolm asked eagerly.

Shirley shook her head.

"A mountain lion? Anything?"

Shirley laughed. "It's been a long time, Malcolm. Give up on it. No, no disaster. She's just been appointed President of Colossoverse

Telephone, Television, Natural Gas, Savings, Radiation, Electricity, Insurance, Steel, and Extortion. Newspaper says her salary will be $500,010,000."

"It figures," Malcolm said disgustedly.

"It was just on the local television news. She was interviewed. She said something about Colossoverse buying the last radio station it didn't already own. She also announced a corporate name change. In keeping with the new, advanced, customer–friendly nature of the company, it will now be known as Universal Tibbs. Company motto will be, 'We rule.' She said she owes her business success to scrupulously following the principles explained in, quote, my brilliant ex–husband's stupendous breakthrough book, *Business Secrets from the Stars,* end quote. The news anchor said that she was a great favorite with all the guys at the station, and they all wished her the very best of luck."

The only sound that came from Malcolm was the grinding together of dentures.

Shirley took pity on him and decided not to tell him that the news item had included the detail that Marlene would be working closely with Big Buck Grossbuck, the Supreme Big Guy at Universal Tibbs, Ted Jones, the Vice Big Guy, Wallace Tenhut, the Vice President for Recreation, and the new Chief Presidential Playpal Marlene had just hired, Fred Seicht, who had recently been allowed to return to the United States after completing his term at one of the Northern Union's Junior Big Guy Institutes.

"She looks and sounds like an interesting person," Shirley said. "I think I'll arrange an introduction for myself. Maybe we can compare notes. Now that our two organizations have merged officially, we'll need to work closely with each other, anyway." She returned to the house.

Carol watched her go and sighed despite himself. Shirley always reminded him of a young Hispanic girl he had known decades ago, during an uncharacteristically tumultuous period of his life. That had been before Bess, of course. "She's still showing up?" he asked. "Still coming to visit?"

Malcolm nodded. "Every six months, approximately," he said. "Whenever she gets tired of dealing with strong, deadly people who're just like her and feels the need for my groveling worship, gratitude, and fear." He had often imagined a lifetime relationship with his dream girl, but he had never imagined it quite this way. Sometimes, toward the end of Shirley's visits, he caught himself staring at her mouth—at her teeth—in fearful expectation.

"Um, Carol, you probably shouldn't mention to anyone that you've seen her here. Safety first."

Carol turned slightly paler than usual. "Whatever you say."

Malcolm sometimes wondered what position Shirley occupied these days. Head of the CIA? Head of some much deadlier agency whose existence the public didn't even know about? She didn't let information slip. Not unintentionally, anyway. She said just enough to keep Malcolm in a constant state of fear—and, paradoxically, and even to his mounting self-hatred, of desire.

The months between her visits stretched interminably. Then she would show up unannounced, bringing Malcolm a few nights of passion and terror. When she was done with him, when she had gained whatever it was she gained from these visits and had left again, he was happy to see her go and relieved that he was still alive and well. A few days later, he would begin longing for her again.

There were times, brief moments, when he didn't think she was real. Had he imagined everything? Had the last however many years been a fantasy? Was he in reality confined in a straitjacket in a mental asylum, living inside his mind in the world of his own fiction? No: the sheer physicality of her brief visits made that impossible to believe.

Carol shook himself. "I have to go, Malcolm. Have to go tend my garden."

"I didn't know you had a garden."

"That's a metaphor, you heathen, atheist, anti–Christian devil spawn. What I really have to do is work on my sermon for tomorrow's broadcast."

"Are you finally going to going to give in to temptation and speak your mind?"

Carol sighed. He looked around quickly before talking. The gesture was unconscious. Everyone did it. He lowered his voice. People did that a lot, too. "Don't be silly. I like breathing."

"So what will your topic be?"

"I think it'll be something about this being after all the best of all possible worlds."

Malcolm laughed. "I might actually watch you this time."

He watched Carol drift away across the lawn to his own mansion, noticing how frail his friend had become. At least I'm not that badly off, Malcolm thought. Yet.

Lukas? he called out silently.

Still no answer.

Malcolm sighed and shook his head.

Well, yes, Carol was right. Malcolm had been Vice President of the United States, even if for only six months and during the administration of an insane dictator. He had had one immense bestseller. He had even changed history. Surely that was enough for any man. He was rich, he was still somewhat famous, and most of his body worked adequately.

Above all, there was Shirley

So what if Marlene was more successful than he was? Marlene was still a bitch.

So what if Joe Hoffman had attained the kind of permanent

literary success that Malcolm had longed for but failed to achieve? Hoffman was showing his age, too. Nor did he seem to be a happy man.

The last time Malcolm had seen him, Hoffman had seemed filled with self–loathing for having turned his back on Larry Lefkowitz after the latter's suicide. "I was frightened," he had confessed to Malcolm. "You should never be frightened."

"It's natural to be frightened," Malcolm had assured him, driven suddenly to pity. "That's human nature. It's evolution. It's how we survive."

"Well, yes" Hoffman had said, "but we must never let it make us betray ourselves."

Malcolm, who felt that betrayal was the basis for much of human society, had patted the other man on the shoulder, noticing for the first time how bony Hoffman felt, how the muscles that Marlene had once admired had shriveled away.

Instead of triumph, that too aroused a feeling of sympathy. After all, Malcolm was also getting older. No, not older: old. Lately, when he looked in the mirror, it seemed to him that he was wearing someone else's skin, and it was a half–size too large.

Nothing worked properly nowadays. Oh, not just the parts of Malcolm's body, but the machines he was surrounded by. Even computers.

Especially computers, for God's sake!

He had spent years programming those things, learning how to make them do the specific tricks he wanted them to. He had, he thought, gotten to be damned good at it. Maybe he hadn't had what it took to be a Grade A+ programmer, but he had made himself into a very solid and reliable Grade B, and sometimes he had even managed to rise to somewhere between B+ and A–. Which, he had always been convinced, still made him better than ninety per cent of his colleagues.

At times, he had thought it a silly way to make a living. At all times, he had taken pride in his competence.

But where were the skills of yesteryear? It wasn't really a skill he needed now or had needed for many years. Thanks to *Business Secrets from the Stars,* Malcolm would never again have to lift a finger. He could hire someone to lift it for him. Even though he hadn't had another literary success, he had nonetheless earned the right to call himself a writer—in terms of dollars, anyway, if not in terms of recognition by the literary establishment. He had no need to bother about computers, or at least about the programming of them. That kind of work was beneath him now.

He had once read that Henry James had said that the only proper pursuit for the intelligent man was the writing of novels.

Was it Henry? Or was it his brother? Had whichever James boy it was come up with that line during a hiatus between robbing banks? Or had someone else said that, someone not even named James?

That didn't matter. Details, details. The sentiment was a good one, in any case.

The writing of novels. Or the thinking about the writing of novels. Or the daydreaming about the writing of a novel that someone—some publisher, some reviewer, damn it, some fellow writer—would regard with just a bit of admiration.

So who cared about computers and the art of programming them? Not Malcolm!

From time to time, he would buy a magazine or book written for those who did care about that arcane art, because of a vague feeling that he ought to keep up with what had once been his field.

He could never get more than a few sentences into the damned thing.

What the hell were these kids doing nowadays? None of it made any sense. The publications were filled with words and phrases and even concepts—concepts, damn it!—that meant nothing to him, that he couldn't even begin to wrap his mind around. The latest one was something called Layer Connections. All computer programs were now supposed to be written in the form of Layer Connections. This would guarantee that they'd take five minutes to write, they'd be esthetically and philosophically superior, they'd be bug free, and the world would be an immeasurably better place. Layer Connections was the new paradigm.

Paradigm. That word had become popular again. But only new paradigms counted. If you wanted to sell something, you called it the new paradigm. In with the new paradigm, out with the old. Buddy, can you paradigm? Nope, sorry. I'm fresh out.

The Layer Connections paradigm. What the hell did that mean? Might as well call it Fleegle. Fleegle programming. That made just as much sense, God damn it.

Maybe what made it worse was that the articles were all written by smug young people who were so sure they knew everything and to whom Malcolm's years of experience and accomplishment counted for nothing. God damn them.

Even the hardware was weird and absurd nowadays. Computers were silent and completely sealed. Tiny little Goddamned boxes. You couldn't even look inside them. By God, Malcolm remembered when you could open them up and stare at the stuff inside and pretend that you knew what it all was.

You were even supposed to talk to the Goddamned things, instead of typing!

He remembered that back when he was in high school, he had really liked the talking computers on that TV show, Star Trek, the original one, the real one. In real life, he couldn't stand the damned things' stupid fakey voices and patronizing manner. They knew they were so much smarter than Malcolm Erskine, and they didn't bother trying to hide it. And they always pretended to keep misunderstanding him and displaying the wrong words on the screen, instead of the ones he spoke to them, no matter how loudly and distinctly he said them. So he'd find himself yelling and swearing at the stupid things, and even though they were featureless little boxes, he just knew they were laughing at him. Fuckers.

So he'd always order his computer to pop up a keyboard for him. Deformable plastic with telescoping carbon nanotubes inside it, or some such thing. They had a good feel to them, he had to admit that. Adjustable, too.

Adjustable. Deformable. The whole damned world had lost its solidity. No sooner did Malcolm think that he understood what was going on around him than it all melted into something else.

Deteriorated into something else.

Deteriorating. Everything was deteriorating.

Deterioration. Maybe that was the word that best described the universe, not betrayal. It was one or the other of those. Malcolm was sure of that.

So he had felt quite a bit of sympathy for Joe Hoffman's sad deterioration, even though Malcolm was sure that he himself had not deteriorated anywhere near that much. Still, what could he say to the man? "You're right, Joe. You're a deteriorated coward. That must be tough to live with. You should just go find a lamppost now, just like your protégé." No, that would have been inappropriate.

Instead, he had said goodbye to Hoffman and had returned to his mansion in Redland Heights.

And here he was, in that mansion. All in all, Malcolm had managed to get a pretty big chunk of the American Dream, and he was fairly satisfied with the path he had followed to achieve it.

He checked his watch. Early yet.

With a spring in his step, he headed for one of the side doors of the mansion.

He had his own garden to tend to. Malcolm had indeed been thinking about writing his memoirs. Not a single book of his since *Business Secrets from the Stars* had sold well. None of them had sold at all, to be truthful It was time for another bestseller.

He knew in his heart that his memoir would be that bestseller. It too was to be titled *Business Secrets from the Stars,* but with the subtitle *The Real Story.* It would tell the truth about the original book, about the fakery and cynical silliness of it. This new book would blow the lid off the whole con game—Malcolm's scam and the many political scams it had given rise to.

America would eat this book up! Eager for the truth at last, tired of centuries of self–deception and play–acting, his fellow citizens would buy his new book by the millions and would love and praise Malcolm Erskine for telling them the truth about themselves and for forcing them to face their own gullibility.

Perhaps Malcolm should have been thinking of lampposts as he sat down at his desk, ordered the computer to pop up a virtual screen and create a keyboard, and began to type:

> *It all came to me while I was eating lunch in a Mexican restaurant.*
>
> *I was there alone. I always ate lunch alone. I never wanted my thoughts about writing interrupted by the inane chatter of shallow companions.*
>
> *I was taking a break—brief, always brief—from writing. I had just completed the latest in a succession of critically praised novels, each of which had earned me the profound admiration of my fellow authors, and I was trying to choose which of various enticing literary projects to next pursue. Which would be the most*

satisfying, the most intellectually and artistically fulfilling?

Or should I, to divert myself and amuse my admirers, write something light, frothy, purely entertaining, a jeu d'esprit? No, I decided, the writer's life is too short to spend any of it traveling such byways.

I had lately been considering a number of non-fiction writing projects. I had so much to say, so much to share with the world. What would be the most effective way to accomplish this?

I will admit to you readily that my mind was not completely occupied with matters literary. I was diverting myself by chatting with my waitress, an extraordinarily beautiful young Mexican-American woman who was blessed with just the sort of looks I have always favored. Although the restaurant was crowded for the lunch hour, she seemed unable to tear herself away from my table and my conversation. Let us be frank: "flirtation" is possibly more accurate than "conversation." Even now, I still feel some residual guilt at the thought that perhaps I unintentionally encouraged her hopeless yearning.

I was recently divorced from the now-famous Marlene Erskine. (Note that after all these years she still retains her married surname!) That marriage had been a melding of two profound souls, meeting, harmonizing, almost on an ethereal plane. Alas, our busy lives and absorbing interests had drawn us in separate directions. Please be assured that Marlene and I have never lost our deep regard and friendship for each other. At any rate, I had of course been utterly faithful to my sweet and beloved Marlene during our years of marriage, and I retained to some degree a feeling that, even after our divorce, any intimacy on my part with another woman would have been in some sense a betrayal of what we had shared.

In time, I hoped, both Marlene and I would find happiness with others, even though it could never approach, either spiritually or physically, what we had had together. Certainly, however, any woman with whom I eventually formed a liaison would have to be—to the degree possible—on an intellectual and artistic level close to my equal. No one would have thought that this charming young waitress, with her lovely dusky skin and shoulder-length black hair and almond-shaped eyes and dewy lips, could ever fill that role. But I am human, and I am a man, and I have the same needs as other men, and so I was pleased by her attentions and amused by her simple conversation, and so I indulged myself. I do hope she has had a satisfactory life in the decades since then and that, wherever she is and whatever her station in life, if she chances to read this book, she will remember our brief encounter with a fond smile.

In the midst of that conversation—I won't go so far as to call it a dalliance—it struck me that what America needed most was a slap in the face.

The nation had become obsessed with the idea that there are easy steps to wealth and happiness, that processes and methods can be detailed in popular books that will inevitably lead those who follow the directions to a state of bliss. How silly! We all know that only hard work, steadiness, application, and a firm adherence to reality, to seeing things as they really are rather than as we wish they were, can earn us the happiness we desire.

As a patriot, as an American, as an artist and intellectual filled with love for my fellow citizens, it was my duty to make them understand this.

But how to undertake this heroic mission?

Why, of course! It was suddenly clear to me. I would create the grandest hoax in American history. I would pretend that I had received self–help business secrets from a galaxy–spanning consciousness, a being of immense knowledge and ancient experience. I would pretend to "channel" his thoughts in the form of a book.

If I did all of this convincingly enough—and I was confident in my ability to do so—then the book would be read by millions, all of whom would take the supposed "channeling" seriously. They would take seriously the existence of the invented cosmic being—on the spot, I decided to call him "Lukas of Aldebaran"—and my contact with him.

The eventual revelation that the channeling and Lukas and the book and all the rules contained within it had been nothing but an enormously clever hoax, a mighty joke, would constitute the slap in the face that my countrymen needed.

As you know, I followed this plan and achieved the huge readership that my selfless goal required. All that remained was to wait until the appropriate time had arrived to tell the truth. That time has now come.

Malcolm leaned back and reread the words glowing in the air above his desk, and, being Malcolm to the end, grinned happily and said, "Wow!"

About the Author

David Dvorkin was born in 1943 in England. His family moved to South Africa after World Two and then to the United States when David was a teenager. After attending college in Indiana, he worked in Houston at NASA on the Apollo program and then in Denver as an aerospace engineer, software developer, and technical writer. He and his wife, Leonore, have lived in Denver since 1971.

In addition to non-fiction, David has published a number of science fiction, horror, mystery, and Star Trek novels. He has also coauthored two science fiction novels with his son, Daniel. For details, as well as quite a bit of non-fiction reading material, please see David's Web site, http://www.dvorkin.com.

www.ingramcontent.com/pod-product-compliance
Lightning Source LLC
Chambersburg PA
CBHW060553310726
48982CB00008B/1109/J

* 9 7 8 1 7 3 4 5 6 3 6 3 4 *